Looking
for Love in All
the Haunted Places

CLAIRE KANN

BERKLEY ROMANCE

NEW YORK

BERKLEY ROMANCE
Published by Berkley
An imprint of Penguin Random House LLC
penguinrandomhouse.com

Library of Congress Cataloging-in-Publication Data

Names: Kann, Claire, author.
Title: Looking for love in all the haunted places / Claire Kann.
Description: First edition. | New York: Berkley Romance, 2024.
Identifiers: LCCN 2023035702 (print) | LCCN 2023035703 (ebook) |
ISBN 9780593336656 (trade paperback) | ISBN 9780593336663 (ebook)
Subjects: LCGFT: Romance fiction. | Paranormal fiction. | Novels.
Classification: LCC PS3611.A549375 L66 2024 (print) |
LCC PS3611.A549375 (ebook) | DDC 813/.6—dc23/eng/20230815
LC record available at https://lccn.loc.gov/2023035702
LC ebook record available at https://lccn.loc.gov/2023035703

First Edition: May 2024

Printed in the United States of America
1st Printing

Book design by Katy Riegel

Because if they wanted to, they would.

*Looking
for Love in All
the Haunted Places*

1

Voluntarily choosing to live in a haunted house took an extraordinary amount of desperation. Or perhaps *determination* was the better word. Either way, Lucky Hart possessed an ample supply of both.

"Next." The receptionist—Gayle, according to her nameplate—signaled her forward. "I need to see your ID. Glasses off, please."

"I have an appointment. Lucky Hart." She removed her dark sunglasses as requested.

Gayle's hair had been cut into a severely angled bob that framed her equally sharp jawline. She dressed as if she'd walked right off the page of a high fashion editorial spread with her glowing, sun-kissed skin and svelte figure. Her eyes and smile were kind, but unfortunately also betrayed precisely who she was. She lived with an insidious type of exhaustion that no amount of sleep could remedy. It burrowed into her bones, hollowed them out, until she had nothing left and yet somehow continued on.

She relied heavily on ambition to keep from collapsing. No matter how many times she crossed that line of living to survive, her endless desire for more, for better, for everything, would never allow her to fail.

Interesting.

That was the thing about Lucky—she had an uncanny knack for first impressions. Looking at someone's eyes told her nearly everything she needed to know about them.

After completing a visitor's sheet, Gayle escorted Lucky to a back office and then excused herself.

"Ah, Miss Hart. Please have a seat."

Three people sat around a table inside the room and, well, that was two too many new windows for Lucky's liking. She couldn't control her ability, so she swiftly slipped her dark sunglasses back on. They managed to block her first impression readings a solid ninety-five percent of the time.

"Thank you," she said as she sat down.

"My name is Castor Paulson." He was a white man with a round body and chubby cheeks, and he wore a suit that fit him like a dream. His most distinguishing feature was a walrus mustache—brown sprinkled with salt and pepper, same as his hair.

"Castor doubles as our casting director and HR manager. I'm Stephen. We spoke on the phone." Also a white man, except he was bald with a muscular build and could double as Bruce Willis's *The Fifth Element* tethered.

"That's quite the face you have," she joked.

"I'm aware." His indulgent, welcoming smile made her like him instantly. She didn't need to know anything else, which was saying something considering what she could do. "And this is my business partner, Xander Hennessee."

"Hello, Ms. Hart." Even though he was sitting she knew he was a giant—long limbs, strong bone structure, and lean muscle. His hazel eyes warmed his pale skin, and he also wore a suit, deep cerulean in color with shining gold cuff links. "Is it too bright in here?"

"No."

"Is there a particular reason why you've chosen to wear sunglasses indoors?"

"There is."

"Do you plan to share that reason?"

Lucky considered her answer. Point-blank, her career hinged on this meeting being a success. She needed to keep a clear head and some readings were harder to shake than others.

A firm, undeniable feeling told her that grief clung to Xander like an old, tattered coat in a snowstorm—useless but better than nothing. He needed to eat something delicious, warm, and home-cooked, and get a good fortnight's sleep . . . and there she was, channeling again. Delaying reading someone's first impression, and choosing to stay near them, occasionally resulted in their surface feelings seeping through. As if her brain were impatient and needed a snack.

Those suspected grief-filled feelings might not be a part of his core personality, but if they were strong enough to punch through *her* defenses? *Before* a reading? Odds were good they had begun to alter his being in a significant way, which rarely happened because people didn't fundamentally change. Evolve and grow, yes. But change? Almost never. Over the years, she'd learned there was a very clear and very distinct difference between the two concepts.

Lucky tossed him her most playful grin. "Only if I get the job. Make me an offer and I'll take them right off." She leaned toward him, stage-whispering, "I promise it'll be worth your while."

Stephen laughed softly and Castor's glorious whiskers twitched as he tried to hide his smile. Xander, however, remained unmoved. He checked his watch and said, "Why don't we get started? I have another meeting in an hour."

Tough crowd. Unfazed, she continued smiling at him, mentally vowing to find a way to win him over.

"All right," Stephen began. "As you know, we're looking for someone to star in our latest production, centered around a haunted house. If chosen, your role would be that of the caretaker. While acting experience isn't necessary, we did hope to find someone with some retail or property management experience, which you also don't have."

Xander frowned. "According to your résumé, you don't have any work experience."

She grinned. "According to my résumé, that's correct."

"You're twenty-five and you've never had a job?"

"That happens more often than you'd think." Not to her, but that was beside the point. "Trust-fund babies, perpetual and professional students, SoundCloud rappers—I mean the list could go on and on."

Xander narrowed his eyes but kept his thoughts to himself. She suspected he was on to her schtick. Giving him a non-answer wouldn't work again. "Why did you apply for this position?"

"I need a job and I need housing. Isn't it incredible how this is the answer to all my problems?" She paused for a beat, slouching slightly with a little sigh. They couldn't see her eyes—making sure they could easily read her body language and interpret her tone was crucial. "I was . . . a student. A really, *really* good student. I dedicated almost twenty years of my life to my education. Yes, I count kindergarten because that's when I learned how to read, and reading is one of the single greatest joys in my life. I wasn't prepared to not be a student. My whole identity had to shift when I got my degree. And now I'm here. Hoping to try something new and exciting. To use my skills in an unexpected way."

It had taken two days to revise and perfect that speech. A taut balance between meticulously selected facts from her life and a little something she liked to call earnest lies. She decided it'd be best to pretend to be an almost-blank slate. She wanted them to project their casting hopes and dreams onto her.

If they thought she was an overqualified know-it-all, they'd reject her. If they misread her confidence for arrogance, they'd reject her. They might not do it on purpose, but the second they unconsciously assumed she was uppity, they'd definitely reject her. But fate was smiling on her that day, because Stephen's eyes hadn't stopped twinkling since she walked in. He saw something special in her. He wanted to give her a chance.

"I'll be honest with you. You're sitting here right now solely based on the strength of your audition tape," Stephen said. "We agreed that we needed to meet you in person before making a decision. Something we rarely do."

Xander continued to stare her down, unconvinced. "There are plenty of jobs that provide housing. *Why* do you want this one? Please be specific."

For the briefest of moments, Lucky considered how this scene might look to outsiders. Three white men hiring a Black woman to be the caretaker for a found-footage haunted-house TV show. It was the ominous opening sequence to a horror film before the real final girl showed up. A bonus scene rescued from the cutting room floor to be used as teaser marketing. She was being set up to die, or if they were culturally competent and subversive, scared shitless and traumatized for life.

But what they didn't know was Lucky was the furthest thing from a naive college graduate willing to work anywhere to land on her feet. She'd done her research. Her next steps absolutely involved forming an alliance with No Qualms Productions. They had a diverse workforce both on and behind the camera, had a great insurance policy, and treated their employees well, and once she'd read them, she'd know if she was in good hands or not.

To be fair, bad hands wouldn't stop her from making this deal. Unless they were murderers. Fun fact: she could read that in someone too. True murderous intentions had an unmistakable stench to them.

Under the table, she discreetly rubbed her increasingly clammy palms on her pants. She had to be careful here. "Because it's mutually beneficial. I get what I want, and you get the novelty of me. I'm here for my community. Black people are largely underrepresented in the supernatural industry. You know there's an eager and dedicated audience waiting for good content. I know because I'm part of it. I'm here because you're looking for the next Maverick Phillips, your big breakout star. And while no, I don't believe I'm destined for stardom, I do believe you will not find someone better than me for this project *specifically*."

"What makes you so confident about that?" Xander. Again.

Shit. Him using the c-word meant she'd accidentally gone too far. Should she backpedal or lean into it? Which option would be best for the show? She licked her lips, nerves beginning to get to her. Instinctively, she wanted to lean into the truth . . . and to give them a hint. They might not catch it, but—

"Almost nothing scares me. I can rationalize my way through anything. And now that I've said that, I know you're *feeling* eager to prove me wrong. It's too tempting. Too perfect." She shrugged—mostly to appear nonchalant but also because Stephen's enthusiasm was beginning to burn through her glasses. She used the movement as an excuse to coyly look away. "Besides, I'm here, aren't I? You said it yourself: I've mostly won you over with a five-minute audition tape. Now that you've met me, please use this moment to imagine what I could do for your show and company." She held her breath, hoping, praying, and wishing for the best.

Xander exchanged a look and an entire silent conversation with Stephen in under ten seconds. Those two must've known each other extremely well. However, it was Castor who decided for them by sliding a manila folder across the table and opening it for her.

Lucky exhaled into a dazzling, triumphant smile as she flipped through the glossy pictures of a three-story Victorian house with a large front driveway, an incredible yard, and beautifully decorated, fully furnished rooms. Castor used phrases she'd never heard before like "pediment porch" and "polygonal towers" and pointed out the turrets, gables, and cupolas. She picked up a photo of a bedroom with the largest bed she'd ever seen, complete with a four-poster frame and canopy. Beautiful rugs complemented the gossamer drapes that glowed from the sunlight.

If they were going to try to scare the unholy hell out of her, at least it would be in the height of luxury.

"This is the haunted house?" A pile of paper, several sheets thick, was stacked under the photos. "Is this the contract?"

Stephen answered, "Yes. It details everything of importance for both the show and your stay in Hennessee House."

"Will I have to sign an NDA?"

Xander said, "Failure to keep the details of production confidential will result in the immediate forfeiture of your wages."

Honestly, she'd be willing to be on the show for free. Hell, she'd pay *them* to get unrestricted access to the house.

He continued, "The exterior is thoroughly monitored. You'll be given a layout of the security system for your safety. Conversely, the interior is not. There are no permanent cameras, mounted or otherwise, anywhere."

"Well, that seems odd and not at all like an interesting premise for a setup." She laughed, happy to play along. "If there are no cameras in the house, and no one there to record it, do the spooky shenanigans actually happen?"

"They do." Xander's tone was unyielding, reinforced with concrete.

Stephen said, "For the first week, you'll be required to give interviews every morning about your experience in the house and must agree to be filmed throughout the day by production. However, you will be alone at night. Every night from sundown to sunrise." He leaned forward, placing his forearms on the table and clasping his hands together. "We live in an era of special effects and deep fakes, and yet, nothing is more horrifying than someone's imagination. Nothing we capture on film will be half as compelling as the way you tell your story. We want to hear what happens to you, from you. You're welcome to film on your phone or camera and share that footage with us, but we're content to take you at your word."

"The house must be booby-trapped, then. It's set up to scare me?"

"No. That defeats the purpose of the show." Xander placed a tablet in front of her. A digital résumé and photo for someone named Eunice Choi was on the screen. "Swipe through. You're actually caretaker number four. Those are your predecessors. No one has lasted longer than three nights."

"Four is my favorite number. Imagine that," she said absently. Most of her focus remained on reading the profiles. "Can I have copies of these? Their videos too?"

"Why?"

Oops.

They had actual footage of subjects recounting their super-natural experiences! Of course, she *needed* to watch them. Alas, it was way too early to give herself away. She needed to be patient. Slipping back into character, she said, "Referencing previous caretakers could create a sense of continuity. Might be interesting for the show."

"We'll take that into consideration," Stephen answered. "But your primary objective will be to live in the house for thirty days. You are free to quit anytime. We will not stop you. We will not attempt to convince you to stay. The shoot and you residing within Hennessee House are and always will be completely voluntary."

"So, what's Hennessee House's story? Did someone die there? Did a lot of people die there?" she asked.

Thanks to a contact within NQP she already knew the answer but figured it would seem strange if she didn't bring it up. Asking also provided her an opportunity to pretend to be surprised.

Xander answered, "Not that I know of."

"Former cemetery?"

"Not that I know of. However, it is the last Victorian house in the area. All the others were torn down and a gated community was built around it. My family refused to sell to the developers."

"Good. I'm honestly not a fan of ghosts. What about séances? Headquarters for a top secret supernatural cult? Those were prolific in the early 1900s."

"There's no record of that. Public or that I know of."

"Built on a veil? Portal to the other side in the basement? Attic?"

He considered his answer. "If there is, I haven't found it."

Lucky skillfully pretended to hide the frustration in her voice. "Okay . . . so what's the deal? Just general spooky business? What kind of a haunting is it?"

"The best way to describe it is that Hennessee House has a personality, and it isn't always friendly."

"Is that the show's angle? A haunted house, not sane and unfriendly?"

Stephen looked impressed. The fact that he'd most likely picked up on her reference was a sign she was absolutely in the right place. Her plan would work.

Xander said, "The only angle is the human one."

Castor, who had noticeably remained silent for some time, said, "I must say, I'm curious. Do you really believe in ghosts, Ms. Hart?"

"As the great Winston Zeddemore once said, 'If there's a steady paycheck in it, I'll believe anything you say.'" She smiled at him. "Mainly, I believe ghosts don't need us to believe in them to be real, so anything is possible. And please, call me Lucky."

2

Hennessee House stuck out like a Victorian sore thumb trapped in suburbia.

It was three stories including the attic, painted dark brown with cream trim, and had a startling number of windows and a short but wide set of stairs that led up to the front door. Most of the cul-de-sac sidewalk framed the expansive front gate, which blocked the entrance to the half-circle driveway.

Up close it loomed much larger than Lucky thought it should. She'd known it was the biggest house on the block by far, but taking in its perfectly green grass, expertly trimmed hedges, and blooming red rose bushes felt strangely intimidating. A quickening in the pit of her stomach warned her to leave while simultaneously daring her to enter.

"Relax." She made the command through gritted teeth, hands white-knuckling the steering wheel for dear life. Her sense of self-preservation was too damn strong. More than once she'd ended up fist-fighting it in abandoned mines and the like.

Ignoring her gut often came at her own peril. But Hennessee House would be worth the risk. Eventually.

The truth was Lucky didn't get into her graduate school of choice. Twice. It was small, exclusive, and the only accredited program specializing in parapsychology in the *entire* country. One school. One program. Zero slots.

To make her lifelong dream of legitimizing the supernatural come true, she'd been forced to take matters into her own hands. Two years of self-funded investigations—everything ranging from harmless interviews to dangerous overnight expeditions— making acquaintances, establishing trusted contacts, and getting her name out there within the community had all led to this moment.

Lucky had given up the security of her day job as a nanny to become . . . a reality TV actress. In her defense, it seemed like a great plan when she mapped it out in her journal.

Her phone chimed in the front pocket of her purse—a new number with the correct area code appeared on the screen.

"Hello?"

"Hi, is this Lucky?"

Melodic and smooth, the caller's voice resonated with her like a tuning fork. She sat up straighter, immediately searching her memories for a match as she looked out the window. "Are you watching Hennessee House remotely?" she asked after spotting three of the *many* exterior cameras Xander promised.

"No?"

"Then how did you know I was here?"

He paused. "I didn't."

"So, you just happened to call me at the exact moment I pulled up?" Give or take ten panicked minutes. "Sure."

"You're there? Right now?"

"I am." She glanced at Hennessee House's front door, thoroughly committed to ignoring the resulting chill that ran through her. "Xander told me to expect a call from production with this area code. He's an extremely surly man. Must be lovely to work with."

"Haven't had any issues so far." He laughed. "I mostly work with Stephen."

"Huh. This might sound odd, but why do I know your laugh? You sound *so* familiar. Who is this?"

He laughed again and she swore she felt something in her chest flutter.

"Well, my name's Maverick."

Lucky gasped softly, then whispered, "Phillips?"

He whispered back, "Yes."

The phone slid clean out of her hand, bouncing off the seat and onto the floor. "*Shit.*" She leaned down, face smooshed against the wheel, still hush-swearing. Her fingertips brushed the sides and the stupid thing flipped over. She sat up quickly, pushing the seat back and picking the phone up just as Maverick said, "Hello? Are you still there?"

"Yes! Hi! Hello! Sorry! I—um— Sorry!" She squeezed her eyes shut. *Stop apologizing!*

She thought she'd meet Maverick Phillips *someday* because they shared a production company now. But she didn't think, not in a million haunted years, that he'd be the one to call.

He asked, "Is everything okay?"

Her heart hammered against her rib cage, temples pulsing with the start of an adrenaline headache. She squeezed her free hand into a fist until her knuckles hurt to get her splintered focus under control. If she could survive the hell week after listening to a "cursed" audio recording, talking to Maverick Phillips paled in comparison.

"Yes! Um." She cleared her throat to get her pitch back from distressed territory. "I'm fine. Everything's fine."

"I have no choice other than to believe you, but you can tell me if it isn't."

"Walking and talking is truly an advanced skill for my clumsy ass. I tripped and dropped my phone. That's all," she lied, smooth as butter. If they were watching, he'd know she was lying and then she'd know he lied. "So, Maverick Phillips. Hi, I've seen your show. Which you obviously guessed by now. I don't know why I told you that."

She'd been following his career for years. His show *Beyond a Reasonable Doubt* was No Qualms Productions' flagship project—a paranormal investigative series focused on interviews rather than spectacle. Its popularity had been what encouraged NQP to branch out and create *The Caretaker* in the first place.

He laughed again, this time soft and breathy. "I'm calling to introduce myself anyway and confirm you received the email with our production schedule."

Our?! Lucky's entire being froze from shock. The hell did he mean *our?!* Was *he* part of the crew assigned to *The Caretaker*? Yes, using Maverick to ensure some audience crossover made perfect sense, but they could've given her a heads-up about it. Rude.

He continued, "We didn't get a reply."

"I did get it. Yes, sorry. I'm the worst. I'll read something and think I responded, but really, it's been sitting there unsent the whole time—wow, you really didn't need to know all that."

What is wrong with me?! She wanted to rip her hair out. Could she stop making insipid comments for five seconds?

"Context is always helpful," he said kindly. "Have you gone inside yet?"

"Not yet, no."

He paused. "Are you all right?"

"Yeah, totally. Trying to psych myself up, say a couple of prayers, you know, the usual," she joked. "Not every day you get to meet a haunted house. I want to make a good first impression. Have you been here before?"

"Yes."

"Right, yeah, I knew that. I'm caretaker number four. Of course, you've been here." Her eyes nearly rolled back into her head because she was absolutely *sick* of herself. She planned to be earnest and endearing, not empty-headed! And of all the people to lose her shit around, why did it have to be *him*?

"Lucky?"

"Maverick?"

"Don't be nervous. You're going to be fine."

"I'm not nervous," she said and then added, "About the house."

"Hennessee House is particular, but nothing ever happens the first night. It likes to take a day or so to assess you before deciding the best way to scare you off."

"You think *the house* wants to scare me?"

"I think Hennessee likes to test people, and everyone keeps failing."

"Good thing I've never failed anything in my life."

"Oh, really?"

"Straight As since kindergarten. If I think of this as a massive practical exam, it'll be a cakewalk."

"Nothing will happen tonight but don't underestimate Hennessee," he said, sounding worried. "I shouldn't even be telling you this now. We'll talk more about it tomorrow. Stephen is convinced you're exactly what the show's been missing. Everyone in production is excited to meet you."

Tomorrow. *Tomorrow.* Talking to him on the phone had scrambled her brain like eggs in a hot skillet. Meeting him might put her in an embarrassment-induced coma. She asked, "Just curious, how many people does production translate to?"

"Four including myself. Oh—plus an intern." He laughed lightly. "We have a young but very talented intern on the team now."

She pinched the bridge of her nose. "That sounds great." Except it didn't!

Reading five people in rapid succession had the potential to put her out of commission for half the morning. The first impressions had to go somewhere, so they formed a queue in her face. Her sinuses to be exact. They seemingly clustered there, clogging up her ducts like a backed-up sink while waiting to be filed away in her memory palace.

When she was younger, every doctor her parents had taken her to swore up and down she suffered from sinus headaches. Some had even upped the ante to chronic sinusitis. The medicine never worked, and no one had any real idea what was making her head hurt so badly she routinely blacked out. The doctors had done their best to give her family answers, but she didn't have a *medical* condition. She had ESP and needed to learn how to live with it.

Lucky owed her life to Mr. Alm, her third-grade teacher. One day he led the class through an enrichment exercise called the method of loci—visualization techniques to help store and recall information. By high school Lucky had gotten so good at it, she'd created small, automated workers who retrieved, archived, and stored the first impressions for her. She didn't have to think about anything except retrieval, which was as fast as any thought took. But reading too many people in a row still remained a tricky feat. She'd have to be careful.

"Great," Maverick repeated. "Well, I'll let you get on with your afternoon, then."

Lucky got out of the car and hauled her suitcases up the stairs, one at a time. A green envelope with her name on it had been taped to the door. She pulled it off and held it in her hands. This was really it—her big break finally come to fruition.

She refused to build a platform by making videos of her reading "real" scary stories lifted from the internet or theorizing about "unexplainable" videos. Paranormal investigation shows had become a dime a dozen. While some were more earnest than clearly staged others, finding ghosts and hunting cryptids didn't interest her.

Lucky's heart belonged to the supernatural—the extraordinary side of reality shimmering right under the surface *for humans*. Growing up with ESP, extrasensory perception, all but sealed her passionate interest in it. She believed things like magic and miracles existed as such because science hadn't caught up yet.

Of course, not everything *needed* to be explained. She respected faith and the solace it provided the human brain and soul. But a lot of things *could* be explained if someone worked hard enough.

Unfortunately, funding streams for supernatural researchers were bone-dry. The legitimate investors she managed to find rarely returned her emails because she lacked experience. They were usually millionaires-plus, searching for the key to eternal life, interested in harnessing mysticism to increase their power, seeking proof of the great beyond to begin securing their future *over there*. As outlandish (and self-serving) as they sounded, they were typically reasonable. They'd want to work with her once she proved herself.

Investigating a haunted house that had no known record of tragedy would be novel enough to get everyone's attention. Something made this place different, and she planned to find out exactly what that was.

"Okay, Hennessee House," she said. "Let's do this."

3

Lucky—

Welcome to Hennessee House. Upon entering you agree to follow five rules:

1. *Walk straight into the kitchen.*

2. *Retrieve your picnic basket.*

3. *Go upstairs, turn left, and enter the primary bedroom suite on the right.*

4. *Stay in your suite until sunrise.*

5. *Do not explore the house for any reason.*

—Xander

4

Three different kinds of dead bolts stood between Lucky and her goals. That felt excessive. Xander must have been worried about break-ins, but . . . why? The maintenance schedule ensured someone would be on-site at least once a day, every day of the week, not to mention the installed over-the-top security system.

Motion detectors guarded the house's exterior and both yards. Cameras recorded every entrance and window. Xander had spent a solid half hour going over the location of each one, hammering it home that there wasn't a single unmonitored spot outside of the house.

She'd laughed and asked, "Why stop there? Why not have cameras in the house too?"

He'd pursed his lips into the unhappy grimace she'd come to know, love, and openly mock during preproduction. "Because they all mysteriously stop working within a week."

"Maybe someone is breaking them."

"No one has lived there as a permanent resident in years.

Because of its unfortunate location and . . . *proclivities*, the most my family has ever used it for were temporary getaways. Every repair tech reports the cameras are functional during tests and for the first six days post-installation. Something makes them go offline on the seventh."

She'd begun vibrating with excitement by that point, barely able to hide her fascination. "*Wow*. How long has that been happening?"

"We made the decision to stop trying a few years ago."

As soon as Lucky opened the door, the alarm began beeping directly on her left. She entered the code on the first try, brought her suitcases inside, and shut the door, pushing firmly against the old wood despite the latch sliding home without resistance.

Not a creak, not a groan, not a hint of warped wood to be found.

She'd read somewhere that dogs understood everything their people said, and relatedly, that plants responded to warm, soothing voices. An alleged haunted house might appreciate the effort as well.

"Hello, Hennessee House." She smiled. "My name is Lucky Hart."

Every curtain had been closed. She surveyed the foyer, the stairs directly in front of her, the rooms on either side, and the hall to the right of the stairs that led farther into the house.

Temperature—warm, almost perfect.

Notable smells—hints of a pine-scented cleaner and fresh laundry.

Appearance—identical to the pictures.

Her instructions said to go straight. She assumed that meant the hall next to the stairs.

No rugs on the aged hardwood floor. No paintings or pictures on the walls. One lone table rested in the middle of the hallway with a flowered vase on top. The same exact purple flowers dotted along the light brown and cream wallpaper.

"At least it's not yellow," she mumbled absently.

After passing the length of the stairs, and the intriguing door in the wall underneath it, the hall suddenly split into two. On her left, a short perpendicular offshoot led to a dead-end window with a door on each side.

Her eye twitched in defiance. She wanted to go that way. She *needed* to go there.

Xander could've lied about the cameras not working in the house as a test to see how well she followed directions. They absolutely had some method of keeping tabs on her—she didn't believe for a second they didn't. Alternatively, her forced first night imprisonment could've been to ensure the mechanisms designed to make the house moan, the doors slam, and the vents whisper her name in the night stayed a secret.

Her palms began to sweat. Temptation was a real bitch sometimes.

She also had to at least consider Xander's rules might belong to Hennessee itself. Wandering might be unsafe. Maverick said he'd explain more in the morning, but in the next breath claimed nothing happened on the first night. The implication being she'd be protected only if she did as instructed.

If one wanted to rob a bank, the inside man couldn't immediately begin casing the safe and interrogating the manager on their first day of work. They mastered their job *while* keeping their eyes and ears on everyone else's. Their patience would pay off eventually, organically through trust.

Logic won that afternoon. She'd follow their damn rules for as long as her patience would allow.

Half against her will, she marched forward into the kitchen. A large brown picnic basket with a red gingham trim sat on the center island. The room was decently sized, filled with colorful retro-style appliances, a small round dining table for four, gorgeous windows, and a Dutch door to the backyard.

Her jaw dropped. A large white gazebo partially blocked the view of what had to be an orchard—an actual, honest-to-God orchard thriving with flowering bushes and gloriously colorful fruit trees. She grabbed the counter to stop herself from sprinting outside. That wasn't in the pictures! Even from where she stood its allure curled around her sweet as smoke, nearly overwhelming, as if it were calling to her, inviting her to walk along its paths, pick its fruit, take naps in its shade—

"*Go upstairs. Go upstairs. Go upstairs.*" She continued chanting under her breath as she picked up the picnic basket. Eyes narrowed into slits, she flew like a bat out of hell straight to the foyer.

Her abysmal self-control wouldn't last much longer! She didn't want to see anything else! It took two painful trips to get all her stuff upstairs. Curiosity pawed at her like a mischievous cat, begging her to break the rules the entire time, but she made it.

Unlike the orchard, the bedroom was the very same she'd seen in the pictures, all dark wooden furniture with rich plum-colored bedding and curtains. She put her clothes away in the walk-in closet and decorated the room with a stack of books on the nightstand, comforting pictures and a jewelry case on the dresser, and a hot pink stuffed lion and her laptop on the bed.

Now this was the part where Lucky was supposed to call

someone to let them know she'd arrived safely and gush over the beautiful house.

Except she had no one. No point in scrolling through her contacts pretending she did.

Someone somewhere would care if she died. Probably her brother. He'd do the right thing and claim her remains. Until then he, and the rest of them, cared very little about her day-to-day life. Thinking of her family hurt like a recurring muscle twinge, easy enough to massage away. She'd stopped being sad about it a long time ago.

Having friends required dedicating time to cultivating a social life. Her messages used to be filled with all kinds of check-ins and invites. She'd decline—choosing to spend her time research-ing instead, going on expeditions, conducting interviews, writing papers, and publishing anonymous blog posts with her findings. She made time for her dreams by sacrificing everything, and everyone, else.

And now she was in Hennessee House. Right where she wanted to be with no room for regret.

The attached bathroom was wonderfully equal in size with a clawfoot tub and a separate shower. Drawing perfect baths was as delicate a science as her supernatural research. She'd been forced to master it after years of nannying. She was a hands-on—playtime, cartwheel competitions, trampoline, hide-and-seek—active kind of nanny. Dollar store bubble bath, lavender baby oil, and a sprinkle of Epsom salt hadn't failed her aching body yet. Carefully, she lowered herself into the hot water, groaning with pleasure as she went. Her feet barely brushed the drain at the head of the tub, and she reclined her head on the rim.

"I could get used to this," she said to absolutely no one.

Lucky had never lived anywhere with a tub big enough to fit her entire body with room to spare. She always had to bend her knees, or it was so shallow the water barely passed her waist. She'd punch a ghost, unprovoked, dead in the face for this tub alone.

Perhaps that was the thought that caused the bedroom door to slowly drift open wider.

She pretended to not notice, humming as she casually reached into her toiletries bag to get her nail brush and spare switchblade. Under the water, she dropped one and flipped the other open. She might die, but she was sure as shit taking her attacker with her.

A merciless, relaxed calm flooded her taut muscles with purpose. She cleared her mind of everything except her self-defense training. Xander promised there'd be no people running around in sheets or special effects makeup to scare her. She'd warned him she knew how to fight if there were. Learning how had become a necessity after a group expedition in a condemned basement laboratory went sideways. Her self-defense instructor taught her "you don't have to get ready if you stay ready." A lesson she took to heart.

But instead of an intruder, a gust of wind blew toward her as if she were standing directly in front of an air conditioner. It cut straight through her, making her shiver, and instantly cooling her bathwater.

It disappeared as quickly as it had arrived but left something behind.

In the bedroom, a mason jar with a purple flower inside sat on top of the old chest directly at the foot of the bed—the same kind of purple flower as on the wallpaper downstairs.

She grabbed her towel, thinking quickly as she headed into the bedroom. That jar hadn't been there before. She *would've* noticed.

A welcome gift?

A *warning* gift? No different than an abusive partner trying to soften her up for the blows to come later.

Her hand stalled with hesitation before ultimately reaching out to pick the jar up. She'd started with respect and would see that plan through. "Thank you." She swallowed hard, forcing her uncertainty back down. "This is so nice. I'll put it on the dresser for now."

Bath ruined, she dressed and unpacked her picnic basket, ate dinner, and swapped the cotton pillowcases on the bed for her satin ones to protect her hair. She'd always been a light, restless sleeper. Bonnets, scarves, wraps, you name it, never lasted longer than an hour on her head because she tossed and turned so much.

Her eyes had begun to drift closed as she read a book in bed when her phone rang.

"Hello?"

"Hi, Lucky? It's Maverick."

She sat bolt upright instantly, stomach somersaulting into oblivion. "Oh. Hi."

He laughed, a husky and amused staccato chuckle. "You sound disappointed."

"I'm not. It's a defense mechanism. Can't be let down if your hopes are never up," she answered without thinking and squeezed her eyes shut in regret. "Sorry. I shouldn't have said that."

"No, that's fine and smart. Although, I don't know if I could live like that. For me, having hope makes life worth living."

She smiled, lowering her head as if she wanted to hide the

sudden burst of expression. Unexpectedly, though, her brain betrayed her by deciding to answer his honesty with nihilism. "The only thing that makes life worth living is the fact that I'm not dead. It's like I'm being forced to survive."

He laughed again, softer that time. "I definitely have questions about that, but I think I'll save them for tomorrow's interview."

"Will you really be here at sunrise?"

"That's the deal. How are you settling in? Still nervous?"

"All settled and tucked into bed." Nerves got to her all the time. She'd felt them in the car, but so far, not at all in the house. Creepy or unsettling feelings weren't following her like a threatening shroud. Getting the flower was . . . strange, at most. Fighting against her desire to do as she pleased had been the most distressing part. "The house hasn't gobbled me up yet."

"I told you nothing happens on the first night."

She glanced at the mason jar. "You sure about that?"

"Did something happen? Wait, no, you can't tell me. I shouldn't even be calling you right now."

"Then why did you?"

"Honestly?" He exhaled into a sigh. "I was . . . worried."

"You . . . you were worried about me?" After three hopeful beats of silence, common sense kicked in. He didn't mean that personally. "Oh, because I'm number four, right? I know my predecessors didn't last long."

"No," he said matter-of-factly. No room for anything else. "I didn't call them. I didn't even think to. Earlier, you sounded a little panicked and I honestly haven't stopped thinking about it."

"Shit, sorry. I promise that wasn't because of the house. I'm fine here. I don't feel unsafe. I don't feel scared. It's a little jarring being somewhere with so much space and no one to share it with because I'm used to my tiny room in my tiny apartment, but other than that I'm okay."

"If it wasn't the house, what made you so nervous?"

She sat stuck in the moment, struggling to find her next words. How could she explain to him that her dreams, plural, were literally coming true without giving herself away?

NQP hired a struggling and aimless not-quite-young-adult who was supposed to learn that she'd bitten off more than she could chew. Telling the truth to reassure Maverick had been a rookie mistake. So, why did she do it? Why did she *keep* doing it?

A small, purple dot moved in her peripheral vision. She turned toward it, watching as the flower in the mason jar spun quickly in a circle at the bottom, moving faster and faster as if caught in a twister.

The hairs on the back of Lucky's neck stood up. "Maverick," she said with perfect, practiced calm. "I'm not afraid, but for the sake of the show, I think I need to hang up now."

A beat of silence on his end, then, "Is something happening?"

Stephen wanted a story. As much as it pained her, this would have to be a part of that. "Good night. Don't worry about me, okay?"

"We all live about an hour away," he said quickly. "Promise you'll call me or even Stephen if you need to?"

"I promise."

"I'm choosing to believe you again." He paused. "Good night."

Lucky smiled softly. "I'll see you at sunrise."

The purple flower began to levitate.

5

To Lucky's eternal disappointment, nothing more happened in Hennessee House.

She'd slid off the bed, hurrying to the dresser only to watch with complete devastation as the flower drifted back to the bottom of the jar. She'd stood there willing it to move, concentrating so hard she gave herself a headache. Confirming, once again, that telekinesis would continue to be her great white whale.

Eventually, she'd fallen into a dreamless sleep with her phone clutched in her hand. Hennessee House wouldn't catch her slacking again, but the only action the phone saw was ringing.

"Lucky?"

It took a full three seconds before she remembered where she was, why she was there, and realized who was calling. "Maverick. Hi." She buried her sleepy smile into her pillow.

"You're okay?"

"I am. Wait, hold on, let me actually check." Her full-body

stretch ended in a yawn. "My muscles are in working order, I can wiggle my toes and fingers, and I have all my senses. I think I just might have survived my first night."

"Good. I wasn't worried. Not even a little bit. Didn't think about calling you again at all."

She snickered. "That's very sweet. Thank you."

"Yeah. Well." He cleared his throat. "We'll be there in about an hour. Don't leave your room until you hear the doorbell."

Lucky glanced at the window. The first colors of rising dawn had barely crested over the horizon. Great. More waiting. She'd planned to use at least a few minutes of her sunrise-provided freedom checking things out solo. So much for that.

She started getting ready, from her usual morning journal session to agonizing over what to wear. Her picnic basket provided an assortment of snacks and prepackaged breakfast foods because they *really* didn't want her leaving the room a millisecond before she had to. With time to spare, she ended up sitting on the bed, bored and all but twiddling her thumbs while waiting to meet Maverick Phillips.

Beyond a Reasonable Doubt, *BARD* for short, was entertaining, thoughtful, well written, award-winning, et cetera, et cetera. On the show, Maverick interviewed people claiming to have had paranormal experiences. Whether they'd been haunted, tormented, or comforted by their encounters, he gave them the space to exist free of judgment or ridicule. He asked questions that expertly exposed the hearts of their stories, allowing their truths to finally be seen. Afterward he attempted to investigate their claims with his team to support a larger narrative based around his character, but that was neither here nor there.

Those interviews with Maverick's empathy, compassion, and

respect on full display were what captivated viewers. Lucky could easily binge-watch it for hours on end if she had a day off or was too sad to move. It honestly didn't matter. She was always in the mood for it. But that was the show.

Maverick was a very real person whom she'd already seen up close, in night vision, being alternately pensive and playful, and even scared and seconds away from screaming. He exuded a protector kind of confidence and there was a keen, seeking intelligence behind his dark brown eyes—alert and focused, driven by his curiosity, and with an open mind constantly spinning with ideas to explain the unexplainable.

Lucky hoped he'd be like that in real life too.

She gnawed on her thumbnail as anxiety acted like a hook crocheting her organs together in disgusting knots. Getting overexcited and making mistakes was forbidden. No matter what or whom she encountered, she vowed to be the epitome of focused. She refused to let a celebrity disappointing her change that.

The doorbell rang and Lucky shot out of that suite like a runner at the start of the race. Common sense kicked in right as she touched the first dead bolt. She slid on her ability-blocking dark sunglasses in record time.

"Hi, good morning." Lucky stepped to the side, gesturing for him to enter. "Welcome to my haunted house. Please come in."

Amazingly, Maverick was even more attractive in person.

Nothing surprised her about how lean and muscular his body was, his cool brown skin, or his closely cropped beard. While his hair had grown out some, he was exactly as tall as she'd thought he'd be. With the right pair of heels, they'd stand eye to eye. All of that she expected, but there was . . . more. She couldn't quite put her finger on the difference. Almost as if the camera only caught a fraction of his radiance, enough to draw the viewer in, and gave up on capturing the rest because it couldn't. With no filters or lenses, he was just . . . more. Whole and mesmerizing.

Her brain felt empty. No thoughts. No words except *more*.

More to him. More of him. More Maverick in her life, please and thank you.

Getting starstruck apparently existed in her emotional wheel-house. Who knew? She sure didn't!

"Everything okay?" Maverick remained on the porch. A large black bag rested at his feet.

"Why wouldn't it be?"

"You're wearing sunglasses."

"Yeah, because I'm not ready to take them off yet."

He eyed her carefully, as if he were searching for something. "You also seem a little . . . flustered."

"Impossible. That's something that happens to other people. Not me." She glanced outside, spotting Stephen and two others near the back of a black van. "Are they not coming in?"

"The team is reshooting some exterior shots. Stephen is directing under the guise of producing. They'll join us once they're done."

"Oh, perfect," she said, genuinely relieved. "Are *you* going to come in? Unless you planned to interview me here?"

Maverick stared at her for a beat, face unreadable. "Let's do it in the library."

"I love libraries." She cringed so hard she almost bit her cheek. Shit, she *did* sound flustered. And breathless. And *starstruck*.

"Perfect. Follow me." Maverick smiled, clearly amused.

As he led the way, she gestured to his camera bag. "Are we

filming right away? I was only able to change my outfit six times. I'm not sure if I want to make my *Caretaker* debut looking like a long-lost Super Mario sibling."

Pointing out her blue overalls and purple sweatshirt seemed like a cute way to make a joke. Hopefully he'd think she'd been acting funny on purpose instead of being betrayed by her brain on the biggest day of her career so far.

"We can go audio only if that's what you prefer. You look fine, by the way."

"Fine?"

"Yeah. Very . . . wholesome."

She laughed at that. "I'm not, though." Her thoughts were growing darker by the second. If she embarrassed herself one more time, she was going to throw herself down a well.

"Film and TV are all smoke and mirrors. You'll fit right in." He shrugged, seemingly not noticing her despair, and turned left at the previous night's perpendicular temptation.

Lucky had no idea Hennessee House had a library. Stephen wanted her to discover the home layout gradually and wouldn't let Xander tell her much. Even the map he'd used to show her the security cameras used generic labels like *downstairs room three*.

"*Ooh*," she breathed.

Fully stocked bookshelves wrapped around the entire room with breaks only for the door and windows. Non-matching armchairs draped with decorative pillows and throw blankets had been staged over a circular, slate gray rug that covered a large section of the floor. A modest chandelier hung in the center of the ceiling, but there were also standing lamps with curved poles that created intimate overhead spotlights above a few of the chairs.

"It's nice, right? It's my favorite room in the house."

"I love it." She nodded, wandering farther inside and ending up standing at the window facing the orchard.

The compulsion to run out there hit her again like a shot of pure dopamine. Small miracle that she didn't press her hands and face up against the glass, breathing heavily through her restraint.

Interesting. Perhaps her reaction meant something other than her usual impulsive desires getting out of hand. She made a note on her phone—create an outline for orchard sub-investigation. Include sensation map as it relates to being inside HH and out.

Maverick appeared next to her. "Ready?"

"Yep." She switched documents to her prepared outline for the day.

The Caretaker would be Lucky's official, main stage debut into the supernatural industry—and she needed her ESP to be spotlighted in the show. Years of being ostracized had taught her to hide her ability at all costs, but it was time. She felt ready (or at least had convinced herself she was).

Her plan involved establishing that while she was familiar with Maverick, she could prove her first impression ability by knowing things only he would. He'd then hopefully vouch for her before she read the rest of the team.

When they inevitably asked why she hadn't disclosed her ability during the interview, she already had her answer prepared.

The main objective of *The Caretaker* was storytelling—an ordinary person relaying their supernatural encounters over time. Her contact at NQP disclosed production was rapidly becoming a shit show. No one had anticipated Hennessee House's darkly enthusiastic participation. In short, the house had been taking things too far.

NQP wanted people from all walks of life that they could mold to fit their narrative. A college-educated, super believer, ESP girlie like her wouldn't have made it past the first round. But now that she was there, she'd make it worth their while. As promised.

Lucky's ability only worked on people. Humans, to be specific. A haunted house might be impossible . . . but what if it wasn't? What if she found the equivalent of its eyes and willingly stared at it?

Three caretakers couldn't hack it. She'd not only be the exception, she'd also be able to explain why. Lucky began, "I've always wondered how much of the real Maverick is in the show version. Is it really all an act?"

"Show Maverick's backstory is made up." He spoke slowly as if he were considering each word. "I've never been married. My parents are alive. I'm nowhere near an only child. I'm more interested in writing stories than being one."

She nodded, unable to resist looking out the window again. A black cat was curled underneath one of the fruit trees.

"I purposefully made his life the opposite of mine to keep myself grounded. I had a feeling I would need that space," he continued, the words tumbling out of him now. "But I think we're both lethally curious. It's a sickness really. We both want to understand everything. If there's a reason for something, he wants to know what it is and won't stop until he gets an answer. Personally, I'm okay if an answer *doesn't* exist. I care more about what I can learn from an experience and how I can move forward with that information."

"*Oh.*" That got her attention. Bit of a rarity for people to be that self-aware.

She'd made it a point to not get that deep into the *BARD* fandom. Her own adventures were more important to her than discussing his online. Still, she'd known about the long-standing debate on whether Maverick was playing a fictional character or a thinly veiled self-insert. No one knew for sure.

The answer resided somewhere in the middle like a rabbit in a magician's hat—the illusion in place well before the audience arrived. The notable details about him were probably true: the deep empathy he displayed while interviewing, how inquisitive and brave he could be, and the unwavering hopeful look in his eye whenever he was unable to solve a case after giving it his all. He *wanted* to believe.

Lucky had been right in deciding to play it this way. Everything truly began with Maverick. *BARD* viewers trusted him *and* his character. NQP was banking on that crossover audience. If Lucky could convince him, everyone else would fall in line and *believe* her.

"I suspected as much." She nodded. "Would you like to know more about yourself? I can tell you if you're up for a little challenge."

He frowned, confused. "What do you mean by that?"

"Is that an on-the-record question?"

"Doesn't have to be."

"It should be. Turn on your camera. It'll be good for the show."

They repositioned a pair of armchairs in front of the windows to make use of the natural lighting, setting them next to each other at an angle to ensure they'd both be in frame. After handing her a small microphone to hold and a quick sound test, he made some preliminary notes for someone named Therese.

He asked, "Have you ever been interviewed before?"

"Probably not in the way you're thinking."

"What makes you think you know what I'm thinking?"

"Oh, it's way too early for you to have all my secrets. You only get one today and that's not it."

His eyes narrowed quickly before relaxing. "Do you always make cryptic little remarks like that?"

"No." She grinned, leaning toward him. "I'm trying to be mysterious. Is it working?"

"It's not *not* working," he admitted. "Before we officially begin discussing your first night in Hennessee House, could you tell me a little about yourself? Specifically, what you were referring to earlier."

"I'm not psychic," she said immediately. "I can't tell the future, and no, I don't know what you're going to do next, but I can read people. *People*, not their auras or anything like that. I'm talking about personality, likes, dislikes, core beliefs, important events that shaped them, repressed memories, and their secrets—the ones they know about and some they might not. First impressions truly tell me everything *I* need to know."

Surprise rippled across his face like a wave before subsiding. He smoothly transitioned back into his usual neutral interviewer expression she'd seen dozens of times. Kind of impressive to see it in real time. "I have to admit, I wasn't expecting you to say that."

"No one ever does." She gave him a rare, wistful smile. "I don't know why or how I can do it. I just can. And I'm almost never wrong."

Maverick glanced at the camera, purposefully displaying a concerned look. She knew he wanted to create tension for the audience. She also knew he wanted them to know he knew what was coming and, against his better judgment, decided to share it with them.

"I would never say that I don't believe you," he said, measured and certain. "Is there any way you can demonstrate this ability for me? Would you be comfortable doing that?"

He was so delightfully wonderful at his job. She felt herself beginning to relax, sinking back into the chair, a contented sigh waiting to leave her lungs. This was how she felt watching his show. Something about the way he worked always set her spirit at ease.

When she didn't answer, he pressed, "Lucky?"

She looked away, staring at the floor as if they'd rehearsed it. "I could read you. If you want." She removed her glasses, folding and hanging them on her front pocket. "I normally don't warn people before I do this, so if you're game, I'm going to read you now."

His nervous laugh didn't sound entirely fake. "How does it work?"

"Once per person. Repeat first impressions highly unlikely. Individual experiences may vary." Her delivery implied a joke, but it wasn't. Especially that last point. "Really, I'll just look at your eyes and then I'll know."

"Don't look at me yet."

She almost did, reflexively jerking toward him. "Okay?"

"Do you mind if we pause for just a second? I thought of something, and I don't want to lose it."

She kept her gaze down, using her hand like a shield on her forehead to block herself from accidentally looking at him. His nimble thumbs typed expertly fast as she leaned in closer to see . . .

"It's just some notes," he said, still going.

"I saw my name."

"Because I'm writing about you."

"Interview questions?"

"Nope."

"A true-or-false personality test to see if I'm not *psychic* psychic?"

He laughed. "No, again. That's an interesting way to phrase it. Is that what you call your gift?"

"Only when I'm being funny. I don't vibe with words like *clairvoyant* or *psychic*. Formally, I've dubbed it a 'first impression ability.' Informally, I'm an ESP girlie."

"And what made you decide to tell me about it?"

She heard the smile in his voice and relaxed that much more. "Because you believe people. Everyone always thinks I'm lying. I thought you might give me the benefit of the doubt like you do to guests on your show. Which you did, so thank you."

His phone rang—Stephen's picture appeared on the screen. "Ah, hold on, I have to take this. Don't look at me yet," he said playfully.

"I won't." She laughed.

"Hey, what's up, we're in the library— No, why would she be with me—? What do you mean she's gone?" He stood up, speed walking toward the hall. "Lucky, I'll be right back!"

"Okay. I'll wait here," she said to the empty room.

A few moments later, she heard a chorus of voices yelling outside but couldn't make out what they were saying. From the window, she didn't see anyone in the backyard. They must have been on the side or toward the front of the house. Part of her thought she should go see if they needed help. Then again, if they needed it, Maverick would've asked. Overstepping on her first day seemed like a bad idea.

Besides, and most importantly, sunrise had officially come and gone.

6

Ten minutes. Lucky decided to give Maverick ten minutes to come back before she left the library. That seemed fair. Coincidentally, that was about how long she projected it would take her to inspect the room.

There wasn't much else to it, and she felt fine being in there. She started at the door, walking the right-side perimeter, and touching random places. No cold spots. No change in energy. She passed the windows with her back turned, eyes closed—and immediately felt a pinch between her shoulder blades and at the base of her neck.

Whatever lure the orchard used still had its claws in her. She bit her lip to disguise her gleeful smile as she opened her notes again:

Might be a visual-based compulsion? Also capable of retaining access through proximity.

She'd have to be careful out there, but make no mistake, she was fully prepared to give in to the pressure. Her gut didn't even disagree.

It had taken her a considerable amount of trial and error to find a balance between her instincts and her reckless desire for knowledge. If a location felt dangerous, but she wanted something that could only be found inside? Eight times out of ten, she'd be in there. Hopefully along with several contingency plans in place including two clear paths for exit.

Hopefully. Almost never always.

Once, she'd needed a quick escape and jumped out of a window on the second floor of a multistory building. She accidentally discovered the trick to not breaking one's legs when falling—hit the ground at an angle and roll with the momentum.

Getting trapped in an orchard surrounded by neighbors with a production crew nearby wouldn't be nearly as bad. Probably.

Lucky moved on to browsing the books neatly arranged in the built-in bookcases. The collection had its fair share of literary classics, an entire section of mass-market romance paperbacks, and a few popular titles she recognized that'd been published in the last few years.

At home, every single book in her collection had already been read—her choices curated from borrowing library books first. She always bought physical copies of the ones she loved best. If they had a space on her shelf, then they had a place in her heart. She couldn't imagine having a whole room dedicated to a personal library full of books she'd never read, waiting for her to choose them.

Like any sensible bookworm, she'd brought her e-reader and a small carry-on bag full of physical books. Gothic manor willing, she was going to be there an entire month. She needed to keep busy! She needed options! She'd already unpacked them upstairs but could use a few more. As she searched reviews online for the titles that caught her eye, a muffled voice stole her attention.

Her entire being went still as a deer caught in headlights, eyes wide and searching. The sound was coming from directly in front of her and had a slight echo.

She brought her ear as close as possible to the back panel of the shelf.

Footsteps. Someone was walking around in what sounded like an enclosed space.

Years of discipline had taught her to jump to plausible conclusions before entertaining supernatural ones. Even as her heart hammered with excitement and adrenaline flooded her system, she forced herself to think through the situation rationally.

Someone in the walls leaned toward improbable because there wasn't another room next to the library . . . unless it had a false wall with a secret room behind it.

Lucky sprang into action, efficiently measuring by walking heel to toe from the doorway to the shelves, repeating the process in the hall until she hit the dead-end window. The shelves, which were the length of her hand from palm to fingertip, were nowhere near deep enough to take up the extra measured space in the hallway.

A secret room was in fact the likely solution. But who, or what, was inside?

Lucky frowned, standing in the doorway with her hands on her hips as she considered her options. Trusty switchblade in her overalls pocket, she walked to the window at the end of the hall again. She didn't know how the intruder got in, and if they made a break for it, she wanted to watch them do it. After clearing her throat, she shouted, "Whoever is in there, you better come out right now before I call the police."

She wasn't going to call the police. If anything, she'd call the private security company number Xander gave her to handle this.

"Right. Now." She ground her teeth—it better not be a damn ghost. She was *promised* no ghosts. "You too, Casper! The order still stands. Out here, right now, front and center. I don't have all day."

Rapid footsteps. Something knocked against the wall. A tiny whispered "*Ow.*"

"Don't make me count to five!"

A loud click sounded from inside the library—Lucky darted back to the room. She pushed past her rattling nerves and the dread crawling up her throat like a scream. Being in tune with her body and her fear kept her alive. Searching for the supernatural came with risks she was willing to take . . . up to a point.

In the far left corner, the smallest section of shelving moved away from the wall like a door. A brown face framed by braids appeared in the opening. "Casper?" she chirped hopefully, eyebrows raised.

Lucky continued to frown as her jaw dropped.

There was a little girl in Hennessee House. A little girl walking around inside the walls talking to herself.

Everything about the intruder screamed adorable. From her sweet little voice to her wide brown eyes to the cluster of freckles on her nose and forehead. She reminded Lucky of a strawberry shortcake with her khaki shorts, white shirt, and bright red bandana. It'd been folded into a headband, with the ends sticking up like bunny ears atop her head. She wasn't scared. Or worried. Or apologetic. Instead, she was bursting with stubborn hope and daring magic in equal measures. Childlike wonder and mischief personified, but not the kind that faded over time. She'd only grow brighter, more inquisitive with each passing year.

Reading children occasionally threw Lucky. For the most part, a person's core almost never changed. Personality? Yes. Core? Unlikely. People were who they were, whether or not they discovered it yet. However, sometimes children felt a little . . . soft. All the ingredients were there but hadn't finished cooking. This girl, however, seemed to be done.

"Well, at least you're not a sickly Victorian child." Lucky pointed to one of the armchairs. "Sit down."

The little girl obliged. Head slightly bowed, she plopped down, sitting all the way back with her feet hovering above the ground.

"Don't move."

The room beyond the shelf door was small, rectangular, and exactly the length of the unaccounted-for slice of library. Empty with no direct source of light, it smelled like dust and grass, and didn't seem to have any other way in besides where she stood. No trap doors in the ceiling. Nothing on or near the floor.

Lucky glanced at her unexpected guest. How in the hell did she get in? Her clothes were clean and pressed—someone had ironed pleats into her shorts. And those suckers were *crisp*.

Kids, and their clothes, didn't stay neat like that on their own. The millisecond they got dressed, stains and wrinkles mysteriously appeared out of nowhere. Once while working as a nanny, she had to stop one of her former kids from wearing tights full of runs to church because she "didn't care" and another from wearing a dirty dress fresh out of the hamper because it was her "favorite." On the same morning.

Looks could be deceiving, but Lucky felt confident enough to bet that this little girl was well cared for. She wasn't a missing kid living in the walls of a usually empty house because she had nowhere else to go.

She closed the door. "What's your name?"

"Rebel."

"You lying?"

"My dad said he thought I was going to be a boy and he wanted to name me after him, but I'm a girl so he decided to give me my own name that was like his but different."

"Uh-huh. Are you here by yourself?"

"Umm, well, right now I'm here with you."

"Don't be cute. That doesn't work on me, Shortcake," she lied. Most regrettably, it did. Her one true nanny-weakness. "Answer my questions. Are you here by yourself *and* how did you get in there?"

Rebel grimaced, clearly weighing if she should divulge her secrets. "You know that small red square on the side of the house?"

She didn't but said, "Go on."

"Well," Rebel said, dragging out the word and tilting her head. "It's actually a door. There's a crawl space thingy and if you go through there it takes you to that room. I saw it on the house pictures but nobody else seemed to, so I thought it'd be okay to check it out for my show."

"*Your* show? Why do *you* have pictures of the house?"

"Well, *I* don't have them. I saw them during the meeting this morning. They were talking about 'external shots.' That means outside videos."

Realization clicked into place at light speed—Maverick. *Rebel*. Now that Lucky connected the dots, she couldn't unsee it. They had the same eyes and a similar smile. "You must be the young but very talented intern Maverick told me about."

Rebel nodded enthusiastically. "I get to be the intern instead of going to summer camp in Massachusetts."

"So, then you must know that part of being an intern means telling your team where you are and not wandering off. I'm pretty sure they're looking for you right now."

"I didn't *wander*. It sounds bad when you say it like that." Rebel shrugged, beginning to resemble a flower in mid-wilt, drooping and gloomy. "I asked Georgia if we could go see the red door together and she said no, that I should wait in the gazebo, so I did that and then I got bored. I was *working*, not wandering."

"Ah, Shortcake, you might be too much for me." Lucky smiled gently. "Come on, let's go put them out of their misery."

In one of the front rooms, Lucky and Rebel peeked around the curtains to spy on the adults through the window. They all stood by the van, no doubt panicked out of their minds. "Okay, Shortcake. We're gonna play it cool. They're mad but you're fine so we're going to try distracting them, okay?"

"Oh, okay," Rebel said, brightening.

"Be happy. Excited. Jubilant. Follow my lead." Lucky put her sunglasses on before opening the front door and calling out, "Hey, you'll *never* guess who I found safe and sound inside the house."

Rebel helped by yelling "Hi, Dad!" and waving. "I met Lucky! You're right, she's really nice!"

"Did any of you know there was a secret room in the library? Because she did!"

"And there's a ghost! Lucky said so!"

She stared at Rebel. "Whoa, whoa, I never said *anything* about a ghost."

"You said 'Casper.' He's a ghost."

Man, this kid was quick. "Again, I never said ghost. Don't put words in my mouth."

Rebel giggled. "My grandma says that to me too."

"I bet she does." She grinned.

By then, Maverick had reached the top of the porch. "Lucky." He breathed her name as if it were an enraptured, thankful prayer.

Meeting him felt like the thrill of a lifetime. Hearing him say her name like that threatened to send her gasping into the afterlife. So strange. So bizarre. So dangerously against her nature that she felt a little lightheaded from the emerging dynamic.

But his grateful smile vanished as his gaze drifted from her to Rebel. His entire body deflated with relief-tinged disappointment. She'd seen that look dozens of times. Rebel was safe. She wasn't hurt. Still, ten minutes might as well have been an eternity.

Maverick asked, "Why didn't you answer your phone?"

The situation was worse than Lucky had initially thought. Rebel had turned on airplane mode. Once reconnected, an avalanche of messages pinged one after another.

Rebel shrugged. "I didn't want my video to get messed up."

Maverick's expression slid into a passive mask, but she read the tension in his eyes with ease. A speechless parent who mastered self-control out of sheer determination to be better.

"Not cool, little miss." A young woman, presumably Georgia, stood next to Maverick. She was only a little bit taller than Rebel, with golden skin, bone-straight black hair, sharp features, and dark eyes that dominated her face. She crossed her arms while glowering. "Rule number one?"

Rebel mumbled, "We don't go no contact."

"No radio silence. No airplane mode. And number two?"

"Answer when called and always call for backup."

"Oh, so you do know what you're not supposed to do."

"Sorry, Georgia."

Stephen said, "Chase, why don't you and Georgia go inside? We'll be in shortly."

Chase guided the still-brooding Georgia toward the open front door. Average height and stocky, his immaculately styled curly red hair matched the freckles on his fair-skinned face. As he passed, he said to Rebel, "Thanks for the heart attack. Been wondering what one of those felt like."

"Sorry, Chase."

Stephen clasped his hands together and addressed Rebel directly. "You obviously have to stay here but are hereby being symbolically sent home with no pay." He gave her shoulder an encouraging squeeze on his way inside. "We'll try again tomorrow."

Watching them each talk to Rebel was fascinating. Under the hurt and disappointment, Lucky realized they were taking Rebel seriously. Being an intern wasn't some fun, honorary title because Maverick couldn't find a sitter. She really was a part of their team, held to the same standards as everyone else. Progressive discipline and all.

She respected them for it instantly. Anyone who saw fit to treat tiny humans as such were all right in her book.

"Lucky, can you give us a minute?" Maverick asked.

"Of course." She turned to Rebel, saying, "See you on the other side, Shortcake."

7

Hennessee House's interior looked different when touched by sunshine. The wood seemed brighter, tinged with a reddish hue Lucky didn't notice before. The air felt lighter, as if pulling the curtains back finally allowed the house to breathe.

Georgia, the curtain culprit, had opened them in the parlor room to the left and Lucky watched as she finished in the sitting room on the right. Chase and Stephen stood nearby behind a loveseat with dark green velvet cushions and carved wood trim.

"You forgot one." The final curtained window was dead center on the far wall. Lucky headed for it with the aim of being helpful.

"Oh, no point in opening it. House wants it closed."

Lucky froze, hands hovering near the thick drapes. "Really?"

Georgia nodded as she took the camera Stephen was holding, leaving him empty-handed. "Walk out the room, come back, and it'll be closed."

Chase added, "It'll stay open as long as someone is in here. Hennessee isn't that rude." He also had a camera.

"Maybe you should try it," Stephen said. "See what happens for yourself."

Challenge accepted. She inspected them first—a matching velvet, albeit a darker shade of green than the couch, and soft to the touch. A bold choice. The cleaning bill must have been outrageous. Xander better not be expecting her to dust while living there.

"My guess is they're on a timer or there's a mechanism to close them remotely." The moment she pulled them aside, a strong cinnamon scent blew into her face. "Did they put perfume on these?" She sneezed twice in a row.

"No." Stephen's tone was noticeably flat. "Why?"

"You don't smell that?" She waved the air in front of her face. "It's like a milky cinnamon latte with extra cinnamon shoved right into my nasal passages." It was so strong she could taste it, and she began to cough a little.

"That's specific. I don't smell anything," Stephen said, and Georgia nodded in agreement before adding, "Must be for you. Nice glasses."

"Thanks. Never go in public without them."

Georgia raised an assessing eyebrow as she gave Lucky a once-over, who returned the gesture. She never played girl hate games but knew that wasn't true for everyone. Georgia might have been used to flying solo on their team and saw her as a threat instead of a potential ally.

"I like your outfit too." Georgia's grin didn't feel entirely harmless. "It's so quirky."

"I like your . . . *everything*. Captivating suits you."

Georgia, taken aback, seemingly glanced at Stephen for help.

"I tried to warn you," he said, shaking his head.

Countering with unique compliments never failed Lucky, especially when she meant them. Charm didn't come naturally to her. She'd put in a metric ton's worth of effort studying how to be the kind of person everyone liked. Learning how to work a room by using innocuous flirting had been a big part of that.

A name like Lucky came with certain expectations. There was a story there. It made people stop and smile. Do a double take and ask questions. Lighting up a room with her presence, and all it entailed, became her default.

Chase cleared his throat. "Lucky, have you had breakfast yet? When Maverick comes in he's going to cook as part of the show."

"Only picnic basket snacks. I wasn't allowed to leave the room."

He seemed surprised as he led the way. The sitting room, dining room, and kitchen were connected, only separated by beautiful open archways and differing décor. "And you actually didn't? That'd make you the first."

Her pleasant smile grew strained on her face. ". . . what?"

"Oh yeah." Chase paused to *laugh*. "The next morning everyone else fessed up to wandering around."

Sonofa—

Lucky's swear-filled thoughts came to an abrupt halt as they crossed under the archway into the dining room. Peppermint, stronger than the cinnamon had been, flooded her senses. It stung her nose, burned her eyes, and tingled on her skin. "*Oh my god.*" She regretted speaking because it coated her mouth with an overpowering frosty aftertaste. "What is *that*?"

"What's what?" The three of them stared at her.

"It's like one of those scented wall plug-ins exploded in here." She gripped the back of the closest dining room chair to stay upright, fingers squeezing into the wood to keep from overloading into a blackout. "You don't smell that? *At all?*"

Chase's camera was suddenly trained on her as Stephen said, just as monotone as before, "I don't smell anything."

She squinted at him through her discomfort. When she eventually made her way through reading the team, he'd be first. That couldn't be the same man from her interview. He'd turned uninspired, as flat and dry as a water cracker.

"The house does that sometimes." Georgia's relenting sigh was a welcome sign of solidarity. "Makes you smell things that aren't there."

Stephen cut his eyes at her—a clear supervisory glare meant to shut her up.

Olfactory hallucinations! If Lucky weren't in pain, she'd be thrilled. "But I don't just *smell* peppermint. It's like it's invading me."

"What does peppermint mean to you?" Maverick stood behind them with Rebel at his side, both their faces pinched with concern. "If you're the only one who smells it, then it's specifically for you."

"Nothing?" She answered honestly and then realized what he'd said. "Even if it did, how would the house know that?"

"Why don't we have breakfast?" Chase said loudly. "The kitchen is right there. Let's just keep moving. Come on. Let's go." He waved them forward as if he were directing traffic while deftly continuing to film.

Rebel darted forward, grabbing Lucky's hand. "Do you want to sit together? My dad is making omelets!" For someone so small, she could double as a mini tow truck. They passed under the second archway together, entering the familiar kitchen, and the overwhelming scentsation instantly faded.

"Better?" Rebel asked immediately.

"Yes, actually." She blinked, suddenly feeling perfectly fine, as if the peppermint scent hadn't nearly incapacitated her entire body. "How did you know that?"

"My dad said the smells don't travel from room to room unless they're leading you somewhere." Rebel waved her down and whispered, "That was supposed to be a secret, but it looked like it was hurting a lot."

She grinned and whispered back, "I see. Thank you."

Secrets turned out to be the theme of the morning.

Chase and Georgia set up their cameras on opposite sides of the kitchen to get a full view of . . . whatever they expected to film. Stephen proclaimed no one was allowed to tell Lucky anything else about Hennessee House until *after* she'd had her interview with Maverick, which made breakfast a spiritless affair with everyone eating in near silence. He didn't want anything else to potentially influence her testimonial.

One thing became clear to Lucky.

Okay, two things.

First: Maverick could *cook*. Seasoned and sautéed mixed vegetables with buttery cheese wrapped in impeccably fluffy eggs with a side of grilled red potatoes—hands down, the best omelet she'd ever had the pleasure of devouring.

Second: Manufactured or not, the production team decided to commit to the bit. Everyone behaved like Xander had during the interview: wholeheartedly certain of Hennessee House's activity. This was fantastic for two additional points.

If the house wasn't haunted, she won—that'd be an automatic

platform to set herself up in opposition to manufactured haunt-ings. Call her Houdini.

If the house was haunted—all the better. She'd be the one to get to the root of it. And again, an automatic platform to talk about her experience and how she planned to continue, parlaying thirty days of sacrifice into a career.

For the time being, she decided to accept that the olfactory hallucinations hadn't been a stunt. She couldn't figure out how no one else had been affected. It'd been so intense, the only way to avoid it involved not breathing, but every single person had spoken at some point.

Post-breakfast, Stephen, Georgia, and Chase resumed their work in the backyard, hoping to film something called *pre-bloom*.

Lucky was once again denied context.

Rude.

Before heading back to the library, Maverick made a pit stop, depositing Rebel in the room across the hall. The office was com-parable in size to the library, except with fewer bookcases and the addition of a fireplace. A wide desk and stately chair sat front and center facing the door. An antique floor globe, empty glass vases, and oddly shaped lamps were the only other items in the strangely minimalist room.

"You're in here." He pulled out the chair for Rebel.

"But, Dad—"

"I don't wanna hear it. You, right at this desk. Bathroom breaks only." He set a laptop down in front of her. "Make me a rough cut using your talent show footage. Any style you want. Think you can do that?"

She nodded glumly. "Can't I work in the library with you?"

"That's my set. Guess where you're not allowed?"

"But I said I was *sorry*."

"Sorry isn't some magic word that makes people automatically forgive you. I know you know what you did was wrong, otherwise you wouldn't have done it behind Georgia's back. How are they supposed to trust you if that's how you choose to behave?"

Lucky began creeping closer to the door to give them space and experienced an immediate change in the room's temperature. It was colder but subtly so, as if a few degrees had been swiped from the air by a skilled pickpocket. One would only realize the absence if they were concentrating. Her preoccupied companions didn't seem to.

Rebel eventually answered, "I don't know."

"Not having an answer yet and needing more time to think about it is okay." He inhaled, filling his lungs, holding it and exhaling as fast as he could. "Let's just put this conversation on pause for now. We'll talk through it some more when we get home."

Lucky had made it across the hall, and was standing in the library doorway when Maverick joined her. She showed him the secret room. He remarked that the camera had been on the entire time. And they sat in their respective chairs again.

It didn't take much more than that to realize something was wrong.

"Hey," she said quietly. "She's fine. Sitting in the next room." They could even see her from where they sat.

Maverick had held it together at breakfast and in front of Rebel, but his internal turmoil began seeping into Lucky the second they were alone. He was spiraling—distant, almost robotic, and ensnared by a mental loop.

"I know. I—" He squeezed his eyes shut, slightly shaking his head.

She placed her hand on top of his to ground him. Occasionally she'd let her nanny care extend to parents. While this wasn't what she'd been hired to do in Hennessee House, taking the time to help him wouldn't hurt anything. She made tight circles with her thumb along his wrist.

His attention snapped back to the present, focusing on their hands and then her face. The look in his eyes made her heartbeat jolt from normal to erratic in what had to be record time, but under her thumb, his remained strong and steady.

"Thank you for finding her." He used that tone again, the same one from earlier when he'd said her name.

"I didn't," she said honestly, automatically. "It was pure coincidence."

"There's no such thing in Hennessee House. I was terrified it lured her away—maybe it did, I don't know."

"Rebel told me she saw the red square in some pictures. She even asked permission first, but Georgia said no. I think she was making her own choices. A bad one, but a choice."

All at once he took a deep, shaking breath, entire torso moving with effort as he returned to himself. "Yeah, that's what she told me too."

Lucky casually pulled her hand away under the guise of fidgeting in her seat. She tried to hide taking the deep breath she needed as well. Did he have any idea how *intense* he felt? "I am in no place to question you, but I'm wondering if it's safe for her to be here?"

"It should be." He scoffed lightly. "The house doesn't mess with children and Xander was adamant that it's dormant-reactive during the day."

Lucky noted the phrase, *dormant-reactive*, and tucked it away to ask about later. It sounded straightforward enough for now. "How does he know that?"

"Neighborhood kids dare each other to break in all the time and Hennessee safely escorts them back out. Usually through the front door—we have footage of it opening on its own and them leaving," he said. "I think that's why they thought the show would work, but apparently, the safety features don't apply to adults."

"That is . . . *interesting*." He really sprinkled in that revelation like it was a garnish to add a little extra flavor. It took every ounce of willpower she had to remain calm and not bombard him with questions. She had to focus on him. On helping him like she planned. And *then* she'd ask. "Anyway, um, Rebel's very special. You're doing great with her."

"Special, yeah." He exhaled into a laugh.

"Oh, no, I wasn't being sarcastic. She's very creative and—"

"It's okay." He held up his hand. "You don't have to do that. Rebel is . . . her namesake, in the best and worst way. I know she's not sorry because she didn't apologize to *me*. That would require lying, which she doesn't do. Dance around the truth? Bend it until it warps? Omit important details? Yes. Without hesitation. But she never flat out lies to me."

"Ah, so she's a tiptoe trapper."

"What's that?"

"It's when they tiptoe around the truth so well, they trap you with semantics and all you can say is *Well you're not wrong*, which makes them think they're right even when they're not."

A quiet, triumphant thrill shot through her as the right side of his mouth *quirked*. "Did you make that up?"

"I did. Saw it enough and figured it needed a name."

"Saw it where?"

Not only had she walked right into that, she'd been the one to open the damn door. How did he keep doing this to her? *How?* Maverick's eyes held the kind of intensity she usually avoided. A true penetrating gaze, he could probably see straight into her soul and tell her exactly how many lies she'd told in her entire life. If she weren't sincere, she suspected he'd know it immediately.

She needed to read him. Soon.

Reluctantly, she said, "I used to be a nanny."

"When?"

"During college. And after."

"Stephen said you never had a job before."

"I said, 'according to my résumé.' I never confirmed that. They hired me to be a storyteller. So, I made one up about myself."

"Right." His disappointment lanced through her, hot then cold.

"I really wanted this job and being a nanny isn't relevant work experience," she said quickly, eager to explain. "People see 'live-in nanny' and automatically reject. It's not my fault society doesn't value childcare."

His eyes softened. "How long were you a nanny?"

"Six years, and I was damn good at it."

He nodded, considering her answer. "Why the career change, then?"

"Because this is where I want to be." With a deep breath, she took off her glasses and looked at him. "This is what I'm meant to be doing with my life."

8

Maverick had a busy interior life. He was extremely guarded, and control and caution calmed him. He was driven by a type of raw, authentic honesty Lucky didn't come across often. Desires mired by awareness. Darkness restrained by accountability. Neither taking the lead in favor of bargained coexistence. The empathy she'd sensed in him well before they met felt livelier, as if it routinely and frequently renewed itself. A constant work in progress.

"I was right about you," Lucky whispered, feeling instant relief.

Now that she'd read him, the surface feelings that had transferred from him and into her faded away. A startling surprise, seeing as how she hadn't even noticed *some* of them in the first place. She'd thought her flustered and embarrassed missteps all belonged to her, but no. That morning it was him too.

Maverick was attracted to her *and* successfully hiding it.

"Right about what?" He smiled. "What did you see?"

"Well." Lucky hadn't tried to translate her readings in years.

There were words, yes, but they also came to her as concepts with images attached to provide context. If she weren't careful, what made sense in her head would break down into candor-flavored word salad coming out of her mouth.

She took a deep breath, closed her eyes to concentrate, hoped for the best, and began, "Through your work, you aim to help people find their truths, just like you were able to. You search for the truth not because you're scared you'll die, but because you *know* you will. Being supportive is important to you—you want to do as much as you can for everyone while you still have time— but you'll only allow certain people to return the favor."

When she opened her eyes, Maverick stared at her with clear skepticism. "Their . . . truths?"

Heart in her throat, she tried to backtrack immediately. "I mean, that's just what I think. Half the time what I read doesn't make sense outside of my head, so my translations are off from time to time. I'm sorry."

His brow furrowed. "Why are you apologizing?"

"Because it didn't make sense?"

"Did I say that?"

"Your face did."

He noticeably glanced at the camera. "Honestly, you sounded like a psychic. A low-grade medium, at best. Nothing you said felt like it was specifically about me. Am I allowed to ask questions?"

Low-grade medium stabbed at her pride like a rusty serrated knife—and made her feel like she had something to prove. She nodded.

"Why did you close your eyes? It's interesting that you have to look at me to perform the reading but not to relay it."

"Oh, that part isn't required." She fidgeted and added quietly, "I was nervous."

He gave her the softest, most reassuring smile, but it was so quick that if she blinked, she would've missed it. Without breaking eye contact, he shifted in his chair and leaned toward her. "Try it again."

"Translating?" She searched his face, unsure what she was looking for.

He nodded. "But don't close your eyes this time. Look at me."

She could *feel* herself breathing too fast. Her cheeks were overheating, which meant her armpits were next, and what in the hell made her wear a sweatshirt in the summer? Her gaze dropped to her knees.

"Don't look away. If you're talking about me, you should focus on me. Again," he persuaded.

Her heart rate accelerated as he delicately lifted her chin, winning her attention.

"Tell me again."

She knew his eyes. Before that, she knew his voice. And now she thought she knew what to say. Familiar, calm purpose settled into her bones. She leaned in too, but only enough to meet him where he was.

"Your caution will be your undoing. You have a deep-seated fear of disappointing people that will only fester into resentment if you don't do something about it. Running away and isolating yourself will only make things worse because that's how you cope, but you don't like who you become when you're all alone, and if you don't like yourself, you will lose hold of the shields you built."

"That won't happen." His gaze flicked to her mouth and

abruptly back up again—his restraint on display, banishing his thoughts.

The tension in his denial beckoned her nearer. She balled her hands into fists to keep herself from touching him. "The monsters *will* get out."

"What monsters?"

"The monsters in your dreams. I *saw* them."

Maverick's sharp inhale caught her off guard. He jerked backward as if he couldn't get away from her fast enough. "How did you know about that?"

She sat up straight, setting her shoulders back and lifting her chin. "Apologize for calling me a low-grade medium."

"I'm sorry," he said instantly, but the sincerity in his voice couldn't be plainer. "I shouldn't have said that."

"Apology accepted." She grinned, feeling splendid. "Are you okay to finish the interview? We could take a break?"

"No. No, let's finish. I'll count us down." He shook his head, slightly clearing his throat and righting himself in the chair. "Three, two, one." With a deep breath, Maverick effortlessly slid back into interviewer mode, as magnetic as ever. "As of this recording, Lucky, you've spent one night in Hennessee House."

"Yes."

"Alone?"

She hesitated, for show. "I don't think there was another human here with me, no. Something is definitely amiss in Hennessee House."

"Could you elaborate?"

"I think it'd be easy for someone to think their mind is playing tricks on them, but I have an exceptional memory and I trust myself." She recalled the night before—the orchard, the bath, the flower—in an animated style, speaking quickly but clearly and emphasizing with her hands. She'd practiced her delivery in the mirror.

He asked, "Were you afraid?"

"No. Almost nothing scares me."

"Everyone is afraid of something," he pressed. "Nothing disappoints you. You don't get flustered. Now you're telling me you're fearless."

"Unlike most people, I am exactly who I say I am." Lucky shrugged. "Also, I said 'almost nothing scares me,' which to me, doesn't equal fearless. I have limits."

"But those limits don't include haunted houses?"

She thought about her answer carefully, wanting to make sure she expressed her stance clearly for the show. "People get scared when they have a supernatural encounter because what they're actually facing is their own limited view and mortality. They're being forced to confront being wrong and sometimes, one of the worst things that can happen to them: they'll die. I think that's why people scream or go into shock during those moments—they don't have the words to express all that existential dread. I've already faced those things. Dozens of times with my own eyes and through others."

"Your gift."

"Exactly."

His gaze remained fully fixed on her, anchoring her to the spot, and linking them together again. Nothing else existed outside of where they sat.

"Dad!" Rebel didn't wait for permission, stomping straight into frame as if the camera weren't there. She dramatically threw herself at him and he effortlessly caught her. "I'm *bored* and falling asleep."

He laughed and kissed her forehead, taking the interruption in complete stride. "We just finished. Stand up, please."

"There's plenty of beds upstairs if she wants to lie down," Lucky offered.

Rebel yawned. "I'm not allowed to sleep in the house. That's how it gets you."

"Oh?" Lucky's gaze slid smoothly to Maverick.

"It's only an educated guess. We don't know for sure."

"Yes, we do," Rebel said, oblivious to her dad's discomfort. "Xander said so and you said we had to listen to him about the house."

Lucky said, "Personally, I'd love to hear more."

"Rebel—"

"When you go to sleep, Hennessee House digs around in your brain, takes out all the bad stuff, and shows it to you. It's supposed to be *really* scary," Rebel said, fully ignoring Maverick. "That's why I have two *unbreakable* rules. No sleeping in the house and I can't be here after sundown."

Lucky raised an eyebrow. "Interesting how nobody warned me about that."

"Stephen sent me home. I'm not working. I can say whatever I want."

Maverick, bless his heart, was seconds away from laughing but expertly smoothed his features into a poker face instead. "Not quite, honey."

After packing up, they found the team outside in the front yard. Rebel pointed to the large tree and asked her dad, "Can I go swing?"

"Go for it."

That was the fascinating thing about kids. One second, they needed a nap. The next, they had enough energy to skip across the lawn at full speed. The tree had a wide trunk, which said nothing of the overhead branches or the age of the rope.

Lucky asked, "Is that thing safe?"

"It's new. Xander installed it for her last week."

"Ah. Xander."

He snickered. "He's a good guy."

"I'll see about that," she promised. "Do you usually bring Rebel to work with you?"

"No." He shook his head. "This was the compromise to an eleventh-hour meltdown. We had summer plans but Rebel . . . changed her mind. It was too late to sign her up for literally anything else so here we are. I honestly didn't expect her to take it so seriously—she's *excited* to be here and make her show. I'm gonna have to figure something out."

"Worried about disappointing her, eh?" She gave him an expectant look before grinning.

He laughed quietly, reluctantly even, while looking away to avoid her gaze. "I already apologized, remember?"

"I do."

"Hey!" Stephen called, finally noticing, and waving them over.

"I'm sure you'll come up with an idea," Lucky said, slipping on her glasses as they descended the porch steps.

"You're not going to read them?"

"Not right now. It might wipe me out if I'm not careful. It's actually one of my limits," she admitted.

9

When the sun had finally begun to set on Hennessee House, Georgia announced they needed to leave.

Lucky watched as they packed the van. "So," she began, aiming for casual. "Am I free to move about the cabin tonight?"

Georgia looked uneasy. "Do you plan to?"

She nodded. "The library piqued my interest. There might be other secrets in the walls to discover."

"Why didn't you do that earlier?"

Because they'd been quite serious about filming her all day. Not used to having two cameras, a producer, a host, and an intern following her every move, she sort of . . . sat down. In the living room. And didn't move until lunch. She switched it up in the afternoon, relocating to the porch to read a book. No one objected or suggested she do something else. They all loitered around watching her be boring.

"I thought it might be better for the show," she lied. "Chill summer days and frightening summer nights has a ring to it. Like a theme park."

"If that's how you want it, we won't stop you," Stephen said. "There are some supplies in the closet under the stairs you may find useful."

"You're a brave one. Godspeed." Chase jumped into the driver's seat.

Georgia gave her a pitying look. "If I don't see you tomorrow, it was nice to meet you."

"You're not coming back?"

"More like *you* might not be here." Georgia laughed as she got in the van. "History isn't on your side."

"Bye, Lucky!" Rebel waved from the back seat. "I hope I see you tomorrow."

Maverick stood next to her, stalling. He kept his voice low, no doubt hoping the others didn't hear. "You don't have to find anything. It's okay if you stay in the suite."

"No, I do. Don't tell me good luck—it's in the name." She pointed to herself and joked, "Now, say goodbye. You can do it."

"I can't. I won't. Because this isn't goodbye," he said. "I'll see you at sunrise."

She smiled. "Sunrise it is."

Lucky spent the rest of her evening getting ready to explore Hennessee House after dark. Stephen had been right about the closet. Inside, she found plenty of candles, flashlights, batteries, and, interestingly, a life alert necklace for emergencies. The directions stated that once pressed, it notified Stephen, Xander, local law enforcement, and a neighbor she hadn't met yet.

For her part, she wanted to keep things low-key, only using items it'd made sense for her to have. Production asking why she had an electromagnetic field radiation detector would only make things awkward for everyone.

She sold a piece of her soul-shaped savings to buy a small camera with excellent infrared and night vision and attached it to a makeshift chest harness (created from a repurposed sweater-vest) to keep her hands free. Her shopping spree also included a backup hard drive with a ridiculous amount of memory, two recorders—digital and analog tape for comparison in case her electronics failed—and a smartwatch to monitor her heart rate and temperature while investigating.

Her body's response to fear would be an important determinant. Fear altered one's perception. And according to Rebel, fear was Hennessee House's aim.

She'd stay upstairs, only exploring the bedrooms. Primarily because she wanted to pace herself. It'd be all too easy to get overexcited, do too much, and miss something. Secondarily because she wanted to get plenty of sleep.

Approximately two hours after sunset, she performed one final equipment check, said her affirmations, and reached for the doorknob, just as her phone rang loud as all hell in her front former-sweater-vest pocket.

"Damn it," she mumbled and exhaled to calm herself. She'd set the volume to the highest setting with vibration as a safety precaution. If lost, she, or someone else, would be able to find it. "Maverick."

"Lucky." He laughed lightly.

"Are you watching me or something?" She whirled around, searching her suite. "How do you always do that?"

"Do what?"

"Call me with suspiciously perfect timing."

"Well. Rebel just went to bed, so this is actually the first chance I had to call. She's probably not even asleep yet." He paused. "What are you doing?"

"Fairly positive I'm not supposed to tell you that until our interview tomorrow."

"I thought so."

Tense silence stretched between them until she said, "I should get going—"

"Or I could stay on the phone with you. I'll keep you company while . . . you do whatever you're doing."

Feeling spicy, she joked, "Oh yeah? I could be masturbating. What then? You still want to stay on the phone with me?"

"Uhh—" He stuttered for a few seconds before recovering. "I don't kink shame. If that's what you're into, um, okay. Yeah."

"You don't sound too sure." She laughed. "I'm sorry. That was inappropriate. I'm not doing that." As she checked the time on her watch, she could've sworn she heard him sigh in relief.

"Earlier you mentioned your plans, and after what happened with the flower and in the dining room, I figured—"

"Thank you, but I'll be fine. I don't need a babysitter, Maverick."

Having a clear head felt *marvelous*. Without his emotions doubling the intensity of her own, focus returned to her. Priorities lined up in order. This was why she moved into Hennessee House—Maverick was a bonus. A very attractive, kind, and considerate bonus, that she would most definitely be thinking about later. But not now.

"I never said you wouldn't be, but that doesn't stop me from worrying."

She sighed. "Why are you worried?"

"I want to make sure you're okay."

"Why?"

"Because Hennessee House is legit. You shouldn't be alone."

"Not sure if you heard, but that's the premise of the show."

"Doesn't mean I agree with it. There's safety in numbers. On my show, we stay together for a reason."

"Well, I'm used to going at it alone. This is what works for me and how I want it on my show."

When he didn't immediately reply, she realized her mistake. She could practically feel him processing her words through the phone, putting two and two together and adding one to finally make five. A hot wave of frustration flooded her face and chest. How did he keep tricking the truth out of her?

Softly, he asked, "Have you done this before?"

She decided to play it cool. "Last night, I stayed in my room, as instructed."

"And before that?"

"Before that . . . maybe."

"Let me be your second," he said. "You deserve to have someone watching your back."

Lucky blinked in surprise. She expected him to be mad and threaten to report her to Stephen, not continue to offer his help. "Is that even allowed?"

"It's better to ask for forgiveness than permission."

"Like daughter, like father, I see."

"Seems that way." He laughed. "Don't tell me what you're doing or anything that happens. I'll stay on the line as your outside contact until you go back to your suite."

Nearly all her group expeditions ended in disaster. At the first hint of activity, everyone started screaming, crying, throwing up.

Meanwhile, she stood in the middle of it all, staring at them and getting more irritated by the second. What did they expect? *That* was what they signed up for—the entire point of the trip. What did they *think* was going to happen?

Solo investigations cleared that issue right up. Some people were meant to be alone. She'd made her peace with being one of them.

"I don't know if I'm up for that. Other people only hold me back."

"A good partner wouldn't."

"Bold of you to say that, never having worked with me before. My style clashes with literally everyone." Her tone unfortunately betrayed her beliefs, making her sound bitter. First her honesty, now this. How was he ripping open her healed wounds too?

"I'll prove it to you, then. Give me tonight. If it doesn't work, I'll step aside and let you be."

One night out of thirty. She bit her lip as she considered it. "Promise you won't distract me?"

"What counts as distraction?"

"I don't know yet. We'll play it by ear."

"Sounds good."

"I'm leaving my suite now."

Hennessee House had turned off its lights. Either that or they were on a timer. She'd ask Stephen about that tomorrow. The long hallway stretched the darkness past the stairs. Three doors on the left, her door and two more. Four on the right, which included the communal bathroom.

A cloud of peppermint blew into Lucky's face. She instantly recoiled back into her room. Not doing that again, nope. She swallowed hard against the memory, resisting the urge to blow her nose to get it out. Why could she still smell it? Not as strong, but unmistakably present, it felt pleasant as cooling mint now.

Rebel said the smells didn't move between rooms unless it wanted to lead someone somewhere. Was that why Hennessee House attacked her earlier? To train her to follow it?

Lucky squeezed her eyes and mouth shut as if that were enough to stop the peppermint from obliterating her senses. She stepped back into the hall, cracked one eye open, then the other, and slowly began to relax. Still tolerable—pleasant. She clicked on her flashlight, took two more steps down the hall, and stopped. The smell vanished. She stepped back—there it was. Forward again—gone. It seemed to want her in front of her suite.

She eyed the bedroom door across from hers. "In there?" she whispered, shining her light on it.

The door slowly drifted open in response.

"*Oh, shit.*" Her entire body shivered, skin erupting in goose bumps.

"Everything okay?" She'd almost forgotten Maverick was there.

"I am *great*," she answered honestly, grinning within an inch of her life.

This bedroom was significantly smaller than hers but furnished almost identically. A bed, a chest, a chair, and two nightstands. Cream-colored bedding and curtains, accented with marigold.

Maverick asked, "Can I ask you a question?"

"Shoot." She felt along the wall for the light switch, keeping her eyes and the light forward.

"Why did you want to be on the show?"

"Hmm, I think I already passed this interview."

"Considering new developments, I don't know if I believe your initial answers. Sorry, I meant story."

"Cute." When she found the light switch, nothing happened, even after flicking it several times. She even tried the bedside lamp to no success.

Hennessee wanted the lights off—confirmed.

"Why did you apply? Be honest with me, please."

Lucky made her way farther into the room, sniffing as she went. The peppermint unerringly led her to the window. It reminded her of those old cartoons, where characters would float on the air lured like a fish on a hook by a scent. She pulled back the curtains on the street-facing window to make use of the moonlight. "If I do, can it stay between us?"

"I don't have any issues with that."

"I didn't lie during my interview. This really is the job I want." Public perception made *paranormal investigator* synonymous with comedians hunting for ghosts and cryptids. She dubbed herself an *academic supernatural researcher*. A mouthful for sure, but far more accurate. "Our brains are incredible and there's more to the world than what we can see. I want to find it—any of it. I want to prove it's real."

"There aren't any ghosts in the house."

"I'm not looking for ghosts." From where she stood at the window, she swung her light in a wide arc. Why would it lead her here? "All signs point to Hennessee being sentient, not haunted. Someone must've led it to enlightenment. It also wants . . . something."

"It wants to scare people away."

"No. That's not it. That's too simple." She frowned at the room. What was she supposed to find? Do next? "Your turn. Why did you call me?"

"I told you I was worried."

"Why are you worried about me? There are three caretakers' worth of history here. What changed your mind?"

"Eunice. I hate the way she left. When they told me they had cast someone new and I saw your picture, I knew I had to do something."

She checked the closet—empty and unremarkable.

Under the bed—clean, not a single dust bunny to be found.

The chest—also empty.

The nightstands—Kleenex, a pen, and a notepad. Amazing. Incredible. Life-changing.

Lucky sighed. "And?"

"And"—he paused—"I swore to myself I wasn't going to let anything happen to you on my watch."

She was about to give up when she passed in front of the window again and heard a solid *click* under her left foot. Her thoughts immediately went to *booby trap*, preparing for the worst. She froze in place, heart pounding as she slowly looked down.

A square of flooring had sunk about an inch below the other slats. She kneeled quickly, investigating with hesitant touches to figure out if she'd accidentally damaged the floor or—was it a *handle*? The entire slat came free with a hard upward yank. And then she did it again.

Lucky sat on the ground, holding all four displaced slats on her lap. The resulting rectangle was two by two feet wide, three feet deep, and extended into a passageway leading clear under the floorboards toward the door. She breathed in—peppermint once again indicating the way.

Her brain screamed *crawl space!!!*, urging her to go inside.

I can't fit in there.

Yes, you can!! You won't know until you try!!

. . . shut up.

She could fit. She *could* fit.

But this was one of those times where common sense needed to have its day. Even with Maverick on the phone, it'd be immensely stupid to wriggle in there and army-crawl her way around the house, with no one around to cut her out if she got stuck.

She'd wait. She had to wait.

. . . right?

She'd been wrong before—she absolutely needed a distraction to keep her out of that crawl space. "Why do you do it?" she asked Maverick, common sense barely hanging on. "Why are you interested in the supernatural?"

"Originally? Money."

Shock snapped her out of her indecision. "*Money?*"

"Yep." He laughed. "I usually don't tell people that, but I asked you to be honest. It's only fair I do the same. I started my podcast on a shoestring budget of zero dollars, a hope, a prayer, and the strange stories I pulled out of my dreams."

"I *loved* it. I listened to it all the time."

Lucky came across Maverick's podcast *Hypnopompic Remnants* while in college. She always listened right before bed, purposefully trying to scare herself. Any self-respecting supernatural researcher had to be ready for anything, which she'd erroneously interpreted to mean desensitizing herself to fear. Nightmares would be nothing.

Two episodes later she was basically addicted to Maverick's smooth and emotive narration. Wearing headphones, she'd drift off to sleep, comforted by his voice telling her his unusual and enthralling supernatural tales.

He continued, "The details are a little fuzzy now, but I re-member thinking *five hundred dollars*. I'd moved out of my par-ents' house. I had primary custody of Rebel. I was working full-time at a warehouse. We just needed an extra five hundred dollars a month and we'd be okay. Things wouldn't be so tight all the time. I couldn't get another job and still be a dad, you know? I had to find something I could do at home at odd hours. So, I started writing. I wrote in the mornings during my commute, recorded at night in a closet after Rebel went to bed, and edited on the weekends during her quiet time."

Lucky glanced at the crawl space entrance before forcing her-self to look out the window. "Then what happened?"

"My audience grew steadily until the snowball effect took over. Timing was on my side, I guess," he said. "The right person on the right day boosted one of my episodes and almost two years' worth of weekly content went viral overnight. That's how Xander found me. A couple of meetings later, he offered me a job."

"I remember that announcement post. I was so happy for you."

"It was a good day." She could hear the smile in his voice. "I really did start on this path because of money but it isn't what keeps me here. I'm not sure when it—*I* changed but I think I've known it for a while. I hadn't actively thought about it until this afternoon because of you."

"What?"

"You said 'truth' but I realized that wasn't quite the right word. It should've been stories. Their stories. *My* stories."

"Oh yeah, that happens," she said, hot with embarrassment. "It's really easy to get lost in translation. Sorry."

"I'm not correcting you," he said gently. "You *were* right. I write stories to help me process my truths and to make sense of the monsters I dream about. On my show, it doesn't matter if the ghosts or hauntings are real because that's not the point. The people are the point. Finding ways to help them tell their stories about their lives is the point. Everything else is just fascinating noise because that's my true purpose. Thank you for helping me see that."

Lucky was utterly speechless. She'd never been thanked for one of her readings before. *Ever.*

Most people didn't like hearing the truth about themselves. Trying to translate what she'd seen was hard enough. Add people snapping at her, thinking she was weird, talking about her behind her back, and she'd given up on telling anyone anything. It'd been so long since she tried, she honestly didn't know if she'd even be able to handle trying to convince production without panicking, but she *needed* to do it—for her career and for herself. So, she'd started small. She'd started with Maverick.

And he thanked her. He thought she'd helped him.

"You're welcome." Her voice was less than a whisper. Stunned beyond all hope for recovery, she locked the slats back into place to reseal the crawl space. Peppermint escorted her the entire walk back to the suite. "Change of plans. I think I'm just gonna go to sleep tonight."

"Really?" He sounded skeptical. "Are you okay?"

No. "Yeah. I'm just tired. Today was a lot. I don't want to push myself too hard." And she desperately needed to hang up before she started crying. "Thank you for wanting to look out for me."

"Of course," he said. "That's what I'm here for."

10

Early the next morning Lucky was deep in analysis mode. She slouched down in her work nest—laptop balanced on her thighs, and surrounded by equipment, research books, and journals. She'd taken a nap to reset her emotional state and allow Hennessee House some time to do its thing before getting to work. Her footage wasn't going to review and take notes of itself.

Exploring the remaining rooms at 3:47 a.m. had been regretfully uneventful. The house must have decided it didn't have anything else to show her. No thumps in the night. No moans through the walls. Nothing except the crawl space, making it her top priority. She'd been awake for hours by the time Maverick called.

"Are you going to do this every morning?" she asked in lieu of hello.

"Affirmative. We're only scheduled to be there for this week, and I don't like showing up somewhere unannounced. How are you?"

Emotionally compromised! "Why only this week?"

"In a few days, if you stay that long, we'll start you on the transition to self-tapes."

"I'm staying."

"I believe you," he said. "Odds are good I'll continue to call after that. Even if you answer, say 'I'm fine,' and then hang up on me. I'll still do it."

She laughed gently. "You don't have to worry about me. I promise."

"I worry about everything. I can't help it." He sighed. "You being in that house has inexplicably shot up to my top five so"—he paused—"hearing your voice makes me feel better."

Lucky frowned, biting her lip. She wasn't used to being worried about. She wasn't even used to having people in her life long enough to get to that point. "Oh, well in that case, you may continue. See you soon?"

"I'll be there."

Maverick, and his perfect timing, arrived as she emerged from the incredibly clean and organized basement full of yardwork and home repair supplies. The setup down there honestly put Home Depot to shame. She recorded herself while browsing the aisles only to be met with more nothing, but she did find the circuit breaker and a toolbox, which she needed.

"There's a package out here for you." He pointed to a large brown box on the porch.

"Perfect. I didn't think it'd get here so early." She brushed past him—he smelled like cocoa butter and minty aftershave—and squatted down, only to quickly realize she couldn't pick it up.

Ten struggle-filled seconds later, he mercifully put her out of her weak-muscled misery, saying, "Allow me."

She pouted as he easily lifted it on the first try.

"*Oof*, this is heavy."

"Liar." She pouted harder—she knew he said that to make her feel better. Like people who said *you loosened it for me* after someone struggled with a jar for too long. "In my defense, I never skip leg day. My arms are just noodly."

He laughed. "Where do you want it?"

"Kitchen. By the back door." She walked beside him.

"What is it?"

"Supplies. I decided to test your *Xander is a good guy* testimonial and emailed to ask him for some things. Is everyone else outside again?"

"No, they dropped me off and went to the grocery store. Stephen was insistent there not be any interruptions for your interview today."

Just the two of them. Perfect. She removed her glasses. "Library? Or should I show you what I found last night first?"

"First, let me get the camera and mics," he said, smiling for some reason. "Then you can show me."

Lucky watched his face as he clipped the mic to her sweater. On the whole, she didn't exactly pay attention to whether or not she liked the look of any given person. Contemplating attraction barely held water against conducting telepathic experiments. That was not the case for Maverick. Something about his face had always felt distinctly magnetic, as if it'd been designed specifically for her brain to appreciate—which was ridiculous.

Her clear head didn't even make it through the night. She'd somehow looped back around to where she'd started, flustered and mere seconds away from giggling. He looked up, meeting her gaze. They smiled at the same time.

"I decided to stick with wholesome," she said, as if he cared about her outfit, swiftly despairing because he probably didn't. And then despairing further as she realized *she* wanted him to care. A lot of thought went into selecting her slightly baggy sweater, skirt, and knee-high socks. She'd even curled her hair in loose spirals and pinned a beret in place.

"I noticed. Very nice."

He noticed. "Thank you."

"Are you wearing perfume?" he asked.

"Yeah, a little. It's nothing fancy. Just some random, cutely named floral combination I found at a store. I thought it smelled nice."

"It does." He anchored the camera to the tripod and held it up toward her. "In three, two, one"—he paused—"This is Maverick Phillips, checking in for morning number two with Caretaker Lucky Hart. How are you feeling? How was your night?"

"Feeling great." She beamed, memorized monologue ready to go. "Last night was *incredible*. You will not *believe* what happened to me."

"I think you'd be surprised what I'm willing to believe."

"Oh, really? Stop me if you've heard this one, then." She gestured for him to follow her through the house. "Okay, so, I knew I wanted to explore the house. I had to try it at least once. First thing I experienced? Hennessee turns off *all* the lights. It does not want anything on at night. The circuit breaker was fine when I checked out the basement this morning and there's no timer to save energy or anything like that. As far as I can tell, Hennessee was in full control."

"What about your suite? Was the power off there?"

"No—that's strange thing number two. Power worked in my

room *and* as soon as I stepped into the hall, I smelled *peppermint* again. It wasn't beyond either side of my door. I could only smell it in the pathway directly from my room to the room across the hall. Right here." She mimed the surface area where the smell had been contained.

"Do you smell it now?"

"Nope. It faded after I found what Hennessee wanted to show me. I think it made the smell so intense earlier in the day so someone would explain the rules to me, and I'd know how to recognize what it wanted me to do later."

"That's giving the house a lot of credit. Premeditation implies thought."

"*Exactly*. Come on."

Lucky led him into the room, demonstrating how to access the crawl space. She set the slats down next to her as Maverick panned the camera inside the hole, and then positioned the tripod to get them both into frame.

"Did you know this was here?" she asked.

"I didn't."

Lucky mentally prepared herself to launch the next part of her plan. She fidgeted in place—the newness of it making her slightly nervous. He said he wanted to be her second. He said he wanted to be partners. He'd kept his word last night. After agonizing over it, she decided to try and meet him halfway. "I'm gonna pitch something. Hear me out?"

"Okay." He focused on her, expression open and waiting.

She took a deep breath. "What if I went in?"

He looked around the room, confused. "In where?"

"The crawl space." She gestured to it for good measure. "I'm pretty sure I can fit and—"

"No."

"What do you mean *no*? Don't cut me off." She frowned at him. "As I was saying, I measured it and ran the numbers. If I'm careful, I can slide in at an angle and shimmy down, flip over, and army crawl to see where it goes. I was going to do it last night, but then I thought better of it, which is rare for me, if I'm being honest. Now that you're here, it should be perfectly safe."

Maverick stared at her for five full seconds before asking, "May I speak now? Just want to make sure I don't interrupt you again."

"Yes," she said, but then decided to add a summary. "I firmly believe I can fit. It's daylight. There are other people in the house. I should be safe."

"Got it. I understand." He nodded. "No."

Lucky instantly deflated—*of course*, this happened to her. The one time she went out on a limb to work with someone else, they suddenly thought they could tell her what to do the moment things got dicey. Typical.

Except Maverick was supposed to get it. He was supposed to understand and be on her side, not stand in her way. She watched him reach into the opening, pressing down on the bottom and the sides.

Preoccupied by her feelings, Lucky almost didn't see the window silently crack open beside them. Her gaze slid to it then back to Maverick as an idea for an experiment formed.

"I already did that," she snapped, resolving to ignore the window for the time being.

"Second opinions don't hurt anything." His voice echoed down the shaft. "I can't tell if it's load-bearing. You might fall through, not to mention there's no way to tell if there's a secondary exit or if it remains a consistent size."

She'd already thought of that too and deemed those risks to be within acceptable limits. "I'm willing to take my chances."

He sat back up with dust now sprinkled across his forehead and the tip of his nose. Her hands twitched on instinct. "Duly noted," he said. "However, insurance has denied your request."

"Hennessee led *me* here," she insisted, unwilling to back down. "I *have* to do this."

Maverick's gaze sharpened, glinting and protective. "*You* are not going in there." His tone, however, remained as understanding as ever.

"You can't stop me from exploring the house."

The window inched upward again.

"You can do whatever you want as long as you do it safely. I meant what *I* said." He mouthed the word *second*.

Second. Her second. He was asking her to trust him again. No one else on the team knew about the promise he made to her and the vow he made with himself. This was their secret. He wanted it to stay that way.

He continued, "I'll get you a remote camera. Probably a drone."

All at once, her internal warring ended. Using a drone hadn't even occurred to her because she couldn't afford it. So far, she'd managed to fund her supernatural research entirely with her nanny paychecks. After bills, every single extra dollar she had was split evenly between her emergency savings and future investigation expenses. A drone would've taken months of saving, whereas strapping a camera to her forehead was well within budget.

"Really?" she asked.

"I'll talk to Xander and Stephen. I've convinced them to do much worse. This'll be easy."

"Worse like what?" she asked, simultaneously hoping she didn't sound too eager and knowing full well she did.

"I'll tell you later." He nodded to the camera. "Let's focus on your stories for now. Did anything else happen last night?" Ever the professional, he'd slid them right back on track after her near derailment.

"No, this was it." Oh, *shit*, she sounded *breathless* again. That man really bewitched her with a promise of a damn drone.

The window continued to climb upward, faster now. Maverick still hadn't noticed.

"Nothing else?" His expression dipped for a moment. "Nothing else at all?"

Even through her happy haze, she picked up on the hint. "Should there have been?"

"Not necessarily. Your predecessors all experienced a . . . noticeable uptick in activity," he said, using his presenter voice. "The kind that made them want to leave. If anything, this discovery seems to have encouraged you to stay longer."

"You're right about that. I'm not going anywhere." She grinned. "By the way, you have some dust on your face."

He began wiping, making it worse.

"Here, let me." She grabbed the Kleenex out of the night-stand, and he held still as she cleaned his face with light strokes. "Much better."

Neither one of them moved back, staying closer than they should've been. She was pinned by his gaze yet again.

He asked her softly, "Do you smell flowers?"

No, but she smelled cocoa butter—and the faintest notes of peppermint.

A mild early-morning breeze flowed into the room. Maverick looked away and did a double take. "Was the window open like that when we came in here?"

11

O h my god." Georgia paced in a tight circle. "Oh my god. How did you not see that? How did you not feel it? *Oh my god*."

"Ehh, they seemed a little preoccupied," Chase said conversationally.

Lucky glanced at Maverick, who stood with his arms crossed while staring at the playback. Stephen replayed it again as if they all hadn't seen the window move the first four times.

"Does it mean something?" Rebel asked. Being in a demonstrably supernatural house didn't seem to faze her.

"It means the house woke up." Maverick covered his mouth with his fist.

Lucky said, "That's so interesting. Are you all operating under the belief that the house *sleeps* during the day? Maverick said it was dormant-reactive—I've never heard of that before."

"Xander explained that it's closer to being in power-save mode," Stephen said. "Daytime activity is exclusively reactionary.

Something, usually intense emotions, triggers it to respond and then it quiets back down."

Rebel stared at the footage for a moment before side-eyeing Lucky. She then squeezed closer to her dad, reaching up to hold his hand. "What triggered it to open the window?"

"Uh, we don't know yet," Maverick said, and Georgia *coughed*. "But you don't have to stay. I'll take you home the second you give me the word. It's up to you, sweetie."

"Mmm . . . I want to stay for now." Rebel fidgeted. "The house is nice. It wants us to be nice too."

What a strange thing for Shortcake to say. Lucky exchanged a concerned look with Maverick, who shook his head slightly, eyes tightening. A move she recognized from her nanny days. She'd leave it to him. Some things were better for parents to handle.

Maverick asked, "Did you get the pancake ingredients at the store?"

"And we got sprinkles too!" Rebel pulled her dad to the kitchen, bursting the bubble of the meeting.

Voice lowered, Georgia said, "You need to tell Xander about this. He'll want to know."

Stephen nodded, exhaling irritation.

Chase asked Lucky, "Are you really okay?"

"Totally fine." She regarded him for a moment—he was wearing a dark gold long-sleeve top. "That's a lovely shirt. The color looks fantastic on you."

Georgia said, "You do understand that this is definitive proof that the house is targeting you, right? I sincerely hope you can handle what comes next because it's going to try to take you out."

"I appreciate your concern but I'm not leaving. So."

"You say that now, but no one makes it past the third night for a reason."

"Which is?"

Georgia hesitated, glancing at Stephen, who had nothing to say.

Lucky sighed theatrically. "Look, if you're not going to tell me, stop bringing it up. Whatever is gonna happen, is gonna happen and I'll deal. But I'm not leaving." She turned on her heel, pleated skirt twirling as she walked away to join Maverick and Rebel.

Behind her, Georgia muttered, "Famous last words."

Lucky volunteered to put the groceries away while Maverick and Rebel began cooking. The refrigerator had been stocked with the foods she requested during her onboarding. Basic items like bread, cheese, milk, eggs, and tofu. Pasta, cereal, and ramen had been stored in the pantry and there was also a full spice rack. She'd been on her own awhile and yet had never quite mastered the art of feeding herself. A compulsive snacker by nature, she often didn't realize she needed to eat something besides Hot Cheetos until she was starving, and by that point her food had to be cooked as quickly as possible.

Rebel must have been in charge of the grocery trip. The team had purchased juice boxes, chips, fruit snacks, oatmeal cookies, and maple syrup. Kind of adorable the way they all doted on her, even after her stunt yesterday.

Growing up, if she'd done anything like that . . . she shook her head to clear the memories away. She didn't get to choose her parents. They didn't get handbooks on how to be perfect caregivers. They gave her what they could, and she appreciated them for it, but that was as far as their relationship went these days.

Lucky watched as Georgia sidled up beside Maverick, asking, "Ooh, can I have a triangle pancake?"

"Why a triangle?"

"Seemed like it would be difficult. Gotta keep you on your toes, Super Dad."

Maverick scoffed and continued cooking. "Any other special requests?"

Stephen and Chase had already settled in at the dining room table, sharing the laptop between them. They both shook their heads, barely sparing him a glance.

About twenty minutes later, Maverick finished making the heart-shaped pancakes, which were apparently Rebel's favorite, and placed one single triangle pancake onto Georgia's plate.

"Now, that's just rude. Show-off—you gotta be kidding me. Why does this taste so good?"

"Secret daddy recipe," Rebel said, happily drenching her pancakes in syrup. Maverick settled into the seat next to her.

"Lucky," Stephen began. "We were hoping we could talk about your interview yesterday."

All eyes were on her. Just as she'd planned. "What about it?"

"You made a fairly interesting claim regarding having ESP. I'd love to hear more."

"Not a claim," she clarified, smiling. "Not a party trick. Not a hoax." After thorough experimentation and research, she'd decided her personal flavor of ESP was a mixture of the following abilities:

Advanced explicit memory—her complex storage system
    of information
Eidetic memory—total recall of every first impression
    she'd read
Mild synesthesia—some cores and intentions had a smell
Temporary empathic absorption—short-term
    internalization of outside emotions
Intuitive body language and patterned behavior
    recognition

And a . . . little something extra. She was still working on
defining what enabled her to access someone's primary nature, as
well as the magnetic compulsion to read them.

"My apologies." For a split second, Stephen's gaze twinkled
briefly with amusement. He smothered it quickly. Interesting.
"What I meant to say was you demonstrated your ability on Maverick, which he confirmed to be accurate. However there was
a"—he paused—"*discrepancy* in how he reported it happening
versus what was filmed."

"The hell does that mean?"

"That's what we want to know," Georgia said, thankfully
jumping in. Lucky appreciated the way she always cut straight to
the heart of things. "Maverick made it seem like it was a once-
in-a-lifetime, magical experience but it looked boring as shit. You
two were just talking. There was more chemistry in the footage
from this morning."

Chase added, "We'd like it if you could demonstrate reading
one of us with everyone in the room. For comparison."

While Stephen was high drama, Georgia was as blunt as a
court transcript. Chase seemed to ride somewhere in the middle,

balancing them both out. Lucky exchanged a look with Maverick, who said, "Only if you're up for it. You don't have to."

And he was the one who made sure everyone was comfortable. Safe.

Rebel asked, "Can you read me too?"

Lucky smiled. "I already did. When I first met you."

"Oh." Rebel pouted a little. "I didn't feel anything."

"Because you're not supposed to."

"What did you see?"

"Well, you . . . are a little troublemaker."

"No, I'm not." Rebel giggled.

"You're going to give your dad a lot of gray hairs," she teased.

"*Noooo,*" she giggle-whined. "Tell me *good* stuff."

Lucky hesitated, unintentionally looking to Maverick for permission to translate for Rebel. He nodded. She didn't need to remove her glasses to recall the reading but did it anyway for the drama. They were recording after all. She also wanted to try the technique Maverick encouraged her to use again.

"Look at me, please," she said while focusing on Rebel's face. Everything behind her instantly transformed into an impressionist painting, a blur of softening colors and shapes. "You possess a unique point of view. It will not age even as you do, but you will grow together. You'll always see the world in a way that most won't because they've forgotten how. They're not going to like that you can do what they cannot so they will try to take it from you—in any way they can. Don't let them break you. Okay?"

"Okay," Rebel agreed, eyes wide.

"And you're an artist. You haven't found it yet, but the medium you're most *drawn* to won't be a natural talent. You'll have to work hard to master it even if it scares you, and it will sometimes." Lucky inhaled, squeezing her eyes shut as the reading slotted back into its place within her memory palace. Glasses on, she blinked several times to clear her vision . . . only to see the entire table staring at her. Stephen was even recording on his phone.

"Oh my *god*," Georgia breathed, before turning to Maverick. "You weren't kidding."

"What? That's what I read—the gist of it, anyway."

Stephen asked, "Did you know your voice changes when you do that?"

"Um, no? Changes how?" Stephen played his video, but she didn't understand what he'd meant. "What are you talking about? I always sound like that."

"That's not how it sounded, though." Georgia pointed to the screen. "This sounds normal. You didn't."

Lucky swallowed hard. Unease pressed against her spine like she was being backed into a spiked corner. "I don't know what you're talking about."

"Sorry," Maverick said immediately, flashing warning looks across the table with ease. "It's not a big deal. Thank you for demonstrating, Lucky. We appreciate you."

"Would you be willing to do it once more?" Stephen asked. "Since you admitted to already reading Rebel, it might be a good idea to capture the entire process, beginning to end."

"I'd rather not." No one was going to experiment on her. No one was going to pressure her to do readings. She did them on her terms only. "I'm not a party trick," she repeated, tone firm as stone.

A low groan rolled through the ceiling overhead, spreading out and down the walls of the dining room.

"That better be the fucking pipes," Georgia angrily whispered.

Lucky stood up, grabbing her plate. "Thank you for breakfast, Maverick. Excuse me." She hurried away from the table, dashing through the kitchen and out to the backyard, not stopping until she stood on a dirt path between two orange trees, breathing in and out, trying to calm down. It took thirty seconds longer than it should've for her to realize she'd made it to the orchard.

She spun in a circle looking around—she didn't even have shoes on. "*Shit.*" Cold mud seeped through her thin socks and in between her toes. "Calm down, calm down," she commanded. Her heartbeat thundered in her ears. "Walk yourself through it."

She remembered standing up. Excusing herself. Picking up her plate . . . and now she was outside. Half-empty plate and all.

How did it pull her outside? Every second of every day she'd felt the tug of the orchard but had compartmentalized it to measure the duration of her resistance. It must've had enough of her doing that and found another way in.

Was the orchard separate from the house? Or did Hennessee want her out here? She sniffed the air—grass, dirt, flowers, citrus, sweet-smelling fruits, and the faintest notes of peppermint. It was fading fast as if it were running away from her.

"Lucky, hey." Maverick hustled toward her, breathing as if *he'd* been running. "There you are. Are you okay?"

"I don't . . . know." She hoped she didn't look as bewildered as she felt. "But I think I'm going to stay? Out here? And do stuff?"

"Why are you barefoot?"

"I don't know. Yet."

Maverick sighed, then pressed his lips into a firm line. "What kind of stuff?"

"Gardening? Trimming bushes, I don't know—oh, pet house!

I'm going to build a pet house," she said confidently. "There's a cat somewhere. That's what's in the box. Cat supplies courtesy of Xander."

"Are you going to build it right here?" he asked calmly.

"No?"

"Okay, how about we set you up near the gazebo, then?"

"Well, I—"

"Distance doesn't make a difference," he said, gently taking her plate from her. "Let me guess: You got upset and don't remember walking out here?"

Her reading and translation had gone so well with Maverick, and yet she still landed right back in the dark place she'd shaken loose after college. She thought she'd be able to handle being treated like a shiny new toy, but no. The second they started interrogating her, she'd felt cornered again, rapidly losing control of the situation. She wanted people to believe her without forgetting she was still a person with feelings.

Lucky eyed him, wary. "How did you know that?"

"Because it's happened before," he said. "I think, and this is the only time I will ever admit to this, the house thought being out here would make you feel better. It did the same thing to the first caretaker, Bobbi, when she was crying. She got news that her guinea pig died. Old age."

"Oh, I don't think that's it," she said. "When I first arrived, it felt like it was pulling me outside. I ignored it and—" She stopped because Maverick was nodding.

"Sorry to disappoint you, but that happens to everyone. Xander suggests thinking of it as the house being proud and wanting to show off its best feature. Come on."

Lucky groaned as she followed him back to the house. "Rational explanations are the worst."

"To be fair, it's only half-rational. The house temporarily hijacked your body to lead you somewhere it thinks of as peaceful."

"In comes Maverick with the silver lining. What would I do without you?" *Shit.* Why did she say *that*?

He laughed. "Did it at least help? Are you feeling better?"

"Sure," she lied.

"We're used to working a certain way," he said, apologetic. "I wouldn't say we're skeptics, I mean look where we're at, but it's not every day we meet someone like you. I'm sorry we got carried away."

"It's okay," she said. "I put myself in that situation by using a half-baked plan and leaving things too open-ended. I can't blame other people for saying things they don't know will upset me."

The back of his hand brushed against hers. "What was your plan?"

"In hindsight, it was pretty bad," she said. "I thought I was ready to share my ability with the world, but surprise, surprise, I can barely handle five people."

"Everyone has to start somewhere." He held a low-hanging branch out of their way, allowing her to pass under it first. "You just need more practice."

"Maybe. Anyway, thank you for running out here to rescue me. The wilds of the orchard are fearsome indeed," she joked.

He regarded her with a serious expression, eyebrows pinched with worry, but said, "Anytime."

12

Lucky fully believed Maverick's explanation once Hennessee tried it again.

When she'd gone inside, she felt an invisible force gently tugging her back. Maverick had to escort her up the stairs so she could get cleaned up and change her clothes. Everything felt normal inside of the suite, but the second she stepped back into the hall, the tug returned.

"*Fine*. I'll go! I wanted to be out there today *anyway*," she relented and then noticed Maverick staring at her. "What? Why are you looking at me like that?"

"No reason," he said. "Come on."

"So, you admit it: you're giving me a *look*."

"In that I'm looking *at* you, yeah." He gestured for her to go down the stairs first like a gentleman. "None of this gets to you? You're just fine with everything that's happened so far?"

"Someone has to be." She shrugged. "Might as well be me."

"Georgia is flipping out because it seems like you're triggering reactions too often." He shook his head, clearly worried as well. "You can tell me if this is too much."

"It's honestly not," she said. "This is what I meant when I said my style clashes with everyone. People expect me to panic, I never do, and then they get scared of *me*. It always plays out like this."

"She's scared *for* you. There's a difference," he said. "Would you even tell me if it was too much?"

"You're my second, right?" She grinned at him. "I wouldn't even hesitate."

The team, Maverick included, set up shop in the gazebo. They stationed cameras on both sides of the backyard to get a full panoramic view from two angles, with strict instructions for Lucky to announce if she planned to travel deeper inside the orchard. For the time being, she only wanted to build the pet house. She picked a spot near the fence, right where the backyard grass ended and the orchard began.

"Hi." Rebel's shadow arrived before she did. The sun beamed overhead at the perfect angle.

"Hey, Shortcake."

"What are you doing?"

"About to start building a cat house. See?" She held up the instruction booklet.

"I like cats."

"Of course you do. You're a young lady of taste."

Xander didn't ask a single follow-up question when she emailed him requesting a bag of top-quality cat food, throw blankets, a stainless-steel water fountain, and a medium-size yellow house she'd found online. He'd only replied with "OK" and like magic, the box arrived. He must've known that black cat lived in the orchard. She'd spotted it a few more times and had a feeling it was currently in the bushes watching her.

"Does it have a name?" Rebel asked.

"I think it's a stray so probably not. I'm leaning toward Gengar. Every haunted house needs a haunted cat."

"That's a good name, I guess. Can I help?"

She glanced at the gazebo. "How's interning going?"

"I'm on break." Rebel squatted down, hugging her knees to her chest. "It's kind of boring. I wanted to film more of my show, but they said no."

"What's it about? You never said."

"Behind-the-scenes vlog stuff. You're the main show and I'd be the side show. I was gonna call it *Spooky Scary* but now I'm not allowed to go anywhere unsupervised." She made a face and rolled her eyes.

"Oh, wow, I wonder why. You've been nothing but responsible and mature since I've known you."

"I understand why they said no. My dad explained it." She pouted. "I'm not mad but I still don't like it."

"Much better."

"They're just sitting there. Someone could go with me through the house and stuff."

"It might look like that's what they're doing, but I'm sure they're working. Tell you what, if they say it's okay, you can make your vlog with me."

"Really?" Her face brightened like sunflowers turning toward the sun.

"Only if you agree to stay with me on my agenda." Which included testing Hennessee House's reactivity to moods at some point. "We go where I say."

Rebel jumped up, sprinting back to the gazebo and returning moments later dragging Maverick by the hand.

"Lucky, tell my dad what you said." She was nearly breathless with excitement. What a sweetheart—it truly didn't take much to make her day.

"I said *if it's okay* she can tag along with me today and film some of her show. I don't mind."

Maverick looked unsure. "Oh, I don't know about that."

"I have references available if you're worried," she teased. "You can call my former family. They'll vouch for my nanny prowess."

He laughed. "Ah, no. That's not the issue. Rebel constantly being in the shot is. She won't be in the show. She'll be fully edited out before it airs."

"How much footage do they need? Surely, they have enough for today by now. I mean, I already got hijacked. What more do they want from me? Should I hold a séance to try channeling the house directly?" she joked.

"Please, Dad? Pleeeeease?" Rebel begged, bouncing on her tiptoes.

Lucky almost laughed watching Maverick lose the battle against Rebel's sweet little face. Helen of Troy had nothing on her.

"I'll talk to them," he said, finally. "No promises. Their answer is final. No appeals. Deal?"

"Deal!" They locked pinkies and Lucky about perished.

Stephen agreed to let Rebel film her vlogs as long as Maverick was an "on-site supervising producer," aka if anything supernatural happened, he'd quickly get her out of the shot.

"I expect to see my name in the credits," Maverick said to Rebel.

"You got it."

In addition to that morning's orchard stunt, Hennessee had reacted to happiness in the bathtub, curiosity in the sitting room, and . . . whatever she and Maverick felt in the bedroom. And when she was on the phone with him. *Ahem*. Her plan consisted of experimenting with different emotions in new locations. Rebel fit into that project quite nicely—Lucky couldn't have planned it better herself.

She slid into nanny mode, altering her schedule the tiniest bit to make it fun for Rebel, who narrated and filmed as they assembled the pet house. Afterward, they placed small bowls of dry cat food in various spots around the orchard.

Maverick temporarily took over filming duties while Rebel used the small ladder, the entire top half of her body hidden by the tree, to fill up brown baskets with fresh oranges, plums, and figs for about an hour. Lucky held her steady, while singing along to the pop music she played for atmosphere.

Identified feeling(s): joy, excitement. No visible response.

Lucky's lunch plans evolved to include her signature playtime menu she'd perfected with her previous family's kids. She taught Rebel how to make sophisticated mimosas (Diet Sprite and fresh orange juice), experimental tea sandwiches, and homemade fruit popsicles using molds they found in the kitchen.

Identified feeling(s): nostalgia, amusement. No visible response.

They moved the furniture out of the way in the parlor room to film dance videos, which then turned into a cartwheel competition, resulting in Stephen's veins popping out of his neck when he found out. Apparently, there were lamps in that room older than all of them.

Identified feeling(s): competitiveness, exhaustion. No visible response.

Properly chastised for "not respecting a borderline historical monument," they moved into the library. Turned out, Rebel was a reader too, and that was how their day ended—both curled up in an armchair, reading together with soft jazz playing at a soothing volume.

Identified feeling(s): contentment, happiness.

"We should head out," Maverick said, checking his watch.

Rebel glanced at Lucky and then asked, "Can we spend the night?"

"Absolutely not. Get your stuff."

"*Fine*." Rebel grumped as she stood up. "Can I borrow this book, then? It's about a super smart girl with really mean parents who develops superpowers."

Lucky said, "As long as you bring it back when you're done."

"I will. I always return my library books on time."

"She does," he confirmed.

"I'll walk you out," Lucky said, completely missing the two purple flowers on the windowsill. She walked right by them as they softly glowed in the early-evening sunset.

THAT NIGHT, HENNESSEE left the lights on for Lucky.

"How considerate. You wouldn't happen to be cousins with Motel 6?" she joked. Suited and booted in her gear, she traversed down the stairs to investigate the first floor. Her expectations for finding anything interesting were low, so she revised her initial plans to involve talking to Hennessee.

Sentient supernatural activity had been confirmed ten times

over. Establishing a reliable method of communication was the next logical step.

"Is it okay if I open this curtain?" she asked while in the sitting room. "Are you hoping people would ask first? Ooh, are curtains your eyelids and we're just ripping them open every day? But not this one—this one is yours?"

Silence.

She didn't care how silly she sounded. Pride had no place in her experiments.

"If you've been rummaging around in my brain like everyone suspects, you've probably found my memory palace by now." She walked into the dining room, the last place of confirmed activity between them, and leaned against the wall. "You'd also know that I read first impressions of people. If you showed me your eyes, or what you consider to be your eyes, I could try to read them. You know me and I'll get to know you. It might give us a better understanding of each other."

Lucky's phone rang loud as all hell, interrupting her moment. "Aren't you sick of me yet?"

"Not even close," Maverick said, rolling with it. "Besides, you have to know you're easy to talk to."

"Occupational hazard. You can't bullshit most kids and survive in the childcare industry. Before I knew it, I developed a skill I could use whenever I wanted."

"It works. Rebel really likes you. She recapped her entire day with *you* as if I weren't there the entire time."

"I have that effect on kids. I think I give off intense big sister energy."

"No, that's not it," he said, confidently. "I have a question for you. I've been trying to puzzle through something, and I can't quite figure it out."

"About me?" she asked, intrigued. "All right."

"What are you aiming for? You're obviously choosing to be there for a reason, but I think everything I've come up with is wrong."

"Aww, did you think I was trying to be *America's Next Top Medium*?"

"Yeah, right up until you panicked. I'm not new to this. I know what it looks like when people are trying to fool me and show out for the cameras. That's not what you're doing," he said thoughtfully. "What's your goal? Why Hennessee House?"

Lucky tried not to smile but being seen so clearly, by Maverick of all people, was exhilarating. Her heart reacted as if she'd suddenly sprinted around the block. "Well, this is an opportunity for me to discover and possibly define something new, which I love," she said honestly. "I've already figured out I'm not interested in ghosts, cryptids, and a host of other phenomena through experiments just like this—putting myself on the line. The only way out is through.

"But ultimately, Hennessee is a means to an end. I want people to take me seriously. I know what I'm up against. Skepticism, sexism, racism, people like my family thinking I'm weird for wanting to work on supernatural cases because that's white people stuff. But it's not. It's for *everyone* because these kinds of phenomena happen all over the world. I'm respectful, smart, inquisitive, talented . . . and I really think I can make a difference, not to mention that I have a unique perspective to offer the field. I just needed a chance to prove it to private investors."

Maverick remained quiet for a handful of rapid heartbeats. "Why didn't you say *any* of that during your interview?"

"They wouldn't have hired me." She truly believed people only liked her when she strategically hid parts of herself. As a result, she'd gotten pretty good at figuring out how to blend in for most situations, but it was hard to keep it up for long periods of time without burning out.

"That's not true," he said. "A TV show is admittedly a great way to get your foot in the door, but you'll need to start thinking about next steps to cement your name and what you can do into the public consciousness."

Lucky's eyes widened. Was Maverick giving her career advice? "Like what?"

"What about writing a book? Nothing says respectable like getting published, especially if you can pull it off without a ghost writer." He laughed. "No pun intended."

She chuckled. "Oh, no. I'm not that kind of writer. I'm not like you. I don't think I could do that."

"I was suggesting nonfiction. Once the show airs, I can help you develop your social platform," he said. "But since you brought it up, why not? You can do whatever the hell you want."

"Because I already tried and it was really bad," she said. "I used to love it when you read guest stories on your podcast. I wanted to submit one for consideration, so I shared it with a creative writing workshop. They met weekly on campus and . . . were not interested." She laughed against the memory. "My ideas just weren't very good, I think. After that, my creative well dried up. I stick to factual essays and blog posts these days."

Peppermint swirled underneath Lucky's nose. She pushed off the wall ready to follow—the kitchen.

"They were wrong," Maverick said, firmly. "You can tell a person who they are after meeting them once. You're *full* of stories waiting to be written."

Hennessee led her directly to the walk-in pantry. Inside, she clicked on the overhead light. Everything seemed to be in place. "But that's not interesting. Not compared to what you were doing."

"Sure, it's not."

Lucky scoffed, shaking her head. "Most of the time, I can't even translate what I've read in a way that matters. You said it yourself—it should be specific. Anyone can say 'you're stubborn' or 'you have a good heart' but I read all the pieces that make them into the person that they are. I can't even articulate just how daunting *that* is, never mind trying to turn it into a story comparable to what I've seen." And because that felt a little too vulnerable, she added, "I'm exceptional at a lot of things and I have no shame in claiming that. Not being able to translate is just one of the many ways my ego succeeds in keeping me humble."

"You did it with me and Rebel."

"Twice out of thousands. Not exactly the best odds." Since the peppermint hadn't faded, she began inspecting the shelves one by one. Moving things out of the way, tapping the wall to check the sound, inspecting the baseboards for gaps. "How does it work for you? You said you pull your stories out of your dreams, right?"

"I can't tell the future, and no, I don't know what you're going to do next, but I am a lucid dreamer."

She snorted. "Cute. Go on."

"That was brilliant, by the way. Stephen's soul left his body when he watched that footage. He thinks you're perfect," he said. "I always know when I'm dreaming. I can manipulate things. I remember everything that happens. I take pieces from there and turn them into my stories." He laughed, dryly. "I had a severe case of dreamer's block for the past couple of weeks. As luck would have it, seems to be gone now."

Lucky thought of his supernatural story time podcast, *Hypnopompic Remnants*, the first thing that ever connected her to him. "Those dreams must be intense."

Something *click*ed directly above her head. Startled, she hopped to her feet, searching for the source.

"They can be, but like I said, I'm always in control. They don't affect me. They creeped everyone else out, though."

"Not me." She found it hidden behind the pasta. A red handle had been embedded into the wall.

"Because almost nothing scares you."

"I listened to every episode of your podcast. It was my absolute favorite."

"What did you like about it?"

It took some trial and error to find the trick for the handle, but she did. Push in on one side, grip the other, and then pull out. The entire wall moved forward, revealing a narrow staircase leading upward. Cold air slowly flowed into the house, chilling her almost as much as the discovery.

"I found something," she whispered, knowingly breaking the rules. "A *big* something."

Lucky closed her eyes, once again using the sound of Maverick's rhythmic, steady breathing to help her stay calm and distracted. She didn't decide to answer so much as the words found their way out of her. "I liked how your podcast made me feel."

He didn't miss a beat. "And how was that?"

"I don't know. I've never been able to describe it."

"Could you try? For me?"

"I don't know if I even have the words for it. All I know is I needed to listen to it. For a long time, I couldn't go to sleep without replaying my favorite episodes. Something about hearing your stories and your voice told my brain, *It's okay. You can rest now. I'll be here when you wake up.*" She opened her eyes, ready to die from embarrassment. "Ew, sorry, that doesn't even make sense. Please forget I said that."

"Why would I do that? It made perfect sense to me."

"It did?" She stared at the staircase.

"Yeah. It's probably the greatest compliment anyone has ever given me about my work." He paused. "I've never told anyone this either, but I think I'd like to write a novel."

More silence and breathing and then, "I think I'd love to read it. If you'd let me," she said, feeling so raw and exposed it made her chest ache.

Thinking of his podcast reminded her how bad things used to be. Living in a college apartment with two girls who relentlessly ostracized her had been hell. She walked on eggshells, kept to herself, and developed a severe case of anxiety. She literally needed his podcast, his voice, to help her sleep at night because she spent her days so wound up.

Maverick had no idea how much he'd helped her and was still helping her. So far almost every time Hennessee House shared something with Lucky he'd been there too, unintentionally splitting her focus or guiding her away. Making a habit of relying on him instead of herself to make safe choices seemed like a bad idea.

Besides, Lucky wasn't used to needing other people anymore. She didn't want to need it.

"I'm sorry but I have to hang up now."

"Lucky, wait, no—"

"I'm sorry! Don't call me back until morning." She wanted to experience whatever Hennessee had in store for her with a clear mind—to comply or resist of her own volition. "I'll see you at sunrise. I promise."

She took several deep breaths and began walking up the stairs. Alone.

The passage didn't have built-in lights to guide her. Dust had settled on every surface. "This is fine. This is good," she whispered, carefully avoiding years-old spiderwebs and dead bugs. "There could be rats instead. Or jumping spiders. Oh god, why did I think of that?" Peppermint surrounded her every step of the way, easing her queasiness, but not erasing it. Just enough left to keep her steady and focused. As long as she felt that, she'd steer clear of true recklessness.

The red door appeared almost suddenly, burning in the near darkness. Her hand shook until it wrapped around the shockingly warm doorknob, which twisted with ease.

"Hello?" Lucky stepped across the threshold and found nothing but an empty attic. It was completely barren and swept clean save for one black fountain pen laid in front of a wall. She only spotted the pen because moonlight streamed in from the circular stained-glass window directly onto it.

She paused, giving herself a moment to check in. Sweating, sore legs, rapid breathing, stomach roiling . . . nerves steady. No indicators of fear response. Good. She reached for the pen—it rolled closer to the wall and flipped upright as if pointing.

"All righty then." She almost laughed but sobered up when

she noticed the writing on the wall. There were names, *several* of them in a list. She held her light over each one to give the camera time to record it. At the bottom, one name had been *carved* into the wood with short, slanted lines.

XANDER

13

Stephen finished inspecting the narrow staircase for the third time, entering the attic with a bewildered, "I cannot believe this has been here the whole time."

"My guess is the others used the ladder. Like any normal person would." Georgia filmed the wall with much steadier hands than Lucky used the night before. "Brian said he planned to lock himself in the suite on night three. Hennessee must have lured him up here somehow because by morning, he didn't want anything to do with us. Not even a final interview."

Stephen said, "We'll need to compare handwriting samples before jumping to conclusions."

"I didn't *jump*." Georgia whirled around. "You heard what she said. The goal was clearly to get her up here by any means necessary, *which* included giving her access to a secret passageway because it *knew* she'd willingly go for it."

No objections to that. Hennessee had Lucky's number and they all knew it.

"Whatever happened after that must've been what scared Brian off for good." Georgia turned her laser-focused gaze on Lucky. "Why didn't you write your name?"

"It seemed optional," she lied. Frankly, she deserved an award for winning against her impulsiveness, especially while paired with Hennessee's influence. The second she picked up the pen, the compulsion to write her name slammed into her like a sledge-hammer. Resisting the orchard had primed her for that moment— she'd forcefully said *no* and walked back downstairs. "Nothing happened after I decided not to. I went back to my room and slept."

"What are you thinking, Mav?" Stephen asked.

Maverick opened his mouth to speak but ended up pressing his lips together and shaking his head. He'd fallen into contemplative near silence from the moment she'd shown him the hidden staircase. Everything had been normal up to that point and then he changed, visibly shaken up. He even refused to let Rebel join them in the attic, banishing her to the backyard with Chase.

Lucky's focus had split clean down the middle. She wanted to give every ounce of brainpower to Hennessee House's list of ex-caretakers, and yet, her gaze kept sliding to him. Why couldn't he see how fantastic this find was? That list provided direct evidence of Hennessee exerting its will. It had led them all there on purpose—a conscious pattern of behavior.

"We should head down. Rebel hasn't eaten yet." Without waiting, Maverick descended the stairs ahead of them.

"Is he okay?" Worry infiltrated Lucky's tone, mortifying her to the bone, but she had to ask.

"He'll be fine." Stephen gave her a weak smile. "Let's go."

Maverick volunteered to cook again—another round of Rebel's favorite pancakes. They settled around the dining room table like a big, happy production family with the shadow of Lucky's discovery looming over them.

"I wanted to avoid looping Xander in." Stephen sighed, shaking his head. "I don't think I have a choice now."

"Xander, Xander, Xander," Lucky sang. "He's quite popular."

"He built this team. Handpicked everyone here except me," Chase said.

"Why not you? The man clearly has taste." She gestured around the table. "There's no way he'd overlook you without regretting it."

Chase's face reddened. "Because technically my wife did. Therese has edited *BARD* since the beginning and asked Mav to personally request me for this shoot so I can get more title credits under my belt. All he did was agree."

Xander must've been deeply invested in this project, then. Lucky asked, "Did he use to live here?"

"Sort of." Stephen winced, clearly uncomfortable. "It's complicated."

"If you'd listened to *me*, he'd already be here," Georgia said.

Half in the conversation, half out, Lucky stared at Maverick, waiting for him to notice. He sat directly across from her focusing on his plate with a distracted expression. Every few seconds, he pushed the food around as if he remembered he was supposed to be eating but couldn't bring himself to do it.

Most people could sense when they were being watched—a fairly common sensory phenomenon. It'd been one of her first investigations. One by one, she'd asked "innocent" and "random" questions to members of her nanny support clique to secretly compare the reports of their experiences. A chill. A pressure cloud. A prickling on the back of their heads. An undefinable awareness explained away by "I just know."

For Lucky, it was always a deep itch under her skin. If she was being stared at by someone she hadn't read yet, the itching intensified. She hadn't discovered exactly how those two things were related but she had a long-standing note to figure it out someday.

Maverick either felt nothing or was deliberately avoiding acknowledging her. Granted, trying to catch someone's eye while wearing sunglasses wasn't exactly the easiest thing in the world. So, she "accidentally" dropped her napkin. She retrieved it quickly, peeking under the table as she did. Once upright, she tapped his foot with hers to get his attention. She had it instantly.

No looking around. No checking under the table. He knew it'd been her. Or maybe hoped it was.

She mouthed, *Are you okay?*

He nodded with a fake smile that didn't have a hope in hell of reaching his eyes.

She lowered her glasses long enough to glare at him. *Don't bullshit me.*

That worked—he tried to hide his sudden smile behind his hand, quietly clearing his throat.

Pleased with herself, she mimed a phone to her ear and subtly pointed from herself to him. *Can we talk?*

He understood perfectly and nodded. *Later.*

Lucky's attention suddenly snapped back to the conversation. "Did you just say *illusions*?"

"Yeah," Stephen confirmed, frowning at her.

"Illusions? Not hallucinations?"

"My apologies," Stephen began. "We have our own terminology here."

"*Illusions* are changes the house makes to itself," Georgia said. "Like if it wanted to right now, it could create a face in the wall." She pointed to a section behind her. "It would warp the wood, change the grain pattern, and move the flowers in the wallpaper. Some of us would see it like a magic eye illusion. The rest wouldn't see it at all because those don't work for everyone."

Chase spoke next. "There's also *scents*, which you've experienced. Those are tailor-made specifically for each person. No one else will smell your . . . smell." He laughed.

"So, the cinnamon and the peppermint for me?" Lucky asked. "Anything else?"

"Much more than that," Stephen said. "Being in this house will always produce unique experiences."

"What about the flowers Hennessee gives me? What are those? Maverick has seen them, I took pictures, *and* my collection is growing. The jar is almost half-full."

An uncomfortable silence floated around the table until Maverick answered, "No one else reported receiving flowers."

"I have a question." Rebel cutely raised her hand—the one holding her fork speared with pancake.

"Yes?" Stephen asked.

"If I have a bad memory and my dad was there so he saw it too, and the house showed it to me, would he see it because he was there?"

Maverick attempted to clarify. "So, you were with me when something bad happened. If the house chose to show you that specific memory, you want to know if I could see it too?"

She nodded. "That's what I said."

"I know. It's a very good question." Maverick gave her such a *dad* smile, doting and amused. It made Lucky ache in a way she hadn't felt in years . . . She crushed that feeling down, back to the dark corner of her mind from where it had risen.

"I suppose that's possible," Stephen said. "It's not something we've tried before, but Xander might know for sure."

"Bad memories? What does that mean?" Lucky asked, mind already shifting and spinning with new ideas.

"It means exactly what she said." Stephen sighed, finally beaten. "We call that type of occurrence *specters*."

"Ghosts? That means ghosts."

"Specter also means something unpleasant that can haunt you. That's the form of the word we use."

"Interesting." Lucky took a sip of her orange juice. "This is really good. Is it from the orange trees outside?"

"It's store-bought." Maverick stared at her, unspoken questions in his eyes.

"Hmm," she said. "Still good."

The day continued much like the one before it. Lucky agreed to let Rebel tag along with her, filming their day. Maverick hovered around them, brooding and distractingly handsome. The other three waited in the wings for any supernatural signs.

Unfortunately, much to Lucky's dismay, Hennessee House had gone quiet.

Night four, she dared to spend time in the orchard accompanied by Maverick on the phone. He still hadn't told her why he'd been so upset but gave her a reason: he wasn't ready to talk about it. Outside, she finally found a curious Gengar watching her from a tree branch. Smaller than she'd thought, with white paws and large, glowing yellow eyes, he had obvious bald patches and a snaggle-toothed grin, and his left ear had been clipped.

"You can come inside," she said. "I don't think Hennessee will mind."

"Lucky?"

"I'm fine, Maverick. I'll introduce you tomorrow."

In the morning, she awoke to find Gengar fast asleep at the foot of her bed. No idea how he'd gotten in, but stranger things had already happened.

Night five, with nowhere else to explore, she stayed in her suite with the doors open. An invitation that went unanswered.

Or so she thought until she came up with an idea.

Night six she set up her camera on the dresser to film her suite through the night. She posited that Hennessee didn't like round-the-clock monitoring, but intermittent filming appeared permissible. She'd previously noted the increasing length and refreshing quality of her sleep. In less than a week she'd gone from restless to unconscious, sleeping harder than she ever had in her life. It was wholly possible she'd been sleeping through Hennessee's nighttime activity.

No dice. She'd been right the first time. Nothing was happening at night.

On her final morning with production, after Maverick finished her quick interview, he showed her how to self-tape. NQP issued her a laptop, a camera, several memory cards, and access to their server. She'd be required to upload her raw footage every twelve hours and back it up to an external drive.

"There's something off about that cat." Maverick glanced at Gengar, who sat on the windowsill supervising them in the office. He was kneeling beside Lucky's chair, their heads bowed closer together than necessary, work going completely ignored.

"I know," she agreed. "He doesn't have fleas. Super odd for an outside cat."

"You know what I meant."

"Did I?" She laughed. "He's obviously not friendly, but he seems to like us. I don't think he'd be in here if he didn't."

"No, he likes you *and* is hiding from Rebel. She's obsessed with him."

"How could she not be? He's so handsome."

Gengar had two default settings, scowl and scowl harder, but seemed to flick the tip of his tail at the compliment.

"I thought about getting Rebel a kitten after she tried to lure a neighborhood raccoon into the house. She wants a pet."

Lucky met his gaze, grinning as she imagined Rebel doing that. "That sounds rough. I'll see your bandit cat caper and raise you the time one of my kids—I called her Muffin—decided it was time to learn how to fly and started jumping from the highest places she could find."

"Damn." He glanced at Gengar again. "I'm gonna let her adopt one. I'm waiting until she's a little older. I don't know if she's ready for that kind of responsibility yet. I was thinking twelve?"

"Are you asking me?" She raised her eyebrows in surprise.

"Yeah. What do you think?"

"Well, Rebel seems pretty on the ball, especially if she wants something. It's less responsibility than a dog but requires more attention than a fish." She thought about it. "You two could sign up to volunteer at an animal shelter. It'll give her a good idea of what it's like to care for cats, cleaning litter boxes, playtime, and all that."

"That's a great idea. I think she'd love that. Thanks."

"Of course. Happy to be of service."

She was really going to miss this.

No more morning interviews, just the two of them. No more production family breakfast. No more spending her days with Rebel. And if Hennessee House remained dormant, no more Maverick calling her every night and morning. He wouldn't have a reason to.

He'd filled in his backstory blanks throughout the week—where he went to school, a little about his family, where he hoped to go in life, and everything she could've possibly wanted to know about Rebel. He was that dad who had pictures in his wallet, not just on his phone (baby's first big-girl Halloween trick-or-treating as a bumblebee). Of all the things she liked about Maverick, that was still her favorite. He loved Rebel with his entire being.

The impending loss of them felt like it was eating her alive, creating a hole where they should be in her life. She'd been racking her brain trying to think of a way to keep them all around but had come up empty.

This was why she never let herself get attached to anyone. She always ended up wanting too much, too quickly, and always ended up disappointed. They'd be gone and she'd be alone in the house. Exactly what she'd wanted before she realized she didn't want that at all.

"Any questions about any of this?" Maverick gestured to the setup he created for her.

"Nope. I got it." She leaned toward him, elbow on the armrest and chin in her hand.

He mirrored her slouching posture, drawing closer. His position resulted in him looking up at her. "Are you hungry?"

"Only if you're cooking. I do believe you've spoiled me, sir."

He laughed lightly, eyes crinkling at the corners.

"It's true. You're too good."

"I either had to learn how to cook or feed my kid McDonald's every night."

"Even chicken nuggets can lose their ineffable charm if you eat them too many times in a row."

"Exactly. Fortunately, Rebel is easy in the food department. She's not picky, no allergies, and she'll try anything once." He lightly tapped her arm. "And you're not so bad yourself. I am not looking forward to trying to replicate your high tea time. Rebel loves it."

"I'll send you a copy of my recipes. The trick is pretesting and making the selections seem random when they're not. All the flavors go well together no matter how they're combined."

"Ah, gotcha." He breathed into the silence between them. "You have beautiful eyes."

Her eyebrow quirked in response. "Maverick. They're brown."

"And I rarely get to see them."

Lucky never wore her glasses when they were alone for that reason. Even now, they were sitting on the desk. She didn't know if he realized it, but every time they made eye contact without her glasses between them, he smiled. Every single time.

She sighed, feeling a growing softness inside of her that matched his tone. "Don't try to feed me lines, okay? That doesn't work on me."

"You think I didn't mean that?"

"I think if you meant it, you could do better," she challenged.

"I've already read you. I've seen you. I know you. All up here." She tapped her temple as she recalled the reading. "That was a line—you're testing the waters to see how shallow they are. You're cautious, almost to a fault . . ." And she wasn't.

His caution mixed with her impulsivity like oil and water. They both inherently knew it, but he wanted to bypass it anyway because of how deeply he believed in people—in them. He would until the very end.

"*Oh.* Oh no." She pulled away from him, saying, "It won't work out between us. I'm sorry." In a matter of seconds, she was on her feet and nearly out the door.

"Wait, hold on—"

Lucky rounded the corner, following the voices she heard in the sitting room. She needed an out, a way to avoid having that conversation with Maverick because she wasn't ready. As annoying as they were, she'd rather keep her stupid crush-like feelings forever than deal with the certainty of knowing their relationship would end with him regretting everything and her being alone again. He couldn't ask her to talk about it in a room full of people.

"Lucky!" Rebel spotted her first. She was sitting on the couch next to someone. An obviously tall, dark-haired, and pale someone.

Xander Hennessee had finally arrived.

And Lucky looked right into his eyes.

14

Xander Hennessee read like a skeleton. Harsh, clean bone structure, empty eyes, and bared teeth. Exposed and cold save for a fragile, friendly warmth using his rib cage as a shield from a snowstorm. Only certain people turned that single flame into a raging fire. And he was searching for them. Always searching.

But he wasn't always that way—Xander's core had changed. He'd been stripped down to almost nothing by overwhelming grief and steadily rebuilt himself one bone at a time. He nurtured an unmatched resilience buoyed by a sentimental and loving interior. And he had an inquisitive and understanding disposition.

Lucky had been right before about the snowstorm and his grief. But he was healing by embracing it. She barely had time to breathe before accidentally making eye contact with Stephen, too.

Stephen carried a soft determination that he wielded like a weapon. A pushover who'd learned to stand his ground, but whose heart would always be in the right place. He'd been born with a strong desire for knowledge and was burdened by the rigidity of his beliefs. His greatest motivations in life were connections and family and creating art that would outlive him.

Horrific pain bloomed in the center of Lucky's face as if she'd been punched by a professional boxer. She simultaneously gasped and closed her eyes. "I need my glasses!" She used the heels of her hands to press down on her eye sockets to counteract the building pressure.

It'd been literal years since she'd felt so much agony. She'd forgotten how cursed she truly was. The throbbing dull ache in her forehead and temples, her inflamed skin stretched too tight across her face, the fire behind the backs of her eyes and the searing pain between them—

"Here. Come with me." Maverick's insistent, hushed voice sounded close to her ear. A hand on her waist and another on her back gently turned her around until she felt his crisp linen shirt against her forearms as he held her to him. His presence enveloped her, slashing through the pain. She inhaled—the comforting scent of cocoa butter soothed her like a balm. "Let me put your glasses on," he said. "Put your hands down."

"My eyes," she whimpered. "Are my eyes okay?"

"I don't know. Let me see," he coaxed.

She lowered her shaking hands.

"Oh—*shit.*"

"Is it bad? Is it both of them?" Burst blood vessels should've taken more than two back-to-back readings to happen. Judging by Maverick's expression, they must've looked terrible, but at least they didn't hurt. The rest of her head, however, hadn't been so fortunate.

"Yeah. It's both," he said, caressing her cheek.

"Shit." She held still while he helped her with her glasses. "My head hurts. I need to lie down. And I need an ice pack. Please."

"Bring her here." Xander's stoic ice-king façade had melted into pure concern. Maverick didn't let go so they escorted her together to the newly empty couch.

"I got frozen peas!" Rebel appeared at Lucky's side, handing her the bag.

"Thank you, Shortcake." She smiled weakly before tilting her head and placing the peas longways, from chin to forehead.

"Take these," Georgia said.

Lucky felt a hand on hers, turning it palm up. She temporarily displaced the peas to take the two Tylenol with some water. "Thank you."

"What the hell happened?" Georgia asked.

"I'm not sure," Lucky said. "I accidentally read Stephen and Xander back-to-back. Something must have gone wrong inside my memory palace."

Her automatons never failed her. They usually retrieved her readings so fast they rarely ever backed up like that anymore. And it had only been *two*—she should've only felt a little tired, not like this.

"Memory palace?" Stephen whispered, clearly not to her, but she answered anyway.

"You try housing over a thousand readings on top of all your other memories and see how you feel without one." She pointed at the room at large to emphasize her point. "Once I read someone, it stays with me forever. I needed an efficient filing system to keep my head clear."

Stephen said, "My apologies. I didn't realize that's how your power worked."

The room seemingly fell silent, but she knew they weren't just standing around staring at her. "I can hear you trying not to talk. I don't have that kind of headache."

Maverick said, "I'll get breakfast started. You should eat something since you took those pills. Rebel, come on."

"I want to stay with Lucky."

"No, come on. I need your help with a special project."

"Holler if you want me," Georgia said, voice fading into the distance. "I'll come right back."

Lucky listened to a procession of steps as they left her alone to recover. She waited a moment before saying, "I know someone is still there."

"I am," Xander said. "Is it all right if I sit next to you?"

She shrugged. "Anybody else?"

"Just me."

Lucky sat up and removed her glasses to give the peas contact with her eyelids. The burning and pressure were fading, but the persistent ache unfortunately kept rolling right along. "What do you want?" She quickly lifted the bag to look at him, nearly laughing as he sucked in a breath, eyes widening. "The rupturing takes the normal amount of time to heal. Should be back to normal in a few days."

"Does it still hurt?"

"I'll be fine."

"I fear I owe you an apology as well. I honestly believed you wore the glasses as a comedic bit."

"Nope. It's all in the name of self-preservation. And occasionally fashion. I like to match them to my outfit for fun," she said. "So. They finally called in the cavalry . . ."

He nodded. "They had some rather interesting things to tell me. Primarily concerning you."

"Hey man, I warned you. Did I not say I was uniquely qualified for this job?" she joked.

"You did. I believed your assertion was rooted in an abundance of hubris."

She removed the peas to squint at him, regretting it immediately when her sore facial muscles protested. "Where in the hell are you from? Do you always talk like that?"

"Whenever it suits me." He smirked. "Don't worry—it'll grow on you."

"Does that mean you're sticking around?"

"For the time being, yes. If it's all the same, I'd like to ask you some questions." He retrieved a tablet from a satchel resting on the end table next to him.

"Sure, if you agree to answer mine. I only operate on two-way streets."

"I'll do what I can." His placating smile felt like condescension.

"Looks like we're taking turns, then." She set the peas on the table and whipped out her phone with a theatrical flourish, ready to transcribe. Intense head pain, swollen face, and bloodshot eyes be damned. She'd conducted interviews under far worse conditions, like the one time she'd been sick with a flu straight from the pits of hell and had to stay up until two a.m. to meet a potential contact in Romania via Zoom. "I'll be generous—you can go first."

He regarded her for a moment, gaze assessing her from head to toe before nodding. "I've watched all your interviews thus far.

I noticed Maverick rarely inquired after your physical state. How have you been sleeping?"

"Fine." Realizing he was clearly waiting for her to say more, she added, "I slept fine. Do you need complete sentences or something?"

He exhaled in what could only be described as a regal huff. "Could you elaborate? Please."

"Could you give me specifics?" she shot back. "Look, I'm not trying to be difficult, but I answered the question." Until she felt satisfied that he'd make good on their little quid pro quo deal, she'd answer exactly what he asked. No more. No less.

"Have you noticed any changes from your normal sleeping habits?"

"Yes, actually." She grinned. "Why is your name on the attic wall?"

"Because I wrote it there." His icy tone could give the arctic tundra a run for its money. "Please list all the changes you've experienced while sleeping."

"I sleep longer. I've stopped waking up during the night. I don't really move either, like whatever position I go to sleep in, that's exactly how I am in the morning. I haven't had a single dream since I've been here. When I wake up, I am fully awake and extremely well rested," she said, ticking them off on her fingers. "Did Hennessee ask you to write your name on the wall?"

"No," he said. "Do you experience headaches or sudden overwhelming bouts of exhaustion in the evenings?"

"No," she said. "Did you know the other caretakers had written their names on the wall? The team didn't."

Xander paused, unable to keep the sudden surprise off his face.

Lucky gave him her cheeriest smile. She probably looked mad in the British sense—a Cheshire cat with bloodshot eyes. "Do you need me to repeat the question?"

He shifted in his seat, surprise giving way to his usual steely expression. "I suspected as much," he said. "Does the smell of peppermint truly not mean anything to you?"

"I have an exceptional memory, medically speaking. I'd remember if it did," she answered honestly. "Has Stephen slept in the house before?"

"No. I don't believe so." His measured response nearly sounded like a question. "Do you hear voices at night? Blatant or subtle ones that are easy enough to explain away as paranoia?"

She almost answered *Just Maverick's* as a joke but had a feeling Xander wouldn't find that funny. He was as much the boss as Stephen—being flippant might get Maverick in trouble. "I haven't heard any unexplainable voices. Did you use to live here?"

"Intermittently. My family used it as a vacation home," he said. "Have you seen anyone who isn't supposed to be here? Glimpses in the mirror, your peripheral vision, walking through the orchard, sitting on the stairs—anyone at all?"

"No." The hairs on the back of Lucky's neck stood at attention. "Don't lie to me: Are there ghosts in this house?"

"Not that I know of." He held out a hand as a peaceful gesture. "Please calm down. I am not attempting to deceive you. I was simply referencing common places where specters have manifested. The caretakers recognized each manifestation, most of them matching people who were still alive. Hennessee seemingly pulled them from their memories."

"Not ghosts?" Her brain was stuck.

He smiled gently. "No ghosts. It's all right."

She nodded, sitting back against the couch. "I haven't seen any specters. I found the cat I emailed you about, though." She pointed beside him where Gengar quietly sat. As if on cue, he jumped onto the couch and sat directly between them, his back to Lucky as if to protect her. "I named him Gengar."

"What an atrocious name."

"Thanks." She snorted. "Pretty sure he was abandoned."

Xander frowned. "He needs a haircut. I do not want him shedding on the furniture. I'll find a groomer who accepts cats and make an appointment."

"Oh," she said, surprised. "Thank you."

"He should visit a vet as well. I will email you the details by tomorrow."

Lucky laughed. He reminded her of one of those *I don't want no dog* dads who ended up falling in love harder than anyone else in the family. "Welcome to the good life, Gengar. Prepare to be spoiled for the rest of your life."

Xander frowned at her. "I'm assuming you will be taking the cat with you upon your departure."

"I'm not leaving," she said. "Speaking of, can I have access to the previous caretaker files now? I'd like to hear the firsthand accounts of their specters in case I'm missing something. Maybe I'm overlooking mine somehow."

Xander considered it. "Sure."

"Can I have one more favor? Do you think you could cover for me? I'm going to sneak upstairs to go lie down for a bit."

"Of course," he said immediately. "Get all the rest you need."

Lucky retired back to her suite like a true Southern belle in a Gothic house. Her delicate disposition required some time to recover. An email from Xander pinged when she was halfway up the stairs. That man was prompt—he'd given her a link to access the footage.

Settled on her bed with Gengar, she opened her laptop only to snap it closed a moment later when someone knocked on the door.

"Yes?"

Maverick poked his head inside. "Hey."

"Not you, visiting my sickbed," she joked.

She smelled his delicious food before she saw it—a buttery croissant breakfast sandwich and hash browns with a generous side of ketchup, a small jar of honey, sliced sweet peaches and tart apples from the orchard, and a glass of water, all on a little breakfast tray.

He set it down on her nightstand. "I noticed you're an avid ketchup person."

"It's true. I am," she said. "But I hate tomatoes."

"May I?" He gestured to her face.

"Yes?"

She watched his face as he felt her forehead and cheeks with the back of his hand. "Tylenol is working—you don't feel as warm. Eating will also help."

"Thank you, doctor."

"And the teasing continues." He sighed. "Are you trying to convince me you're feeling better?"

"Is it working?"

"No, but I think that's a me problem." He hesitated, worrying at his palms. "You forgot your glasses on the desk. I had them in my hand when I heard you scream."

"Oh no, I'm sorry." She crawled closer to him, sitting on her knees. "It shouldn't have been like that. I don't know what happened. It hasn't hurt like that in a long time. I'm fine. I promise."

"You really don't know what happened?"

She shook her head. "I used to routinely test my limits. One time, I was in class and spontaneously decided to read everyone. Made it to like twenty in a row before I had to stop." She made jazz hands, but he didn't laugh. "Anyway, I spent three days feeling like my brain was leaking out of my ears, but that was *twenty*. Two shouldn't have done that to me. It's like my tolerance reset to zero or something. That's what it was like when I was a kid."

"Maybe the house had something to do with it."

"I doubt it."

"Why? You looked upset when you ran out of the room. Maybe it was hijacking you again."

Lucky frowned. She'd felt in control—leaving the room had been her choice. Hennessee might've been *trying* to hijack her, but then her ability kicked in around the same time to read Xander and Stephen. That must've been too much activity at once for her brain and everything short-circuited.

"If it was trying to, what happened was an accident," she said. "I don't think the house wants to hurt me."

"You don't know that." He continued staring at his hands, head down. Lucky balled her hands into fists to keep them to herself. She didn't think they were familiar enough with each other to touch so casually.

Were they?

That first day when she touched his hand to distract him felt like a million years ago. Now there was so much of everything between them. If she were to touch him again, it wouldn't have the same meaning.

Maverick looked at her, unable to hide the flinch from seeing the state of her eyes again. Lucky wasn't ready. Not yet.

"I'm sorry I ran out of the room like that. That was me." She gnawed at her lip. "I got overwhelmed and I—"

"You don't have to apologize to me. That's not why I'm here."

Lucky didn't dare move as he reached for her hands, uncurling them, holding them, rubbing the backs of them with his thumbs. He touched his forehead to hers. "Feel better, okay? Call me if you need anything?" he whispered.

She closed her eyes. "Okay."

15

Lucky positioned her camera at the foot of her bed to record her reactions as she watched the previous caretaker footage. She shared small pieces of her apple slices with Gengar while taking notes on her phone.

Caretaker Number One: Bobbi Grayson. Cheery disposition. Main character energy. Aspiring actress with various work experience, primarily retail. Slept extremely well on night one. Experienced sudden headaches in the early afternoon. Felt compelled to leave the suite but resisted due to overwhelming fear on night two. Abruptly left in the middle of **night three**. During follow-up inquiries, recounted waking up to her deceased guinea pig curled in the crook of her neck and having a conversation with her grandpa, who begged her to stay in the house forever. Confirmed specter: Her grandpa currently lives in Austria and is in decent health.

Caretaker Number Two: Brian Ford-Mackenzie. Very self-assured, borderline arrogant. Family owns a bed-and-breakfast where he worked part-time in high school. Former athlete transitioning to acting. Slept very well on night one. Reported multiple physical ailments including headaches, nausea, and exhaustion in the afternoon. On night two, immediately had difficulty sleeping, with reports of voices speaking to him through the vents, seeing multiple women roaming the halls, and a strong compulsion to walk out the front door. Resorted to locking himself in the suite and turning on loud music until a power outage occurred. Turned in the keys the morning following **night three**. Refused a final interview.

Caretaker Number Three: Eunice Choi. Claimed to have a connection to the "other side" that runs in her family. Exuded a calming presence. Well-traveled with an open mind. Immediately experienced a sudden headache upon entering Hennessee House. Did not sleep night one due to pain. Reported constantly smelling eucalyptus—the exact scent of the candles she used to help her relax. Unable to sleep on night two. Reported hearing the voice of her deceased mother warning her to stay awake. Nearing sixty hours without sleep, reported specters inconsistent with previous Hennessee House activity and acute forgetfulness—deemed to be due to insomnia. Passed out in the kitchen at some point during **night three**. Admitted to the hospital with a diagnosis of exhaustion and severe dehydration. Reportedly does not remember anything from night

three but refused to return to Hennessee House. States
her "ancestors don't want [her] there." Has
subsequently returned to good health and agreed to be
a consultant as needed.

No wonder Maverick approached Lucky with protective guns
blazing.

Lucky's brain was reeling with information, processing
through scenarios and proposed answers faster than she could
write them down. She began pacing the room, talking into a
recorder to catch it all.

This changed everything. Eunice likely had ESP. She was up-
front about it, and they hired her anyway—had Lucky been
wrong about NQP's plans? What *else* did she and Eunice have in
common? What made them different? Did Hennessee's experience with Eunice make it change its approach?

She speculated that Hennessee hadn't attacked Eunice so
much as clashed with her. Protected by her inherited abilities,
Hennessee never got access to her since she never slept. But how
did it know what to use to produce a scent for her? And why did
she write her name in the attic?

Writing on the wall *must* have created some form of binding
agreement with Hennessee because everything escalated past the
point of no return afterward. The inverse appeared to be true as
well. Lucky resisted writing her name and the house went dormant, save for continuing to give her flowers. A gentle reminder
that the offer, whatever it may be, was still on the table.

What, then, was Hennessee's end game?

Lucky came to a sudden stop in the middle of the room and
stared at the wall behind her dresser. She brought the recorder

closer to her mouth and said quietly, "I think I'm seeing my first illusion? It's in the wall, but it's not clear. I think it looks like letters. An *X*? I don't know how to do the magic eye thing—unfocusing my eyes isn't working."

Afraid to look away or even blink, she squinted and turned her head, holding it at different angles. It appeared exactly as Georgia said. The wood suddenly *looked* different, as if the grain had changed. "I think it's definitely an *X*. Two intersecting slashes and there's a curved line too. Like an *S*." Strangely, she didn't smell peppermint or feel anything at all, so if it was a message from Hennessee it might not have been a direct one.

She needed more information. Immediately. Fortunately, a gut feeling told her exactly how she could get it.

A FEW HOURS later, Lucky spied on everyone from the shadows of the staircase, creeper-mode fully activated.

They'd gathered in the sitting room again. Coworking created an astonishing kind of harmony—alone, together, noses buried in their computers. The soft clicking of their keyboards. Music from their earphones, too faint to discern but distracting enough to notice. The occasional grunt, cough, and sniffle.

Maverick sat in the sunny corner near the window, laptop balanced on his knees. Every so often, he'd pause long enough to bite his thumbnail or rub the pinched frown lines in his forehead. She didn't realize she was smiling until she felt herself sigh like a lovesick teenager.

Lucky tapped her head against the baluster to knock some sense back into it. Terrible idea considering the lingering pain from her earlier readings, but it got the job done. Incompatible on an actual fundamental level, their romantic "future" wasn't bleak—it didn't have a single hope of existing. He didn't know it yet, but he didn't want someone like her complicating his love life. No one did.

Rebel lay in the middle of the floor, staring at the ceiling. Right where they could all see her. Poor Shortcake looked bored out of her mind while the adults busied themselves with anything but paying real attention to her.

"*Psst!*" Lucky waited before doing it again louder and longer. "*Pssssst!*"

Rebel spotted her immediately and gasped.

Lucky pressed a finger to her lips, waving her over.

"Dad, I need to go to the bathroom." She walked out of the room, looking over her shoulder before excitedly running up the stairs. "Are you feeling better now?"

"I am. What've you been up to?"

"*Nothing.* I am *so* bored. I can't film anything. I can't go anywhere. My dad won't stop writing *and* he won't let me help yet. This is the worst last day of work *ever*."

"I think I might be able to do something about that. Want to help me with a top secret project?"

A year ago, if someone told Lucky her experience being a nanny would inevitably lead to making a ten-year-old her partner in crime in a sentient house, she absolutely would've believed it.

Rebel cased the sitting room in record time, assessing the best angles through her camera. She secured a spot beside her dad's chair and sat next to him. Her job entailed filming the entire room while strategically keeping Xander in frame.

Lucky flounced down the stairs to prove she was as good as new. "I have returned," she announced and ended up lingering by the sofa, where Georgia reclined with her feet up. No one else seemed to notice her arrival.

Georgia uncovered one of her ears. "Oh, hey. Did you want to sit?"

"I'm good, thanks. But I did want to talk to everyone for a sec."

"I got you." Georgia typed something quickly—several chimes sounded around the room.

"When did you get here?" Chase asked, removing his earbuds. He grabbed the camera next to him, aiming it straight at Lucky. "How's your head?"

"Just now. Back to normal." Lucky checked in with Rebel, who gave her a thumbs-up. "I have an idea for something. It came to me while I was upstairs resting, but mostly thinking about the house. Hennessee seems to be after something that it gets from us, people, but only under specific conditions."

Georgia grimaced. "What makes you say that?"

"During my interview, Xander said Hennessee isn't always friendly. When I got here, Maverick said Hennessee takes a day to assess someone before deciding the best way to scare them off—a test everyone keeps failing. I think you're both right, in a way, but we're all viewing things through a human lens.

"Everyone sees things differently. We're all taught that, right? Through my ability, I've experienced it. I know for a fact that's true. So, why would Hennessee House be any different?" She paused to let her question breathe. "What if Hennessee House isn't scaring people because it wants them to leave? What if it's challenging us to stay? Its version of a litmus test."

"Okay," Stephen said. "I'm following, but why would it do that?"

"Your guess is as good as mine," she admitted. "I believe it values fear in ways that we don't."

"Then why hasn't it tried to scare you?" Georgia countered.

Lucky barely caught her surprised grin before it erupted on her face. She anticipated Xander asking that question. But Georgia came in hot, proving once again she was as quick as everyone else. "Because Hennessee lost interest in me when I didn't write my name on the wall on my third night," she lied. "I didn't agree to take the test, but now there's someone in the house again who did."

All eyes turned to Xander. Impassive as ever, nothing in his stance indicated she'd caught him off guard. He was far too good at being secretive for that. She hoped Rebel's footage might say otherwise.

She continued, "I'd like to hold a little experiment. If Hennessee reacts to Xander being here at night, then it proves the wall is the key. Writing your name guarantees continued supernatural activity that will escalate in intensity for as long as you remain in the house. Otherwise, Hennessee just . . . allows you to stay, peacefully and mostly unbothered."

Lucky outlined the four integral steps she'd come up with thus far:

One—Subject falls asleep, granting Hennessee access to their mind.

Two—Subject experiences events that confirm they are susceptible to Hennessee's influence. Can include general body discomfort, scents, illusions, and hijacking.

Three—Subject will be guided to the attic to write their name on the wall.

Four—Hennessee begins using specters to scare the living bejesus out of Subjects to weed out the weak like it's a game.

"You," Georgia began slowly, as she tilted her head to the side.

"You make dumb decisions, but I had a feeling that was an act. You're actually a lot smarter than I thought you were."

"Georgia, really?" Chase asked, clearly exasperated.

"I'm gonna choose to take that as a compliment," Lucky said with a laugh, before flowing back into the momentum she built. "For the experiment, Xander will be the post-wall control. Through him, we find out what happens next. Will the house keep trying to scare someone forever or is it only a temporary means to its true desire? Because I believe the litmus test is only the beginning. Hennessee has more secrets to discover, but no one's gotten that far yet."

Xander's jaw tensed as he stared at Lucky. He crossed his arms and audibly huffed through his nose before looking away.

"That means he's in," Georgia explained, sounding impressed.

"Stephen?"

"Yes, Lucky?" He was already grinning.

"I need you to be the new sleeper—a mock caretaker number five on their first night. I want to see what happens."

"Okay."

"No, not okay, *Stephen*." Georgia glared at him before turning back to Lucky. "Why? Explain it."

"So far, I've been the only caretaker who's had a vastly different experience," Lucky said, happy to oblige. "My first night I followed the rules, stayed in the suite, and Hennessee gave me a flower—it's still giving me flowers. That alone is a clear deviation from its usual MO, most likely because of its previous failures. Everyone kept leaving too quickly. I think it hoped I would see it as friendly, which I have, and although I haven't left, I didn't write my name on the wall. It still hasn't gotten what it really wants. Another failure."

Because the house still very much wanted Lucky in the attic. The compulsion was subtle, but she felt it continuously. Even now.

"You're thinking it'll try something else again?" Stephen asked. "Still okay, by the way. I've been rooting for you since day one."

Lucky laughed. "The house adapts and changes based on its experiences. If its core value is fear, I believe it will return to being silent and unfriendly. You won't get a gift tonight."

Maverick said, "Lucky, you also claimed 'almost nothing' scares you while in the house. Repeatedly. That could've been what triggered it to try a different approach instead of randomly deciding to be friendly. Your confidence changed its mind."

Lucky held Maverick's gaze. In that moment, she knew he wasn't only talking about Hennessee House. "That's very possible."

Except one fear in particular would be right up Hennessee's haunted alley. Her guess was the house hadn't found it yet because her memory palace was too massive, and she kept that fear hidden for her own protection. It might also explain why she continued to sleep so deeply beyond the first night, unlike the other caretakers. Hennessee was still having the time of its life in her head.

Rebel added, "When it looked in your brain, it thought, *Oh no! She was telling the truth!* My grandma says all girls deserve pretty flowers. Maybe the house thinks that too."

"I don't think the house cares about gender, Shortcake. I believe the flowers hold personal meaning for Hennessee and it tried to share that with me," Lucky said.

"How did you come to that conclusion?" Xander asked suddenly.

"Educated guess." She grinned. Interesting how that was the only topic he deigned to comment on so far. "My experiment also requires a third person. I'd like to see what happens when someone is here at night, on their first night, but does *not* sleep. I believe the house will do everything it can to lure them into doing so, thereby solidifying sleep assessment as the vital first step. It'll also provide a contrasting set of data to pair with the sleeper."

And Eunice.

"Oh, I see," Georgia said. "And just who exactly are you thinking could be lucky number three?"

Lucky faltered under Georgia's smug stare, changing course to ask, "Any volunteers?"

"Respectfully, no fucking way." Georgia held up her hands, and then conceded, "I'm in favor of the experiment, though. It just might solve our production problems."

Chase said, "I'll end up falling asleep. Hennessee will start whispering sweet nothings and I'll be out like a light. Unless I swap with Stephen? He can stay awake, and I'll be the sleeper?"

Lucky bit her lip while pretending to consider his offer. "Well." She held her breath, trying to not look hopeful. She'd wanted Maverick there from the moment she'd thought of the plan. She wanted to do this with him backing her up for real. They locked eyes again.

"I'll do it," Maverick said immediately, as if he'd been waiting for her.

"Of course you will," Georgia muttered.

"We're spending the night?!" Rebel's jaw dropped.

"No, I am," Maverick said. "You're staying at Uncle Max's house."

16

Georgia refused to be physically present for experiment night but found an ingenious way to contribute. Matching pajama sets. For everyone.

"Since you wanna be test subjects so bad, you can dress like them too," she said, passing them out. "All the same design but different neon colors so it'll be easier to spot each other at night if anything goes down since we know Hennessee likes to play with the lighting."

"How thoughtful," Xander said, masterfully blurring that line between genuine and sardonic.

Georgia pointed at him and threatened, "You better wear them. I'll know if you don't."

Xander generously gave her a lazy smile. "Then what will happen?"

"It'll hurt my feelings." She switched it up on him so quick it almost gave Lucky whiplash. "I'll cry."

"Well, I wouldn't want you to do that." He leaned down slightly, head bowed. "I will wear them. You have my word."

Sibling vibes sparkled between them, so vibrant Lucky felt like she could touch it if she tried. Interesting.

After dinner and sundown, they decided to separate immediately to give the house as much time alone with them as possible. Xander took the room directly across from Lucky, with Maverick and Stephen shacking up in opposite rooms at the end of the hall. Each person had a camera set up to continuously film the room and a second for self-tapes, if they chose to do so.

Gengar silently judged Lucky as she did everything and anything to burn off the anticipation anxiety keeping her awake. Jumping jacks, dancing, push-ups, wall-sits, handstands, yoga—for literal hours.

Around midnight, after a third failed attempt to walk out of a back bend, she asked, "Do you want to go outside? I haven't tried that yet."

Gengar jumped from the bed and sat by the door, staring at the doorknob.

"Do you understand me? Blink once for yes," she joked.

Outside was one of Gengar's words. He also recognized *hungry*, *snackies*, and *Rebel*. That last one often sent him running for his favorite hiding spot. According to Maverick, he knew Lucky's name too.

Gengar entered the hall ahead of her, trotting toward the stairs at a quick pace. Overall, he seemed to be adjusting well to being a house cat, but Lucky didn't think he'd ever want to give up roaming around the orchard, climbing the trees, and chasing the rodents to his kitty heart's content.

"Lucky. Hey."

"Maverick." They met at the top of the staircase in their matching pajamas as if they planned it. She leaned against the banister, pathetically happy to see him. "Still awake. Well done."

"Barely." He held up a mug of what smelled like coffee. "I tried everything else. If I start reading, I'll fall asleep. If I try writing, I'll fall asleep. If I listen to music or watch a movie, I'm definitely going to sleep."

"But we talk every night for hours. I figured you were a night owl."

"Only for you."

"Stop. You have not been staying up just to talk to me."

That indulgent grin looked so good on him. "Was I allowed to call you tonight?"

"Technically, no."

"Thought so." He nodded. "I made coffee to keep me awake because otherwise I. Will. Fall. Asleep."

Lucky's cheeks began to warm. She realized she was always the one to hang up first. She always accidentally fell asleep before him. She always teased him if he called even five minutes later than normal.

He'd really been staying awake for her the whole time.

Gengar yowled at her from the bottom of the stairs.

She laughed, grateful for the reprieve. "Go on. I'll catch up."

Gengar paused for a second more before dashing off for his newly installed kitty door.

Maverick asked, "What are you two up to?"

"A midnight stroll around the orchard. I can't sleep."

"Well, we've already broken the experiment rules. Might as

well keep going." He sat on the top step, gesturing for her to join him.

"That's like saying I have a crack in my phone screen, might as well shatter the whole thing." She sat down anyway.

The staircase was narrower than average, barely enough room for two adults to walk side by side. Lucky held her hands between her thighs, hoping to take up less space. Their shoulders and hips met in the middle despite her efforts—a comforting warmth radiated through his clothes.

She asked, "Anything exciting happen for you yet?"

"Not really. I smelled flowers again when I was in the kitchen. I followed it but it might have been leading me back to my room. I think it faded when I saw you. I stopped focusing on it so I'm not sure."

"Interesting. What kind of flowers?"

"I don't think it's a specific one. It's more like a pleasant floral perfume."

"Is it familiar?"

"Yep." He nodded, clearing his throat. "Very."

"I wonder what the parameters are for scents. Can the house make them for anyone it wants to? It made one for Eunice and she hadn't slept yet either."

Maverick sighed, shaking his head.

"What?" After accepting he wasn't going to elaborate, she said, "At least yours isn't like mine and completely random. Hennessee hasn't shown me anything personal at all." If Hennessee House wanted to get her attention now, it should use Maverick. He always smelled so good. She'd follow even faster than with the peppermint. Currently, his usual cocoa butter scent was stronger than normal, still lingering on his skin after his shower.

"That's a good thing," he said seriously. "I'm never sleeping in this house. With the way my dreams work, I'm low-key terrified what it'll show me."

"With a mind like mine, it should be having a field day. It could have tried to put the fear of everything in me a million times over using the things I've read in people. And yet? Nothing. It doesn't make sense."

"Maybe it has other plans for you." He shrugged. "I get where you're coming from, but no one person can know everything. Sometimes things just won't ever make sense, no matter how you spin it."

"Well, I can't accept that."

"I know." The resigned look on his face made her heart sink. Words fell to the wayside as they stared at each other until he said, "Your eyes are starting to look better."

"Ah, going for my eyes again, I see," she joked. "I promise I'm fine."

"What's it like?"

"The pain?"

"No, being able to read people the way you do. What's it like living with it?"

"Oh, um." No one had ever asked her that before. "I don't really remember what life was like before I could do it, so I guess you could say it changed everything for me. I've never met a person I couldn't read. No matter how old or young, confident or shy, good or bad—I see them for who they were. Who they are. Who they want to be. Who they will be if all their stars align. Sometimes it feels like cheating." She looked away, concentrating on her knees, and felt him move impossibly closer.

Their temples nearly touched, and he didn't need to use more than a whisper. "What do you mean?"

"Life gave me a cheat code, but it wasn't free. I have to pay for it." She shrugged. "No one wants to be around a know-it-all. No one likes it when you know their secrets, sometimes before they do. My family doesn't like me very much because they think I'm too self-righteous, among other things. Keeping friends is difficult when you start being too weird or too driven. I see everyone and my payment, my punishment, is no one sees me." She smiled at him to keep from crying. She'd never said that out loud before. Easy to forget how much it hurt when she forced herself to never think of it.

He shook his head, frowning and concerned. "Having a gift isn't a punishment." His fierce whisper was almost enough to convince her.

"A gift. Sure. I wish whoever gave it to me left a note so I could return it." She laughed.

"Who would you be without it?"

She stared at him wide-eyed, slightly in shock.

"Don't misunderstand," he said gently. "I'm not saying you'd be nothing without it. I'm asking who would you be instead? What would your life be like? Would it be better? Would it be worse? Who would you want to be? It's obviously had a profound effect in shaping who you are. Would you be the same person without it?"

She shook her head. Of course, she wouldn't be. Her ability was tied to her existence. Not to be dramatic but losing it would be like staying alive after giving up her heart—she didn't know how she'd function. That was why it hurt so much to be rejected so thoroughly by her loved ones. Changing for them meant deny-ing a part of herself.

He asked, "If you could really give it up, right now, right this second, would you?"

"It was just a joke, Maverick."

"I know that. But why did you make it? It came so quick, like it was nothing. Rolled right off the tongue. Why? I don't think it was to make me laugh."

Because when she pretended it was a burden people felt sorry for her and stayed a little bit longer. Pretending to hate parts of herself made her relatable. But she said to him, "I don't know."

"You do know."

"I don't—I don't know. I was just being stupid."

"No, you weren't."

"It doesn't matter."

"I think it does," he said. "Maybe you feel like no one sees you because you don't let them. I ask you a personal question, you almost always try to dismiss it at your expense. You think it's stupid. You don't know why you said it. You ask me to forget what you said. It's like you want to erase any traces of you genuinely being yourself. Why?"

Because sometimes you make me forget how to think.

Because you make me let go of who I trained myself to be.

Because I'm trying so hard to be normal. Because I'm better in small doses.

Because no one wants the real me.

For the first time in a long time, Lucky couldn't figure out the perfect lie to answer his question. Her brilliant mind had finally failed her, a moment she never thought would happen. It'd gone blank—every word and quip and pun and turn of phrase wiped clean. Nothing remained except her feelings.

The raw burning of unshed tears. The lump in her throat. The persistent, phantom ache in her chest that grew stronger every time she looked at him. The bottomless pit of inevitability in her stomach ready to consume any hope she dared to have.

She was so close to falling apart and he just sat there next to her. Patiently waiting and refusing to let her fake her way through an answer.

A loud *bang* echoed from downstairs. Maverick and Lucky shot to their feet, fully alert. His hand found hers as if it were always meant to.

He asked, "Just checking: You heard that, right?"

Heart hammering in her chest, she glanced at their joined hands and then his face. "I did."

"We stay together." A statement not up for negotiation.

Wind howled downstairs, whistling and demanding attention as an endless cascade of purple flowers flowed into the house like an evening tide. They hit the front door, curling up and around and out, swirling with every gust.

Lucky smiled as if it were the most magical thing she'd ever seen, but said, "I hope that's an illusion because I'm not cleaning that up."

"It isn't." Xander stood behind them, wearing his pajamas as promised. Maverick gently pulled Lucky toward him and out of the way as he wordlessly squeezed by them, down the stairs, and toward the kitchen.

"Come on!"

"Lucky, wait—"

But she wouldn't hear him. Possessed by the spirit of Rebel

herself, she pulled him after her. If he didn't move, he would've fallen. "We can't let him go alone."

"We can actually. Wait, wait." Maverick gently gripped her other arm—she allowed it, holding momentarily still in the hallway. "He told me this might happen. He doesn't want us to follow him."

Dutch door wide open, flowers continued to spill inside seemingly from nowhere. She barely caught sight of Xander's back as he disappeared into the orchard.

"Why?"

"You'll have to ask him. I'm sorry."

"Will he be safe out there?"

"Probably. It's his house. He knows more than any of us."

"Maverick, do you understand what this means? Look." She gestured to the ground as flowers whirled around their feet and up their calves. "It gave him flowers. This is his welcome home. Hennessee has been waiting for him to come back."

He looked uneasy and skeptical.

"Don't be like that, please?" she pleaded. "This is good. This is *so* good."

"We don't know what it's showing him," he said. "We don't know what comes after this. I know you want to believe the house has good intentions, and I'm sorry, but I don't. Neither does Xander. And if he says that, it means something."

She shook her head, taking a step back.

He took a step forward. "Just wait until you talk to him before deciding if this is actually a good thing. Please? In the meantime, we'll stay down here until he comes back or if something happens and he needs us. Okay?" They sat together at the small kitchenette table in front of the window. The vibrant colors of the orchard were no match for the oppressive darkness, but the white gazebo glowed in the moonlight next to it. Maverick pulled their chairs together, as close as they'd been on the stairs. Fifteen minutes of silently waiting passed before she said, "I hope he's okay."

"Me too." He paused. "I want to tell you something."

She tore her attention from the window for him.

"Since I've met you, I've started dreaming again. I've written more in the past week than I have all year," he said. "I really do believe you have a gift. The kind that helps people see the best in themselves. You guide them toward where they would be happiest. You're a muse, Lucky."

"That's very sweet, Maverick. It's not true, though."

"That's what I see in you," he said. "I also see that you're a know-it-all and a little self-righteous. And you lie all the time. I see everything and I'm still here. Because I want to be and I'm not going anywhere unless you tell me to."

She scoffed. "Sure, you say that now."

"Because that's how this works. This is how it starts." He huffed in frustration. "You're so brilliant it's ridiculous and yet you think it's okay for you to make decisions for me." He paused. "For us. Why can't we do that together?"

"Because it won't work."

"But you're not psychic, remember? You don't know how this will end until we live it, but we'll never find out if you keep running away," he said. "I want to see where this goes. What do you want? Honestly. Not based on what you think will happen or how you think I'll react. What do you honestly want?"

She didn't even need to think about it. "I want to be wrong about us. You don't know what it was like for me when I tried to be with other people." Her voice was shaking as badly as her hands. She didn't want to cry. She didn't want him to think he made her unhappy because he didn't. Not even close. "I want . . . I want to take things slowly. I need slow."

"Slow," he repeated, wiping her tears. "We can do that."

Lucky sniffled, laughing as she smiled, but then *something* made her yawn. She felt it, like a command in her head telling her body what to do. The edges of her vision began to blur and darken as she looked at Maverick and whispered, "I think I'm tired."

17

Lucky jolted awake as if something forcefully ripped her from unconsciousness. She barely moved an inch before feeling the awful cramp in her neck. And legs. And her right arm—why was she so achy?

Because she'd slept on a makeshift bed made from pushed-together kitchen chairs, the wall, and Maverick's body.

Maverick, who was still asleep.

Shit.

"Maverick, wake up," she said, heart beating too fast. "You have to wake up." She shook him gently.

He woke with a start, inhaling sharply on high alert. "What is it? What's wrong?"

Panic danced in his eyes as she held his face, trying to stay calm. "When did you fall asleep? Was it after sunrise?"

"I didn't sleep." He shook his head, looking past her around the kitchen. "I didn't . . . *You* fell asleep. I almost carried you upstairs because you passed out so hard—you just turned off like someone pushed your power button. But I didn't want you to be upset that you weren't down here, and I was fine. I felt fine. I don't remember going to sleep." He closed his eyes, grimacing. "But I think I did. No. *No.*"

"Did you make it past sunrise first? It might not count if it was during the day."

He shook his head. "I honestly don't know. I don't remember."

"Maybe it wasn't that long. It might not have been enough time for the house to see anything. It's probably fine."

Lucky felt terrible. This was *her* experiment. She was responsible for keeping them safe. He explicitly stated he never wanted to sleep in the house—she should have been there and awake to make sure this didn't happen to him.

"Hey. It's okay." He began rubbing circles on her back.

"No, it's not. Don't comfort me." She gently pushed his arm away. "I should be doing that for you." She hesitated for a split second before leaping—his chair skidded backward from the force of it. "I'm sorry. This is my fault," she said, hugging him tightly and rubbing *his* back.

He chuckled into the crook of her neck as he wrapped her in his arms. "It isn't, but thank you."

"Did you two sleep in here? I thought we were supposed to stay separated." Stephen stood in the kitchen doorway fully dressed.

Lucky regretfully detached herself from Maverick and they both stood up. "We were. Hennessee had other plans." He began fixing the chairs back into position.

"I take it something happened." Stephen kicked up a plume of flowers and they oddly took their time floating back down. "Xander mostly mumbled at me on the way to his room."

"You've seen Xander?"

"Yeah, like a second ago. He said he's going to sleep for a couple of hours. Well, that's what I think he said on account of the mumbling."

So much for that. Lucky asked, "How did you sleep?"

"Fine." He grinned. "No complaints."

After going upstairs, Lucky took a bath, got dressed, and then passed out in the middle of the bed when she mistakenly decided to rest her eyes for a few minutes. Falling asleep hadn't been on the docket, and yet . . . her body refused to be denied. Again.

She didn't know what to expect by the time she made it downstairs but found them all in the sitting room again—by far Hennessee's most popular location. Surprisingly, Maverick hadn't gone home. More powerful than a jump scare, the sight of him sent her reeling headlong into her feelings.

"Sleeping Beauty finally decided to wake up," Xander quipped.

Lucky gasped. "You think I'm beautiful? Oh my god, Xander, stop it," she said, instinctively falling back on old habits. "So sorry to inform you that you're not my type. My condolences."

Stephen laughed. "He jokes, but we were starting to get worried."

Her gaze found Maverick's, immediately fearing he'd been the root of that worry. He was sitting in the sunny corner armchair again. Early-afternoon light streamed through the gauzy curtains, giving his skin a luminous glow. Seeing his face, noticing all the subtle ways his expression shifted as he looked at her, was remarkable in a way few things were.

"I feel fine. I think I overdid it by staying up too late," she said to him and sat on the couch.

A silent conversation passed between the three men like they were playing catch with a secret. Stephen to Maverick to Xander.

Back and forth and back again. No one saying anything aloud. She began to suspect they already discussed the night before among themselves and decided to keep her in the dark.

As if she'd just let that happen. "So, Stephen, earlier you said you slept well? How was everything else?"

"Uneventful."

"Wow, what a riveting account. Felt like I was there."

His reluctant smile felt like a victory. "Nothing happened. Truly. I fell asleep around ten or so. Slept through the night. Woke up at four-thirty when my alarm went off."

"No flowers? Any other surprise gifts?"

"Nothing out of the ordinary," Stephen said. "I didn't go out of my way to search or anything because I figured it would be in plain sight."

"And how are you feeling now?"

"I actually have a banging headache." He laughed despite his discomfort. "A little queasy too."

Lucky nodded solemnly. "Xander? I notice the floor is devoid of the flower tide pool."

"Because I cleaned it up. You're welcome, by the way. As care-taker it was your responsibility to see to it."

"I said I wasn't cleaning them up. Oh, you thought I was jok-ing. How adorable of you." She winked at him. "Anything else you'd like to share with the class? I was right, wasn't I? The house showed you a specter. It called you outside."

Xander exhaled in a huff, crossing his arms. He was the only one standing—well, leaning against the wall near the empty por-trait mantel. "Yes. That was exactly what happened. You were right." He regarded her with a steely gaze. "Is that what you need to hear?"

"What did you see?"

"That's irrelevant. You're the star of this show. Not me."

"Then why did you participate?"

"Because I am willing to entertain your little side quests up to a certain point, which you are rapidly approaching. You work for me—not the other way around." His tone was firm but had no bite. "Is that clear?"

"Unfortunately." She shrugged, hoping her petulant pout would read as if she'd felt chastised. He wasn't going to fire her.

Calling her the star of the show hadn't been sarcasm on his part and they all knew it. Production needed her as much as she needed them now.

Xander turned his attention to Maverick. "And you're positive you want to keep working with her?"

Lucky's ears perked up. *Keep?* Maverick wasn't leaving the production? She looked to him for confirmation, and he nodded, holding her gaze.

Stephen cleared his throat. "We'd like to discuss the pitch for a new show with you. It'd be a limited series. Three episodes max. Filmed concurrently with *The Caretaker* as a promotional prequel."

Lucky asked, "How? What's it about?"

"They would be related—you acting as the bridge between the two shows," Maverick said. "I wanted to do something for Rebel. She's really passionate about making her videos and she's gotten so much good footage from being with you in the house. I want to help her make something special with it."

"And we both fully support Rebel." Stephen pointed to himself and Xander. "Everyone's been working overtime to put the show together as a surprise early birthday present for her. Xander is personally funding it. Not investors. The rights will be split between NQP and Rebel's trust. Fifty-fifty."

"Wow, okay. How can I help?" she asked, stunned into seriousness.

Maverick said, "It'll be a found footage–style series of her exploring a previously rejected *BARD* location—Penny Place Amusement Park. We couldn't use it because there isn't a single heart behind the haunting to build the narrative. It's fairly unique, but also kid-friendly. The initial idea came to me after watching the video she made finding the library safe room."

Stephen jumped in. "All Rebel did was narrate what she knew about the house's history and her actions, and it was compelling to watch. She's ten, brave but also scares easily. We can't have her running around by herself, which is where you'd come in. You're brilliant both on and off camera, have this intensely calming presence, and are also capable of these unexpected moments of vulnerability."

"First Xander calls me beautiful, now you're complimenting me like that? My head won't be able to fit through doorways soon."

"It's true," Maverick said. "You're perfect for her show. We even decided to call it *Shortcake*."

On one hand, Lucky really wasn't an actress. Her planned characterization quickly dissolved into flustered failure. *The Caretaker* evolving into an "unintentional" investigative show wasn't what Xander intended, but he saw the potential in letting her continue. She suspected he wanted answers, and he knew she was willing to get them for him. Being in the house as much as possible was crucial to her finding long-term funding post-Hennessee.

On the other hand, the opportunity to explore other supernatural locations on someone else's dime was ridiculously tempting. She liked the team, even more so now. They were giving Rebel a tremendous gift. Asking Lucky to be a part of it humbled the hell out of her ambitions.

"The *premise*," Xander said with a surprising amount of emphasis, "involves an unnamed young girl and her *nanny*, whose faces are never shown." His eyebrow quirked—her secret job history was out in the open now. "Each episode will include them providing narration, seemingly speaking to someone about her adventures as they happen. They'll seem innocuous at first, but something will feel slightly off. The final episode will reveal she's had multiple supernatural encounters and the nanny is there for her protection. Maverick wrote a loose script for both of you to follow."

If she had a third hand, she'd add that Maverick used his talent for skillfully blending reality and fiction to create on-screen characters for her and Rebel. That was what he'd been working on all week—he wrote the story and script because he claimed she'd inspired him to do it.

"The hope is that dedicated viewers will investigate the clues and lore presented in *Shortcake*, only to realize that the nanny is also the final caretaker living in Hennessee House," Stephen said.

"Final? Wait, am I the final girl?" Resisting a good joke simply wasn't in her DNA.

Xander regarded her coolly. "We're not casting anyone else. Production officially wraps up when you decide to leave."

"Good to know. I'll make sure my exit is as dramatic as possible."

His dignified snort almost made her laugh. "Of that, I have

no doubt. If our offer is acceptable, you'll be granted temporary leave from your Hennessee House obligations for an entire weekend."

Stephen said, "We'll give you some time to think it over."

"I don't need it," Lucky said, looking at Maverick. She failed him last night, but she'd make it up to him with *Shortcake*. "When do we leave?"

"Soon. Georgia is finalizing the last few details as we speak," Maverick said, standing up. "I should get going. Rebel already called twice." He nodded toward the door, giving her a look.

"I'll walk you out," she said smoothly.

"I should get going too," Stephen said. "I can't remember the last time I felt this . . . *off*. It really does feel like there's something digging around in my head."

"I'll walk you both out. Xander?"

"We need to go over your *Shortcake* contract. It's ready."

"Oh. I'll be right back, then."

Outside a heatwave had landed with the full force of a flaming meteorite. Lucky squinted through her sunglasses, which were barely enough to block out the blistering light. She began sweating almost instantly, growing more uncomfortable with each step toward Maverick's car.

"Bye, Stephen," she called after him. "Thank you!"

He waved before hopping in his car.

"Hennessee's air-conditioning is unmatched. I didn't even realize it was this hot out here."

"Probably the best money can buy." Maverick laughed. He shielded his eyes with his hand. "It doesn't usually get this hot. Once-in-a-lifetime freak event and all that."

"That's what they say. Every time it happens like we forgot about the first time."

"Right." He nodded. "So, I probably won't see you again until we leave."

"I figured," she said with a sigh. "How's *your* head?"

"Not as bad as Stephen, but also not great. It could honestly just be one of my normal headaches. I can't tell."

"I'm really sorry I didn't stay awake. I don't know what happened."

"You said, 'I think I'm tired,' and then closed your eyes. That was it. I've never seen anyone fall asleep that fast. Not even Rebel when she was younger."

"Interesting."

"That's not the word I would use," he said. "I think the house made you fall asleep."

"I think so too," she admitted. Because if the house wanted him to sleep and he clearly stated she was the only thing keeping him awake . . . but she didn't dare hypothesize out loud. The experiment was a success, but Maverick had obviously reached his limits with Hennessee. "I guess that means you won't be coming back to visit."

"No," he said. "I will. Just . . . not in the evening or at night. And I'll probably stick to outside, here or the backyard, to be safe. If I did fall asleep, I don't want to risk the house showing me anything."

"I understand. You'll still call me?"

"Same time?"

"Both of them, please. Don't forget about sunrise," she said softly. "If that's okay?"

"Whenever you want." He grinned and said, "I'd hug you but I think Xander might be watching."

Challenge accepted, she hugged him anyway. "If he says anything about it, I'll offer him one too."

"Be careful," he whispered, lips pressed near her ear. "Be safe."

Lucky remained in the driveway until Maverick's car turned the corner. After heading back in, she found Xander in the kitchen making a sandwich. He asked, "Do you want one?"

"Sure." She leaned against the doorframe. "How kind. How generous. Can I ask you a question?"

"No."

She ignored him. "Who came up with the idea for *The Caretaker*?"

"Creative team. We have brainstorming meetings once a week. This was one idea of many."

"Why this house?"

He looked at her as if the answer should've been obvious. "Using property I own saves on production costs."

"So, you expect me to believe that your creative team came up with an idea based around a 'haunted' house, completely unprompted, and you just happened to have one in your portfolio?"

He stared at her. "You can believe whatever you want as long as you do your job."

"Which is?" She eyed him, inching forward expectantly. "Admit it: you want me to investigate."

"We hired you to spend thirty days in the house and give a detailed account of your experiences. If you feel investigating should be a part of your time here, then yes. I do. Simple as that," he said. "However, going forward I expect you to do your job alone as intended. No more using my team as guinea pigs."

"And what if I need *you*? You probably have the strongest connection out of all of us."

His cool stare was as impassive as ever. "Make it worth my while again and I'll consider it."

Lucky smiled. "You're really not going to tell me what happened in the orchard, are you?"

"No. Once again, I want to hear about *your* experiences."

"I hope you know this means I'm gonna have to research you now. I need answers and the internet always provides."

He *almost* chuckled—he literally stopped himself, covering his mouth. "Good luck finding anything."

"Don't need it." She grinned. "It's in the name."

Xander met her at the doorway. He loomed over her like a powerful storm cloud, an intimidation tactic that most definitely worked on other people, but he'd never be able to fool her again. "Don't forget to make your self-tape about last night." He handed her a plate with a perfectly acceptable turkey sandwich cut diagonally, as it should be. "And it better be good. I'll be watching."

18

Bags packed. Automatic feeder set for Gengar. Maverick on his way to pick her up.

Lucky used the drop-down ladder to get to the attic this time. She sat down in front of the wall, taking a moment to read each name. Emotions, thoughts, and actions seemed to be the house's preferred language, but she knew it understood words too.

"Hennessee."

For the first time in days, peppermint instantly coiled around her like an embrace. The fountain pen she twirled between her fingers began to feel warm.

"I'm leaving for a little bit. Maverick needs me for an important project, but you're not rid of me yet. I promise I'm coming back."

The other caretakers couldn't handle whatever Hennessee did after it had their names, but Xander could. And if he could, so would Lucky.

She wrote her name directly under his to prove it.

19

Lucky had never flown before. She'd never even been to an airport.

Her heart belonged to driving—the longer the road trip the better. She'd had her rusty brown Toyota Corolla since she'd packed up and left home for college, very rarely ever looking back.

On the plane, she'd closed her eyes during takeoff and next thing she knew they were landing at an airport four states over.

Penny Place Amusement Park was owned and operated by Georgia's uncle. He also graciously offered for them to stay in his guesthouse for free. However, when Georgia used the word *Podunk* to describe her tiny hometown, Springstop, she failed to mention that her family had the kind of money that owned property large enough to have a main house *and* a guesthouse, which itself was house-size—multiple bedrooms, a full-size kitchen, and two bathrooms. Not to mention the massive pool, giant tree-house, and barn with horses that resided in the space between the two homes. The weather was perfect blue skies above endless flatland, and the warm summer air carried the distinct scent of *cows* from somewhere nearby.

Maverick asked, "Your uncle wouldn't happen to be interested in being an investor for a promising new production company, would he?"

Georgia laughed as she led them up the walkway to the guest-house. They passed a hand-painted sign that read *Horizon Cottage*. "I already asked. Media isn't his thing. But *you* can try my aunt. Fair warning, though, she'll try to hit on you."

"Ah."

"Oh, don't worry. My uncle will be cool with it. They're s-w-i-n-g-e-r-s."

"What's swingers?" Rebel asked.

"You *know* she can spell and read. Come on." Maverick stared Georgia down, who only smiled.

"Calm down, Super Dad. Little miss, that's only for consenting adults so forget I said that, okay?"

"Okay." Rebel shrugged.

A vein in Maverick's forehead began pulsating. There was no way Rebel wouldn't ask him about that later. Knowing him, he'd find an age-appropriate way to answer her curiosity.

Georgia continued to be unbothered. "I'm thinking Maverick and Rebel in the primary bedroom—the bed in there is huge, excellent for jumping. And me and Lucky together?"

The four of them were on their own. Chase would've joined but had already been put on the schedule to assist with filming a scripted production. Stephen and Xander gave their blessing and their money, respectively, but didn't feel they needed to be on set. NQP had multiple arms and projects running at any given time and they'd already devoted so much to Hennessee House.

Lucky nodded.

"This way, roomie."

Their room was big enough to comfortably fit two full-size beds. That shouldn't have been shocking and yet, Lucky had to force herself to not comment on it.

Georgia lugged her suitcase onto the foldable rack and unzipped it. "How do you feel about bars? There's a couple in town. I was thinking we could head over, check out the scene, get dinner and some drinks? Maverick's not a bar kind of guy and has Rebel, which leaves you and me. Together again."

"Oh, I'm honestly not really a bar person either. I don't do well in large crowds and people asking why I'm wearing sunglasses indoors gets really old, really fast . . ."

Disappointment filled Georgia's eyes as Lucky spoke.

"But you know what? To hell with it. Let's go." She had an entire weekend ahead of her to spend time with Maverick and Rebel—the actual reason why she wanted to stay behind.

"I knew I liked you. Are you going to wear that?" Georgia didn't wait for an answer, pulling clothes out of her suitcase. "Do you want to borrow something of mine?"

"I think I want to shower first. Get the feel of airport off me and then I'll decide."

Decide meaning letting Georgia have her way and squeezing into matching little black dresses.

"This is the only reliable way to stand out among the aggressive self-tanner, cowboy hats, and boots," Georgia explained as she drove them downtown. "Minus tourists, almost everyone there will have practically grown up together. They expect outsiders to dress like this and make fun of them when it happens."

"But you're not an outsider."

"True, but I left, which is an entirely different beast. You're my way back in. They'll be forced to talk to me because they'll want to talk to you. A new hot girl in town will always be the great equalizer."

Lucky snorted. "And here I thought you wanted to hang out because of my sparkling personality."

"That too. We all have ulterior motives. Some people are simply more up-front about it than others. Like us."

Lucky's phone buzzed in her purse. She side-eyed Georgia before silencing it—unknown call. She never answered those on principle. "What do you think my motives are?"

"For tonight? I think you agreed to have dinner with me because you want to be friends." Georgia grinned. "You're weirder than I'd usually like, but I'm strangely into it."

"Wow. Thanks." The word *weird* felt like a weapon formed to be used specifically against Lucky. It followed her everywhere, beating and berating her until she internalized it. Okay, fine, so she was weird—why did that have to be seen as a bad thing?

"No, for real. I used to know this one girl, who was also weird, but in a bad way because she did it for attention. It wasn't a part of her, you know what I mean? I thought she didn't know how to fit in or something, so I tried to be nice to her," she said. "Plot twist: she was just a huge bitch."

The parking situation turned out to be awful. Georgia found a garage a good distance away from the restaurant she'd chosen after charitably deciding to skip the bar crawl. They walked over, passing other shops, pubs, and bars that were ignored in favor of going to Ditto Road—because her family also owned it.

"We get to eat for free and have as many drinks as we want," Georgia said, waving her hand. "Stop looking so shocked."

"You're as bad as Xander."

She shook her head with a serious look. "I may be small-town princess rich, but that philanthropic asshole is fucking loaded."

At Ditto Road, they were seated right away by a hostess with reddened, sunburned skin and a teal ear-length bowl cut. Lucky immediately channeled her indecisiveness. From the scale tattoo on the inside of her wrist to the way her shoulders naturally sloped downward as if they were bowing from the pressure of dealing with too many choices—she was a Libra, left to her own devices for too long.

"She must be new," Georgia whispered as she left with their drink order.

"Have you spotted anyone you know?"

"No one worth talking to." Georgia glanced around the room. "Or worth a new introduction."

Interesting. "Are you hoping to pick someone up?"

"Never hoping, no. My options are wide open if you know what I mean," she said. "I have a feeling I'm going to meet my future spouse here or somewhere mundane like a bar or a grocery store. Don't ask me why."

"Aren't you supposed to despise your hometown and all it represents? No one worthy of your time kind of vibe."

"Why would I do that?" Georgia laughed.

"I don't know. Sorry. I haven't read you—that was my best uneducated guess." She cleared her throat. "Sorry."

Georgia gave her a funny look, but it didn't last. "If I could've networked and got work experience from here, I never would've left. But I want to make movies—when Xander offered me a job as an intern I was on the next flight out of here, no questions asked. I thought I'd go the usual route by slogging it out as a PA to work my way up and writing my scripts whenever I could, but then I met Maverick. He started sharing some of his story ideas with me. They were so atmospheric and cerebral, but also viscerally heartfelt and sensual, all wrapped in an intriguingly horrifying bow. I knew immediately I wanted to be the one to interpret them visually."

"He wants to make movies?"

"He wants to tell original stories. I want to adapt said stories. We work really well together. He gets me." Georgia smiled. "He was the one who pushed me to lobby for a promotion to coproducer on *BARD* after I'd only been with them for a few months." She playfully rolled her eyes. "He's the worst. I hate him."

"Yeah," Lucky agreed, fully aboard the sarcasm train. "It's kind of annoying how much he believes in people. How dare he."

Georgia snorted, grinning now. "When he practiced pitching *Shortcake* to me, I immediately volunteered. If Stephen had said no, we would've found a way to do it ourselves. We're planning to strike out on our own as partners."

So, that was what Maverick meant when he asked if Georgia's uncle wanted to invest in a new company. Lucky had thought he meant NQP.

Georgia continued, "For now, though, NQP is great. Rebel needs stability and health care, which Maverick gets from working there, and it still aligns with my current goals." She continued talking about how she started filming makeup tutorials and school vlogs in high school. She was a self-taught editor, majored in film and TV in college, and transitioned to working full-time after interning at NQP.

Lucky asked, "Did you leave your videos up?"

She snorted. "Hell no. I privated *everything* after I got hired. I'm not trying to be judged by work I did as a teenager. Fortunately, my channel never took off. Those videos were for me. They're cringy as hell, but I'm proud of them. They're how I found myself." The waitress returned, smiling and setting down their drinks with practiced hands before flitting away. Lucky checked her phone during the interruption—three missed calls, all from the unknown number. She raised her drink to toast. "To new opportunities."

"New opportunities." They clinked glasses. Lucky was in mid-drink when Georgia asked, "So how long have you and Maverick been fucking?"

Half of Lucky's drink sprayed out of her mouth and the other went down the wrong pipe. She stared at Georgia in disbelief while gasping and forcefully coughing against the burn of her whiskey sour. "Why would you ask me that? Are you trying to kill me?"

"What? We all know you are. I just want to know when you started because I haven't been able to figure it out. It's been driving me up a wall."

"You don't know anything." She continued coughing as she cleaned the table.

"I'll get you another one." Georgia gestured for the waitress's attention and pointed to Lucky's drink. "It's fine if you don't want to tell me. No need to be dramatic about it."

"I'm not being dramatic. We're . . . not. I don't really date." That seemed like the safer word.

"I wouldn't have guessed that." She eyed Lucky, a curious expression on her face as she sipped her martini. "But you're obviously into each other. At first, I couldn't tell if you were genuinely flirting or being overly friendly. I knew a girl like that once. Confused the hell out of everybody."

"I, um, I see it more as me actively trying to be . . . charming. That doesn't have anything to do with Maverick specifically. I want people to like me. I also want to get my way. The details of how that's interpreted are for the devil, not me."

"I see you"—she raised her glass in salute—"but no. That's not what I mean. We had a team meeting before deciding to offer you a spot on *Shortcake*. Stephen put it in perspective for me: friendly with everyone, flirting with Maverick."

"Uh, no?" If anything, it was the opposite. The first few days around Maverick she'd been a damn disaster. Skills she'd developed from years of reading and people-watching suddenly flew out of her brain like a murder of startled crows. Something about him consistently knocked her off her game.

"Uh, yeah." Georgia laughed. "You're different with him than you are with the rest of us."

"Different?"

"You're softer. More serious. You talk to him like you mean it, like if you had to lie to one hundred people in a row, you'd only get to ninety-nine if he was in line. That's how *you* flirt for real— painfully earnest with your heart so far down your sleeve it's almost in your hand."

Lucky opened her mouth to object, but no words came out.

Georgia full-on witch-cackled, snapping her fingers. "Finally got you, bitch. I knew it."

But Lucky still hadn't recovered from the revelation. "Is that what's happening?"

"*Yes*. I might not have ESP, but this is my lane. I can spot it from a mile away," Georgia said. "Anyway, the only rule we have is no dating between employees and upper management. You two are good to go."

"We're not dating."

"Well, when you are it's fine. Super Dad is way too perfect and uptight. He needs someone like you to shake things up—what?! You look like you're struggling to remember how to blink."

Lucky focused on her drink, taking a hearty chug. She needed time! Lots of it! Slow was not dating! "We're not dating."

"Fine, you're exclusive." Georgia winked and grinned. "Same difference, babes. Get over it."

There was nothing to get over. Lucky cleared the reluctance hurdle but got tripped up on nerves. She *was* nervous, which was perfectly okay.

But people like Georgia expected Lucky to move the same way, and at the same speed, as everyone else. She knew the expectations—at her big age, dating shouldn't be a big deal. They rolled their eyes, gave pitying looks, hit her with the *Girl, it's not that serious*. Except it was.

Lucky finished her drink, hoping to take the edge off.

"Do you want another one?"

"No, I'm good. I should stick to water now."

"Suit yourself." Georgia was on her second of what would probably be many.

"I know that's not Georgia," someone called out.

"Something tells me you've been spotted," Lucky deadpanned.

Georgia smiled into her drink and then whispered, "Watch this." She set her glass down and flipped her hair over her shoulder. "Who's asking?"

"You're gonna act like you don't recognize me?" A tall sunburned white man wearing a plaid shirt, blue jeans, and cowboy boots approached their table.

Lucky winced. Did no one in this town invest in sunscreen? She'd never experienced sunburn a day in her life, but it always looked so painful. Maybe they'd just gotten used to it.

"It's not an act." Georgia laughed, flirtatiously delicate.

He grinned. "You move away, leave us all behind, and suddenly you're too good for us."

"Speak for yourself," Georgia chided. "I was too good for *you* while I was here."

"I thought you didn't know who I was."

"I don't." Georgia shrugged. "Don't be rude. Introduce yourself to my friend."

He ran a hand through his thick dark brown hair, which had a healthy sheen to it. The color even matched his kind eyes and noticeably wispy eyelashes. "Excuse my bad manners, I'm Randall. It's a pleasure to meet you, Miss . . ."

"Oh, I'm Lucky."

His eyebrow quirked, eyes alight with sudden interest. "Is that right?"

"Oh my god," Georgia complained. "Randall, you are shameless, and she's taken. Go away."

He winked at Lucky. "She hates not being the center of attention. Anytime you want to get under her skin, just ignore her."

"Don't listen to him. He doesn't know me."

"She's been like that her whole life. Since we were babies." He laughed, leaning over to plant a kiss on Georgia's forehead. She surprisingly let him do it, playfully rolling her eyes.

"How's your mama? Is she here?"

He shook his head. "Me and Jake are on our way to Outpost. He's the one who spotted you through the window."

"And he didn't come in? He's always such a bastard."

Lucky couldn't use Georgia's life story to understand her choices. Every second of her interaction with Randall felt like a delightful surprise because despite Georgia's insistence, they did know each other. Very well. The way he softly gazed at her was filled with loyalty and affection—years and years' worth of it. And she smiled at him as if she'd watched him hang the moon and was determined to appear unimpressed but was slowly losing the battle for the millionth time.

"Are we ready to order?" Their cheery waitress returned holding a small notepad.

"I'll let you two get on with your dinner," Randall said. "Call me before you leave town again."

"No," Georgia said sweetly. "Bye, stranger."

Dinner arrived in three courses accompanied by a slew of drinks for Georgia. People continued approaching their table in a steady stream. Strangers wanting to shoot their shot. Old friends and acquaintances wanting to make plans to catch up. And never once did Georgia forget Lucky or pretend like she wasn't there.

20

True to her promise, their entire lovely dinner was free. Georgia announced her departure by blowing kisses at the staff and swearing to strong-arm her aunt into giving them raises. Her tanned face had taken on a flushed undertone from all the alcohol.

Lucky asked, "Can you do that for them?"

"Sure can." Georgia giggled. Off the clock, her personality still had a blunt edge, but she was also louder and harsher. She talked faster, swore constantly, laughed with her entire body, and did the cutest little shimmy at the most random times. "I own twenty-five percent of Ditto Road. I'll fight for them and win."

"Wow."

"I know, I'm privileged," she said with a playful sneer. "I never said I wasn't. My family worked hard so I don't have to but choose to anyway. I want my own shit to pass down to my kids. That's why we're helping Rebel, you know? Collectively"—she held up her hands—"we all have resources to devote to that precious little miss and nothing will stop us. Our company is small but mighty and we take care of each other and our families."

"Sounds like a slogan."

"I'm drunk. I'll do it better when I'm sober. Oh, shit!" Georgia grabbed Lucky at the waist, pulling her toward the street chanting, "Cross, cross, cross!"

Lucky caught on and took the lead, helping the increasingly wobbly Georgia, who then made them crouch down behind a parked car to spy on a small group as they walked down the opposite sidewalk.

"What was that for?" Lucky asked.

"I don't want him to see me!"

"Who?"

"Elvin. That's him in the gray hoodie."

Lucky didn't bother to look, instead checking the time on her phone. Late enough for Rebel to be sleeping, but Maverick might still be up. She also had two more missed calls from Unknown. Once Georgia was positive Elvin had no chance of turning around and spotting her, they continued walking to the parking garage.

"How can you see through those things at night?" Georgia asked.

"Lots of practice. The tint isn't as dark on these glasses." Lucky could still see everything clearly—the downtown city lights were bright enough for that—but her ability-blocking effectiveness dropped to forty-five percent. She kept her gaze on the ground or the sky to avoid accidentally making eye contact with anyone. "So, what's wrong with Elvin?"

"Nothing."

"Uh-huh."

Georgia sighed. "It was Christmas. I was lonely. Things happened in an outdoor shed, and he hasn't moved on. You know how it is."

"No. I don't."

"But you know what I *mean*. Don't get all judgey on me."

"I'm not judging you." She smiled to show her sincerity. "But I honestly don't know. Can't relate."

"Oh, really?" Georgia's irritation faded to suspicion.

"Really." Lucky thought quickly, trying to come up with a simple way to explain without getting too into the weeds. "I don't have any experience with, uh, inclinations that would lead to spontaneous hookups. It's not for me."

Georgia's jaw dropped as she slapped Lucky's arm. "You are not asexual. Shut up!"

"I—*what*? You know what that is?"

"Stop being so shy, oh my god. *Inclinations*, are you kidding me?" Georgia looped her arm through Lucky's as if they'd been friends for years. "My cousin is ace and he's told me *all* about it."

If she'd been drinking, she probably would've started choking again. But instead of being horrified, Lucky was elated. She started laughing, straight from her belly, very nearly a cackle.

"What's so funny?"

"*How* did you even guess that?" she managed, through her laughing fit. "I thought I was being *vague*."

"Girl, I said the words 'Maverick' and 'fucking' and you almost died. I mean, I could've been dead wrong. You could've said no and explained but . . . you haven't denied it." She pinned her with a glassy-eyed stare.

"Because it's true." Lucky had to take several deep breaths to calm herself before she could continue. A couple going the opposite direction passed by them with a cordial greeting, but Georgia claimed to not know them. The parking garage was still a good distance away. "I really wasn't expecting you to figure me out like that. I haven't laughed that hard in a long time."

Georgia, still holding on to Lucky's arm, squeezed in closer to her. "I told you this is my lane and I make it a point to be open-minded."

"I wish more people were like that."

College was hell on both the friendship and romantic fronts, but Lucky did have one boyfriend—Louis. He appeared seemingly out of nowhere while she was at the grocery store and asked her out on a date. She still had fond memories of it because it'd gone so well. He kept trying to make her laugh, repeatedly told her she was pretty, and even asked good questions. After a few more dates, he asked her to be his girlfriend. At the time, all she could think was *Someone actually likes me? Welp this'll probably be my only shot.* In hindsight, she should've thoroughly thought things through before saying yes.

"So, where do you fall on the spectrum?" Georgia asked conversationally.

"You are way too excited about this," Lucky said, trying and failing to keep a straight face. How was Georgia able to ask that question like it was nothing? She didn't sound judgmental or invasive—she made Lucky feel like they were just two friends gossiping.

"No such thing and *you* don't have to beat around the bush about your sexuality."

"I'm not. I just feel a little uncomfortable, like I'm not supposed to talk about it."

"Why?"

"Because people always say stuff like *I don't care if you don't want to have sex* or *That's not a real sexuality because everyone feels that way at some point*, but that's not how it works. It makes me feel like I'm not allowed to have a spot in the conversation. What I say doesn't matter so I just keep it to myself."

"*Pfft.*" She snorted. "That's bullshit. You can talk to me about it all you want."

Lucky wanted to take her up on that offer . . . just not on the street in front of so many random people walking around. She waited until they made it to the car, taking the keys from Georgia, who was way too drunk to drive. She aimed for casual as she programmed the GPS. "Is it really okay if we talk about sex and stuff?"

"I said it was." Georgia yawned.

"Well, I think sex sounds good in theory. In practice, not so much. I categorize it as the triple *p*'s. I'm not interested in the performance and politics of sex. The pleasure part can stay."

"You're such a nerd." Georgia cackled with a signature shimmy. "Talk nerdy to me."

Lucky laughed as she drove them out of the garage and back to the house. "That's pretty much it. Although, I am low-key fascinated by the flip side of things. What it's like to rip off someone's clothes in unbridled desire, to be so lost I can't think straight, and I need them right at that moment. Nailing someone to the wall with smoldering gazes while my lower body quivers and jumps with desire unleashing a waterfall. Romance books really sell it. They make it all sound so . . . fantastic." She scrunched her nose. "But I don't experience any of that. I don't think about people in that way. And I really *hate* pretending that I do, so I don't. Ever. I am who I am."

"Amen to that."

"People really discount how important acknowledging attraction, *or* lack thereof, can be in a relationship. They can pretend like it's not until they're blue in the face, but at the end of the day someone's going to end up getting hurt way worse than if they'd been honest and communicated in the first place." She'd been holding that in for a while and now that she started, she felt like she had to get it all out. "I *know* they're scared of being seen as superficial or shallow because it reads like a moral failing. I understand where they're coming from, but I was rarely extended the same courtesy."

Georgia held up a hand. "Okay, hold on, you're at about a nerdy level ten. Can you scale it back to like a three?"

"Sorry," she said, embarrassed. "I get carried away sometimes."

"No, no, it's only 'cause I'm drunk. *Sober* me can handle your nerdy level ten. Test me tomorrow. I'll prove it." She giggled.

Lucky considered taking her up on that offer too. She never had a chance to talk about her feelings on the topic aloud before. It was strangely . . . freeing. Dating and romance and relationships had been on the back burner for so long they disintegrated into ashes. She'd accepted that she'd end up sacrificing more of herself than her partners and that simply wasn't what she wanted for her life. Why chase happily-ever-after rainbows when she could seek out the supernatural?

Still, she did have some regrets. One, specifically.

"I think this might be level three?" Deciding to try being as frank as Georgia, Lucky admitted, "I've never had romantic, sensual sex. I think about it sometimes."

"Candlelight. Roses. Massages. Silk sheets? Hmm?"

"Ehh, no. That seems like it's straying a bit close to performance for me."

"Foreplay?"

"No." Lucky concentrated on the full moon for strength before turning her gaze back to the road. "I've never fallen in love before. I meant having sex with someone I'm deeply in love with. I wonder if it would feel different. What would it mean to me emotionally? Would it be better? *Worse?* I don't know."

"Ooh, that's a good question. It feels different for me. Let me try to explain." Georgia's brow furrowed in concentration. "Outside of overwhelming desire it's like there's this mental tether between us, keeping us perfectly in sync."

"Really?"

"Yeah, I think so. I mean, I'm not one hundred percent sure. It's honestly hard to separate each individual feeling and put them in little boxes like I think you'd do—remember, level three." She tapped her forehead and hiccupped. "It could also be the alcohol making me sound like a dumb bitch, who knows? But there was this moment with my first boyfriend after we'd been having sex for a couple of weeks. It had just stopped being awkward and we finally got to a place where we had it down, you know? We were in the middle of it and he said *I love you* for the first time and it was like my brain exploded. I remember being so shocked and I just . . . I just started bawling my eyes out.

"I'm crying like somebody died, he's flipping out because he doesn't know what happened, every inch of my body is so overwhelmed I feel like I'm never gonna recover. Think about it: I was seventeen, extremely hormonal, and on birth control for the first time. I didn't stand a fucking chance." She added softly, "I loved him with all of my heart, body, and soul."

"Oh, wow. I can see how that would have such a memorable impact on you. Has that feeling happened again?"

She nodded. "Yeah, and I only know it because with that person, the lust was out of fucking control, and when it calmed down, I stayed anyway because I wanted to. Wild."

"I wish I understood lust and sexual attraction outside of theory."

"You're definitely missing out." Georgia laughed.

"I don't think I am," Lucky disagreed, with a headshake. She couldn't miss something she didn't experience in the first place. "To me, it's like watching everyone enjoy eating chocolate cake but I'm deathly allergic to chocolate and wheat. I'll be fine without that *specific* cake. There are countless other types and substitutions I can try so I can find something that I like *if* I want to. I just wonder about that one from time to time because it's everywhere."

"Well, if that's the case, I wouldn't. You're ace and nerdy, babes—you gotta find a way to make that work for you."

BACK AT THE guesthouse, Lucky found Maverick sitting in the window seat nook. The cozy kind with a firm mattress, throw blankets, and built-in overhead lights.

"Georgia good?"

He looked sleepy, as if he were once again staying up just for her, but his eyes brightened as she sat in front of him, pulling a pillow into her lap. "Tucked into bed with a bucket just in case."

"She'll be fine. You'd be surprised how much she can drink and work the next day with no issues," he said. "Ready for tomorrow?"

"Ready for you to regret wanting me here. I'm really not an actress. You'll see."

"The script is more of a guide. Don't worry about delivering the lines as written. If it doesn't feel right, improvise."

She'd read through it ten times even though she'd memorized it after the first. "Right. Got it."

"The most important thing is to follow Rebel's lead. Georgia will keep you both on track."

"Wait, where will you be?"

"Georgia and I have to wear multiple hats since we're running this thing with a skeleton crew," he said. "I'll be scouting a second location that we got a lead on: a perfectly ordinary, abandoned office building. There aren't any reports of supernatural activity, but it supposedly has a Backrooms feel. We agreed it would look good in the show, and I want to personally make sure it's safe for Rebel to be there. Tomorrow, we'll meet up for dinner before heading back to the park after closing."

"Oh. Okay." She nodded. The Backrooms was an internet urban legend about a seemingly infinite maze outside of reality. "Got that too."

"You're cute when you're nervous."

"I'm neither of those things."

Maverick rubbed his face, grumbling as he looked out the window.

Lucky snickered. "Sorry. I'm working on the whole *accepting your compliments* thing. Be patient with me."

"That I can do." He moved closer to her and frowned. "I didn't notice this before." His thumb traced the long, jagged scar on her arm. He didn't ask.

She chose to answer the question in his eyes anyway. "I shredded my arm on barbwire while running from security guards trying to detain me for trespassing."

"I'd ask why, but I don't know if I can handle it." His fingers passed her wrist and lingered near her palm.

"Investigating a lead. It all started with an allegedly telekinetic man and his goat and ended with a trip to the hospital for stitches and a tetanus shot."

"The goat is the wildest part of that story, isn't it?" He chuckled, unsurprised. "All that but no ghosts, huh? I was waiting for you to change your mind about coming here, right up until we boarded the plane."

Penny Place was a bona fide hoax. Rooted in the false myth of a tragedy, the urban legend belonged to the town. Mostly tested by teenagers at night with nothing better to do.

"There shouldn't be ghosts at the park. Besides, wanting to help Rebel outweighed my reservations." She shrugged, but then eyed him seriously. "But if they are there, please understand that I *will* flee for my life. If we're alone, I'll grab Rebel and run, otherwise don't expect me to stick around."

"It's that serious?"

"Incredibly." She was always down for a supernatural adventure but could run faster than Jurnee Smollett did in *Lovecraft Country* away from those monsters when she needed to. That scene had made her proud because it showed people how it was done. No tripping and falling and breaking an ankle—just pure purpose and an unbreakable will to stay alive.

"Why?"

"Because it is. It won't make sense if I try to explain it." Lucky leaned against him, resting her head on his shoulder. She tilted her head upward until her face was in the crook of his neck and inhaled.

"Come here." And just like that, she was in his arms again.

Her new favorite place to be. He leaned back against the wall, breathing deep and even as if he were about to fall asleep. She faced the window, her legs across his lap. "Tell me anyway," he said. His lips brushed against her forehead.

"Because they come from humans. I can read them." She sighed, squeezing her eyes shut.

"And that's bad?"

Might as well tell him all of it. "Ghosts are vessels for strong emotions anchored by unfinished business, but their cores are gone. That's what I read. That's what I take into me—copies of who people are. Ghosts don't hold on to who they were. I can't even describe what they feel like instead. I—"

He shifted slightly, pulling back until they faced each other. Him gazing down at her. Her looking up at him, framed by the clear night sky. "The words are there. I've seen you do it. The way you translate your impressions feels like a dream to me. I can almost imagine the storyline. How lives will play out, the choices being made, the way it all connects together."

"But I'm so bad at it."

"You're not, I promise. There's an undeniable art to your impressions, Lucky. Concentrate on the feeling and paint me a picture. Give it shape. Tell me its story."

"It's like . . ." Her gaze shifted beyond him. The answer gently came into focus. "Imagine space."

"Okay," he encouraged.

"There are all these beautiful stars exhibited in a perfect filing system." She smiled but it didn't last. "Then comes this black hole. It can't touch the stars. It doesn't even warp around them or bend their light. But when I try to touch it, I can feel something desperate to pull me in. It wants me inside of it.

"I can't forget impressions. The best I could do was lock it away, but I still feel it, drifting around in the deepest depths of my memory palace like a constant threat." She looked at him again. "If one ghost did that, what would more do? If I ever got possessed by a ghost, I'm terrified I would disappear completely."

His expression folded into worry. "Can you see ghosts?"

She sat up, caught in his gaze and refusing to let go, eager to reassure him. "I suspect I see them the way a regular person would: only if the ghost is strong enough," she said. "Most people don't have that kind of ESP. They just think they do but it's incredibly rare to see a fully realized ghost. It happened to me once and that was enough. I avoid anywhere I think they might be."

"Good. That's good to know." His smile was fleeting. "You always seem so eager to put yourself in dangerous situations. You have no idea how much I worry about you getting hurt."

Lucky almost couldn't believe that Maverick *believed* her. She saw it written all over his face. He wasn't going to call her dramatic or stupid or weird. He wasn't going to laugh or text his friends to make fun of her. An old, weathered piece of hurt she'd been carrying for years began to dissolve.

Everything felt like it was moving in slow motion.

She cupped her hand against his left cheek and softly kissed him on his right. He didn't move as her fingers caressed across his jaw until she tried to pull away.

Maverick caught her hand in midair, kissing her knuckles. His second set of kisses turned into a smile against her palm at the sound of her surprised gasp. And then, he placed her hand back where it'd been against his cheek, holding it there.

All at once, she rushed forward and it was happening and

then it wasn't because she suddenly inhaled, stealing the literal last breath of air between them.

Reeling backward at the last minute, she ran to her room. "I have to go. Good night!"

Lucky dove into bed, burrowing under the covers. *Shit*, she'd done it again. She *asked* for slow. She *told* him slow.

Why did she feel like they were going a hundred miles per hour?

And why was she suddenly okay with not slowing down?

There was still so much she needed to tell him.

Lucky made the mistake of rolling over and locked eyes with Georgia, who was awake and staring at her.

Georgia read like an active war zone. A natural assertiveness complicated by extremism versus a deep fear of being docile— broken. She craved genuine human connection as if it were a basic necessity, enjoying the weight of other people's lives when held against her own. Parts of her were also prone to falling into darkness but felt compartmentalized. Unable to fully take root.

"Not dating, huh?"

"Talking isn't dating," Lucky whispered.

"Late-night talking after everyone is sleeping is secret affair territory. How scandalous of you."

"It's not a secret affair." She summoned her courage and whispered, "We're taking it slow."

"Not for much longer, if that look on your face has anything to say about it." Georgia grinned. "Good night, babes."

21

Lucky woke up before sunrise when her phone vibrated against her boob with yet another unknown call. She really had to stop sleeping with the damn thing.

Last night she'd almost kissed Maverick.

Never in her life had she ever made the first move. She never even wanted to before. Her first crush wasn't until sophomore year of college—Holly Jenkins, who she sat next to in Religion and Mythology—and she would've chosen death over confessing. And now here she was almost *kissing* people first. Look at her go. Moving on up.

After Louis broke up with her, she just couldn't bring herself to try dating again. She had truly convinced herself it'd never be worth it. But Maverick was proving her wrong.

Georgia's gentle snores in the background kept her grounded lest she float away from feeling too buoyant and optimistic. For the first time, in a very, very long time, she felt disgustingly, overwhelmingly hopeful.

Was her abundance of good feelings solely because of Maverick? Or was it because her life was suddenly filled with a kaleidoscope of different people who were all kind and interested in her, in one way or another? The answer, she knew, was both.

Their room's door forcefully swung open, and Rebel marched in wearing pajamas covered in cartoon koala bears. She stopped beside Lucky's bed. "Oh, you're awake."

"Disappointed?"

She shrugged.

"She likes to poke people repeatedly until they open their eyes." Georgia sat up. "I heard she slaps Super Dad on the forehead."

"She does," Maverick added as he walked past their open door. "Rebel, leave them alone and go finish getting dressed."

"Okay," she called after him. "We're having savory oatmeal and eggs for breakfast and lasagna for dinner. He's gonna get ice cream at the store too."

"It was a good day if my dad made me Pop-Tarts for breakfast." Georgia threw her blankets back, gracefully gliding out of bed as if she never heard the word *hangover* before. "You don't even know how good you have it, little miss. Dibs on the shower."

Rebel watched her go and then turned back to Lucky. "Yes, I do."

"She's just teasing. I don't think she meant anything bad by that."

Rebel nodded silently, gaze drifting to the bedspread. Oh, shit. Georgia must have struck a nerve.

Kids were far more perceptive than adults gave them credit for. Lucky didn't know Rebel well enough yet to automatically zero in on the issue, but knew she was quite sensitive when it came to her dad.

Surprisingly, Rebel's magical, fairy tale gaze didn't extend to Maverick. She had a steady, realistic grip on who he was and what he meant to her. She wasn't possessive; rather, devoted and protective were the better fit.

Lucky asked, "How are you feeling?"

"Fine." Rebel shrugged.

"Would you like to talk about it?"

"No."

"Okay. We don't have to," she said. "Do you want to talk about logistics for the shoot today?"

"We do that during the team meeting."

"Oh, see, I didn't even know that. Hennessee House is different since I live there. This is my first time on an official shoot, so I don't know all the rules. Would you be okay with helping me out today, so I don't look silly?"

"You won't look silly. You're allowed to ask questions if you don't know something, but I'll teach you everything you need to know anyway." She nodded. "My dad said you're supposed to follow my lead. I'm a good leader."

Lucky smiled. "Thank you, Shortcake. I appreciate it."

After breakfast and their first meeting, Lucky was in the middle of putting on her socks when she got another unknown call. She stared at the screen, not quite at her breaking point. Yet.

"Are you going to answer that?" Georgia demanded as she walked into the room.

"Wasn't planning on it."

"Is someone harassing you? I swear I heard your phone buzzing nonstop last night."

"It might be telemarketers. I started a spreadsheet to track what times they call. So far, there's no discernible pattern other than often."

Her money was currently on an automated bot trying to reach her regarding her car's extended warranty.

Which was very nearly hilarious considering her car was so old the warranty probably ended before she'd even learned to walk. It was a small miracle the hand-me-down car hadn't totally broken down from old age yet. Every time she started it, the engine sputtered to life and sent its usual barrage of pleading telepathic signals: *LET ME RETIRE! LET ME DIE!*

In return, she patted the sun-bleached dashboard while thinking, *You're fine. You've barely hit your Toyota prime.*

"That is such a *you* thing to do. Wait, where are your glasses?"

"Don't need them in the house. Unless we're having a visitor?"

"Since when?" Georgia gasped, hand flying to her mouth. "You weren't wearing them when you came in the room last night. You read *me*? Oh my god, don't tell me. I don't want to know."

She seemed genuinely panicked about it so Lucky said, "Sure. That's actually how it's supposed to be, I think. Starting to tell people what I've read again is kind of a new thing. Before Maverick, I hadn't done it in years."

"Why did you stop?"

"People didn't like it." She slid on her shoes. "Once, in high school, I had this art teacher who asked if anyone wanted her to sketch their portrait. When no one responded, she started calling on us. She asked me. I said no. And she said, 'Not ready to see the truth, eh?'"

Georgia's jaw dropped. "The fuck was she implying?"

"Take a guess. For a long time, whenever I read someone and considered translating for them, I'd think of that moment. She really thought it was okay to use her talents to insult a confident teenager in front of the whole class," she said. "I think people used to react badly to me because I must have been insulting them too."

"No. No way. I don't believe that. You're not that kind of person."

"I might've been. It's also possible I made them feel like I was. Both have the same result. All that to say, I respect your decision. If you don't want to know, I won't tell you."

"People are the worst. Not you. That raggedy bitch who had no business being a teacher."

"All right." Maverick met them near the front door. "Are we ready?"

Lucky grinned at Georgia before sliding on her glasses. "Ready."

"Let's go! Come on!" Rebel yelled from outside, standing near their rental car.

Penny Place Amusement Park's main selling point was that it was one of the last standing and fully operational vintage parks. A family business since the early 1980s, Georgia's uncle had taken it over in the mid-2000s with hopes of modern renovations but ended up leaving it as is, following in every one of his predecessors' footsteps.

Tourists reportedly came from all over the world to enjoy the nostalgia. It helped that the park's aesthetic looked fantastic on social media because it wasn't run-down. Georgia's family treated the park as a historic site, maintaining it with the utmost care.

"It's tradition at this point," she explained. "Only fix what's broken. Touch up the paint here and there. Any new rides or attractions have to be in line with the spirit of the park. That kind of thing."

Lucky didn't know what living in the 1980s was like, but the staff dressing in decade-appropriate clothes certainly enhanced the experience. They even wore buttons noting the year their look was based on.

The majority of their production schedule consisted of . . . Rebel being a kid with a camera having fun at an amusement park.

Now that, Lucky could do. She effortlessly slipped into nanny mode, ready to make this day everything Rebel wanted and more. She wasn't privy to the budget for *Shortcake*. She'd thought it'd been shoestring-tight since they were staying with Georgia's family, but prior to their departure Stephen handed her a credit card with instructions to "buy Rebel whatever she wants, courtesy of Xander."

They trekked around the park, running through the hall of mirrors, bouncing through a questionably challenging funhouse, riding the giant swings, and yelling (and praying) on rickety roller coasters that clicked a little too often for Lucky's liking. They ate thickly battered corn dogs, salty giant pickles, crunchy brick fries, sweet funnel cakes dripping with ice cream on top, and enough cotton candy to get Lucky in trouble with Maverick later. All the while, Georgia trailed them, filming shots from an outsider POV as if they were being watched. That set of footage would have a distinct editing style and would be spliced with Rebel's.

The anonymous vlog style tripped Rebel up a little at first. Lucky ended up stopping her multiple times from turning the camera around out of habit, often with a sharp "Shortcake. No."

That was a part of the script. Lucky was only supposed to refer to Rebel as Shortcake on camera. Rebel's vision entailed her nanny being calm and mysterious like a tour guide full of secrets. They settled on her using a moderate tone in Lucky's chest voice, but she would speak slower and more deliberately.

"But why?"

"Because it's not for us." Which also was in the script.

She managed to say every one of her lines at random moments as a natural response to something Rebel was doing.

In the afternoon, they found a large tree to sit under while waiting for Maverick to pick them up.

"I'm wiped. How did you do that full-time?" Georgia lay flat on the grass, arm thrown across her eyes.

"Not getting drunk the night before a shift helped immensely."

Georgia snorted. "I am a consummate professional who can also hold her liquor. This has nothing to do with that. It's her."

"It's the sugar."

Rebel, still revved up on cotton candy and maybe the chocolate-dipped pretzels Lucky caved and bought her on the way out, spun in circles while staring at the sky until she collapsed, laughing.

Georgia continued, "I didn't realize how much energy a ten-year-old truly had. How does Super Dad do it?"

"Quite well."

Rebel collapsed again after spinning round number two.

"Shortcake. Look." Lucky gestured toward a group of kids, probably around Rebel's age, playing some kind of tag game in the adjacent open field. The poor grass looked dry enough to start a fire if someone ran too quickly. "Do you want to ask if you can play with them while we wait? Make some new friends?"

Rebel, perhaps unconsciously, moved closer to Lucky's side. "No."

"Eh, friendship is overrated anyway," she joked, ignoring Georgia's sudden sharp glare.

Rebel scrunched her nose in doubt. "Really?"

She shrugged. "Sometimes, it just takes some of us a lot longer to find our people."

"I have people. Um, person? People? Person." Rebel nodded, finally confident in her word choice. "Riley's my person, not my people. He's just one person."

Georgia said, "Little miss and little menace."

Rebel began to smile, high beams on. "He's ten like me. We're exactly three months, two weeks, and one day apart. Isn't that cool?"

"The coolest," Lucky agreed.

"He lives in the apartment building across the pathway from mine. Our windows face each other and everything."

"Oh, wow."

"Where do your people live?"

Lucky hesitated. "I, uh, haven't found my person-people yet." Not a lie, but maybe not the entire truth.

Georgia was more than willing to correct her. She sat up, openly glaring. "You're gonna stop insulting me to my face. I am *sensitive*. We're friends now, damn it. No more of this pity party shit, got it?"

Guess that meant she was off the clock. She hadn't said a single swear word the entire day while filming.

Rebel giggle-whispered, "I think you made her mad."

"I think so too," she whispered back.

Georgia continued, "And that goes for the rest of the team. You're one of us now. Get over it because it already happened."

Lucky said to Rebel, "I guess I missed the memo."

"You did. I signed it and everything. My dad too. I wish he were here." She side-eyed Lucky. "He's *really* fun."

Not quite having mastered the art of being surreptitious yet, Lucky sensed where Rebel was going before she got there. "There might be time for you two to spend the day here before we go."

"No," Rebel whined. "The three of us together. That would be the most fun."

Georgia said, "You see what you started? Now she's insulting me too, acting like I wasn't even there today. I get no respect. None." She dramatically lay back down, arms crossed and pouting.

"A group trip would be nice. Chase would come. I feel like we could all bully Xander into it. Stephen might be harder," Lucky said. "He probably needs a day off."

"Stephen doesn't even know what that means," Georgia said. "You'd catch him typing an email on a roller coaster, completely calm."

Lucky's phone vibrated for the sixth time that day. The unknown caller once again.

"Maybe we can go to Canada for the group trip." Rebel stood up and resumed her spinning game. "I want to see the northern lights!"

"What made her think of that?" Georgia asked.

"The sugar." Lucky laughed. "She'll come down soon."

Rebel continued spinning and falling until she decided to sunbathe on the grass, face up with her eyes closed and arms stretched at her sides. Lucky remembered most of her life because her brain wasn't set up to forget. She knew for a fact she'd never felt that free and happy growing up. Her decision to become a nanny came from an unshakable belief that all kids deserved to experience that kind of peace. If she could give it to them, even if it was for only a few hours, then she'd done her job.

"Hey, Lucky?" Georgia's voice was unexpectedly quiet. "Did you see something bad when you read me?"

"I thought you didn't want to know?" Lucky sighed, busying her hands by plucking the dry grass. Having a sort-of-friend was fun while it lasted. She knew her terrible odds were bound to kick in eventually. Interpreting her readings almost always ended with her being ostracized.

"I don't. I really don't. Ignore me."

Lucky glanced at her. She was covering her eyes again. "If it's stressing you out—"

"I'm not stressed about it."

"—don't think about it as good or bad." Lucky didn't. Mostly. Sometimes, some people were objectively bad. Nothing to be done about it. That wasn't the case with Georgia.

Maverick believed she was meant to help people. If she believed it too, how would it look? Georgia wanted to feel reassured without knowing anything about what Lucky read. There was a tenderness to her reading—rife with insecurities and burdened by doubt. She would hate feeling as if Lucky were judging her.

"How should I think about it, then? Something obviously changed."

"Changed when?" Lucky frowned as she stared at Georgia, who didn't answer and kept her eyes hidden.

She must've missed something. They'd had a good night and day, but something shifted—she quickly relived the conversation, using Georgia's reading to sift through any subtext.

I'm sensitive. Stop insulting me.

Georgia *always* stated her feelings plainly. Her truths were just wrapped in a playfully dramatic protective veneer. Like when Georgia told Xander it would hurt her feelings and she'd cry if he didn't wear the pajamas on experiment night. He *believed* her because he knew she was being honest.

I think you want to be friends.

Georgia must've assumed the reading changed Lucky's mind. "I—" She paused, a little unsure. "Reading you didn't change anything for me. I liked who you were before, and I still like who you are now because you're the same person. I can provide insight into who you are and maybe explain a couple things you might not understand about yourself. That's all. Ultimately, what you choose to do with that information is up to you."

"I don't want to know. Don't ever tell me." Georgia was quiet for a moment before saying, "Thanks for giving me a choice."

Lucky hesitated too. "Thank you for wanting to be my friend. When I said I didn't have any earlier, that was me trying to not be presumptuous. It's hard to leave the pity party when I've lived there for so long, I started paying rent."

Georgia sat up. A delicate frown graced her features. "You're too cute to have low self-esteem. Stop it."

None of that was true, but she said, "I'm working on it."

22

Night had fallen on Penny Place Amusement Park hours ago. A few minutes before midnight, the last park employee handed Georgia the keys to the main gate.

Rebel yawned, then proceeded to jump up and down.

"Time to split up," Georgia said, handing Maverick a map.

"Why?" Lucky asked, slightly frowning.

"For the ghosts. Team B will keep them distracted so Rebel can film her night scenes safely."

Legend had it that a couple decided to have their wedding at Penny Place because they met there as park employees. The details were fuzzy because they were fake, but somehow the couple died right after saying their vows. Now they haunted the park at night testing couples who dared to walk the wedding's procession path. If their love was deemed worthy, they'd feel cold and get a love token from the enchanted tree stump. If not, they'd be tormented for the duration of the walk and cursed to break up in seven days.

Lucky's palms began to sweat. "What are you talking about? There aren't any ghosts in this park. No one died here—I checked the town records myself."

"How did you do that?" Maverick asked.

"Most of the town's newspaper archive have been digitized. I pretended to be a new resident, signed up for a library card on-line, and got access. When I didn't find anything, I called the police department, got the contact info for the retired sheriff who would've handled the investigation at the time if it had happened, and told him I was a journalist working on a story about small-town urban legends. He confirmed—it's all a lie. What?" She looked at the group, all staring at her. "I don't go anywhere without researching the location first."

Georgia's scoff ended in an affectionate laugh. "Instead of doing all that, you could've asked me. I used 'ghosts' as shorthand. The legend itself isn't real but that didn't stop an entire town from repeating the story, passing it down for generations, testing it, keeping it alive. Our belief in the legend made it real. It's not ghosts, but it's definitely . . . something."

"Oh, shit. I didn't think of that. Why didn't I think of that?" She turned to Maverick as if he had an answer.

"Not gonna lie, I assumed you did. That's why I didn't bring it up."

"And you're sure about this?" Lucky asked Georgia.

"I've done the walk. It's not fake."

Lucky gasped. "Did you pass?"

"If you must know"—Georgia pursed her lips—"no, I didn't. They scared me so bad a patch of my hair turned white and we broke up a week later. Anyway, as long as Rebel stays off the path while a couple is walking it, they won't mess with her."

Lucky nodded, trying to temper her growing discomfort. "Who's on what team?"

"Well." Georgia dragged out the word as if she were stalling. "If it's me and Maverick, the incest alarms will start blaring immediately. We're practically family at this point. Lucky, you and me, we could go but it's not the *best* idea. It has to be you and Maverick."

"Even I knew that," Rebel whispered.

"What happened to no such thing as silly questions, Short-cake? Don't betray me like this."

Georgia placed her hands on Lucky's shoulders. "Be cheesy. Keep it cute. Make it sexy. It doesn't matter as long as they believe it and you follow the rules. This isn't like Hennessee House." The fierce look in her eyes killed Lucky's objections before she could even think of them.

"How so?"

"Because if you see something uncanny, no, you didn't," Georgia began with unquestionable authority. "If you hear something strange, no, you didn't. Don't listen to it, don't look at it, don't look back. Stay calm and please do not run unless you are positive you have to because it will chase you. Keep moving forward at a nice, steady pace. Okay?"

And with that, Georgia had stomped her way into Lucky's heart. "Okay."

"*Promise* me."

"I promise."

Georgia turned to Maverick. "You. Eyes forward and focused. Keep her on the path—you know how she gets."

"On my honor."

"Trackers on. Timers set," Georgia commanded, looking at her watch. "One hour at my mark. We meet back here. No exceptions. Safe word: lifehouse."

"Ready," they all said in unison.

Maverick kneeled in front of Rebel. "Remember what we talked about? Let's run through it. Who's in charge?"

"Georgia," Rebel answered.

"What do you do if you get scared?"

"Don't move, count to ten, and if I'm still scared, I can quit."

"What do you do if you want to quit? Do you run away?"

"No, I tell Georgia."

"What if you get separated? What do you do?"

"We don't get separated. I have to hold Georgia's hand the entire time."

"What if there's an emergency and you have to let go of her hand?"

"I stay where I am and call *everyone* for help."

"Good." He clipped a white tag to the front of Rebel's shirt—her tracker. They all had one. It pulsed red at steady intervals. "You know I'm proud of you, right?"

Rebel nodded and lunged at him, trapping him in a bear hug. "This is the best day ever."

"You always say that."

"I mean it this time." Rebel grabbed Georgia's hand as they walked away. "I love you, Dad! Thank you!"

"Love you too!"

Lucky's phone buzzed in her pocket—the unknown caller never slept, giving weight to the automated marketing calls theory. "Maverick, I need a favor."

"Anything." She had his complete attention.

"I know we have to do this, and I'm going to, but you might have to calm me down first."

"What do you need?"

She took a deep breath to center herself. "On the one hand, I am absolutely *buzzing* right now. This is *incredible*. The collective energy of human belief coalesced and manifested this entity. I need to be here. Hennessee House is fantastic, but this is the work I've wanted to do since I was a teenager. This is my dream—investigating humans and our brains and the phenomena we create and the things we can do."

"I wish you could see the way you look right now," Maverick said, smiling.

"But on the other hand . . . it's ghosts. The legend is based around the idea of ghosts haunting the park. If the community believes it's ghosts, who's to say the entity won't have the same composition and functionality as one? Hell, I'm a believer and believing is half the battle. They already got my ass."

Maverick held her face in his hands and spoke calmly. "You're going to be fine. The legend is clear: the entity is rarely seen because it stays behind the couples and in their peripheral. It has rules to follow too."

He was right. That made sense. As long as they all followed the rules, they'd be safe. Except. "If it decides to haunt us, you gotta keep me steady." She pressed her lips together because she didn't want to say the next part, but he needed to know what he might be up against. In her tiniest, hushed voice she confessed, "I might try to talk to it. I'm sorry!"

"I already know," he said with the patience of a saint. "That's why we need to go into this with the right state of mind. Both thinking the same thing, on the same page."

"Which is?"

He grinned. "How amazing our first date is about to be."

Realization suddenly clicked into place. "Maverick, I'm so stressed right now. Don't do this to me." But she was smiling.

"Afraid I'm gonna have to."

"I can't. We can't." But she was seconds away from giggling.

"It's already happening. Our walk awaits."

She narrowed her eyes as he took her hand. "You planned this, didn't you?"

"Mmm, I plead the fifth on that," he said as they took their first steps together. "But hypothetically speaking, if I had, would I have been right in assuming this would make you happy?"

Never in her wildest dreams did she think she'd find someone willing to test a supernatural urban legend in an amusement park as a first date, at midnight no less. Be still her heart because Maverick had hers sprung and soaring.

"Yes." Lucky beamed. "Minus the ghostly potential, but yes. Very happy."

He pulled a single-stem white rose out of his jacket pocket and presented it to her. "I didn't know what kind of flowers you like."

"I—"

"Don't tell me. I have a plan for that. Tonight, I picked that one because allegedly the park security cameras have recorded the entity before. It appears as a large, heart-shaped white cloud."

"That's so precious." Lucky laughed, shaking her head. "I love it—I love that you thought of this." The best mixture of fantastical and cheesy—and just for her. She held it to her nose and breathed in. "No one's ever given me flowers before. Thank you. Your only competition is a house."

The wedding's procession path consisted of a single loop around the park, no detours. The shutters had been drawn on the games. The generators for the food stands sat silent. Every shadow-filled roller coaster loomed in the distance. Springstop was close enough to a big city to have some light pollution but distant enough to be quiet, apart from the noisy chorus of crickets serenading them.

Eerie stillness never bothered Lucky even on her worst day. They had flashlights. They had the full moon. They had each other.

Maverick said, "You should know it's been a while since I've seriously dated anyone. I didn't tell the team. They all noticed I was being . . . different and figured it out."

"What about Rebel?"

"She asked me about you, actually, and gave her blessing with some caveats around daddy-daughter days. You're not allowed. Sorry."

Lucky chuckled. "That's fair and understandable."

"For the most part, though, she's excited to have you around more often. It probably helps that I've never brought anyone to meet her before. I flat out refused. Wasn't doing it."

"Why? I mean, was there no one at all?" Lucky shivered.

"Not really. After Rebecca and I split up for good, that was it for me."

He didn't provide context as to who that was, and she was too nervous to confirm her obvious guess—Rebel's mom. "And you haven't wanted to?"

"More like I didn't think about it for a long time. Then Rebel started going to school and let me tell you, single dads are extremely attractive to some women. I go to PTA meetings, talent shows, book fairs, bake sales, birthday parties—all that, whatever Rebel wants—and I swear they can sense me coming."

Wow, Georgia wasn't kidding about him being a Super Dad. "What do they do?"

"A lot of them give me food or offer to come cook us dinner. There's also the constant playdate invitations. It's like they forget that Rebel should like their kids for us to go, which rarely happens. At first, I naively thought they were being neighborly, but no. Because when trying to be helpful didn't work, some got bolder. They'd get my number and start texting me things I'd rather not read. Or see."

"Suburban sexual harassment? Yikes. How do you get them to stop?"

"The truth. Some are more persistent than others, but usually when I tell them I'm flattered but not interested they back off. There were a few here and there, though. Kind of low-key, casual stuff. Nothing serious. And then, I met you."

"And then, you met me." Lucky shivered again, noting their position—in between the corn dog food truck and a ring toss game. "Ooh, it's cold."

"You were all I could think about. Every moment of every day. Rebel and you."

"I see," she said, feigning seriousness. "So, you're obsessed with me?"

"Unfortunately."

"How terrible for you."

"I've made my peace with it."

Lucky sneezed and shivered again. "Oh, I'm *really* cold. How are you feeling?"

Wordlessly, Maverick shrugged off his jacket, placing it on her shoulders.

"Oh, no, you don't have to do that. I meant like *suddenly* cold." She tried communicating with her eyes, resisting the urge to turn around.

"Oh, that kind of cold." He took her hand again and squeezed it twice as if to say *I got you*. "I don't feel anything."

She moved to take off his jacket, planning to hand it back to him, but he stopped her.

"No, you keep it. I feel fine."

"Well, now it looks like I said that in hopes you'd give it to me."

"Once again, doing the most when all you needed to do was ask," he teased. "Besides, this way if something is making you cold, I'm more likely to feel it now too."

Lucky pulled it around her, holding it closed at the collar. Still warm and smelled like him. "I guess it's my turn now?"

He laughed. "Only if you feel like it. We can do whatever you want as long as we stay on the path."

"Funny you should say that. Georgia is the expert here—I'm deferring to her in terms of what we can and cannot do. Leaving the path is out, but what if we pretended like we were going to?"

"You want to see what happens."

She smiled as sweetly as she could manage. "Yes, please."

Maverick's jaw tightened as he considered, exhaling a sigh through his nose. "All right, *but* we do it my way. I'll lead."

She nodded in agreement, careful to keep her excitement in check.

"Sometimes, I can't believe how much you actually like stuff like this."

"You don't?"

"It's definitely not my first choice." Both his gaze and tone were soft, non-judgmental.

"I know a job is a job, but you could help people tell their stories in other fields. Another company would hire you in a heartbeat."

"I like my company—there's other non-paranormal positions I could apply for. I'm tired of traveling, hosting, and being on camera in general, but the team will fight me if I try to retire."

"They seem more supportive than that," she said. "Georgia knows, right?"

"She's the only one."

He tugged on Lucky's hand as they subtly began walking at an angle toward the edge of the path. With their current pace in mind, she suspected he was aiming for the bumper cars on their left. The cars themselves had been lined up in a neat row next to the operator console in the darkened arena.

"I think you should tell them," Lucky said, softly. "Plan your exit and tell them what you want to do instead. They'll listen."

He grinned. "Is that some extrasensory advice?"

"Yeah," she admitted. "I could tell you more but I think that's enough." She had a feeling he only needed encouragement, not a firm answer like *Xander searched for you specifically and he still believes in you* or *Stephen would follow you anywhere because you earned his trust.* Some translations were better left unspoken—a lesson in balance she'd been steadily learning as of late.

Maverick continued leading the way to finish Lucky's experiment. "Act like we're about to get in line for the bumper cars."

Lucky nodded, catching his drift. They were so close to the ride now, she spotted the cracked paint on the sign.

"We're not leaving the path," he reminded her. "Just pretend like we are."

"Together." She squeezed his hand while holding his arm.

"*Oh, shit*," they said in unison.

The moment they swerved close to the closed gate one of the bumper cars broke formation, swiftly gliding across the metal floor and skidding to an audible stop in the center. Its paint glittered in the moonlight as if dozens of eyes were watching them.

23

Lucky barely had time to gasp before Maverick reacted, promptly guiding her away. "Nope! Keep moving," he insisted.

The bumper car followed, stalking alongside them like a predator until the barrier forced it to stop.

"But do you—did you see?!" Her excitement made her stutter as the goose bumps from being cold multiplied at a steady rate.

"I saw." He physically blocked her view with his body as they continued walking. A loud crashing sound echoed behind them—like an empty metal trash can falling to the ground and rolling. It happened twice more, closer and louder, making both of them flinch. "It's testing us. Don't look back. You can't."

"What if—"

"You agreed to do it my way," he reminded her. "That means we keep going."

Lucky groaned. "Maverick, don't do this to me."

"Don't do what?" He laughed nervously. "Do you *want* your hair to turn white?"

"Georgia said it was only a patch," she reasoned, laughing too. "It'll turn gray someday anyway."

"You're ridiculous."

"I am a well-seasoned supernatural researcher. It takes more than a phantom bumper car to stop me." Her stomach didn't even react. They'd be *fine*.

Maverick led them back to the middle of the path just as it began to make its first curve and the park instantly quieted down behind them.

Lucky grinned. "That didn't scare you, did it?"

His intense side-eye was all the answer she needed.

"I'm sorry," she said, gaze on her feet. "I told you I-I don't really get scared. Stuff like that barely registers anymore."

"Rebel is out there." Maverick was quiet for a moment before adding, "I wasn't scared of the bumper car. I was worried about what you might do because of it. None of this bothers you. Just . . . how?"

"Practice, I guess." She shrugged. "My stomachache system keeps me in check. That didn't feel dangerous at all."

"Stomachache system," he repeated.

"Yeah, you know how like when you can tell something is wrong? You get a bad feeling? I figured out how to reliably use it to my advantage."

"*Mmm.*" He nodded. "How did you even figure out you wanted to be a . . . supernatural researcher?"

"Not sure if I mentioned this but I have ESP."

A rustling pair of bushes directly on their right grabbed their attention. Their flashlights caught three raccoons in mid-scurry. One of them froze in place standing on two legs as they passed it.

"Poor little guy." Lucky laughed.

"You know what I meant," he said. "How did you go from knowing how to read people to living in Hennessee House? I want to understand."

"Everyone has a calling. This is mine." She shrugged. "Thank you, but also no offense. I'm not sure I care all that much if people *understand* my choices as long as they respect them. That's the biggest issue I have."

"You told me that. I remember," he said. "I wouldn't be here if I didn't take you seriously or believe you."

"Yeah because you're in it. You *know* it's real. I don't have to prove anything to you. But outsiders, like my family and the people I thought were my friends? They didn't get it," she said. "That's why I made the decision to just be alone."

Maverick shivered suddenly—their eyes locked. He gave a quick nod for her to continue.

According to the legend and Georgia, the entity had a vested interest in emotions shared between people. Lucky wondered if that meant they needed to be solely romantic in nature. As long as she was genuine, she might get an answer.

"I don't talk to my family," she began. "I don't date at all. I don't think I'm the kind of person who was made for other people. I can be a lot sometimes. Intense. Impulsive. Obsessive in a way people don't understand. No one ever really sticks around, and I don't blame them. It's okay."

Maverick frowned as his teeth began to chatter. "Being a lot doesn't mean you deserve to be alone. Not if you don't want to be."

As he spoke, Lucky's goose bumps returned with a vengeance. "I don't know if I have much of a choice. My ability helps me see people in ways I probably shouldn't. One of the first lessons I ever learned was that people don't really change. If they don't want me, as I am without lying or pretending to be I'm something I'm not, there's nothing I can do to change someone's mind. I can delay it, but never stop it."

"I don't think that's true. People *can* change."

"On the surface it might seem that way," she said. "Everything starts as promising as it should, but then I'll watch as their behavior takes a turn. They're not as nice. They make fun of the things I like only to claim it's a joke and call me sensitive. It'll steadily get worse: they ignore me, insult me, accuse me of things that aren't true. They act like that in response to me. It's my fault."

"No, it isn't," he said through clenched teeth. He was shivering so bad, their hands shook. "No one has the right to treat you that way."

Strangely, Lucky didn't feel any colder. "Your jacket . . ."

"No," he said, with a fierce glint in his eyes. "Why do you believe people can't change?"

"Because I'm helpless as all that stuff happens." If he wouldn't take his jacket from her, then they'd just have to walk faster. She changed their pace to a speed walk, still huddling close together. "I'll be completely clueless as to how to fix it because my impression of them *never* changes. That's how I know people can do bad things and still be a fundamentally good person. They've just lost their way and need time to sort it out. But knowing that doesn't change how much they hurt me in the process."

It also didn't mean she *had* to forgive them or give them a second chance. That was for her to decide.

"If that's the case, I think it's fine if you blame them for leaving. You shouldn't be the only one trying to make it work. If they refuse, then you're right, you are better off without them." His voice trembled, halting and gasping from the cold. "But being alone isn't the answer if it hurts you this much."

Lucky stared at him in confusion. "What?"

"The more you talked, the colder I got and I am *freezing*. I think the entity is on your side." His laugh was a ragged exhale. "I think it's warning me to not fuck this up."

Her eyes widened as she thought of an idea. "It's not *me*. It sides with whoever is more emotionally honest. You had its attention initially, but I stole it from you." And maybe he could steal some of it back. "Share something personal with me, anything as long as it's honest," she demanded.

"Uh." He blinked hard repeatedly as if it would help him concentrate despite the cold. "I can honestly say I've never met anyone like you."

"I said personal!"

"That was personal!"

They couldn't walk any faster without it turning into a sprint, but they were hustling like their lives depended on it. "Tell me something else!"

"I love how amazing you are with Rebel!"

"Maverick!"

"Okay! You make me feel like I don't have to compromise! I don't have to choose between being Rebel's dad and trying to find someone for me! But I don't know if you want us!"

Cold ricocheted through Lucky, from the top of her head down to her feet. Her knees nearly gave out, making her stumble, but Maverick caught her in time. He held her steady as ever as they continued to the end.

By the time they made it to the final stretch, the cold had

penetrated every part of Lucky. It prickled like needles in her bone marrow. She'd never be warm again. Never be able to feel the sun or fire again. "I'm so excited but I'm so cold!"

Maverick had gone silent after his last confession. Could've been from the cold. Could've been shock from what he'd said.

Still, he unerringly guided them into the shadows of the shaved ice stand to find the tree stump, marking the end of their walk. Their token lay in the notched center: a single shiny penny. The second he picked it up, the cold flowed out of her body so fast she needed to lean on him for support.

"It's gone." He closed his eyes in relief, breathing deeply as he pressed a hand to his chest. "My lungs. Oh, they *hurt*."

Lucky balled her hands into fists, wiggling her fingers. "No frostbite. Circulation normal." Her own breaths were deep as well—her chest could fully expand again. "Can I see it?"

He handed her the penny and then proceeded to bend over, hands on his knees.

She inspected it with her flashlight. It was dated 1982, and other than appearing polished, it was unremarkable. "I wish there were cameras. We have no proof the entity left this for us."

"So? We have no proof that you have ESP. We all choose to believe you do." Maverick righted himself, a serious expression on his face. "And I choose to believe that the Penny Place entity believes in *us* too. We passed, Lucky. *We* did it."

This man was impossible.

The same way she'd used her ability to decide they would never work, he found a way to use the supernatural to show her they could. They were literally on the right path—even a decades-old entity thought so.

How was he real?

The penny slipped from her fingers. She was kissing him before it even hit the ground.

Maverick's lips felt just as exquisite as they had on her palm, so the strangely pleasant sensation of his facial hair rubbing her skin surprised her most. He held her so tightly at the waist that when he moved, she did too until her back was against the wall. Her skin felt like it was on fire, burning with a mixture of relief, confusion, and tenderness, and somehow, he burned even hotter as he pressed firmly against her. She'd literally thrown herself at him and he'd given her soft kisses in return.

Soft, but not gentle.

They felt insistent and impatient as if he needed more, he needed all of her, and he would use all of him to get it. His tongue sweetly coaxing hers, his teeth tugging at her bottom lip, his legs carefully sliding in between her thighs, one hand caressing the arch in her back, and the other firm against the back of her neck. Maverick kissed her with his entire body, a contradictory choreographed dance.

And in her kiss-drunk haze, she had a feeling this was only the first step to lure her in. His irresistible kisses were a promise—one she might not know how to accept.

Maverick's timer cut through their haze. "We have to go," he whispered against her mouth.

"Okay."

He kissed her again.

"Okay, now, now we have to go." They ran off into the night back to the entrance.

ℓℓ

24

The next day, at the abandoned office building, Lucky began to realize she'd landed herself in a hell of a situation.

This was why literally everyone advised against dating coworkers—a lesson she didn't think she'd ever need to learn. Maverick was standing right next to her. Right there. So close. And she had to keep her damn hands to herself. They hadn't had a single moment alone since leaving the park last night and the day wasn't looking any better.

Georgia finished checking Rebel's camera and mic. "The concept for this location is to film as if you're sneaking inside. You'll go through the underground parking garage to the elevator then up to the second floor, down to the first, and exit through the front doors where I'll be waiting. That's it, little miss. Are we clear?"

"Crystal!" Rebel beamed.

"All right. Are you excited?"

"Yep!"

"Nervous?"

"A little?"

"Camera and microphone charged and ready?"

"Ready!"

Georgia unclipped a walkie from her back pocket. A gold strip of tape on the front had *REBEL* written across it. "We're on channel two."

Rebel bounced on the tips of her toes as she took it. Lucky briefly wondered why they didn't use walkies last night, but didn't ask.

"That stays on," Georgia warned. "You answer when called and you call when you need backup. Are we crystal clear?"

"Sparkling!"

"Trackers on. Timers set: ninety minutes on my mark for check-in. Safe word"—Georgia paused, grinning devilishly—"happy family."

"That's two words," Maverick complained as he set his watch. "And uncalled for."

"I call it like I see it, Super Dad."

Lucky crossed her arms, leaning away from him. If a stiff breeze blew their way and she smelled a hint of his cocoa butter and mint combo . . . She needed Maverick to touch her again. Now.

Objectively, she knew she was touch-starved. Classic textbook case. Subjectively, Maverick was the only remedy for her. How was she supposed to focus on work under these conditions?

Rebel said, "Dad, you can't say anything. It's not your show."

Maverick mimed zipping his lips, twisting a key, and then handing it to Rebel.

She took it and said, "And make sure you get good footage.

Don't just film *me* the whole time like you did at the talent show. I mean it. You have to get *everything*."

He held up his hands in surrender. It'd be the three of them for the shoot.

Rebel had a clear vision of what she wanted. She began by filming a scene of her quietly deciding where they should go first by listing the pros and cons of her pre-approved locations before announcing they'd go in through the parking garage.

Lucky held her camera steady to create a static overhead shot of Rebel holding the map. Her knees buckled when Maverick pressed his hand gently against her lower back as he watched over her shoulder. She slowly turned her head and blinked at him.

His guilty, amused smile as he stepped back gave him away. He did that on purpose.

They traveled through the parking garage and reached the set of elevators quickly. Inside, Maverick tapped Lucky on the shoulder and pointed to the reflective stainless-steel door. She checked the camera to see if they appeared in it—they did—and silently indicated to Rebel to lower the camera.

At least he wasn't distracted and was on his game. One of them had to be.

On the second floor, the doors opened to a darkened room. They were greeted by one of those cloth cubicle walls extending in both directions. A flyer had been pinned to it, now stiff and yellowed with age: *Misuse of company supplies is considered theft! Reduce crime by recycling!*

Rebel asked, "Which way should we go?"

"Wait." Lucky placed a firm hand on Rebel's shoulder to keep her from going any farther.

Maverick stood at her side. The front of his clothes brushed against her arm, followed by the gentle warm touch of his hand as he held her wrist to check in. *Why are you going off script?*

She forced herself to pull away from him to concentrate. Almost immediately, something told her to leave. Very rarely was her gut so insistent—it felt like it was retreating toward her spine as if that alone could turn her around.

For all its flowers and chills, Hennessee House had never once felt threatening in the way this floor did. Something invisible but tangible in the air pressed against her the moment the doors opened. It slowly tickled up her body like fingers eager to strangle her.

Using her agreed-upon voice, she said, "We can't be here."

"Why not?"

She chose her words carefully. "It doesn't feel right."

Rebel didn't hesitate, leaping to the back wall of the elevator.

Maverick gave Lucky a questioning look—instead of responding, she hit the button for the first floor.

"Did you have a gut feeling?" Rebel asked, wide-eyed.

Maverick had asked Lucky to explain her stomachache system over breakfast. "I did."

"What was it like? People will want to know."

Lucky almost laughed, but her still-jangled nerves held her back. Rebel was truly her father's daughter, interview skills out in full force. "You know I'm not good at explaining."

"Well, how are you going to get better if you don't practice?"

Maverick barely concealed his snort.

She glared at him. Not the whole family treating her like this. She said, "It was like a . . . like a clear bubble. I could feel it touching me. Walking through it would've been a very bad idea."

On the first floor, however, Lucky didn't feel any resistance, so they freely explored the semi-dark office space. It smelled like a mixture of cleaning solution and mildew. Soggy carpet squished under their shoes with every step. Overhead the florescent lights that worked bathed everything in a sickly yellow glow. Laminated labor law notices and employer memos still covered the walls, while desk chairs appeared in random places, like in the middle of walkways.

Rebel stated her line from the script: "Did you see which way they went?" She was supposed to see someone on the second floor and follow them down to the first.

"I didn't," Lucky said, using her calming voice. "I never did. Are you sure you saw someone?"

"I'm sure."

"Why would anyone be here?"

"Well, we are."

Lucky laughed. "Good point. I meant why would anyone else be here, Shortcake? Maybe we should head back."

"What if they're in trouble and they need our help, but they're too scared to talk to anyone?"

"Those are very admirable sentiments," Lucky said. "But I'm afraid not everyone thinks like you."

Rebel turned left toward a conference room. "Let's look in here."

They walked inside a long rectangular room with a large oval-shaped table in the center. As expected, there were no chairs. Rebel narrated as she looked under the table, behind the doors, and inside of an already-open closet. "No one in here. I don't understand how they moved so fast. We should've caught up to them by now."

"Maybe they don't want to be found."

"You're doing great," Maverick whispered close to her ear. His fingers covertly traced the lines in her palm. The surprising intimacy of the moment nearly took her breath away.

Sometimes, she wished she'd been born with that reckless abandon she'd read in some people. The desire for physical connection burning like smothered coal inside of them, the smoke fogging up their brain and blurring their senses, including the common one. So overwhelmed and confused as to how suddenly, the only thing that mattered, that made sense in the world, was the person standing in front of her. But she thought too much. Considered every angle. Her body perpetually stuck in neutral, rolling along.

Her desire for Maverick Phillips wasn't like that at all, but she wasn't empty. It wasn't a passive want. It was *yearning*—a desperate ache pulling her heartstrings taut as hot wire.

Now yearning? That one could make her jump, make her bold and daring, but even still she would never lose control. Make a fool of herself? Sure. Absolutely. But lose control? Never. Being honest, she'd never experienced this specific flavor of yearning before. It was like a new ingredient waiting to be identified and added to her arsenal.

They'd almost made a full loop of the first floor and the elevator doors were in sight when an office door began to open. Light spilled into the hallway from somewhere farther in the room.

Rebel stumbled before backing up against the far wall.

Lucky's attention snapped toward her. On guard, she asked, "Are we okay?"

"Do you think someone is in there?"

"I don't know."

Rebel began to whine, biting her lip while her breathing became uneven.

Lucky could practically feel Maverick shift from producer to dad, ready to tell her she could stop. "R—" The sound had barely left his mouth when Lucky put her hand up. She eyed him seriously, shaking her head. She felt just as in tune as she had on the elevator. Rebel needed reassurance and it was Lucky's job to give that to her.

"Why don't we try a new angle?" Lucky knelt in front of Rebel, carefully pushing the camera away and toward the open door. "How about a bird's-eye view?"

She whimpered, "What's that?"

"I'll give you a piggyback ride. You film, I walk."

"What if there's a ghost?"

"I'll beat him up," she said with certainty.

The smallest smile broke through her terror. "You can't beat up a ghost."

"Oh yeah? How do you know that?"

"They don't have a corporeal form," she said. "And you're not supposed to hit people. Or former people. You're supposed to use your words."

"Well, where I'm from we use our legs, which would technically be kicking. You know what else legs are good for? Running. I'm really good at that too." She lowered her voice to make a vow she intended to keep; ghosts be damned. "I won't let anything bad happen to you."

"Do you promise?"

Lucky smiled. "Cross my heart, Shortcake." She turned around and Rebel climbed on her back. She stood up and asked, "Camera in focus?"

"Yes."

"Ready?"

"Maybe."

"Which way? I'm only going where you tell me."

"Straight ahead, please."

As Lucky suspected, they were able to pass by the room without incident. Rebel made it clear she didn't want to go inside, so they continued on, to the front entrance.

"Phew." Rebel laughed the last of her fears away after turning off her camera. "I think that's enough for today."

Maverick smiled. "Then that's officially a wrap on *Shortcake*."

LATER THAT NIGHT, Lucky quietly walked past a sleeping Georgia and opened their door to find Maverick standing down the hall with his hand still on his doorknob too. In the morning, she wouldn't remember closing the door. The feel of the hardwood floor, the sound of her quick steps, the breathlessness in her lungs—all of it lost to the fickle whims of her surprisingly fallible short-term memory.

But the moment he was within reach, the second it took to jump high enough, the way he smoothly caught her, and the feel of his lips as he smiled and whispered "*I missed you*" against hers would stay with her forever. She'd been waiting all morning, all afternoon, all night for this.

Maverick carried her down the hall. They passed the living room, couches, and the kitchen table, and headed straight outside for the tree house. The cool, post-midnight air helped clear Lucky's head. The amount of time she spent thinking about him . . . *whew*. She shivered, holding on to him tighter.

"We should be okay to talk out here." He retrieved a thick, folded blanket from the corner because he always had a plan. "For you."

A single yellow sunflower. "Thank you."

"Because in that creepy yellow office, you kept your promise to me and Rebel." He shook out the blanket before wrapping it around his shoulders and gesturing for her to come sit with him.

Suddenly feeling absurdly bashful, she watched his face as she slowly went to him to gauge his reaction.

Ever patient, as always.

She sat with her back to his front, cradled by his legs. He pulled the blanket around her, making sure she'd be covered and warm. Her chest felt tight with something she refused to name.

"How did you know something was off on the second floor?" he asked. "I wouldn't call myself sensitive or anything, but I do get bad feelings from time to time on some shoots. I didn't feel anything today."

"I could try teaching you," she offered. "Your lucid dreams suggest you'd have the aptitude for it. You're also very self-aware, which is important."

"No." She felt him shake his head. "No. I don't want to . . . expand my dreams or learn anything new about them. I'm fine where I'm at."

"Okay," she said, a little disappointed. "Well, there are different levels of sensitivity, I think. You might only be able to pick up on the threats that are impossible to ignore. That one was subtle but also too eager, which was where it messed up. I could feel it wanting to latch on to me. I didn't want to risk it spreading to you or Rebel."

Maverick tightened his embrace, pulling her against him as if he wanted to protect her. "What do you think it was?"

"I honestly don't know. It's not something I'd usually investigate, not anymore." She smiled. "I've settled on sticking to human-based supernatural phenomenon. My wild days are mostly over."

"You're living in a haunted house. That's pretty wild."

She laughed. "Hennessee is my last hurrah and it's a good one. Its secrets are worth discovering. I *know* they are. I can feel it."

"Hmm."

When he hooked his chin around her shoulder, pressing their cheeks together, she said, "I really rocket-launched myself at you in the house. I can't believe I did that."

"I'm glad you did. I was dying." He kissed her cheek twice, then moved to the front of her ear and down the side of her neck. Stopping there he inhaled, slow and deep, and sighed contentedly. He whispered, tone thick with disbelief, "My god."

Lucky closed her eyes to savor the feeling of his breath tickling across her skin—and immediately regretted it. Everything about him was overwhelming her. This couldn't be real. It just couldn't be. She balled her hands into fists, pressing them into her thighs to stay grounded. Something deep in the recesses of her brain recognized him as if she'd known it was always supposed to be this way. As if she were seeing him again for the first time after years and years apart, her patience finally rewarded.

She asked, "How do you feel about sex?"

"Right now?"

"In general, please." She laughed.

"Okay, yeah, 'cause I was gonna say I didn't think we were

coming out here for that because . . . slow. We're still going slow, right?"

"Yeah. Slow." Existential panic hit her like a guillotine. "I'm not asking to have sex right now or ever, that's also on the table if that's what you need, but I don't want there to be any miscommunication. It's important to me that we talk about it first. Soon, if possible."

"Is something wrong?"

"No. There's nothing 'wrong' about what I have to say. Honestly, I'm expecting it to be the start of an engaging and enlightening conversation like all the other things we talk about. We have a reputation to uphold, after all."

He laughed, chest rumbling against her back. "I'd expect nothing less. You're really something, you know that?"

"I do not know that but thank you."

Maverick kissed her again and that heady, overpowering feeling flared back to life between them until they snuck back into the house and into their respective rooms.

Unable to sleep, Lucky lay awake staring at the ceiling. How in the hell was she going to make this last?

25

Hennessee House's welcome home for Lucky was . . . lack-luster.

Xander got a river of flowers. She got three in her bathtub. Hardly comparable, and very nearly insulting. She ended up spending her first night back in her suite bonding with Gengar while Hennessee had what could only be described as a temper tantrum. And Lucky simply didn't respond to those.

Maverick, however, didn't let her down, and promptly called at sunrise.

"Good morning. I'm fine." Predictability had never been so attractive.

"You fell asleep on me last night," he said. "I stayed on for a while but—"

"Were you listening to me sleep?"

"I was listening for signs of distress, and I happened to hear you sleep. You were mostly quiet."

"Mostly?"

"That's why I didn't hang up right away. I wasn't sure."

"Did I talk?"

"No, you mumbled a little bit. And I think you snored."

"You're unsure about that?"

"You didn't sound like a chainsaw or anything. They were . . . quiet, like you were congested and trying to avoid breathing out of your mouth."

She laughed. "Nobody likes a mouth breather."

"I'd argue that's subjective," he said. "I have to go. Rebel is already up."

"Okay. See you later?"

"Absolutely."

Gengar yowled, openly judging her from the window.

"Hmm." She propped herself up on one arm. "I can't tell if you're mad because I haven't fed you yet or because you disapprove of my choices. Why do I have the sudden urge to shout *But Daddy, you don't even know him!* at you?"

Her answer came in the form of one dramatically slow blink. Gengar jumped down, swished to the door, and waited.

"Fine. I'll get up. Just so bossy," she said. "What should we do today? Ooh, we could use the drone?"

The cat could not have cared less.

After breakfast, he followed her anyway, back upstairs to the bedroom across from hers.

Lucky had found the gift in the office next to her company-issued laptop. Wrapped in lovely green paper with a bright blue ribbon, it had a card attached.

Try your best not to break it. You seem the overzealous type.
—Xander

Unfortunately, she'd have to make him pay for that.

The drone was heavier than expected. Bigger than her hand, it had four propellers, flood lights, and built-in storage for recording. The controls had a monitor—figuring out how to use it reminded her of playing an intuitive video game. She mastered it in under five minutes.

Crawl space exposed, she sat with her back against the wall as she navigated the drone inside and forward.

Lucky frowned as she heard the window opening behind her. The summer air displaced the house's constant near-perfect temperature. "Not now." She said it as if swatting a fly.

The drone whirred insistently under the floorboards and echoed around the metal passage. At what she suspected was the room's threshold, the passageway made a sharp left. After a few more feet, she could turn either left, right, or continue forward. Choosing left, she maneuvered through the passageway until reaching a dead end in front of a small grate.

The passageways led to the rooms. If one could fit, they allowed someone to spy on other occupants.

A triumphant chill shivered through Lucky despite the heat. She'd uncovered another one of Hennessee's secrets. But why did it show her this? There was no one else in the house.

"Great. Fantastic. Another wild goose chase and for what?" She navigated the drone back to her.

All this discovery did was waste more of Lucky's time, which was running out.

Her experience at Penny Place solidified that her work hadn't been pointless. Whether or not they knew it, people were powerful—as individuals and as a collective. Their place within the supernatural realm existed. There were more ESPers, more urban legends brought to life in the world waiting to be found. She'd thought Hennessee House might have a place within her work too, but if she couldn't find a connection or what caused its sentience, she'd be a failure.

Failures and grad school rejects didn't get funding for their research.

Since writing her name didn't work, she'd have to try something more drastic.

Lucky decided to film her daily self-tape outside in the gazebo. Surrounded by partially cloudy skies, the perfect amount of warm summer breeze, birds chirping and bathing in the small fountain, and the faint sounds of the neighborhood, she'd never felt more content on a lazy morning.

Rebel had taught her quite a bit about framing and drilled into her how important it was to look at the lens and not watch herself on the screen while talking. Pretending to tell a story to a friend made the best videos apparently.

Contractual obligations expected her to make these videos good, so she put Rebel's excellent advice to work.

"I can definitely say, without a doubt, that last night was the most disappointing I've had in the house so far. I know what you're thinking—*but Lucky you heard creaking floorboards and footsteps, banging on the walls, wind screeching in the hallway, doors rattling, windows slamming, literally everything all at once, supernatural activity running rampant throughout the house.* And to that I say, it was . . . boring. Hennessee House is supposed to be exceptional—talk about a waste of potential. It's giving nothing but stereotypical haunted house tripe.

"Granted, maybe if that happened during my first couple of nights, I would've been excited, but this is my *third* week. I resisted Hennessee's formidable compulsion for so long before giving in and writing my name on the wall because I wanted to prove myself. I wanted to show I was strong enough to be here. I haven't seen even a single confirmed illusion or specter. Either I'm preternaturally strong-willed, which is very likely, or my predecessors had it worse than I did. Because so far, I haven't experienced anything capable of sending me screaming into the night.

"I know they say you're supposed to be careful what you wish for. I know there's power in that. But I'm wishing for it anyway. Otherwise, what's the point in me being here?"

Satisfied with her performance, she cut off the camera and turned to Gengar. "How was that?"

He blinked at her, almost asleep. She'd given him some special snackies to sedate him for his vet trip.

"Remember, once means yes. That means you agree with my choices."

"Lucky?"

She whirled around at the sound of her name. Maverick was walking toward her from the side of the house. Every time she saw him still felt as remarkable as the first. She stood to meet him on the steps. "How did you know I was back here?" The sounding breathless part could go any day now, though.

"The house. I was about to ring the doorbell when I smelled flowers." He sighed with resignation. "It's your perfume. That's what it uses for me."

His specialized scent was . . . her? "Hennessee didn't lead you around before I got here?"

He chuckled, shaking his head. "What do you think?"

"*Oh.*" She began to melt as she mentally connected the dots.

The house noticed everything. It must not have needed to have access to someone's mind to create a scent if that someone unintentionally gave it enough information to work with. Hennessee had Maverick's number too—probably from the very moment he met Lucky.

He handed her a coffee and a single-stem flower. "Cinnamon latte with foam and cinnamon sugar. Pink peony because of your name."

Her favorite drink, which she'd told him, and she honestly didn't have a favorite flower. But eventually, hopefully, she would. Not that one, though. "Thank you. Where's Rebel?"

"Afraid you were no match for going to the movies with Riley and his mom."

She gasped. "The betrayal."

"The first time she chose hanging out with Riley over me I was so hurt." He laughed as he reached for her waist. "It's a good thing."

"Mmm, is that what you keep telling yourself?" She draped her arms around his shoulders, following his lead as he pressed her against the gazebo post.

"Every time."

He was still smiling as he kissed her.

Was kissing supposed to make her feel so . . . giddy? It'd never happened before.

They'd been pleasant enough, fine as long as they weren't too wet, but she never got excited about them. Didn't eagerly look forward to them either.

Kissing Maverick was . . . she didn't even *know*.

"We're gonna be late," he whispered in between kisses at her jaw.

He was always the one to stop first. He had more control or didn't feel as intensely as she did. Both were possible.

Gengar had fallen asleep peacefully on the bench next to where she'd sat. "It's me," she crooned. She rubbed between his ears—the one place he tolerated being touched. "We're going to your appointment now. We have to make sure your little body is doing okay and get you groomed. I'm going to pick you up now."

Maverick grabbed the open-top cat carrier from its hiding place. He also put on thick gloves, up to his elbows, in case Gengar woke up and lashed out.

Lucky carefully curled her hands under him.

He growled softly but remained asleep.

"I got you. Don't worry. I'm gonna take good care of you."

He growled louder but it cut off, suddenly transforming into a rumbling purr. She held him loosely against her chest and five seconds later, he was nestled into the soft blanket fort inside the carrier.

Maverick said, "That wasn't so bad."

"If you see me crying in the car, mind your business," she said. "Did you hear him purring?"

"You are my business." He kissed her forehead. "I told you he loves you."

The vet appointment would take at least an hour, longer if they needed to sedate him again. Before they left, the doctor checked for a microchip, but Gengar didn't have one. Lucky signed up immediately, listing herself and Xander as the owners and Hennessee House as his address.

Maverick frowned. "Did you ask him about that first?"

"Sure didn't." She grinned. "I hope it annoys the hell out of him."

"What is it with you two?"

"It's like we bring out the petty in each other. He makes me want to fight him but in a good way."

Was it because he was a skeleton? . . . Maybe.

Yes. What *else* was she supposed to do? He needed *love*. She'd taken a page from Georgia's book, deciding to become the annoying younger sister to her adored eldest.

Maverick treated Lucky to lunch and they headed to a nearby park to wait for Gengar. They sat under a vacant tree with a blanket he had in his emergency car kit. She hadn't spent much time outside the house, but she knew a little something about the area. He lived about an hour north in the city while Hennessee House was in a small incorporated town, both in Sacramento County.

It seemed like a nice place to live full-time. Swans in the pond. Ducks waddling the paths. Kids riding bikes and parents with jogging strollers. Plenty of supernatural activity to investigate. Everything a girl could want.

"Do you have plans after this?" She lay on her stomach, propped up on her elbows.

He was on his back, looking up at her. "Not until Rebel is ready to come home for dinner. You're welcome to join us."

"I don't think I can. Can I?"

"It's technically not my show, but probably not."

Lucky wasn't under house arrest, but they were paying her to be there. Especially at night. "You two can come to Hennessee," she said hopefully.

"Not after dark. No."

"I understand. But for the record"—she paused to grin at him—"literally nothing bad happens. You'll both be safe."

"You don't know that." He still wasn't willing to risk it under any circumstances barring extreme emergencies.

Lucky frowned, unable to hide her frustration. She wanted to spend time with him any way she could, but how were they supposed to make this work? She couldn't go to his apartment. He wouldn't stay in Hennessee House. "I'm starting to think the other caretakers were exaggerating."

"They weren't. You're an exception for some reason. The house just likes you." He rolled over onto his side, gently tugging her closer to him. "I can see how that could happen. I almost feel sorry for it."

"I accept that compliment." She smiled and kissed him . . . and then didn't stop.

"There are children in this park. Behave," he teased.

"I can't. It's like I'm possessed."

"Bad choice of words. Please don't say that."

"Sorry." She kissed his jaw then bit it gently.

"Are you a *biter*?"

"I might be," she admitted. "Is that bad?"

"No." He snorted. "It's just a little surprising."

"Why?" she asked, trying not to sound nervous.

"Just is." He answered a little too fast, gaze darting away. "You asked for slow. I'm honestly okay with that."

Maybe she'd been unconsciously trying to match the energy she sensed in him. She didn't feel like she was performing or doing what she assumed was expected of her. She honestly wanted to kiss him. And touch him. And be close to him. For hours at a time, if possible. Maybe it felt so intense because it was new, and they spent so much time apart. She needed to cram as much affection in as possible to hold her over until she saw him again.

He continued, "Although, if you're up for it, I'd like you to meet my family."

"*Oh*," she squeaked in surprise. "Family. Oh."

"We're having a little get-together this weekend at my parents' house. I thought it'd be nice if you came. Or is that too fast?"

"It isn't," she said, eager to soothe the worried look in his eyes. They hadn't talked about what he said at Penny Place. She didn't want him thinking that she didn't want them, not even for a single second. "It's just . . . it's *parents*. I wouldn't want to impose or whatever."

He laughed. "Lucky, they know who you are. My mom would love to meet you."

She softened. "You told them about me?"

"Yeah. And if I didn't, Rebel would have. Or Georgia."

Georgia knew his family. Oh. That must've been what people did when they had a family to share. A family who didn't hate them.

"Where do they live?" she asked.

"About twenty minutes away from me."

She nodded. "How many siblings do you have? You never said."

"Five. I'm dead-center middle child."

"I love that for you."

"It was hell." He laughed. "My family is of the matching pajamas on Christmas day variety and really traditional. The eldest are responsible for the rest of us and should set a good example. The youngest get away with murder and are spoiled rotten. And then there was me, flying under the radar no matter what I did until Rebecca got pregnant. They cared about that."

Lucky knew how old Maverick was when Rebel was born—nineteen—and how long he'd had full custody—since she was two—but not what happened to Rebecca or where she was. He never really talked about her. Neither did Rebel.

He continued by asking, "Do you have any?"

"Siblings? Yeah. An older brother."

"Where does—"

"I don't really want to talk about my family." She kissed him. "What time is the party?"

"Two to whenever."

"Daylight. Perfect. Xander won't get upset if I'm back at the house before dark. I think. I'm willing to test it," she said, gaze downcast. "I want to go. It really means a lot to me that you told your family about me."

"Of course, I did." He kissed her cheek and then the corner of her mouth. "There are some downsides. I tell them I have a girlfriend, and literally no one will stop bringing up how miraculous that is, but that's family for you."

Lucky's heart stopped and sputtered back to life. She narrowed her eyes, determined to suppress the euphoria suddenly racing through her entire body. "Girlfriend? I'm your girlfriend now?"

"Yes?" Maverick's adorably nervous reaction almost made her laugh and break character.

"And who decided that?"

"I figured it was implied."

She thought the same but really, *really* wanted to have this moment. "I would like to be asked, please."

He moved to sit up and she followed his lead until they sat facing each other. Knees touching, holding hands and gazes, under the shade of a tree in the middle of a beatific park on a perfect summer day.

"Lucky."

"Maverick."

"I didn't realize I'd been looking for someone until you found me," he said. "That's exactly how it felt—I saw your picture and I thought *Oh, shit, there* she *is. She's coming whether I'm ready or not* and I wasn't. I was not at all prepared for how quickly you turned my entire existence upside down. You have no idea how desperate I am to stay with you, to keep seeing where this goes. Be with me."

"That didn't sound like a question," she teased. Meanwhile, the words *be with me* echoed around her memory palace until it found his reading and settled in next to it. Forever.

"Because I'm not questioning it. That's where I stand. I'm asking: Where are you?"

It took every single ounce of self-restraint she had to not crawl into his lap, wrap her body around his, and cover his face with an endless barrage of kisses. He'd given her so much more than what she'd hoped for.

"I'm standing right next to you," she said, meaning it. "Because I'm yours."

26

Back at Hennessee House, Lucky gingerly placed Gengar's carrier on the floor.

Her feral kitty was fully awake and enraged—hissing, growling, and yowling to be set free. The carrier rocked and skidded across the floor.

"Just one minute! One more minute!" Lucky darted to the kitchen to lock the kitty door. He wasn't supposed to go outside for at least twelve hours. Doctor's orders. "I'm sorry! I'm sorry!" With quick fingers, she unlatched the top opening and pulled it back. He was going to eat her alive for this.

Gengar leaped out of the carrier and ran straight into the sitting room. He continued growling and glaring at her from under the couch.

"We had to get you checked out! What if you needed medication?" He didn't, thankfully. "She said you were incredible, never seen an outside cat like you before."

Gengar was approximately six to eight years old with no

identifiable illnesses or physical ailments. The doctor even seemed confused by his clean bill of health.

"And you're registered now. That means we're officially family. I'm responsible for you."

Gengar continued staring at her.

"Okay, I'll leave you alone." She sighed. "I'll be in the suite if you find it in your heart to forgive me."

Lucky sprinkled extra treats on top of his dry food and grabbed a couple of the Squeeze Up treats he loved before heading upstairs. After her bath and dinner she waited around for Maverick's nighttime check-in because that's what her life had been reduced to—waiting for something spooky worth documenting or for him to call. Preferably both would happen at the same time.

She'd been so surprised when he asked her to meet his family. Not because she never expected him to—it just seemed so . . . final. He'd said he never brought anyone he dated around Rebel before and she assumed that rule extended to the rest of his family.

He was sure about her. And she didn't have anything to give him in return.

Maverick would probably never meet her family. She didn't have anyone else worth introducing him to. She didn't have *any* other parts of her life to share. She had . . . her work. That was it. Yes, it was deeply important to her, but how could that possibly be enough?

In a perfect world, she'd have the family she always wanted. A mom who loved her unconditionally. A brother who never stopped understanding her. A dad who hadn't died and maybe still, a stepdad who wanted to be there for her. There'd be daily messages and weekly calls and postcards from all the places she traveled while investigating and big family dinners when she came home. She'd be a good daughter and little sister. Thoughtful, caring, and supportive.

But that wasn't what she got.

Her family never recovered from her dad's death. Her mom remarried, but it didn't do anything to stop how mean she became. That really was the best word for it. She wasn't evil or a narcissist. She was hurting and refused to talk about it. All that pain turned inward and made her mean, especially to Lucky, who was already the black sheep of their extended family by that point.

Lucky understood, in a way, more so now that she was older. But parents were supposed to protect their kids, not hurt them. She didn't know how to heal from that yet. She might not ever. So, she didn't talk or even think about her mom, and although her heart might always want to love her mom, hearts didn't always know best.

Her brother was a different story.

He didn't have ESP and believed she didn't either. She was lying, being weird for attention. He'd stopped talking to her after they graduated high school. The last time he called was to tell her Grandpa died. She could at least count on him for big news like that.

Lucky hadn't seen him in years—did they even still look alike? Where did he live now? Was he married? Did he have kids? When she met Maverick's family, they'd ask about hers and she'd have nothing to tell them except lies. Her phone finally rang and she crawled out of her accidental nest of blankets. "Hi."

Maverick hesitated. "Are you okay?"

"Yeah."

"You don't sound like it. What happened?"

"I'm a little congested." Not a lie. Not the whole truth. "I'll be fine."

Maverick managed to hold every bit of her attention, keeping her barely concealed sadness at bay, until they said good night. And then, right as she was falling asleep, she thought about her family again. Her mom and her brother.

LUCKY HAD THE best, most restorative sleeps of her life inside of Hennessee House. No tossing. No turning. Never woke up in the middle of the night.

Until now.

She gasped awake, sitting up in bed with one hand clutching her blankets and the other on her chest. Cold air clung to her clammy skin—her window was open. She did not do that. She never slept with the windows open out of fear of someone crawling through it.

Yes, she was on the second floor. Old habits stemming from years of being a woman living alone in a first-floor apartment died hard.

Tossing her blankets to the side, she walked to the window and firmly shut it.

Someone knocked on her bedroom door.

She whirled around, heart in her throat.

A voice called out, "Lucky?"

She clutched the windowsill so hard her fingers began to hurt. Carefully, slowly, eyes peeled for any sign of danger, she grabbed her phone and began to record. Because she knew that voice. Fear existed within her like flour inside of a sifter—solid until she forced it through. Was she truly afraid or just startled?

Heart rate—accelerated.

Breathing—heavier than normal.

Stomach—queasy with nerves.

Hands—a slight tremor.

Willpower—steady as a rock.

Not calm, but ready. The doorknob felt warm in her hand as she turned it. Hennessee's peppermint scent beckoned her into the hall.

A woman stood on the other side. Tall with light brown skin and giant dark eyes. Her hair extended around her like a curly halo straight from the heavens. She didn't smile because she rarely ever did when she looked at Lucky.

"Hi, Mom."

"Lucky." Not a hint of affection. Not even a scrape of it. Shit.

"You're not real."

"Oh?" Her eyebrows raised in question. "You could be wrong but that never occurs to you, does it? Stop being rude. Why are you always hiding in your room?"

"I'll come out."

Hennessee House's specter of Lucky's mom stepped back to give her space.

The house had turned all the lights on. Lucky almost laughed. It must not have wanted her to miss a single detail of its work. The hair, her face, her voice—it'd even gotten the small triangle-shaped mole on the front of her mom's wrist right.

Her gaze flicked between the phone screen and the specter as she willed herself to internalize the truth. No matter what happened, no matter what it said, it wasn't real. That wasn't her mom. On the screen, a blurry white smear appeared in her place.

As if reading her mind, it said, "You don't need that. Put it away. Now."

"No. Don't tell me what to do."

"Who in the hell are you talking to like that?"

Lucky nearly flinched. That tone made her feel twelve again, trying to disappear after giving a bad translation to one of her mom's friends. *You speak when spoken to, do you hear me?*

Hennessee was so good, she instinctively knew which bad memories the house had chosen to sustain the specter: *Her dead husband had left her with a weird-ass daughter who wouldn't stop racking up medical debt. A useless daughter who couldn't even be a good psychic to help them cover the bills. What a life. At least her son was normal.*

"You're not my mom."

"Always thinking you know everything." It smiled. "What if I die? Who would want to take care of a self-righteous brat like you?"

"You're not dead. Reggie would've called for that."

"Would he? Are you sure? Maybe he's too busy with a baby now. Maybe you're an aunt and you didn't even know it."

"That's not true."

"A little boy. Reggie Junior. Ten little perfect toes and fingers, fat little legs, and chubby cheeks. He might have your eyes— Hart eyes. Just like Reggie. Just like your dad."

"That's not true. Reggie would've told me. I would've gone home for him."

"You sure about that?"

Lucky closed her eyes in resignation. This is what she asked for. This is what she wanted. A specter of her brother leaned against the wall, hands in his pockets. The waves in his short hair, the nose piercing, the dimple in his chin—a picture-perfect replica. Oh no, this one was going to *hurt*. She blinked back the tears pooling in her eyes.

"You're shorter than I remember," she lied, staring him down.

He grinned in response, gaze dropping to the ground momentarily—a nervous habit he'd always had because ironically he hated eye contact.

Lucky's heart squeezed with fondness for him, but that wasn't her Reggie. It wasn't.

Hennessee House couldn't fool her. Hennessee House couldn't scare her. The most it could do was hurt her feelings, but she'd brought this on herself. She'd gone to sleep thinking about her family because Maverick wanted her to meet his. Technically, she hurt her own feelings.

Lucky would bow to no one—not even an invasive, old sentient house.

Summoning the bravado she always found when she truly needed it, she asked, "So is this it, then? We're going to stand here until sunrise?"

It, Reggie-edition, moved closer to her. Face to face. It tilted its head to the side. "Why aren't you leaving?"

"The others were scared. I'm not."

Specter-Mom's face had gone slack. "Yes, I know, only the ghost scares you."

Lucky frowned. "What ghost?"

Its eyes suddenly turned black, shining with a tiny pinprick of light at the center—a single star in endless darkness. Its mouth hung open.

Formidable, ringing, and clear, she heard it speak directly *inside* of her head—a deep, slow growl with a halting cadence. *"at the bottom of your mind—destroyed—are you not happy—will you stay—will you run."*

Hennessee House needed to use telepathy to communicate!

Lucky's eyes widened. Terror gripped her neck, cutting off her air. Fear so palpable she could taste it burned in her mouth like stomach acid and had her reaching for the door, slamming it behind her.

"Come back, Lucky Bug! Come back!"

A cold sweat beaded on her brow, ran down her face as she sank to the floor in her suite. She curled into the fetal position willing her lungs to relax, to let her breathe, to not pass out. She squeezed her eyes shut.

That voice reverberated in her memory palace. Her great library with reflective tide-pool floors and enormous columns, living water tree bookcases with branches and sprouting leaves, vaulted ceilings covered in vines and giant windows. Her gold-plated automatons that were shaped like starfish and spun like tops to travel, zipping around everywhere. She'd left it unchanged, the exact way her eight-year-old self imagined it—nonsensical, earthy, and wondrous. That voice chased her as she visualized flying down the winding staircases, through the long passageways and secret rooms, past the vaults, and beyond the final boundary to the bottom.

To an empty room.

The first impression of the ghost she'd read, the one that she had to lock away for her own safety, was gone.

But that was impossible. Impressions didn't leave her memory palace. She remembered everything about the ghost, how it felt, what it wanted, how she got it—but it wasn't there. And she couldn't feel it anywhere else.

But when? She had it at Penny Place. It must have been when she came back. Sometime in the past few days, Hennessee House stole it. Destroyed it.

Lucky opened her eyes. She knew *exactly* what her next steps would be. Had to be.

"Lucky Bug." Only Specter-Reggie had waited for her in the hall.

She swallowed hard, choosing her words carefully. "Thank you. I appreciate your intentions, but don't ever do that again. My memory palace is mine. You are a guest. From the moment I walked through your doors, I have been nothing but respectful. I expect the same while you're in my head."

Specter-Reggie's brow furrowed as if he didn't understand.

"And no more hijacking. Don't do that to me again either. Good night." Lucky closed the door.

She unfortunately welcomed the specters back the next night. And the next. And the next . . .

27

"Lucky." Maverick opened his door and immediately hugged her. She'd driven to his apartment for the first time so they could all ride to his parents' house together. "I swear this has felt like the longest week of my life."

"I know exactly what you mean." The feel of his body pressed against hers was as exquisite as she remembered. He was lean, but not naturally so. She knew he worked out regularly to help keep his "anxious levels" down—his exact words. There was almost no give to his chest, all hard lines and shapely muscles. And yet, somehow, she relaxed against him as if he had the softest, most malleable body in existence. How could a simple hug be so comforting? He made her feel like they fit together perfectly without even trying.

He pulled back, examining her face. "Mmm, glasses."

"Better safe than sorry. I'll take them off inside," she promised, even though it wasn't the best idea. Her eyes had taken on a semi-permanent red tint from crying too much and not enough sleep. Progress required sacrifice and she was making headway with Hennessee House, one long night at a time. He closed the door behind them.

"You look tired." She poked him in the side.

"I haven't been sleeping well. I was in the middle of a power nap just now—I feel like I'm still asleep," he said. "I was dreaming about you."

"Oh?"

"Yeah. I'm a little . . . stressed. Lately, real life has been infiltrating my dreams and causing me all kinds of trouble."

"Dreams but not nightmares," she challenged. "Must've been a good kind of trouble."

Maverick took a long, lingering glance at her. From head to toe and back again, stopping at her eyes. "It was." He wrapped her up in another hug. "I missed you."

"Why?" she joked.

"Why did I miss you?" he asked, playing along. "Because I want you here. I wish I could be there. I can't have what I want so missing you is all that's left."

"Booooo! Tomato, tomato! Booooo!" Georgia laughed as she rounded the corner with Rebel. "I didn't know you had that level of cheese in you, Super Dad." She made a show of prying them apart to give Lucky a hug too.

"Hi, Georgia."

"Don't you miss me? You haven't texted, which is so rude. A whole weekend together and not a single follow-up message. I'm hurt."

"I don't think I have your phone number?"

"That's both beside the point and exactly what I'm talking about."

Lucky nodded, giving her an apologetic smile. She understood what Georgia meant. Friendship, like all relationships, required intention. More often than not, it wasn't effortless. It'd never been that way for her, and she didn't expect it to be now. She'd just been ~~suffering~~ busy. Between Hennessee House and Maverick, everything else felt like it *had* to be shoved to the side. Which felt wrong.

"I have her number," Rebel said to Lucky. "I'll give it to you."

"Shall we, ladies?" Maverick laughed, gesturing them toward the door.

"Dad, Beanie said they're bringing Sophie."

"Your uncle Max isn't bringing that puppy." He locked the door.

"Yes, he is!" Rebel said. "I'll bet you five dollars."

"Do you have five dollars? It can't be like last time when you lost and said the money was already in my wallet and that you were just giving it back to me before I gave it to you anyway."

Georgia shrieked with laughter. "That is genius. I'm stealing that."

Maverick glared. "Please don't encourage her."

"Grandma is giving me birthday money," Rebel said confidently. "I'll use that."

WITHIN SECONDS OF arriving at the Phillipses' family home, Georgia seamlessly blended into the crowd, greeting everyone by name and giving out hugs. Rebel ran directly to the backyard, disappearing into a small group of kids.

"Her cousins. She's the oldest and their ringleader," Maverick whispered to Lucky. He told her their names, ages, and which of his siblings they belonged to. "Freddie, my youngest brother, might not be here yet."

"Does he have kids too?"

He shook his head. "He got married a few months ago. I think they're still deciding but leaning toward no."

They followed Rebel into the backyard but headed straight for the dark-skinned man wearing a cream button-up shirt and manning the impressively sized grill—Maverick's dad.

Lucky asked to see pictures of Maverick's parents and siblings beforehand to memorize their faces. He told her his parents didn't tolerate being addressed by their first names or without an honorific by anyone younger than them, something she inherently knew. Her family had the same rules.

Mr. Charles Phillips, Charlie to his friends, was taller than Maverick with a bald head and a face just beginning to wrinkle. He had trickster eyes and a good-humored smile—features belonging to a man who'd fallen headlong into dad jokes and never looked back. "You're late, knucklehead. This her?"

"It is." Maverick sighed. "Lucky, this is my dad."

"Hi, Mr. Phillips." Sounding shyer than she preferred, she added, "It's lovely to meet you."

"Lovely? Well, all right. I'll take that." He turned to Maverick, still smiling. "Your mama's inside. Better hurry up before she realizes you didn't introduce her first." He winked at Lucky.

"You were closer." Maverick shrugged.

They found his mom in the dining room deeply embroiled in an intense conversation with four other women—three Lucky didn't recognize, and one she did. While the group wasn't yelling exactly, they were exceedingly loud. Indoor voices need not apply kind of loud. But when Maverick announced their arrival with a subdued "Hey," it was like all the sound was snatched from the room. Pin-drop quiet in an instant.

Lucky felt them staring at her, itching under her skin and begging to be read. This was why she never went to parties anymore. She wanted it to be a good, happy day, but *wow*. Things were off to a rough start for her.

Everyone in the group had similar features, perks of a strong gene pool, but different senses of style. Track suits, sundresses, jeans and blouses, nothing in common other than the color. They all wore a shade of cream, same as his dad.

Maverick was also wearing a cream-colored sweater and dark jeans. And Rebel looked adorable in her cream-and-brown polka-dot dress. Matching pajamas on Christmas must have been a year-round affair. Any holiday, any party, anytime.

"Everyone, this is Lucky, Lucky, this is everyone. Okay, that's done, we'll be elsewhere, see you later."

Lucky followed Maverick's lead as he abruptly turned around, attempting to whisk her away.

"*Aht, aht!* Get back here." Mrs. Beverly Phillips, in the tracksuit, playfully swatted him on the shoulder. "What's wrong with you?"

"Fight or flight kicked in."

"Don't start with me." Her patient face nearly frowned but smoothed into the friendliest, most welcoming smile as she turned to Lucky. "I've heard so much about you. Let me get a good look at you." She deftly pushed Maverick out of the way, stepping into his place and taking Lucky's hands. She held their arms out wide, assessing her up and down.

Mrs. Phillips took pride in her appearance. The fitted athleisure tracksuit somehow didn't clash with the matching jewelry set she wore—earrings, necklace, bracelet, and ring—or the soft makeup with dramatic eyelashes and blushing lipstick. The muted tones of her perfume settled nicely around her.

No other surface emotions seeped through.

Unsure what to do, Lucky became a mannequin, mirroring her movements. Was this normal? Mr. Phillips had barely glanced at her. Maybe Mrs. Phillips was in charge. Her word determined whether Lucky would be accepted by the family at large.

Maverick caught the exact moment she looked his way for reassurance. *Roll with it*, he mouthed.

Finally, Mrs. Phillips said, "Maverick, what is this?"

"What?"

What? Lucky's stomach dropped.

"What is she wearing? Family wears cream and one accent color. I'm assuming you didn't tell her."

"Didn't want to scare her off," he confirmed.

"Well, now it's going to *throw* off all of the pictures."

She . . . she'd get to be in the pictures?

"Should've known. I'll take her up." Maverick's youngest sister, Silvia, walked into the dining room and headed straight for Lucky. She exuded a bored, sleepy energy. Even her voice sounded relaxed, slightly muffled and unaffected. She had naturally down-turned eyes with dark circles but otherwise was very much identifiable as a Phillips.

"Don't worry about a thing, sweetheart. You're in good hands now," Mrs. Phillips said.

Lucky rolled with it like he asked her to, following Silvia upstairs to a good-sized bedroom with a walk-in closet. The bed had been neatly made with decorative pillows and a throw blanket at the bottom. Nothing seemed out of place or dusty. There were even vacuum pattern lines in the carpet.

"What size are you?" Silvia asked.

Lucky told her. "Do I really have to change?"

"You don't have to, no, but it would make my mom happy. What do you want to do?"

"I . . . don't know."

Normally, Lucky would've thrown herself into the role, being the best and brightest girlfriend, winning over his entire family one observant joke and practiced dizzying smile at a time. But communing with Hennessee's specters to gain access to the house itself had been sucking the life out of her. She'd built herself up to be charming, and now passing for pleasant felt brutal.

This was a big deal for Maverick. She wanted his family to like her, but she only had the capacity to be herself. And her real self was . . . sad.

Sad because it'd only been fifteen minutes and she could imagine the road ahead. Spending time with a loving family, who enjoyed being together, used endearing nicknames, threw parties, and took color-coordinated pictures. Maverick invited her into his world, and she didn't have a single equivalent thing to share in return.

Just sad and sorry and obsessively thinking about her estranged family.

Lucky took off her glasses.

Silvia was filled with an authentic kindness that ran so deep the sheer power of her compassion overwhelmed her. She cried easily. Her feelings bruised regularly. Profoundly sensitive and loving, she protected herself with a cloak of ambivalence.

Silvia smirked. "You're not supposed to do that."

"Do what?"

"Take your glasses off. Maverick made us swear to not ask you about them because you were going to wear them all day."

She nodded. "That's usually true. Did he tell you why I wear them?"

"No. He said you'd tell us when you were ready but that wouldn't be today."

Meaning Maverick expected Lucky to see them again. His invitation hadn't been a rash, last-minute decision. He'd not only told them about her, but he also made sure they'd respect the accommodations she needed. How could one person be so thoughtful all the time?

"I feel like you're overthinking this," Silvia continued. "It's not a *wear the shirt or we kick you out* type mess, all right? Maverick said he wants you in the picture so you're in it either way." She returned to the closet, rummaging around. "My brother is extremely fucking private. My mom started crying when he asked to invite you and the fact that you're here at all is a miracle. This should work." She held up a cream-and-blue cardigan.

The hem stopped near Lucky's thighs and the sleeves extended past her hands if she didn't push them up. It swallowed her whole, but somehow still managed to look good. Slouchy but fashionable.

"I'm not gonna tell you his business because I don't know what he's told you and it's not my place, but like"—Silvia grasped at the air for the words—"I know we look like one big happy family and it's kind of intimidating to outsiders, but we have issues too. For me. My experience"—she paused again—"I'm the youngest. I didn't see my brother for long stretches of time because he didn't want to be around our parents. All I want is for him to be happy. If you can do that, I'll take a bullet for you, honestly."

"I don't think anyone plans to shoot me. You should be safe," she said. "I have a type of ESP. That's why I wear the glasses. They help block my ability."

"Okay. No idea what that means."

"It means thank you for being kind to me."

Maverick pictured having Lucky in his life long-term. If that's what he wanted, she'd do her best to make it happen because she wanted it too. She'd approach his family one person at a time, getting to know them at her own pace. Exactly as she had with the *Caretaker* production team. She did it once, and she could do it again.

Lucky focused on Silvia's eyes. "Your empathy makes you soft in a way you hate because it hurts so much, but it's one of the best things about you. Without knowing I needed help, you knew I needed help. That's why you volunteered to bring me up here before anyone else could. You feel like it's your job to keep the peace in the family, so you do this often. You're very good at it, but don't forget to tell others what you need too. Be careful to not hold your feelings too tightly to your chest because they'll only turn inward."

"I—what?"

Lucky slipped her glasses back on. "Also, you're Maverick's favorite sibling."

28

Properly dressed and finally feeling ready, Lucky was immediately swept into the heart of the party.

Maverick stayed by her side as they mingled with guests. She began keeping tally every time she heard *Maverick? Girlfriend?* or some other variation with the same vibe. He apparently had a reputation as a perpetual bachelor and they'd all lost hope.

"Why do they all care so much that you were single for so long?" she whispered to him, after meeting the fourth auntie in a row.

"Because I have a kid. They've been after me for years to settle down for Rebel's sake. They swear up and down she's going to turn into a tomboy."

"So what if she does? It's her choice."

"That's what I said." He grinned. "Never mind the fact that she gets mad anytime I even suggest she shouldn't wear a dress."

"Rebel knows who she is," Lucky said, nodding. "She figured it out early."

Maverick looked confused for a moment and then kissed her temple quickly. She didn't miss his slightly strained smile or that it disappeared by the time he looked at her again.

"Hey." Freddie appeared beside them, lightly punching Maverick in the shoulder. "They need help putting the food out."

"Then go help them."

"They asked for you. And her. Hey." Freddie was Maverick's height but larger. He had the breadth, stance, and energy of a linebacker. Fitting as he played football all his life until he graduated college with a degree in kinesiology. He recently transitioned to becoming the assistant coach at the same school.

"Hi."

"I don't know how you two met, but you're too good for him. Run while you can."

"I'm fine where I am." She smiled sweetly, voice playfully firm. "Thank you, though."

Freddie cocked a curious eyebrow, measuring her up and deciding his next move.

"Don't try her," Maverick warned. "She's quick."

Freddie considered it for a few more seconds before bowing out. "Kitchen," he repeated as a parting.

"He'll be back," Maverick said as they walked. "Try not to stun him too bad."

She laughed. "For you? I'll consider it."

The kitchen smelled wonderful—filled with the kinds of homemade food Lucky hadn't eaten in years. Steaming rolls fresh out the oven, spicy collard greens, buttery corn cobs sprinkled with salt and pepper, proper potato salad, decadent macaroni and cheese, heavenly candied yams, and more.

She asked, "Is there spaghetti too?"

"Yeah," Maverick said. "Pretty sure there is. Why?"

Lucky had to stop herself from drooling. She hoped this would happen. Every family was different with their own traditions and staple foods, but somehow most Black American families all followed the same cookout blueprint. She couldn't *wait* to *eat*.

Mrs. Phillips instructed Maverick to start carrying the large aluminum pans wrapped in foil to the backyard. Silvia had been assigned to do the same and they walked out together.

"Lucky, here, please." Mrs. Phillips waved her over. "How are you with cakes?"

"Um, fine?"

"That yellow one over there still needs to be frosted. Use the chocolate buttercream and knife next to it."

Lucky washed her hands and got to work, smoothing a generous layer on top. She used an *S*-pattern like she'd been taught. Whenever her mom was in the mood to bake, it'd been Reggie's job to pick the recipe and help with mixing, and Lucky's job to decorate. She was allowed to do whatever she wanted, in any style, using any flavor, with extras like sprinkles and coconut shavings. They always had taste-testing parties after dinner, eating as much as they wanted.

It was easy to overlook those cherished good memories when they were tragically outnumbered by the bad. But they existed too. They happened.

"Wonderful," Mrs. Phillips said when Lucky finished. "Carry it outside for me?"

Lucky did as requested, and spotted Maverick entertaining Rebel and the other kids. He was carrying a little girl with bright pink pom-poms around her pigtails on his back—he'd called her his Beanie Baby earlier. She suddenly understood *and* felt sorry for those suburban moms.

"Super Dad strikes again. He always makes it look so easy." Georgia appeared out of nowhere, holding what smelled like a very strong drink in a red cup. "Being around him upsets my ovaries."

"How much have you had to drink?"

"A decent amount. This is my last one." She bumped Lucky's shoulder. "How are you doing? How's your face? Any accidents?"

"Nope. Everyone's been really nice." She told her what Silvia said.

"Of course, he did that." Georgia grinned. "Super Dad always has a plan."

When Mr. Phillips announced it was time to eat, they all lined up to make their plates. The spread had been set up buffet-style and Lucky made two plates because that was all she could reasonably carry in one trip. She sat picnic-style with Maverick and the kids in a big cluster on the grass.

After demolishing her first serving, she went back for seconds and again for dessert. One of the uncles tried to be sly, saying to Maverick, "She's sure got an appetite."

Lucky answered, "Sure do!" loud and clear. She had every intention of eating until she couldn't breathe, and no one was gonna shame her about it. By the time she finished, everyone else was watching all the grandkids open summer presents—another Phillips tradition.

Suddenly deserted, Lucky leaned her head against Maverick's shoulder and sighed.

He wrapped an arm around her, pulling her close. "Happy?"

"Very," she said. "Thank you for inviting me."

Choosing to give up her family had also meant cutting herself off from large swaths of her culture. Traditions. Recipes. Family functions. The internet—reading posts and watching videos and laughing at inside jokes—helped fill some of the void but not all. Being with Maverick had the potential to give those things back to her.

"I'm glad you're here." He kissed the top of her forehead as a slight phantom summer wind blew through the backyard.

An unpleasant smell tickled the inside of Lucky's nose. "*Ugh.*" She straightened up, scanning the party guests for the cause of the stench. Someone had a rotting core.

"What's wrong?" Maverick asked.

Unlike Xander, who'd been able to embrace the grief that altered him, rot was the result of change attempting to destroy everything in its wake.

Lucky whipped off her glasses.

"What are you doing?" Maverick asked, alarmed.

"Wait wait wait give me a second." She wouldn't need to look at their eyes to find them. They were too far gone. She'd sense it—there. The stench intensified as she observed a short man wearing a black hat speaking with three other gentlemen off to the side. She scrunched her nose. "Who is that?"

"Uhh, one of my dad's coworkers, I think? I'm not sure."

"Remember how I told you people don't really change? I was generalizing. That's not entirely accurate. Significant events can change a person's core." She sniffed again—definitely him—made a face, and put her sunglasses back on. "He's *rotting*. I can *smell* it."

Maverick wordlessly stood up and held out his hand to help her. He guided her toward a secluded bench on the other side of the backyard. "Better?" He waved at the air in front of her face as if that would clear the smell.

She had no choice but to kiss him. "Yes, thank you," she lied. As long as the man was near her, she'd smell it.

"Okay," he said, nodding and rubbing the tops of her arms. "What did you mean by rotting?"

"Let me start at the beginning: changes to a core resemble tree rings or vinyl records. Each groove is pressed with recorded information." She paused to make sure he was following. "Like I said, change comes from significant events. Unmanageable grief is a big one, same as childbirth or becoming a parent. And then, there are some things that can cause what I named *rot*. Because they're rotting from the inside."

Maverick's expression was curiously neutral so . . . she kept explaining.

"I smell it while it's happening. The rot spreads until their core decays, turns to dust, and then there's nothing left to read. I'll feel that a core used to be there, but that's it," she said. "Not all people like that are dangerous but all dangerous people are like that. I won't know which one he is unless I read him while I still can."

"I don't think that's a good idea. We'll just keep you away from him. It'll be fine." That same strained smile from earlier reappeared again, making Lucky's stomach drop. "I didn't know you could do that."

"Surprise," she said with a weak smile. Maverick must not have wanted her to read that man because then he might have to tell his parents, and that'd require telling them the truth about his weird-ass girlfriend with ESP and ruining everything.

"Does anything *else* have a smell?" The tone he used was

unfamiliar enough to make her frown. Not quite irritated or even frustrated, but everything wasn't okay.

Lucky worried at her hands. "Sometimes intentions can. Depends on what they are. I think I can also smell Hennessee House."

"The house? *Specifically?*" He seemed surprised. "Since when?"

"Since the beginning." Lucky wasn't sure if she should tell him more. It'd only been a few days since she realized it herself while making her daily self-tape and recapping Maverick's visit. He seemed a bit shaken but asked, "It's the peppermint, isn't it?"

"I figured it out because you brought me coffee." She nodded. "On my second day, while you talked to Rebel on the porch, I smelled cinnamon first—my favorite cinnamon latte was my initial scent, like how my perfume is yours. I really didn't have a memory associated with peppermint until it accidentally gave me one."

Maverick's reluctance was written all over him—his tense jaw, furrowed brow, the concerned look in his eyes. He wanted to know but also desperately didn't. "How did it do that?" He spoke quickly as if he were trying to bite back the sentence while it left him.

"I think the house lost the synesthesia battle." Lucky kissed the tip of his nose to illustrate her point. She wished she had the ability to calm him, to cover and soothe his worries with her assuredness. Kisses would have to do. "When it tried to make me smell cinnamon the second time, my ability automatically kicked in. It recognized the house's intentions and decided to classify it, but my brain couldn't really handle them both being active at the same time. That's why it hurt so bad—I overloaded."

"Same as Eunice." Remembrance sparked behind his eyes.

Lucky had overloaded *twice*. Her reaction during the readings had been substantially worse, but both were symptoms of the same root cause—she *was* clashing with Hennessee too.

"But it's different for me—listen," she said quickly. "Exhaust fumes means rot. Spoiled meat means dangerous. Sawdust means harmless. Peppermint means Hennessee is up to something." She smiled, wistful and overjoyed to share her discoveries with some-one she trusted. "I think that also explains why I haven't smelled cinnamon again. I can't anymore. My ability overpowers it every time. Interacting with the house is making me stronger."

That admission had officially stressed Maverick the hell out. He opened his mouth, silently closed it, and shook his head. At a complete loss for words, he stared at the ground with his arms crossed over his chest.

"I'm sorry," she whispered.

Her feeble apology seemed to snap him out of it. He exhaled and took her hand as they sat down on the bench. She angled her body toward him, ready to listen to whatever he had to say. Be-cause something was definitely coming. She braced herself for the worst, hoped for the best, and prayed she didn't ruin the day by being too weird.

"You don't ever have to apologize for who you are. Not with me," he said with sincerity. "It's just I, uh, put some precautions in place for today."

"I heard."

He laughed lightly, then looked at her. "But this isn't some-thing you can turn off for a day to relax. It's never going to be 'just work' for you. You can't clock out or quit or walk away. It's a part of your life, all the time, forever."

He spoke to her but she sensed the words were for himself. He was trying—she could *see* him trying to accept it. Her.

"As far as I know." She shrugged, biting her lip. "Yeah."

"Okay." He nodded, squeezing her hand. "Why did you decide to read and translate for Silvia?"

"I was sad."

"Does reading people make you feel better?"

"No, but being myself does," she said. "I've never liked hiding who I am. I did it—*I do it* because I always think I have to. I didn't want to meet your family stuck in that mindset. It was important to me to not be that way for once."

"And I was trying to do the opposite. You seemed nervous about meeting my parents. I didn't want you to have to worry about *anything*." He opened his arms, gesturing for her to come to him. "We really should've talked about this beforehand."

"Lesson learned." She fell into him, holding on as tightly as she could. His scent pierced through the rot, precise and clean, overtaking and then blocking it.

"I fully support you being yourself at all times, but you should know you freaked Silvia out. Her reaction was a lot like Georgia's when you translated for Rebel except funnier," he said. "I told her you're open to questions. I'm sure she'll talk to you soon."

"She loves you."

"I know. She also talks too much."

Lucky wished there was a way to stay inside this moment Maverick made for them, but she knew they wouldn't be alone for long. She kissed him as if they'd never be interrupted anyway—both insistent and languid until time meant nothing.

They thankfully heard Rebel before they saw her.

"Dad, why are you all the way back here?" Rebel and Beanie approached the bench. "I've been looking for you *everywhere*."

Maverick and Lucky had separated, but still sat close together. "Sorry. We needed a minute to talk about something important. What's up?"

Annoyed Rebel was quite the sight. She glared at him, standing closer to Lucky as if she'd be expected to choose a side.

"Uncle Maverick?" Beanie chewed on her ragged cuticles.

Maverick gently guided her to stop, holding her hands. "Yes, my Beanie Baby."

She giggled. "Can Rebel stay at my house tonight? My dad will say yes."

"Do you want to do that?"

Rebel nodded. "Jinx wants to sleep over too."

"Ah, so it's a slumber party," he said. "Where's Uncle Max?"

"I'll go get him." Beanie ran off with Rebel following.

"That's nice." Lucky asked, "Does that happen often?"

"Nope." He shook his head. "I think they made a plan. They're trying to trick one of us into saying yes to use as proof that it's okay, so we'll all say yes. Notice how Rebel said Jinx wants to sleep over, not that she is."

"And 'my dad will say yes.' Genius—not a single lie in sight."

"They're very good, but I'm better." He smirked. "I'm actually really happy they all get along so well. I love it."

Silvia said Maverick stopped coming around them, long enough for it to have a significant impact on her. He must've kept Rebel away too—she was only a year older than Beanie.

"Silvia told me you moved out and didn't come back for a while. Why did you leave them?"

"My parents. I got tired of being criticized all the time.

Nothing I did was good enough for them," he said. "So, I packed my stuff, took my baby with me, and left."

"But you went back."

"I don't think I planned to stay away forever. I didn't have much of a plan at all, to be honest."

Five hundred dollars. He'd said he started writing because he needed a second job that wouldn't force him to sacrifice spending time with Rebel. His family obviously had money and loved him. If he asked, they would've helped—with strings attached. That must've been so hard on him. She wanted to ask what happened to Rebecca but couldn't bring herself to do it.

Max arrived, looking very much like Maverick's double except noticeably older. His hair had begun to go gray at the temples and in his full beard. "You need me to watch Rebel for the night?"

"No, they're trying to have a slumber party. You're the dad of choice."

"It's 'cause of the dog." He turned to Lucky. "I got my kids a puppy for their birthday. They're obsessed with it." Beanie and Jeremy were his fraternal nine-year-old twins.

Maverick added, "Rebel was distraught for a week that I wouldn't get her a pet too."

"I'm fine with it if you are," Max said. "Pick her up around eleven tomorrow? Will that work?"

"Fine with me. Thanks, man."

Once they were alone again, Lucky traced a delicate line down Maverick's neck to the middle of his back. She kissed his shoulder before resting her chin on it.

"What about you?" he asked.

"Hmm?"

"Do you want to have a slumber party too? I had a sudden opening in my schedule tonight."

"I don't think I'm supposed to."

They held each other's gaze.

"I don't think so either."

His hand tightened on her knee—an interesting contrast to the small, delicate circles his thumb made on her thigh. She closed the distance between them with a quick kiss.

"Will you come to Hennessee?"

His eyes tightened in discomfort. "I can't sleep there."

She felt like she needed a break. To reset her priorities and get back in tune with her objectives. One night away wouldn't hurt anything.

"Can we stop at the store before we go to your place?"

29

In the moment, Lucky might not have fully considered what spending the night at Maverick's house would entail.

Her boyfriend asked. She said yes. And now she was standing like an awkward penguin in the middle of his kitchen while he prepped the counter to make donuts.

"What's wrong?" he asked over his shoulder. "This should be easy for you."

"I don't cook. I perfect making other people's recipes and re-use them until the family's kids want something new. Then I learn some more."

Maverick smiled against her lips as his arms slid around her waist. "Ah, your secret revealed." He almost always smiled right before he kissed her. "What is it?"

She rested her forehead against his. "Nothing."

"I know when you're upset. Tell me."

She grabbed loose fistfuls of his shirt to keep herself in the moment. "I'm not sure what I'm supposed to be doing."

"About?"

"Right now. I've been trying to figure out what we're doing, and I can't."

He pulled back in confusion. "You don't want to make donuts?"

"I do. That's . . . fine. But we're here. Alone. For once. With nowhere to go. And you're not—" She took a breath. "I'm asexual."

His eyebrows shot up. "Uh. Okay."

"I don't always read situations like this correctly. I'm not sure if you're waiting for me to make the first move or if I'm supposed to be forward and do it or if you don't want to at all. We don't have to. I just—I don't like feeling confused about this."

"Okay. I hear you," he said. "So, did *I* do something to make you confused?"

She sighed. "Please don't get mad at me because I didn't pick up on sexy time signals or whatever. You have to tell me. I know that's not hot or even romantic, but that's what works for me. I'm sorry."

"Don't apologize." He rubbed her cheek with the back of his hand. "I would never get mad at you for that. I take it that's happened before?"

She nodded, unable to look at him. She used to have sex with her ex-boyfriend Louis whenever he wanted. Whether she enjoyed it was as predictable as a coin toss. Not that he cared. But that still wasn't enough because *she* never brought it up or initiated it, which he said was "really weird."

So, Lucky did what she always did and researched. Turns out, she wasn't weird—she was asexual. And she began to suspect she didn't like Louis as much as she had convinced herself she had.

Maverick gently raised her chin. "Donuts aren't a code for anything. I need to use the dough before it goes bad. I figured we would make them, relax, maybe watch a movie, and then go from there. That's honestly as far as I got. I didn't invite you here to necessarily have sex. My only goal was to spend time with you."

She almost always kissed him as fast and desperate as she felt.

So, they made donuts. He stood behind her as he taught her how, guiding her hands with his as they rolled the dough, cut them into near-perfect shapes, and mixed the filling while they proofed. His kitchen filled with the smell of the warm oil, the crackling bubble of the dough frying, the sweet cinnamon sugar they dusted on top. Her favorite.

Afterward, they settled on the couch wrapped in a blanket. He reclined backward, one leg up and the other bent at the knee, his foot on the floor. She nestled half on top of him, half squeezed into the sliver of space between him and the couch. His arm curved around her back, holding her firmly against him. Every few minutes, he'd kiss the top of her forehead and she nuzzled his jaw in return. Perfectly warm. Perfectly happy.

"That's what you wanted to tell me in the tree house, wasn't it?" He shifted to look at her.

She smiled from the feeling of his voice vibrating in his chest. It'd been so, so long since she'd been close enough to experience it like this. "Yeah."

"That makes sense. Explains a lot."

It took some effort, but she managed to roll over, lying on top of him. He moved with her, hands holding her steady at the hip.

"Do you want to talk about it?" She traced the curve at the hollow of his throat with nimble fingers.

He inhaled sharply in response but said nothing, gaze fixed on her face.

"It's okay to ask me. About anything. I don't mind."

He captured her fingers suddenly and held them in place against his chest. She caught the barest hint of frustration in his expression before it faded.

"It'd be helpful, for me, if you told me whether or not you wanted to."

"What do you want?" he asked.

"I want to know what you want so I can start processing the idea."

"Processing." He laughed, chest rumbling beneath her, but he stopped abruptly. "Wait . . . you're serious?"

Lucky nodded. She hated feeling ignorant. She wanted to be informed and confident in her choices. So, she'd taken Georgia's advice, which led to her researching how to approach a partner about sex. She'd get it right this time.

"I don't handle spontaneous well. I know that's a big turn-on for some people, so I need to mentally prepare for that kind of thing. My libido is also on the lower side. I don't think about sex often, if at all, and I really don't like being surprised." She scrunched her nose, completely comfortable with him. "Now, I know that might make me sound boring, but I promise having sex won't be."

"It won't." He traded the last bits of his smile for a furrowed brow.

"Nope. I'd like to think I'm pretty good at it."

"I see."

She kissed his chin and kept smiling. She'd learned the most important behavioral parts of sexual negotiations were smiling and eye contact. She also needed to be firm but not inflexible. Give-and-take and compromise were crucial to setting boundaries. She wanted Maverick. She wanted to make this work.

So why wasn't it working? Maverick was *frowning*.

"Was that too nerdy? I'm sorry," she whispered.

He frowned harder. "For what?"

"Ruining the mood by talking too much. But if I don't ask, then—"

"You haven't ruined anything." He paused. "I'm . . . processing. I'm not sure if having sex is a good idea."

"Oh, you don't want to."

He shook his head. "That's not what I said."

"You don't want to . . . with me?"

"It's not that I don't want to—"

"Did I do something wrong?"

"Nope, no, you didn't. No." He laughed nervously. "I feel like you're spinning out here and that's not where I'm going. I'll explain. I need a second." He raised one of her hands to his mouth, kissing her knuckles and then her palm.

She pressed her lips together to keep quiet. He let her get everything she wanted to say out into the open and she'd do the same for him. No interruptions. No assumptions.

"You know me," he began quietly. "You called me cautious. I can see how you might interpret my . . . *self-control* for something it isn't. You're so affectionate, and I love that about you. I can't stress that enough—love it. Okay?"

She nodded enthusiastically. "I love that about you too."

"Okay." He bit his lower lip, dragging it through his teeth before continuing. "I feel like you might be sensitive about this, but I don't know how else to explain it."

"Tell me. It's okay." She braced herself for impact.

He took a deep breath. "I don't think we're on the same wavelength. I mean, look how we're laying—it's obvious that I'm the only one struggling right now."

"Oh, shit." She instantly reeled backward, using the back of the couch to sit up. How could she be so selfishly oblivious? She was literally laying between his legs on top of him. *Of course*, he was having a hard time.

But he sat up just as quickly, pulling her back to him. "No, don't go, please. Don't leave."

He pulled her into his lap, at presumably a better angle, holding her against his chest again. She curled her arms under his, placing her hands on his shoulders and doing her best to hide her face.

Faking attraction wasn't hard when the other person didn't see you clearly.

Lucky learned to be a mirror. People saw what they wanted. Their desires reflected.

But Maverick saw through her like a window. She chose to let him see who she was. He chose to see her beyond his needs.

"If I start crying, no, I didn't." He was so, so good to her.

"Okay." He rubbed her back, smooth, gentle circles.

"This is so strange. I worked so hard learning all the rules and taking the time to figure out how to make them work for me." She started giggling. "No one's ever rejected my sexual advances before."

His reluctant laugh made her look at him. "I didn't reject you."

"I know," she said softly. "Thank you for showing me how much you really do see me. I said no one did, and here you are, proving me wrong—wow, you're really wrecking my ego tonight."

"I told you—you don't know everything."

"And you hit me with the *I told you so*?" Lucky was saved from further humbling by her phone chirping across the room.

"What is that?" he asked.

"I chose the most annoying sound possible for Hennessee's motion detector alarm. Otherwise, I won't look at it." She regretfully untangled herself from him. The orchard had frequent visitors like possums and raccoons. More so now that Gengar wasn't constantly patrolling his territory. "Oh, shit."

"Everything okay?" He turned off the TV and was folding the blanket.

"Yeah. Raccoons."

She also had seven missed calls from the unknown caller. In Springstop, the calls became so frequent she tuned them out until she copied the times on her spreadsheet for analysis. And then . . . Maverick happened. She'd been so preoccupied by him that she'd forgotten all about them.

According to the call log, before today, the last call was a few hours before she returned to Hennessee House. Nothing in between then and now—the night she skipped curfew.

Interesting.

The screen changed, signaling an incoming call. "Hello?"

Low-grade static sounded through the phone. She held it slightly away from her ear, purposefully turning her back to Maverick. The noise continued with the addition of clicking every three seconds.

Maverick's hand on her lower back made her hang up. "Come on."

They'd stopped at the store to get the toiletries she preferred, but he let her borrow one of his shirts for bed. She walked out of the guest bathroom post-shower wearing it, holding it to her nose and sniffing.

"Are you checking if it's clean?"

"No." She snorted. "It smells like you." She kissed him, then buried her face in his neck, inhaling to make him laugh.

"You're ridiculous."

"Stop smelling so good, then." She walked to the bed. "Which side do you normally sleep on?"

"The middle."

"Perfect. You can curl around me on either side. I prefer being the little spoon."

"Somehow, I knew that."

Lucky was under Maverick's covers in record time, turning her back to him. As instructed, he curved his body around her, sliding one arm across her chest, holding her close just under her breasts. He kissed the back of her neck before she felt their shared pillow dip when he relaxed. She bided her time by counting his breaths before rolling over to face him. "Maverick."

"Lucky." He was already smiling, clearly amused. He was also topless.

On a scale of one to ten, he broke it because he was the most beautiful man she'd ever seen. She touched his arm, loving the smooth texture of his skin and the way it hugged his muscles. "So, how do you like to be touched?"

"You're doing just fine." He kissed her once and had her in the palm of his hand.

"If you need to—"

"See, that's it though. If *I* need to." He propped himself up on his elbow. "I appreciate what you're trying to do but that isn't what I need. It's not that simple."

"I don't understand."

"I know you don't." His gaze dropped to the sheets, but she wasn't going to let him run away from her. They'd come too far. She pressed her forehead against his, making him look at her. His eyes burned with conflict, seeming even darker.

"Explain it to me."

"I already know it'll make you feel bad. It's not your fault and I don't want you thinking it is."

"Noted," she said. "Tell me anyway."

He caressed her cheek, across her jaw, and down the lines of her neck. She fought to keep her breathing even. It might not have been sexual, but his touch absolutely did something to her. She felt those sensations in vivid detail, every blissful second as he moved across her skin.

No one had ever made her feel that way. No one had ever held her so delicately in their hands that if they were to crush her, she'd come back for more. But he would never do that to her. Because he proved how precious she was to him.

Maybe that was it. The inherent safety in his touch had irrevocably changed her.

"In my dreams, you always talk in riddles," he began. "Everything you say is designed to torment me. You're not even supposed to be there. I dream about monsters and phantoms, demons and misery, worlds with no rules other than pain. I've made my way through, taking what I want, controlling what I can't for years, and now suddenly there's you. Deep in the heart of me every night."

The ferocity in his eyes left her breathless. Mesmerized—no better word for the control he had over her in that moment.

"I can't write about you. Every night I hope you're there so I'll have another chance to figure out how your dream story will end. Because when I'm awake I think about you too much, too often. I can't stop. I'm so desperate for you it's shameful. Every part of me is overpowered by you all the time. I hide it because I don't understand how this happened. I can't write about you. I can't make sense of it."

Lucky grinned. "That's why you said you wanted to see where this goes. How long have you been dreaming about me?" she teased.

He bit his lip. "You know me, and I see you. I don't want to feel your indifference. I can't because I think it'll break me."

She exhaled a delicate laugh. "If I wasn't okay with having sex, please trust me when I say I would have *never* offered. I would've gone out of my way to avoid even talking about it. Wanting you to clue me in doesn't mean I'm *indifferent*."

"The way you keep talking about it makes it seem like that's exactly what'll happen. Your whole focus is on me. Like, you need me to ask because it's some obligation you've convinced yourself you need to fulfill," he said, disbelief on full display. "I have never once brought up sex. You're the one who keeps doing it."

"Because I know *you're* thinking about it and trying to hide it. And it's not an obligation. It's . . . kindness?"

"No, it isn't." His smile had almost returned.

"It's . . . it's . . . understanding?"

"It's *you*, pretending. That's the word you're looking for."

"Well, if I'm pretending, then so are you," she challenged. They needed to have an agreement in place that they could both be happy with. They needed to decide together, openly and honestly. Didn't he understand that? "Pretending you're 'fine' isn't going to do either of us any good. You can't surprise me with this later on. I need you to tell me if this is something important to you because I honestly feel like it is. All my cards are on the table, and you can barely match my honesty."

"Because I only have one card." Maverick hesitated. "I *want* you to want me as desperately as I want you."

"You think I don't want you?" She climbed onto his lap, placing her hands on his shoulders. "I want you to listen to me very carefully. I'm going to speak slowly to ensure you understand every word. No, I don't have a well of unbridled passion to pull from. It's never going to feel like that so make your peace with it now."

"Lucky—"

"Do not interrupt me." She kissed him long enough to make her point. "Do you have any idea how hard all of this has been for me? I have never been this vulnerable in my life. I've shared things with you I planned to take to my grave, alone and unloved. But you ruined that when you promised to keep me safe, because I believed you. I still believe you. I want you to be happy and I want to be the one who makes you happy. *Me.* I want you more than I have ever wanted *anyone*, but I will never sacrifice myself to do that. And now I know that you would never ask me to.

"I know you and you see me. I'm yours and you are mine. Any questions?"

His smile was as criminal as it was transcendent. "No, ma'am."

"Good." Lucky kissed him, as gently as she could manage while caressing the curve of his jaw. His hands finally left her hips to tentatively travel up the back of her shirt. The heat from his hands permeated her skin, reaching down to her muscles. Maintaining eye contact, she whispered against his lips, "Because you make me *feel* safe." She brushed her nose against his. "I want us to get to a place where you *feel* comfortable telling me what you need."

Lucky had told him everything, but she knew from his uncertain touches and hard-won smiles that he'd barely gotten started. Maverick wasn't where she was. Not yet.

30

Lucky felt like a teenager sneaking back into the house after a night out, hoping their parents wouldn't hear them skulking around, which was silly.

Until she made eye contact with Xander waiting for her in the sitting room.

"Hey, what are you doing here?" She smiled as if nothing were wrong. They never explicitly stated she couldn't go out. She hadn't technically broken any production rules. Semantically speaking, her conscience was clear.

His withering glare melted the smile clean off her face. He wasn't mad! He was disappointed! Infinitely worse!

"I can explain," she began.

"I know where you were. I'm perfectly capable of discerning why you were there," he said. "What I do not understand is why you believe it's acceptable not to perform your job as requested. Your presence is required in the house at night, every night. I granted you leave for an entire weekend. Was that not enough of a break?"

Lucky paused, deeply confused. His seething expression contrasted with his concerned tone. "Is that a rhetorical question or are you genuinely asking?"

He sighed. "Come sit down."

She sat on his right on the green velvet couch again.

"I've personally been monitoring your self-tapes daily. Initially, I began to believe the house had no intentions of presenting specters to you, and then you stupidly asked for them."

"Stupidity implies I made a mistake," she countered. "I move with intention inside this house."

He regarded her for a moment. "You're not afraid of them."

"They're not real. Hennessee can't use my brain against me. I thought it might be able to, but no."

"You expect me to believe you're not affected at all, whatsoever."

"I wouldn't go that far. The specters shocked the hell out of me at first." She laughed. "I'm honestly not afraid. But seeing them is . . . upsetting. Extremely upsetting." Her confession came out as a whisper.

"I suspected as much." He nodded. "That's why I instructed Maverick to stop you from following me. I didn't want to risk my experience influencing yours in any way."

"What does it make you see?"

"My stepmom. She asks me to follow her outside." A faraway look clouded his eyes. "We sit at the back of the orchard, and she wants to talk to me about new projects at work. Asks me when I'm going to get married. Wonders why I don't visit her more often."

"Your stepmom, is she . . ."

"She died about a year ago. I know that isn't her. She loved this house, more than the rest of us. I think that's why it uses her to upset me, as you put it."

So, they both saw family members. As did Bobbi, and even Eunice had heard her deceased mom. Was that enough to be considered a pattern? Damn, she really wished she knew what Brian had seen. "It wants something. I can't figure out what," she said, frowning. "What do you think? Any guesses?"

"I don't need to guess." He leveled her with a cool stare. "That's what I'm paying you to find out, isn't it?"

Lucky snorted. "No? I'm supposed to be the titular Caretaker slash Final Girl. You're only getting a two-for-one investigative special because it suits my agenda." She was only half-joking. "It's been my choice. *That* was the deal, right?"

His unexpected wry smile nearly sent her spiraling. "For someone so clever, I'm truly astonished you have yet to figure me out. I suppose the internet didn't provide after all."

"I've been busy," she admitted. "I haven't had time. You're not exactly my top priority, Xander."

"That's a shame," he muttered as he adjusted his gold cuff links. "*The Caretaker* had become troublesome and much bigger than we initially intended. Bobbi and Brian were fantastic on camera but ultimately ordinary. Eunice was exceptional but incompatible. After her departure I knew if we continued on the same path we'd end up with an endless parade of caretakers, never making it beyond three nights. I was venting to an associate during dinner when they mentioned your name. They forwarded an email you'd sent them soliciting private funding."

Lucky stared at him with a bewildered expression. "Which associate? Who shared my email?" Because 'an associate' told her less than nothing. She'd sent *hundreds* of emails over the past two years with her supernatural researcher résumé, begging for a chance. And money.

"Let's just say they're very *invested* in the progress you've made thus far," he said. "It didn't take long for me to find out more about your investigations and I didn't believe any of it. But"—he held up his index finger—"I had a feeling and I couldn't shake it. So, I instructed my employee, your contact, to leak the production information to you. I knew you would apply. And I knew if you could convince my team of your suitability for the show, that at some point we would end up right here."

Xander, the skeleton, searching—always searching. He'd found them all, just as Chase said.

Lucky almost didn't know what to say to any of that. She'd lied during her interview for nothing, but her pride wouldn't let him take credit for her initiative and work. "None of that means you hired me to investigate. I'm doing it on my own."

"Then let's change that," he said, holding her gaze with his determined hazel eyes. "Hennessee has reacted to you in ways it never has with me. You were as right as I was: you are perfect for this job, *specifically*. I need you here at night communicating with the house to find out more about it. I cannot do this without you.

"We'll renegotiate the contract to increase your pay. I'm sure you'll find my offer very generous. Whatever supplies or equipment you require are already yours. Your residence here will last for as long as you need with no interruptions, even if that exceeds your initial thirty days."

Holy shit. This was it. All her hard work had paid off because she officially had an investor on her side. An *investor* with resources who *believed* in her. She grabbed the back of the couch to steady herself.

"But what about the show?" She paused—two sentences in one breath was a bit too much for her overwhelmed state. "Are we still filming it?"

"That will continue as well, yes. Self-tapes every twelve hours, more if you can manage it. Any additional footage you record such as vlogging or incidents will be welcomed but not mandatory."

Lucky nodded. "Okay. Yeah. I—" *Breathe in. Breathe out.* "Thank you. Let's do it. I agree."

"Excellent," he said, looking away. He began staring out the front window. "There is, however, one more thing we need to discuss. I'm thrilled to see how happy Maverick has been of late. I have no issues with your relationship, but he distracts you. Severely so. I need you to separate from him for the time being."

"Excuse me?" She blinked at him, taken aback. "Separate *how*?"

"Physically." Xander turned back to her, expression neutral but immovable. "Maverick cannot come here, and you cannot go there for the duration of your investigation."

What in the Faustian bargain?

Lucky's chest felt tight. "Xander, you can't ask me to do that."

She and Maverick had already made plans. Early-afternoon Sunday dinner. Cheering for Rebel at her first swim meet. Shopping for birthday party decorations. A joint interview with a local medium who claimed to use psychography. A trip to the pier to go on a whale-watching boat tour. Gengar's follow-up vet appointment. Maverick's turn to take Rebel and Riley to the movies.

Xander at least seemed to understand the gravity of the situation he placed her in. "This is, and always will be, a voluntary project. Whether or not you accept is up to you."

LUCKY PACED THE length of her suite, from window to door and back again. She concentrated on her breathing, the feel of her phone in her hand, and the sun-warmed hardwood floor under her feet. Her center, her gut, had been thrown so far out of whack she didn't know if she'd ever find equilibrium again. Because it wasn't one side against the other—each side refused to let the other go. She wanted both. She had to have both.

"Maverick, hey."

"Hey," he answered. "I'm assuming you made it to the house okay?"

"I did. Sorry, I meant to text you when I got here, but I got sidetracked."

"Did the raccoons attack the garbage again?"

"Hopefully not. I haven't checked yet." She sank onto the bed, covering her eyes with her hand. "We need to talk."

"Uh-oh. That sounds serious." His nervous chuckle caught her off guard. "What could've possibly happened in two hours?"

Xander decided to make my dream come true and ruin my life all in the same breath. "We—I—" She clutched her stomach, doubling over. "I need to focus on Hennessee. I'm *so* close to figuring out its secrets—I can't spend time with you right now."

A loud *thud* temporarily jolted Lucky out of her misery. Her mason jar of purple flowers had fallen to the ground. Fortunately, it didn't shatter.

"Right now, as in today?"

The hope in his voice made her so lightheaded she felt faint. Her nearly full jar began to roll across the floor, leaving a trail of flowers as if it were bleeding.

"Right now, as in until I'm done. No more overnights or day trips or anything." She refused to call him a *distraction*. But until she finished her work there was only room for one central figure.

"Two weeks?"

"Or longer. Xander wants to expand the scope of the show. He's funding my research."

"So, I don't get to see you until you figure out—what? Why Hennessee House exists? That's ridiculous."

"I know. But this is my *dream*, Maverick. All my plans are out in the open *and* Xander is onboard. This is *huge* for me. I can't just walk away."

"You can. Finish your thirty days and leave. The job is to live in the house and walk away at the end. You're choosing to make it more than that."

"Because I can do this. I know I can. I'm not making this decision lightly," she said. "We're not breaking up. We're not even taking a break. It'll be like a long-distance relationship. We'll talk every day, just like before. Every morning—that doesn't have to change."

Maverick remained silent for several heartbeats. "What about nights?"

"That's when Hennessee is most active." She paused. "It's been showing me specters."

His harsh, stunned laughter slashed through her. "Why didn't you tell me?"

"I didn't want you to worry, because I'm not afraid. That's a large part of why we're expanding. The specters serve a specific purpose. I don't know what it is yet, but I'm going to find out."

"Setting aside not being able to see you, what about the risks? You'll be there alone. No one to back you up."

She shook her head as if he could see it. "I've worked and trained for this, exactly like that—on my own."

"What if something happens? What if you get in over your head or the house tricks you? That *house* put Eunice in the hospital, Lucky."

"Those are risks I'm willing to take."

That laughter again, undercut by fear and anxiety this time.

"I *believe* in myself. Maverick, *please*—I need you to believe in me too."

"I hate this," he said. "We're supposed to make decisions together and you're deciding for us. I don't agree with any of this. I believe in you, but I don't agree."

After their call Lucky ended up curled in the fetal position on her bed, simultaneously feeling elation and despair. Wallowing at its finest. She lay in that position so long, her hip began to hurt. Reluctantly, she rolled onto her other side and ended up facing the window. The sky had begun to transition to dark blue with clouds barely reflecting the light. Burnt oranges, deep reds, and brilliant yellow stacked together in a neat block as the sun began to set.

Hennessee's specters were coming.

One thought sliced through her wallowing—*not him*.

Not him. Not Maverick.

If Hennessee showed people the worst parts of their mind, if it *really* wanted to make her suffer, she knew in her heart it'd be Maverick now. It'd make him say all the terrible things she'd heard before from others. Because deep down, she knew she'd been waiting for him to say them too. Because eventually, everyone always did.

Abject fear gripped her instantly like icy fingers around her spine. If he . . . even knowing it wasn't real . . . it would *ruin* her.

She refused to let the house taint her memories of him.

Lucky sat up and closed her eyes to focus. The first night she saw specters she'd been obsessing over her estranged family. What would happen if she focused on them again? What if she banished all the thoughts of Maverick from her mind?

Reggie Reggie Reggie Reggie, she mentally chanted. She thought of how he used to push her on the swing at their apartment complex's play structure. How he patiently taught her how to play his video games with him. Waking up in the hospital to him asleep and holding her hand because she'd blacked out and hit her head on the ground. The journal they shared and the secret writing code they used so their parents couldn't read it. How she always helped him with homework by doing it for him. Cheering in the stands at his first basketball game only for him to ditch her afterward to hang out with his friends who didn't like his weird sister. The cruelest thing he'd ever said to her—her final straw and the reason she'd gone low contact.

Reggie, she thought. *I want to see Reggie.*

Lucky recalled his reading from deep in her archive. It was her most prized possession because she'd read him so young. Her ability was still developing and so was he, and they'd grown together.

Before she'd figured out her ring theory, she used to think of layered readings like candy because Reggie had always been so sweet. He personally had a soft six-year-old center, a crunchy ten-year-old middle, and a thirteen-year-old hard shell.

Reggie settled into being a dreamer with big lofty goals of greatness. But while his head was in the clouds, his feet were firmly planted on the ground—a rare combination meaning he had the potential to make things happen. Whatever he wanted, he'd find a way to get it.

Their dad dying changed him. He became more closed off to protect himself, pushing everyone away by any means necessary, never allowing himself to get close to anyone again as he gave in to his intense fears. Death couldn't hurt him again without love.

Naturally, Lucky had to be the first one to go. She knew that and held on for as long as she could anyway because it was *Reggie*.

When the specter knocked on her door, she held her breath as she opened it.

"Lucky Bug," Specter-Reggie said.

Experiment #1 / Status: Complete
Discovery #1: Confirmed

Hennessee allowed her to choose the form the specters took. Choose and despair.

31

As much as Lucky hated it, Xander had been right. She'd never admit to his unnaturally passive face that keeping Maverick contained, so to speak, was the right move. Not because she was distracted, but rather because her desire for him would be too strong for the house to ignore.

Inside Hennessee House from sunrise to sunrise with the exception of a few sleepy hours at dawn, Maverick didn't exist. She didn't think or talk about him. She archived his first impression and resisted indulging in any memories of him. If she felt herself slipping up, pining and yearning for him, she thought of a brick wall instead—something the house instantly picked up on.

No matter how much she focused on Reggie, she knew that if Hennessee figured out the truth it wouldn't hesitate to create Specter-Maverick.

"You've been keeping secrets," Specter-Reggie accused. They sat together, alone in the hallway. Gengar was strangely nowhere to be found. He was probably outside terrorizing the gophers that had recently moved into the backyard.

"Have I?" Lucky played clueless, as she had for several nights in row. Sometimes, she even imagined spray-painting words on her brick wall like—

"I know what you did last summer."

Lucky laughed. "I bet you do." Her days were increasingly depressing. She amused herself whenever she could.

But Specter-Reggie had an iron will, staying on target despite whatever curveballs she threw its way. "We always shared secrets. We could start another journal. Do you remember our code?"

"I remember, but you're mistaken. I shared secrets with Reggie. You're not him. Why are you pretending to be? How does it work?"

"Your life is miserable, but you won't do anything about it."

She sighed. "Is it? I hadn't noticed."

"That's your problem. Negativity. Bad energy. Nobody wants to be around that shit."

"I'm fully aware of that, thank you."

"You'll never change."

"People rarely do," she said. "But I am different now than when we first met. More myself."

Specter-Reggie's eyes brightened. "*How* are you different? Why?"

"There it is. You're becoming so predictable," she teased.

That had been a massive breakthrough—the house coveted information. More accurately put, conversation. Lucky noticed an immediate change when she stopped volunteering details about her life at present.

After gaining access to someone's mind, Hennessee House wanted to have a discussion because it simply didn't fully understand humans yet. But it wanted to, so much so that she felt confident in declaring that its primary driving force.

"Let's play a game," Lucky suggested. She sized up Specter-Reggie, quickly assessing her well-being. She had to perform multiple mental check-ins every session as a precaution.

Initially she'd anticipated an eventual desensitization to the specter process, but that hadn't happened yet! Seeing it hurt! Every night! She suspected Hennessee had a hand in manipulating the experience, ensuring it never lessened in intensity. As equally clever as it was cruel.

"How's my nephew?" Lucky asked.

"You're so stubborn."

"Interesting." She jotted down the reaction in her phone and scrolled to the list of follow-up questions she'd been using. The "game" involved seeing if Hennessee could keep up continuity across specters. So far, the answer was no. "How old is Reggie Junior? You gotta give me something."

Specter-Reggie rolled its eyes. "Always have to be the smartest person in the room."

"Very interesting."

It seemed incapable of using direct lies in its responses and it never responded to questions Lucky herself didn't have the answer to.

She truly didn't know if she had a nephew, therefore an answer wasn't possible. So, it pivoted to insults—words Reggie had indeed previously said to her. Hennessee seemingly lacked a moral compass, willing to say anything to provoke her into continued engagement.

"Does my nephew even exist?" she asked while consulting her phone again. "You claimed he did while using a different specter."

"Because you believed it."

Lucky did a double take, eyebrows shooting up. Oh, that was *new*. She didn't hate her family—of course, she wondered if she was an aunt and if she'd ever get to see Reggie's kids. But she'd never said that to her mom and vice versa. She never said it Reggie either.

Those thoughts were private. *Hers*.

Lying was out. Speculation, however, appeared to be permissible as long as the information came directly from her mind. Suddenly fired up, Lucky opened a new document to create a game to help break this new discovery down further.

"You're hopeless," Specter-Reggie said, drawing her attention. "You don't understand anything."

"Oh, but I will." She was running out of time.

Nearing sunrise, Specter-Reggie had begun to fade. Its face began to take on a tired look—eyes drooping and bleary, mouth relaxed, head bowed as it continued to watch her.

He became more transparent with each passing minute as she timed how long the disappearing act took. Whatever energy its existence used had limits. She suspected communicating with her for so long was draining for Hennessee. It wasn't used to this much attention, needing to rest and recharge too.

"Good night, Hennessee."

She watched as it struggled to reply, face pinching with determination before relaxing again. "Good night, Lucky Bug."

Hennessee House "slept" deepest in the first few hours around sunrise—completely dormant and unavailable to Lucky. It came back around ten a.m., tugging at her mind as if it'd been startled awake and instinctively reached out to confirm she hadn't left.

She suspected someone being there comforted the house,

because once assured, it returned to its dormant-reactive state until sunset.

Unfortunately, that tug also woke Lucky up. Every time.

"*Noooo,*" she groaned, regretfully rolling over into consciousness. Her phone was in her hand, hopes sky-high before she could stop them.

No missed calls. One text message from [Redacted].

"Damn it," she cried, plummeting into despair. "I hate *everything.*"

Gengar was awake and watching her—folded into bread-loaf mode at the foot of the bed.

"Not you," Lucky said to him. "I love you very much."

In between feeding Gengar and her breakfast self-tape session, Lucky liked to go on a daily walk around the neighborhood before it got too hot outside, to clear her head. Among other things.

Each house featured the kind of manufactured uniformity enforced by HOAs and there were at least two cars in every driveway—something big like a minivan or SUV paired with a sleek sports car, which was very telling.

Some of her temporary neighbors noticed her, pausing to point and whisper while watering their lawns, checking their mail, or power walking down the opposite sidewalk. She'd always thought neighbors in small communities like this were supposed to be nosy as hell, but no one dared to say anything to her until she beamed a sunny "Good morning!" at them as she passed by.

Lucky savored the warm air in her lungs and on her skin, the feel of her muscles stretching, and even the slight pain in her shins. She really needed to invest in a good pair of shoes sooner rather than later. But the best part of her walk? Finally allowing herself to think about Maverick.

[Redacted]: Good morning. Please let me know
you're okay.

She'd changed his contact entry to help her stay strong and even forbidden Xander from mentioning him during their meetings.

It'd be safe to talk to him at sunrise if he'd bother calling, but he hadn't, and it'd been *days*. Were text messages all she deserved now? She was so devastated she almost didn't respond the first time he checked in, but knew if she didn't, he'd be at the house within the hour.

She could break his heart seven ways from Sunday but let her be in danger. He'd come running to her rescue because that was the kind of person he was.

Blocking her thoughts about him from Hennessee House wasn't hard. He was too precious to her to fail.

This was hard—not knowing if he was ready to talk about things yet. She hated obsessing over it. She just . . . didn't understand how they'd gotten here. He *knew* how important her work was to her. He'd been worrying about her since day one and she'd proven she could handle herself. Why was staying a little bit longer suddenly an issue?

Restrictive clauses aside. She understood that part. That was all on her.

Lucky: I'm okay. Thank you for checking.

Maverick was in his feelings. He needed time. She just wished he would tell her how much.

She flipped her phone between her hands as she passed the neighborhood library. It had a fountain out front—the strong, nostalgic smell of its chlorinated water made her want to go swimming. She also wanted to call Georgia. But she worried she'd hallucinated the whole having a new friend thing.

Making friends had always felt like climbing an impossible mountain—every time she tried, harsh winds sent her stumbling back into a nerve-shredding and vomit-inducing free fall.

Initially, Lucky believed being rejected would be a singular occurrence. As the black sheep, her family didn't consciously band together to isolate her. It was groupthink. Easier to roll along and use her as the scapegoat for their own issues.

Then she attended college, where it happened again. Instead of a mother hen, warning her dorm mates about the boys with bad intentions at parties, she was a jealous cockblocker. The weird girl with the neat party trick was so *annoying* when she decided she wanted to be seen as a real person.

They weren't the problem—it was her. Lucky needed to change.

After graduation, she joined a neighborhood nanny clique and discovered how to convince people to like her. They gossiped, traded war stories, and covered shifts like real coworkers. None of them knew she spent her off days doing things like wandering around forests with alleged telepaths who made their names trying to solve cold cases. None of them knew she had ESP. She kept her two lives separate until one eclipsed the other.

But Georgia knew everything—and liked her anyway?! Impossible.

The line only rang twice before Georgia answered. "Hi, it's Lucky."

"Well, well, and it only took several days. Honestly, I'm impressed. I didn't think you'd work up the nerve."

Lucky snickered as she pressed the button for the crosswalk. She sensed the unspoken insecurity hiding behind Georgia's bravado. At least they were somewhat in the same boat. "When you said we were friends, did you mean the dinner and small talk kind of friends, or we call each for support kind of friends?"

"Those two things aren't mutually exclusive. I like dinner and constant contact. I suppose I can make an exception for you when it comes to talking on the phone. I'm not against it, but I will say hearing your voice strangely makes me want to see your face. Might have to switch to video." Georgia laughed. "I heard about you and Mav."

"Heard what exactly?" She frowned and then quickly smiled at the prancing mini pinscher sniffing her ankles as it walked by with its owner. *Good morning*, she mouthed to them.

"All of it. He tells me almost everything and Rebel fills in the rest." Lucky could practically hear Georgia's nonchalant shrug. "Oh, Silvia wants your number. Can I give it to her?"

"Why does she want it?"

"Why do you think?" Georgia scoffed. "You're her brother's girlfriend. She wants to get to know you. Really, Lucky, are you okay over there? Usually you're quicker than this."

"I'm—" She paused, deciding to head for the park to sit down for the rest of the call. "I feel like I'm going through a lot, and I would like to not be."

"Hmm, yeah. Xander played the role of wealthy benefactor in a soap opera quite well. It's a shame he doesn't date. I would've married him yesterday." Georgia snort-laughed. "For what it's worth, I'm with you. That man is magic—he always finds a way to give people exactly what they need but he does *not* help everyone. You've made it to the inner circle, babes. If Xander's decided he's on your side, that shit's for life."

"Magic? Do you think he has ESP?" She hadn't read that in him. Granted, she'd never read a fellow ESPer before. Not enough data to make a comparison.

"If you asked me three weeks ago, I would've said no. Now? I wouldn't be surprised if he did. I think he thinks of it as a really strong sense of intuition."

"Interesting."

"Ah, there's my nerdy babe." Georgia sighed, and then said, "Oh, shit, I really *do* miss your face."

"No video. I'm, like, super sweaty right now."

"*Ooh*, I have a better idea. Xander never said you couldn't have non-Maverick company."

Lucky almost got her hopes up. "You'll come to Hennessee House?"

"I have to switch some things around, but . . . maybe? I'll let you know as soon as I can."

In the afternoon, Georgia graced Hennessee House's doorstep as promised, dressed in an electric blue short suit set with sunglasses holding back her hair. Lucky grinned at the sight of her. She'd unexpectedly missed her face too. "I'm leaving at seven o'clock sharp," she said, striding through the door. "I decided we're having a Get to Know Georgia session by watching my old videos. A cringey but necessary step in cementing our friendship."

Lucky closed the door behind her. "Do you do this with all your friends?"

"Absolutely fucking not." Georgia cackled. "I'm doing this to help *you*. A little miss who shall not be named instructed me to give you vlogging tips."

She'd already warned Georgia about the brick wall rules.

Their quality time session was filled with popcorn, embarrassed laughter, guided lessons, and Gengar snuggles. He jumped on the couch and sat right next to Georgia as if people no longer bothered him. Lucky realized that was a part of Georgia's charm—the ability to make anyone feel special and like they belonged whenever she wanted. She also realized that wasn't something Georgia knew about herself yet.

"You're going to make a great director someday," Lucky said quietly. Her friend had the vision, talent, and compassion to lead a crew to greatness.

"Because of this?" They'd reached Georgia's senior year of high school and third year vlogging overall by then. "Don't be so easily impressed, babes. I'm way better than this now."

A FEW HOURS after Georgia left, Lucky walked to the back of the orchard for the first time.

Neat rows of planted trees made it easy enough to find. No twist, no turns, no secret shortcuts hiding under large leaves that needed to be pushed back. Even so, the orchard still felt enchanting—if she took one wrong step, she'd fall into a new realm. Walk too far and she'd be in a fairy hill. She found the bench, intricate white wrought iron and earthly wooden planks, nestled in the center of a pumpkin patch. Thick green twisting vines and leaves had begun crawling up the sides.

Sitting down, only the second floor of Hennessee House was visible. She could see her suite room window—but couldn't see the bench from there. Interesting.

Specter-Reggie appeared as expected, silently and right next to her. Fitting, as she'd chosen *vow of silence* as her first game of the night.

"Lucky Bug."

She refused to respond. Instead, she set up her camera to film herself. Even after Georgia's lessons, she hadn't gotten the hang of vlogging yet. It just wasn't the same without [Mini-Redacted] there with her, but getting footage of her reactions was better than nothing.

She sat resolutely listening as Specter-Reggie's frustration grew and grew until he began spewing every fear, weakness, and horrible thing she'd ever thought about herself. With increasing hostility.

Specter-Reggie wasn't overly talkative—a very Reggie-like quality. He was outgoing and personable but preferred to listen over being the loudest one in the room. But Hennessee House had a temper and was letting it fly something fierce. A very un-Reggie-like development.

Interesting.

Hours later, when Lucky had had enough, she'd said, "You don't believe those things about me."

It blinked at her, a smile tugging at its lips.

"Those memories, those insults were mine. Before tonight, you only repeated things Reggie had actually said to me," she said. "You need to wear someone's memory to be seen, I get that. But why can't you speak for yourself?"

Specter-Reggie's face went slack, and it made Lucky shiver—from anticipation.

32

Experiment #2 / Status: Ongoing
Topic: Communication

Lucky quietly paused for a moment to perform her self-assessment before continuing. "Is it okay if I call you Hennessee? Do you have a different name?"

"My name is Reggie." It sounded anything but sure.

Lucky frowned. "Who made you?"

"Our parents. Why would you ask such a stupid question? We look alike."

"You stole my brother's face. He looks like me."

"I was born first."

"Purely by circumstance," she said, changing tactics to play along. "I can't actively remember, but I feel like you pushed me out of the way. My memories might go back that far, though. Can you see that? Do I have a memory of the day I was born?"

"Yes." Specter-Reggie asked, "Would you like to know the first person you read?"

"*Interesting.*" That was Hennessee answering. It had to be. She needed to keep it on this topic to know for sure. "I remember that," she lied.

"You do not. You remember the first resident of your memory palace. Me."

Shit. It flipped back to Reggie—Hennessee didn't have a reading. What was going on? Why couldn't it stay focused?

"Who was the first person I ever read, then?"

"Our mother."

That was a direct question. It wouldn't have answered if it wasn't true. Lucky *did* have that memory somewhere.

Reggie wouldn't know that. She didn't even know that.

Hennessee appeared to be oscillating between staying in character as Specter-Reggie and speaking as itself. A hybrid state.

"Why aren't you using that other voice?" she asked carefully. Wary. "The super deep voice I heard inside my head. That was you, wasn't it? The real you?"

Specter-Reggie's eyes met hers, shining with mischief so blatant it made her shiver again—and not in a good way. "Because it scares you when almost nothing does."

That voice had made an unforgettable debut on the list of things that unnerved Lucky to the bone. The ghost formerly trapped in her memory palace, being possessed by it, had been Lucky's biggest fear. She wished that Hennessee had asked before deleting it, but she wasn't sorry it was gone, and in the time since, the house had obeyed her wishes. All of her other readings remained untouched, even the ones that caused her a great deal of pain. But why did the house do that in the first place? It didn't make a lick of sense . . .

Unless the house thought it was helping her by deleting it and never meant to replace the ghost with its voice, but it had. And now it refused to use it. Interesting.

Lucky realized she might've been wrong before. "If you don't want me to be scared, what do you want?"

"I want a *normal* sister." Specter-Reggie . . . frowned, face clearly folding in frustration. "*No.*"

"No what?" She held her breath.

"I want—I want—" Its eyes darted from side to side, searching but not seeing. "I want a *normal* sister. *No.*"

Was it . . . struggling? What was it trying to say? She turned toward it, brimming with determination. "You're not my brother. You are not Reggie. Be you, Hennessee. Who are you?"

"No." It shook its head. "*No.*"

Specter-Reggie disappeared before Lucky could say anything else. She sighed, sitting back against the bench. "Well, that didn't go as planned."

But it was good, solid progress, and it only took another week for Lucky to discover why Hennessee had run away.

Reality made specters unravel.

Days later, Lucky was squaring off against Specter-Reggie in the library. "Talk to me, Hennessee! Come on! You are not my brother, and you know it," she said with conviction. "You are not Reggie. This is not real."

When continually denied, Hennessee *glitched* out of the hybrid state and briefly seeped through its specter-avatar. She could force it to speak to her directly, but the connection only lasted for a few costly minutes.

"Who made you?" she demanded. "Where did you come from?"

Specter-Reggie's eyes turned black, jaw slack and mouth hanging open.

She readied herself, waiting for its voice to echo inside her mind. "What do you want?" she pleaded. "I'm not afraid. Tell me, please."

"give me what I want—are you not happy—will you stay—will you run." Specter-Reggie winked out of existence faster than Lucky's eyes could catch. She fell back onto the floor, closing her eyes and trying to slow her heart rate. A fine layer of sweat coated her skin. Her head swam, eyes pulsating in her sockets.

Connecting with the house like that had formed a tremendous psychic link and she routinely collapsed from the stress of standing her ground. Exhaustion stretched between them—infecting and commiserating. Forced glitching had become just as draining for her as it was for the house.

Progress required sacrifice and she was only hurting herself. Every night it got closer and closer to being able to speak to her purely as itself in the hybrid state. It demanded information, consistently struggling to offer any return. She steadfastly refused to give in even when it resorted to insults. Close to sunrise, when the house was at its weakest, it cooperated while she forced the glitch.

Because they were in it together now. For better or worse.

Gengar climbed on her chest, activating bread-loaf mode and staring at her.

"Does the house talk to you too?"

He blinked once and she narrowed her eyes. "You're next on my list, mister. Don't think you're not."

Lucky talked to Gengar regularly for the company. She spoke to Georgia once per day and Xander once per week, but it didn't feel like enough. She'd spent so much time with NQP, she began feeling the absence of *people* more acutely than ever before.

Now that she'd secured an investor (that philanthropic asshole), she also began thinking about her next steps. When she finally unraveled the secrets of Hennessee House, where would she go? What would she do? She quit her full-time live-in nanny gig for the show. She didn't even have her own apartment waiting for her at the end of this.

She'd have enough money to start her own supernatural PI business, but was that really all she wanted? It was—weeks ago, before she'd met NQP and began working with them. Before she'd met Maverick.

In the kitchen, she downed an entire bottle of water in thirty seconds flat and then inhaled a granola bar. Her stomach kept rumbling so she ate two more while making eggs and toast.

Lucky nearly hit the ceiling when her phone suddenly rang. Clutching her chest, she checked the screen and gasped. While not quite sunrise, Hennessee was exhausted. It'd be safe to drop the brick wall. "The world must be ending," she said after answering. "This is your final goodbye."

"Hardly," Maverick said dryly. She hated how her entire body seemed to react to the sound of his voice. "I'm sorry I didn't call. I needed some time to reevaluate where I'm at."

Lucky sighed as she brought her breakfast to the table. "How did that work out for you?" She tried to be understanding but that ship had set sail a week ago. All she felt was bitter and a little hurt.

"I know you can take care of yourself. Trusting you doesn't mean I trust that house. I'm terrified it'll take things too far and you won't want to stop until it's too late."

Lucky glanced around the room—Hennessee House's sublimely retro and inviting kitchen. She thought of Eunice, how the NQP team found her alone and passed out, close to where Lucky sat now.

"I'm trying to balance trusting you and being afraid for you, but one side keeps outweighing the other."

His fear, his caution, was winning. She didn't need him to say it.

"On top of that," he said, "I can't stop thinking that this is just the start of it. It's always going to be like this. You're always going to prioritize your career over our relationship. I've already been down this road with Rebecca, and I can't do it again."

Lucky forced herself to ask, "And where is she?"

"Off studying some super scientific gene sequencing thing in Massachusetts. You'll meet her at some point." His breathy laugh caused an eruption of butterflies in her stomach. She rolled her eyes at herself, because *really?*

He continued, "I didn't want to talk to you about this until I was sure. I know it hasn't been that long, but I'm not interested in anything temporary or short-term with you. Before, it kind of felt like you weren't as all-in as I was."

"Do you need me to say that I am? Because I *am*."

"Yeah, I know that *now*," he said.

Lucky finished her last few bites and cleared the table. "So, Rebecca?" she asked as she began washing the dishes.

"She just had all these larger-than-life goals for herself. Back then, it made the most sense, for our family, for me to take Rebel and for her to continue her education. I had a family to fall back on. Rebecca only had me. If I didn't tell her to go, she would've stayed, but I don't think she would've been happy. I didn't want her to feel like she was wasting her life and end up resenting us."

"And she just . . . left?"

"Rebecca isn't a bad person. I don't want you thinking she is. She's a part of our lives and that isn't changing," he said, defensive. Protective. "We were *really* young. We met, hooked up at a party, and kept doing it until she got pregnant. We tried to make it work but . . . we couldn't. Good sex alone isn't enough to hold a relationship together. You can't build a life on that."

Oh, shit. Lucky immediately began to high-key panic. Did Maverick think the opposite was true—bad sex was enough to ruin it? *Oh, shit.*

Jumping to conclusions before he finished wouldn't help anything. She had to hear him out. While focusing on calming her thoughts, she set out an early wet-food breakfast for Gengar and headed to her suite.

"But that's not what I want to focus on," he said. "The point I wanted to make is I don't know if I could make that same choice with you. I'd be selfish and I'd lose you anyway."

"Well, if I felt like you were standing in my way, *on purpose*, it would change things for me. But I know that's not the kind of person you are." Lucky needed to hold the banister for support. Her legs barely had enough strength to get her up the stairs safely. Communicating with Hennessee drained her in every way imaginable—mentally, emotionally, and physically. She'd even started taking her baths in the afternoon because she was too drained to do anything other than sleep after being with the house all night.

"That's not the kind of person I want to be with anyone, let alone you," he said. "I just found you and I'm already scared of losing you. I know you feel like I'm being unsupportive, but that's where I'm coming from. That's the heart of it."

Lucky's own heart reacted accordingly by losing its mind. Unsure what to say yet, she decided to keep quiet for once. She closed the curtains in her suite to block out the light. If she didn't, she'd wake up well before Hennessee's good morning tug. Pajamas already on, she climbed into bed and covered her head with the blanket.

"I feel like you locked me out," she whispered. "You asked me not to run away and then *you* did. I'm fine waiting as long as I *know* I'm waiting. Don't go radio silent on me."

She should've seen it coming. He had a clear history of it. When Maverick got stressed, he disappeared. Checked out.

Silvia told her so. He let Rebecca go. He even retreated into himself, while standing right next to Lucky several times.

"You're right. I know. It's just . . . that's easier for me. I don't want to make excuses so all I can do is promise to be better in the future," he admitted. "Because sometimes, I really do need time and I don't want to be pushed. The other night, I got super anxious because"—he paused, exhaling into the space he created—"I didn't know enough about asexuality. I thought asexual people hated sex, like as a feature."

Oh. "Well, some of us do," she admitted, worrying at her bottom lip. "That's very true for *them*."

"But I thought that applied across the board. I honestly thought you *were* pretending until you pushed back *so* hard. I believed you," he said. "I knew I needed to educate myself before I fucked everything up. I found some pretty balanced articles and a couple of memoirs that really helped me get a handle on the basic definition. My biggest takeaway was that generalizing is pointless." He laughed. "I was dead wrong and so glad I didn't say anything."

He—he—he researched? On his own? Because he wanted to be proactive and understand asexuality better? Lucky felt like she was melting into a heart-shaped puddle. She'd never find someone like him again.

"I didn't mean to push you. I honestly thought being forward and getting everything out into the open was the right way to do that." She sighed, closing her eyes. No excuses. "When I said I wanted you to feel comfortable telling me what you need, I wasn't only talking about sex. I'm sorry I did that."

"Honestly, I was trying to downplay it because"—he hesitated again, voice thick with frustration—"the things I want to do with you, *to you*, I can't even say them because I can't get past this block of thinking I'm *too* sexual. It'll be too much."

"You're not entirely wrong," she said, thoughtfully. "The truth is I don't know, but I'm very much okay with finding out. I trust you."

And she trusted herself too.

"Let's try it," she murmured. "Start small."

"I want to see you." He hesitated. "I don't want to have this conversation over the phone."

"This is what we have right now. Do you like phone sex? I'm surprisingly proficient at dirty talk," she bragged.

The silence on the other end of the line was *so* loud.

She sighed his name. "Most people wouldn't have given me half as much care and attention as you do. I've told you everything. *Everything.* At some point you're gonna have to believe me about this."

"I do believe you."

"Then be your honest self with me," she said, and then got an idea. "Because if you ever cheat on me, we're breaking up immediately. I will *never* speak to you again."

"I would *never* do that." He sounded sufficiently offended, so she switched up her tone.

"You say that now, but one day little Maverick might get tired of your shit and take over. Repressed sexual desires can lead to people making *wild* decisions. I've heard lust plays you all for fools."

"That's not gonna happen," he said. "Also . . . it's not little."

"I haven't seen it. I wouldn't know," she teased.

"I'm telling you it's not."

Lucky paused, checking in with herself to see if she felt repulsed, which could happen occasionally . . . and nope. She was still good. "How big are we talking, then? Have you measured it? Can *I* measure it?"

"Lucky."

"I'm asking scientifically. For science." She laughed. "I'll even use official scientific tools—like my hands."

He laughed. "You're ridiculous."

"I'm proficient. Give me a chance to prove it," she countered. "I'm not going to judge you for being too sexual, especially since you've been nothing but good to me. You wouldn't believe the shit people say about aces and you haven't said any of it. Not a word, not an insult, not even on accident. If I can't handle it, trust me to tell you and we'll go from there. As soon as you're ready, I'm ready."

"I've *been* ready. I have been struggling since the day I met you." He laughed. "You were wearing overalls and a sweatshirt, but you might as well have answered the door naked."

33

After yet another difficult night with Specter-Reggie, Lucky needed a power nap. Two more weeks had passed, and while the days sometimes blurred together, the nights absolutely didn't. She was sound asleep when her alarm blasted her back into consciousness.

"Shut up," she muttered, silencing it. She'd set it to go off every morning at twenty minutes before sunrise—the average range of time Hennessee House consistently flatlined.

Her eyelids felt like sandpaper scraping against her eyeballs. The rest of her body wasn't faring any better. Skin too tight, mouth dry, and if she stretched too hard, she knew a charley horse would take her down screaming.

Emotionally drained and feeling like she'd been visited in the night by a desiccation demon, the only solution was to take a bath. Maverick called right as she entered the water, sliding down until the bubbles reached her shoulders.

"Good morning." Early-morning Maverick had a deeper voice that felt as rich as chocolate mousse.

"I'm alive."

"Good to know."

Lucky began opening the previous day's flower. Every day at noon, a slender white box arrived in the mail from Maverick. Keeping her mind blank, she brought them up to her room for safekeeping, not thinking about or opening them until their sunrise call.

"Gardenia, oh, it smells wonderful. But I don't think it quite makes it to my potential favorites list."

"I think you'll like today's flower. I have a good feeling about it."

She bit her lip at the familiar sound of the smile in his voice, briefly imagining what he looked like. "Can I have a hint?"

"Nope. How did you sleep?"

"Not the best. I'm trying to relax by taking a bath."

"You're in the bathtub?" He paused. "Right now?"

"They usually make me feel better."

Maverick sighed. "Why did you have to say that? You're trying to ruin me, aren't you?"

"Never intentionally, but if it happens . . ." She trailed off with a shrug. "Is it the bath itself or because I'm naked?"

"Both."

She faux-gasped. "I knew it."

"It's yet another first-day memory that's been haunting me. You painted such a vivid picture of your bath ritual I instantly imagined it—bubbles, lavender, music, steam, you." He chuckled, low and dreamy. "I just know you set the temperature to molten lava."

"It's the only way to get a decent amount of steam. I could send you pictures. Of me. Right now." She grinned her way through feeling bashful. "If you want. I trust you with them."

Maverick groaned, voice straining as he asked, "How much longer?"

"I don't know," she said, sinking lower into the water. "I'm making progress, but no definitive answers yet."

Rarely did they talk about Hennessee and Lucky's mission during their only hour together. The fact that he brought it up meant he'd been thinking about it, and now they were losing precious seconds to dead air. She usually tried to be bright and bubbly, hiding how terribly she missed him. This was her choice. She caused their separation. She had to live with that burden.

And then he said, "When I dreamed about you last night, you said, 'I see the threads in the fabric of you. They're stronger when you thread them through my needle eye. We burn the dull ones like trash.'"

"Are you asking for a translation? Because I have no idea what I meant by that."

After Maverick explained his lucid dreaming process, Lucky began to suspect there might be more to it. But he'd already told her he was happy with what he'd learned about himself so far. His control over it made him feel safe. She had no right to disrupt that.

"You kissed me while you said it then yelled at me to wake up." He sighed. "Not even Hennessee can hide from you. I'll be here when you get out."

"It's not jail." She laughed. Although, she had begun tracking her days with tick marks in her journal to keep herself grounded and those did kind of resemble scratches on a cell wall. "So about the pictures."

"Lucky—"

"I'm just saying we could swap."

"You want me to send you nudes? Why?"

She couldn't stop herself from giggling at how skeptical he sounded. When she explained how seeing little-Maverick-until-proven-otherwise wouldn't do anything for her, he took the news as well as could be expected.

"Maybe not nudes, but you, shirtless, in a tight-fitting apron, baking or cooking something fancy. Or you, wearing that one blue sweater I like and holding a book. Ooh, with glasses—do you have glasses? You could pretend to be a librarian." She sighed so hard she nearly swooned. "Librarian romances are in my top five."

"Stop, I can't take it." He started laughing more than she'd heard in weeks. She'd missed that sound so much. "It's too early."

"Don't laugh." She pretended to whine.

"I thought you weren't wholesome. That's like the definition of wholesome."

"Hey, it's not my fault you're so handsome and I want to see you dressed up in clothes for different professions. That's what I want," she said firmly. "I'll make my pictures artistic, the suggestion of nudity, so it seems fair."

"I'll send you pictures of me. You don't have to send me anything."

"You don't want my tasteful nudes?"

"I want a whole lot more than that," he said, and started laughing again. "Have you ever tried roleplaying? I think you might like it."

"Don't think so," she said. "I'll have to look it up."

"Nudes aside—"

"But—"

"No, we're moving on," he said. "I have a question for you."

"Okay?"

"If I sent you something I've been working on, would you be interested in reading it?"

She gasped. "Is it your book?"

"Not the *whole* book, but yes. I finished the opening. I needed a distraction and ended up writing nonstop again. It's really rough, really, *really* rough, but I feel ready to share it with you."

He sounded so adorably nervous again, if she weren't in the bathtub she would've started gleefully kicking her feet. She needed to be calm. Professional. Encouraging sans the syrupy sweetness. She decided to go with "I'd be honored to read it. Send it to me immediately."

"Thank you," he said. "I usually wait until I'm done and it feels perfect before sending it out for feedback. You're honestly the only person I feel like I can trust at this stage. I couldn't have done it without you."

"*Yes*, you could have," she insisted.

"I told you—you're my muse. You inspired me to face the blank page and just . . . start."

Lucky resisted the urge to grumble at him. "And how did I do that while locked away in my tower?"

"It was exactly that," he said. "Your drive. Your dedication. I think I'd forgotten what it was like to be so absorbed by a goal, you'll do anything for it. You being there gave me the motivation to write my novel. And now I have something to share with you, the way you shared your Hennessee House nights with me."

"I'm . . . honestly not sure how I feel about that. Being alone here isn't—" She stopped herself.

"Isn't what?"

Isn't what she wanted after all. She missed him. She missed the NQP team. She missed working with them and having a second. She didn't want to make these discoveries alone. She wanted to share her progress, triumphs, and failures with him too.

But more than that, she wanted her *own* team. She wanted to mentor and work with other ESPers like herself, who had the same interests and goals.

"Never mind. Forget I said that."

POST-NEIGHBORHOOD WALK, THERE wasn't much for Lucky to do once she made her self-tapes and organized her notes. Even though it would be helpful to gauge her process in real time, she couldn't bring herself to play back her vlog raw footage, particularly the ones she filmed during difficult nights with Hennessee. She knew she looked *Rough*, with a capital *R*, but they would be good for the show. The audience (and Xander) would appreciate seeing how truly worn-out she got.

A busy body meant a busy mind, and she needed to keep Hennessee in the dark as much as possible. She made a schedule, slotting in activities like reading books, wasting time on the internet, doing her own box braids, watching movies, and trying to conquer one new recipe every day. Had she also tried staving off restlessness by talking to a cat? Yes, but things could be *a lot* worse.

Honestly, she was grateful for Gengar's company. She played and took naps with him. Tried teaching him tricks. He'd become her constant companion.

During his front yard patrol time, she supervised from the porch. He'd probably been an outdoor kitty for his entire life, but she'd never had a pet before. Heat exhaustion was no joke. He might *need* her.

She settled into her usual spot—the pillowed bench with her feet up on the banister. To pass the time, she started an unremarkable book with an unremarkable title that she was strangely desperate to read. She focused on the story slowly unfolding, and not at all on the mysterious anonymous writer whose words managed to give her a severe case of chills in the dry summer heat. When the mail arrived at noon, she thoughtlessly set a slender white box aside using a similar technique.

A large box directly addressed to Lucky with no return address had also arrived.

"Gengar, I'm going inside."

The cat ran after her, rubbing across her ankles as it passed the threshold. She brought the box into the kitchen, set it on the counter, and grabbed a pair of scissors.

"Do you think it's from Xander?"

Gengar yowled as she sliced it open to find an assortment of baked goods—cookies, muffins, pastries, an entire loaf of banana bread. He stood on his hind legs, ready to jump in.

"No cookies for you," she said, knowing full well he just wanted the box. "You could be allergic."

Lucky searched around the sides, eventually finding a greeting card–size blue envelope. The handwriting on the front was on the larger side, but neat and evenly spaced. Inside there was a card and when she opened it, something fell out and onto the counter. She'd thought they were postcards—that's why she looked. But they were photos.

A picture of Maverick in the blue sweater wearing glasses and holding a stack of books.

A picture of her, Maverick, and Rebel outside the gates of Penny Place.

"*Shit.*" Lucky clenched her jaw and squeezed her eyes shut, summoning her brick wall to slam into place.

Hennessee House busted through it like the damn Kool-Aid man. She lurched forward from the force of it, gripping the counter to help her stay upright. No longer daytime dormant, it had fully woken up for this, ravenously craving the thing it knew she'd been hiding. It had taken that image of him, the thought of his name, and barreled through her mind like a tornado.

A chair at the kitchen table scraped backward across the floor like nails on a chalkboard. The second one moved, then the third and the fourth until they were arranged exactly the same way as when she and Maverick had accidentally slept in the kitchen. Her memory on display because Hennessee had finally found where she'd hidden them.

Three weeks of control, straight down the drain. Opening the box had been a rookie mistake. She'd gone through incredible lengths to keep Maverick and Rebel off Hennessee's radar and it'd all been for nothing.

Lucky took a deep, shuddering breath. Shoulders hunched, she bowed her head in failure and fear. There'd be no stopping it now. Specter-Maverick was going to break her heart.

Gengar yowled softly in front of her on the counter, head-butting her arm. He sat down, yowling again in her face.

"I'm fine," she lied with a smile and scratched behind his ears the way he liked.

Lucky fixed the chairs, putting them back into place, and sat down with her baked goods box. She realized she hadn't read the letter yet. Might as well.

Dear Lucky,

I made the macarons by myself!

We miss you! I asked Xander if you could come to movie day and he said maybe! You have to finish your work first so hurry up okay? We're going on Saturday. Riley says hi. I told him all about you and he said he thinks you sound made-up. I showed him the pictures we took at Penny Place and he shut up about it. His mom says he has a crush on you now but I don't believe her. Riley likes Cathy at school. Don't tell him I told you, please. It's a secret.

Love, your Shortcake

"Oh, Rebel." Lucky searched for the macarons to eat them first. A little lopsided in shape, they came in a variety of creative colors as vibrant as Rebel, like robin egg blue, pastel green, and salmon pink.

"Good afternoon, Lucky."

She squinted at Xander darkening her doorway for their weekly check-in. "You."

Xander never looked anything less than immaculate. Dark colored, well-fitting suits seemed to be his preference, but not so stuffy that he didn't own jeans and tennis shoes. He probably had his plain white T-shirts tailored, though.

"Would you like some baked goods?" She gestured to her box. "This is a test. You don't strike me as the sugar type. I want to know if I'm right."

"What is a sugar type?"

"Someone who ingests sugar and other bad-for-you foods for fun."

Xander ignored her offering, sitting in the chair across the table. He might've sat next to her, but she had her feet up and had no intentions of being a hospitable host.

He asked, "Did you buy these?"

"Special delivery from Maverick and Rebel."

Upstairs, a door slammed. Lucky sighed.

Xander gave her a questioning look. "I take it that means your embargo has been lifted?"

"Yep," she said. "Lifted. Smashed. Destroyed. Whatever works."

"Maverick continues to be furious with me. He believes I tempted you away from him."

She snickered. "Did he say it like that?"

"I'm not comfortable repeating his exact words. Don't worry—I didn't fire him." Xander stared at her for a beat and then added, "He needs someone to blame other than himself."

She *hadn't* been worried until he said that. "Blame himself? For what?"

Xander shrugged, a disgustingly casual gesture for Mr. Formal. "Your happiness is of the utmost importance to him. He would never stand in the way of you attaining it."

"A non-answer answer? I must be rubbing off on you."

"Perhaps." He shrugged again. "How has the week been?"

Every fiber of Lucky's being dreaded what was coming at sunset. A distraction might be nice.

A *distraction* might actually be the answer.

Lucky grinned at him, a new plan suddenly coming together with ease. "Interesting. I'm thinking it might be time for a little experiment."

34

Lucky wondered if Xander's intuition sensed her plan brewing around him. She needed to find a way to make it worth his while again, and had the beginnings of an idea to start with. "*Whew*, oh gosh, it's so *hot*. I should open the window or something." She began fanning herself, wiping her brow, and visualizing how it felt to overheat.

Behind them, the top half of the Dutch door swung open. A barely there summer breeze drifted into the room and clung to her clammy skin—her dreaded anticipation sweats had begun.

Xander stared with an uneasy look in his eyes, mouth as ajar as the door. He swallowed hard, reigning himself back in. "That's quite the development."

"We're connected now. Prolonged exposure strengthened our psychic bond. During the day while it's dormant-reactive, it kindly responds to my wants, my moods. I also think the house has a sense of humor." She'd been holding on to this discovery like a secret weapon. Good thing, too. She held up her hands to mime the motion as she spoke. "This strange buoyant pressure starts vibrating the air. Belly laughs."

His expression morphed into a neat mix of horrified and fascinated. "What does it laugh at?"

"I'm not sure," she said honestly. "We're still working on effective two-way communication. It took some time to realize it doesn't respond to words so much as images while in daytime house mode. I spoke out loud for your sake, but I was thinking about being hot. Picturing how it feels in my mind and what would help me."

"*Help* you?" he asked slowly.

She nodded. "This might sound shocking, but Hennessee isn't calm during the day *because* it's dormant-reactive. It's downright friendly. It's *kind*—I can feel it wanting to be a gracious host and it costs me nothing to do it."

Xander's brow furrowed as he processed what she'd said. "If that's true, and to be clear I believe you, why does its behavior shift so drastically at sunset?"

"Sunrise too. It's truly tied to night and day. I'm missing . . . something. I know I am." She bit her thumbnail, genuinely puzzled. "Even communicating at night is on the opposite end of the spectrum. Speaking to specters uses an *incredible* amount of energy. Did it feel that way for you?"

"Always."

A feeling of kinship, unspoken and profound, passed between them. It linked them together as the last standing caretakers of Hennessee House.

"Stop me if you get confused," she began. "Hennessee makes a connection with someone's mind. It uses *their* memories to create a specter and gains the ability to speak, courtesy of that connection. It's a loop. Hennessee needs access to language if it wishes to communicate verbally. Does that make sense?"

His eyes tightened, but he said, "Please continue."

"Once the loop is established and a specter is created, it's almost like it uses catchphrases, saying the same things over and over. If it can't use or mimic conversations from your memory, it'll try to speak on its own, *but* it can't do it for long. It'll slip right back into specter-character."

Until she pushed it too far. It was still too soon to tell him about that part.

"You are"—he paused, shaking his head—"moving at an astonishing pace."

"It's hard, tiring work and objectively wonderful," she said, smiling for a moment before slowly letting it fade. "It's great. Having the time of my life."

"At the moment it sounds like anything but." He picked up on her tone change, falling right into her trap.

"You're mistaken," she said, softly miserable. "It's everything I've ever wanted."

"I suspected as much." Xander stood and retrieved two glasses and a bottle of dark brown alcohol from the cabinet. He poured and handed her one.

Lucky accepted it and asked, "You don't eat cookies, but you drink alcohol?"

"I never said I didn't eat cookies."

"You snubbed Rebel's macarons."

"No, I didn't. You seem to need them more than I do. I was being thoughtful." He raised his glass. "Cheers."

"Cheers." She downed the drink and almost choked to death. "*What is that?*" she sputtered, throat seizing up.

"You're supposed to sip it," he snapped.

"How was I supposed to know? You didn't say that." She hit her burning chest, trying in vain to work through another coughing fit. "I feel like I can breathe fire."

Xander poured her another glass, passing it to her. "*Sip*," he repeated with a stern tone.

"I've learned my lesson," she said, suddenly feeling warm and spinny. "Maybe."

"Don't you dare," he warned.

"I'm going to *sip* it." However, doing so barely improved the drinking experience. She scrunched her face, only breathing a small puff of fire that time. "Are we bonding? Is that what this is?"

"I thought you weren't psychic."

She chose to ignore his sarcasm. "I'm not. I just know people. The unchanging and predictable nature of humanity, and all that. You're a collector," she said. "Collector's bond."

Xander regarded her for a moment. "I'm curious about the parameters of your ability. Is it only humans or is it any living being?"

"I can't read the house, if that's what you're asking."

"I am."

Lucky nodded before taking another sip and wincing. She needed to kick her plan into high gear before she was too tipsy to remember it.

Rebel's inquisitive mind had once again steered Lucky in the right direction. *The Caretaker* was designed to focus on one person at a time. Initially, no one knew what happened if two people who shared memories stayed inside the house at night, at the same time.

The answer so far was business as usual. But what if those two people had already experienced specters individually?

Would there be a shared specter experience?

Would there be one for each of them?

Or would it be as Lucky ~~hoped~~ suspected?

The house might be old, but the sheer level of its desperation paired with its glaring restrictions suggested the house was inexperienced. It might not yet be strong enough to use the memories of more than one person at a time. It might not even know how.

Xander was Hennessee's favorite by a wide purple-flower margin. Not to mention, Lucky had a history of not cooperating and challenging it, whereas he didn't. If Hennessee had to choose between creating a specter for her or him, who would win?

Lucky asked, "When did you write your name on the wall?"

"I was seven, I think. We were here for a month in the summer, my stepmom and I. My dad refused, so he took my brother to Spain for their vacation."

"Spain? Over Hennessee House? Unthinkable." She'd earned a sardonic smile from him for that one.

He continued, "The house didn't ask me to write it. I was bored, had a knife, and carved my name into a couple of places, actually. The attic wall. The orange tree. Under the dining room table."

"That's Gengar's favorite tree. Interesting," she said. "Did you see illusions or specters back then?"

He nodded. "I didn't understand what was happening. I thought they were imaginary friends because they were almost always animals."

Bobbi, the first caretaker, saw her guinea pig, but Hennessee used her grandfather to communicate. Why *didn't* it use a person back then for Xander too? Because he was just a kid, maybe?

"Do you know if your stepmom saw them?" she asked gently.

"I don't," he said thoughtfully. "But I do think her connection was similar to yours. I remember her asking for things and then they would happen like magic. We had such a wonderful time. She loved it here."

"You miss her."

"Every day. After the second caretaker quit, production went on a brief hiatus, and I slept here. When I saw her specter, I thought she'd come back as a ghost."

Lucky reached across the table, covering his hand with hers. She knew exactly what he needed to hear. "Ghosts are remnants of who people used to be. That I know. Who we *are* moves on to the next journey, whatever and wherever that may be."

He stared at her hand long enough to make her think she made a mistake, but then he surprised her by covering it with his. Holding her there. "You called me a collector. What is that?"

"That's who you are. You search for people and bring them in, give them somewhere to belong," she said. "I can tell you more but we both know you knew that part."

He smirked, laughing lightly as he looked away. "I wasn't aware there was a term for it."

"Because I made it up. I do that from time to time," she said. "You're doing just fine. As long as you continue on as you have been, healing and not shutting down, you'll keep healing." He nodded in acknowledgment, and she sat back in her chair, taking a deep breath. "I might have another small piece of an answer for you. You should sleep over again."

"You're in luck." He grinned, before downing the rest of his drink with a *completely* straight face. "I plan on being too drunk to drive."

LUCKY AND XANDER continued day drinking until it turned into afternoon drinking, then took a break to watch the sunset from the parlor room. Brilliant orange and amber light filled the space, hitting the stained-glass lamps just right. The room began shimmering with greens, blues, and yellows until darkness descended.

They lay side by side on the floor musing about the meaning of life, ESP, and, most surprisingly, sharing what it was like having an estranged sibling.

Xander also had one—a brother named Sasha. Their dad, Alexander, was apparently as funny as he was vain.

"I've been thinking about calling Reggie," Lucky said, purposefully thinking of him. "An email might be better, though."

"You should."

"I mean, I know *why* he didn't want to talk to me before but what about now? I'm different now. I think I can actually help him now, if he wanted."

"Now."

"What?"

He snorted and began laughing. "Nothing."

"Hey." She teetered as she sat up to glare down at him. "I'm trying to be mulnerable."

"*Vulnerable,*" he corrected with a snicker.

"Shut *up* and listen. Don't make fun of me." Every now and then, her words slurred into mush, and she didn't appreciate him pointing it out. "I'm almost sober."

"No, you're not."

She pointed at him. "Anyway. As I was saying. I made myself believe I was alone by choice when it was circumstance all along. I could show Reggie there's a better way."

Lucky *was* the problem, as were they—her family, her dorm mates, her nanny clique. None of them made a true effort to see and be seen in return. Doing so hurt and it could go wrong, but ultimately, it'd been so, so worth it. "I wish I didn't have to be here alone."

"I'm here."

"Which is fantastic, but I don't wanna kiss you."

"Good. I don't want to kiss you either."

"We're in agreement then."

"Seems like it." He closed his eyes.

Lucky sighed. "I miss Maverick." Not thinking about him didn't matter anymore.

"Are you complaining *again*?"

"You should make an exception and let me see him."

"I'll take it under advisement."

"Don't tease me. I'll punch you."

"I'm not." But he chuckled as he said it. "How about this?" He heaved himself into a sitting position, looking her right in the eyes. "Allow me to stand in as your unofficial big brother: I give you my blessing. I hope you two are very happy together."

"Stop *that*," she said, utterly astonished because he'd meant it. His hazel eyes, tinged with a bleary drunken sheen, somehow burned with sincerity.

"And if he does *anything* less than make you happy, he'll have to answer to me."

Shit, he'd meant that too. "Cut it out! You're going to make me *cry*."

Suddenly, Xander's gaze shifted to behind Lucky. She held her breath as she turned to look, knowing there'd be a specter but not what to expect.

A very light-skinned Black woman wearing a flowing soft pink gown sat on the chaise longue. She was absurdly beautiful—her face a picture-perfect portrait of serenity.

Xander said, "Hi, Brightly."

Lucky almost hit him but settled on hissing, "*You didn't tell me your stepmom was Black*."

He gave her a puzzled look. "Because it doesn't matter."

"It matters to *me*. You *know* how I feel about my people and the supernatural."

Specter-Brightly laughed, drawing their attention with its delicate sound.

"*Oh god*," Xander whispered, nearly gasping with pain.

"Xander," Specter-Brightly called. "Let's catch up in the orchard."

"I'm afraid I'm too drunk to walk out there safely," he said. "Forgive me."

In the blink of an eye, Specter-Brightly joined them on the floor, sitting close to him. "That's all right. How are you? I've missed you so much." It peered at him closely as if it needed to commit his face to memory. He couldn't bring himself to ignore it.

Something felt suspiciously different about this scene.

Lucky observed them, noting the way Specter-Brightly's smiles came easily and eagerly, and its clear obliviousness to Xander's torment.

But it wasn't being mean. It wasn't insulting him.

For every question Xander answered, Specter-Brightly lavished him with praise—telling him how proud it was, how much it believed in him, asking him if he was happy and to visit more often. It was possible those were his memories of her, but it also could've been Hennessee in the hybrid state. It might be stronger when paired with Xander. Their connection was much older.

"Xander." Lucky spoke firmly as if she had his ear. "Tell it it's not real."

He turned to Lucky. "What?"

"Say it. You have to say it. Tell it it's not real."

Xander nodded, turning back to Specter-Brightly. "You're not real."

"Why would you say such a thing?" Specter-Brightly's warm gaze glossed over Lucky.

"Ask something only Brightly would know. Something you haven't thought about in a long time, but *don't* think of the answer yet."

"That's a lot of instructions." His face pinched with doubt. "Did you not hear the *I'm drunk* part?"

Specter-Brightly asked, "Who's your friend?"

Lucky raised an eyebrow. "Cut the shit, Hennessee. You know exactly who I am."

Specter-Brightly blinked, face going slack but recovering quickly. "I like her. She's cute and *very* funny. Where did you two meet again?"

Xander struggled to find a question before settling on, "What color nail polish were you wearing the first day we met?"

"Why would you ask me that?"

Lucky frowned. Still no insults. If anything it sounded *hurt*.

Xander held firm, saying, "Answer the question, please."

"I'm sorry, baby. I didn't hear you. Ask me again?"

Lucky coached, "You have to use repetition or it will outthink you. When you don't play along it drops the façade and you can kind of speak to the house. Ask questions, but *don't* push it too hard."

He nodded, seemingly understanding. "Why Brightly?"

"You missed me."

"I miss *her*. Not you."

"Xander," Lucky warned.

"That is not true. You miss family. I am family."

Lucky and Xander exchanged a look—that was the house answering. He asked, "You think you're *my* family?"

"She called me Hennessee. You are Xander Hennessee."

"Me?" Lucky asked. "Or Brightly?"

For the first time that night, Specter-Brightly turned the full weight of its blank gaze to Lucky. "You *will* stay."

Lucky stopped herself from flinching. She'd said she wasn't leaving multiple times. The house believed her, that's all. That wasn't a command. That wasn't a threat.

"Hey," Xander snapped. "You didn't answer me. Why are you wearing Brightly's face?"

"My name is Brightly."

"No, it's not."

Lucky touched his arm, shaking her head. "Don't do that."

But he pressed on, "Why Brightly? Why are you doing this to me?"

"Close your eyes, hold your wish in your heart, and blow out your birthday candles," Specter-Brightly said.

Xander's eyes went wide. She watched as his fierce expression crumbled into sorrow. "How *dare* you. You're not real. You have no right to do this to me. You're a fucking *house*. You are not *Brightly*."

Inky black darkness filled Specter-Brightly's eyes like a whirlpool, save for that familiar single star.

"You should've listened to me," Lucky said, bracing herself to hear the voice like she always did. "Ask the house one last question—hurry, the connection won't last long."

Xander swallowed hard, the most distressed she'd ever seen him. He reached for Lucky's hand, squeezing it tightly. "Why Brightly? That's all I want to know." He began searching the room, a bewildered expression on his face. "Where is that voice coming from? *What is that?*"

But Lucky couldn't hear it! She breathed a sigh of relief before squeezing his hand back. "It's in your head," she said calmly. "It'll fade. Breathe through it."

"*No.*" Xander sounded horrified as Specter-Brightly disappeared. "What did it say?"

He blinked in disbelief, struggling to speak before managing to. "It said, 'are you not happy, will you stay, will you run, are you not happy,' I think. What was that?"

"The house's true voice," she said, rubbing his back. "You're okay. It says something similar to me every night too. I've been spinning in circles trying to figure out what it means."

"I think that scared me sober." He laughed weakly, but it was good to hear. "You do this *every* night? I am not paying you enough."

Lucky laughed, scrunching her nose at him. "At least something good came out of tonight," she joked, patting his arm. "Welcome to *my* inner circle."

35

Lucky awoke with a raging headache that her insensitive alarm clock could not care less about. Sunrise waited for no one, but Maverick waited for her.

Her mouth tasted like bitter ashes. "Xander, I hate you." She dry-heaved and rolled onto her stomach for safety's sake. "As soon as I remember how to walk, I'm going to destroy you and your evil brown liquor." She spotted him half-seated, half-lying, but all strewn about the round table and chair in the back of the parlor. "Are you alive?"

"I am. Unfortunately." He sat up, complaining about the ache in his back and neck like a stiff old man who'd lived a long and active life.

She looked him dead in the eye. "I'm never drinking with you again."

"We should've just eaten the cookies. Are you all right?"

"No, I'm miserable." She took her time standing, taking stock of her current condition. Headache. Foul feelings. Flutters of queasiness. "I'm going upstairs. If you suddenly hear me squealing in delight, no, you didn't. Mind your business." She wobbled toward the entryway, using the furniture to keep her balance, and turned to him for one more thing. "Thank you for helping with my experiment."

In a wonderful turn of events, her personal crisis had been averted. Hennessee didn't force her to communicate with a specter of Maverick or Rebel. It'd left them alone the rest of the night.

Xander scoffed, shaking his head, but said, "You're welcome."

In her suite, Lucky gently flopped face down on the bed and counted 113 seconds before her phone rang. "I'm hungover. Help."

"Oh no, you sound pitiful," Maverick crooned. "What made you decide to get drunk?"

"It's Xander's fault—he kept pouring drinks. Sipping bourbon doesn't make you get less drunk. It's still the same amount of alcohol in the end."

Maverick was silent for several heartbeats and then, "Xander."

Lucky smiled into her pillow. "Maverick."

"Lucky."

"Why did you say his name like that?"

"Why is he there?"

"He checks in once a week to make sure I'm not possessed."

"That is *not* funny."

"Yes, it is because that's never gonna happen." She giggled. "I showed him something and he started drinking to cope, I think. But *ooh*! We had a breakthrough last night!"

"We? You and the house?"

"All three of us. Xander was too drunk to drive so he slept over."

"He could've called for a ride. He didn't have to stay there."

"Maverick Phillips, are you jealous?" she teased.

"*Yes.*"

Lucky laughed her heart out, headache be damned. "You know you have zero reason to be, right?"

"I know," he said. "But he gets to see you, and I don't."

"I'm technically working. He's technically my boss. Last night was the equivalent of after-work cocktails with a supernatural twist." She closed her eyes, adjusting her position for maximum comfort. "I saw Xander's specter. It's his stepmom. He told me a little bit about her."

"Oh, shit." Maverick blew out a breath. "I know he's been having a hard time since she passed."

"You have no idea. I read it in him—he changed because of it."

"Changed as in he's—"

"No, not even close," she said, quickly. "Xander isn't rotting. He's *healing.* I read the steps he's taken since Brightly passed. He'll be all right eventually."

"You sound proud of him."

"Because I am. You were right—he really is a good guy. Don't be mad at him."

"I'm not." He sounded surprised. "I was just giving him a hard time. Georgia swears his sense of humor is underdeveloped and I'm starting to think she's right."

"No, it's there. It's just *really* dry," she said. "His specter behaved differently than mine. As soon as my head calms down, I'm on the case."

"Why don't I let you go so you can recover?"

"No."

"If you insist."

"I do."

His warm, soft laughter felt like a balm to her soul. She didn't feel half as exhausted as she normally did after a night with Hennessee because Xander had been its primary focus. But if she wasn't careful, she'd fall asleep on the phone anyway. "I read the chapters you sent. I'm letting my thoughts simmer before I read it again."

"You're going to read it twice?"

"Once isn't enough. I don't want to say too much yet, but"—she paused to tease him—"I *loved* it. I was expecting something similar to the style you used on the podcast but that wasn't it at all."

"I'm really proud of those stories, but I'd like to think I've gotten better since then."

"You have. It was *so* good."

"Thank you," he said, and then delicately cleared his throat. "I'm sure there were some parts that were . . . not so good?"

Lucky covered her mouth and held the phone away from her ear. Hearing that voice again—so vulnerable, so nervous—made her want to scream because she almost couldn't handle it. Allowing her to see this side of him meant she'd made it. He trusted her.

"It's a draft," she said carefully. "And yet, as a reader, I was fully invested by the time I finished."

"Really?"

"*Really*. That's why I want to read it again to focus on the craft stuff. I bought an ebook about plotting and character since I'm not familiar with all the terms."

"You—you didn't have to do that. General thoughts and feedback would've been more than enough."

"Oh," she said softly, hoping she didn't overstep.

"I honestly don't know why I'm surprised." He chuckled. "Tell you what, after you've finished studying we can talk about it. You can ask me all the questions you want and I'll teach you how I do it."

Lucky sighed in relief, pressing a hand over her heart. It was okay to be a lot. It was okay to be too much. It was okay to be herself with him. She felt relaxed, settling into the comfortable silence between them . . . sinking into the soft bedding . . . eyes drifting closed to the sound of his even, steady breathing as if it were music.

"You're falling asleep," he whispered.

"*Mmm.*"

"Okay. One last thing—"

"No, many more things," she mumbled.

He laughed again, making her sigh. Again. "I wanted to ask if you were still getting calls from that unknown number?"

"No. Why?"

"I think whoever is doing it moved on to me. I woke up to six missed calls."

Lucky's eyes shot open. She was up and fully alert as if someone poured cold water on her. "What time did they start?"

"Hold on—first one was at 8:43 p.m. I missed it because Rebel wanted to read a book with me before bed. I didn't hear the others."

"Can you do me a favor? If they call again, could you answer it? Tell me what they say?"

"Of course. Did you eventually answer?"

"I did. I think that's what stopped the calls," she lied. She didn't mean to—that was genuinely what she'd thought at the time. Now she wasn't so sure. "Thank you."

LUCKY'S BRAIN WHIRRED with new ideas, throbbed from the bourbon infection, and the combination had a devastating effect on her stomach. She rushed down the stairs anyway, hoping Xander hadn't left yet. After searching in a desperate circle around the first floor, she found him outside in the gazebo with the bag of peas on his forehead.

"Is that a Bloody Mary? I had ingredients for that in there?" she asked.

"Would you like one?"

"Pass. I told you we're never drinking together again." She took the seat kitty-corner to him. "What are you doing out here?"

"Fresh air."

"How are you holding up?"

"How do I look?"

Still in yesterday's clothes with barely a wrinkle in sight. How rich, how annoying. "I meant emotionally."

He glanced at her with reddened eyes. His skin had a subtle green tint, but other than that he seemed all right. "You don't need to worry about me."

"Oh, I'm not worried. You don't pay me enough for that yet," she joked. "Off-the-wall question: Do you ever get phone calls from an unknown number? Specifically one that calls at odd hours but noticeably more frequently at night."

Those pesky peas blocked her from reading his expression as he asked, "Why?"

"Because *I* started getting the calls the weekend we filmed *Shortcake* and they stopped when I came back here. The last one I got was while at Maverick's place, right before you put me on house arrest."

"For the final time, you are free to leave. Do not imply I am your parole officer."

"Focus, Xander," she said, trying to keep a straight face. "I answered the last call but didn't hear anything except clicking and static. If my suspicions are correct, then I'm right in assuming you've gotten them too. Do you answer?"

"No." He sighed, removing the peas. "Two of the previous caretakers reported getting them from a short time as well."

"I can't believe this." Lucky began to giggle. "The calls really *have* been coming from inside the house."

Xander stared at her. "I will walk out right now."

"What? Why? That was funny, come on."

"I'm glad I'm not paying you to be a comedian," he said with no bite. "What do you think it means?"

"My initial guess is the psychic link between Hennessee and its occupants doesn't instantly vanish upon exit. It must fade naturally over time when the house doesn't refresh its access." She bit her thumbnail. "What about Stephen? Has he received any?"

"Not that I know of." He pulled out his phone and fired off a text. "I suppose it's calling us in efforts to get us to return?"

"That's plausible, but kind of silly. It needs us present somewhere on its property to speak."

"Are you sure about that?"

"Ninety-six percent." She grinned. "For example, I know how to make spaghetti. I have the memory, but if I don't have the ingredients, I can't cook it. Hennessee remembers who we are, the memories it absorbs, and its own experiences, but it can't duplicate them from nothing. We are the ingredients. Frankly, I don't believe the house is even strong enough for long-distance communication yet."

"Yet." Xander's phone pinged. "No calls," he confirmed.

"So, either he doesn't have a connection to the house or it doesn't have a reason to call him."

So, why, then, would Hennessee call Maverick? What would it need him for? It had her *and* Xander last night.

"*Oh, shit.*" Lucky leaped to her feet, turning in a circle as if she were chasing her thoughts. If Xander *hadn't* been there, she knew it would've used Maverick as a specter for her. It wasn't strong enough to do *both* so it had to *choose*. She stared at Hennessee House as everything came together, slotting into place like puzzle pieces. Since it couldn't give her a specter, it tried to give her the real thing. "*Holy shit.*"

"What? What is it?"

It made sense. All of it. Everything. She'd been partially wrong again, seeing what she wanted and misinterpreting what she didn't. She looked at Xander, waiting with his eyebrows raised in question.

Lucky swallowed hard. He'd hired her, given her a chance, voluntarily helped with her experiments, but she couldn't tell Xander. Not yet. Not first.

Maverick was her person. Being with him felt the way she always imagined it would. There wasn't anyone else she wanted to share her discoveries with more than him.

"It's too early to tell. I need time to process and plan, but *holy shit.*" She hugged him and planted a kiss in the middle of his forehead. "Don't bother me for the next several hours."

36

When Maverick opened his door, he breathed Lucky's name again as if the very sight of her stole all the air in his lungs.

A more enthusiastic "*Lucky?!*" and rapid footsteps sounded from behind him. Rebel, wearing a darling dalmatian-print pajama set, pushed past her dad and hugged Lucky first.

"Hey, Shortcake." She laughed, truly delighted to see her. "Thank you for my cookies and the beautiful letter."

"Xander let you come over?"

"Uhh, well, no. Not exactly." She looked at Maverick, who was watching them with an expression she'd never seen before on his face. "I needed help with something."

Rebel grabbed Lucky's hand, tugging her inside. "Do you want to see my room? I showed Georgia but you didn't get to see last time."

"We redecorated. She picked out everything herself," Maverick explained. "Sweetheart, I think Lucky is here for a reason. She might not be staying long."

Lucky said, "I promise you can show me your room before I go. I wanted to talk to your dad about Hennessee House." She'd waited for Xander to leave before she packed her supplies. Then after sunset, she waited in her car around the corner from the house for the first unknown call to confirm her theory.

"Everything okay?" Maverick stood at her side, hand finding its usual spot on her lower back. "Did something happen?"

Lucky knew not all couples shared their work or even their hobbies with each other, but it seemed to be true for them. He wasn't as passionate about the supernatural as she was and that was more than okay. As long as he always cared enough to listen, she'd be happy.

"I cracked the code," she said. "And I have you to thank for it."

Maverick and Rebel sat together on the couch while Lucky set up her laptop on the opposite side of the coffee table. After typing up all her thoughts and evidence, she spent the afternoon creating hopefully easy-to-follow visual slides. "It's been a while since I did a presentation. I think I'm a little nervous."

"Take your time," he encouraged.

"I need a hard line. Push back on everything," she instructed him. "I need someone I trust to be my skeptic."

He grinned. "That's a tall order, but I'll do my best."

Rebel said, "I'll help too. I'm really good at solving logic puzzles at school. My team *always* wins."

Her partner and her partner-in-crime. Lucky couldn't even remember the last time her heart felt so full. She spun her screen around for them.

Investigating Hennessee House:

A Study in the Sentience of Haunted Places

"Initially, I believed Hennessee House valued fear. That's no longer the case," she began. "Hennessee is a sentient house, and it will do whatever it wants. There's zero morality involved in its decision making when in pursuit of its goals. However, it does value some things more than others. Value number one: children—young people."

"Like me?" Rebel asked.

"Exactly like you—little kids wandering around alone outside or teens breaking in for fun. The house will react and guide them to safety."

Maverick's gaze slid to Rebel. "Wait."

"Yes," Lucky confirmed. "Rebel knew about the square from the pictures, but Hennessee opened the door for her *because* it would've led her straight to you."

"But I left the library when they called me and you found her instead." He dragged a hand down his face, muttering, "You've gotta be kidding me."

"Hennessee thought it was being helpful. It didn't register how much it stressed everyone out in the process because it doesn't really understand human emotions. Which, unfortunately, is kind of a running theme." Lucky hit the next slide.

"Value number two: regular people. Specifically visitors, occupants, residents, etc. Hennessee House isn't trying to scare anyone away. It believes it's giving us what we desire—the things that will make us happiest."

Rebel raised her hand as Maverick asked, "If it doesn't understand emotions, how does it know what happiness is?"

"Hey, I was gonna ask that." Rebel pouted and Maverick kissed the top of her head.

"You can ask the next one," he promised.

"Excellent question, Rebel." Lucky winked at her. "The answer is positive reinforcement. It has a handle on happiness, anger, and fear. That seems to be it for now." She hit the next slide. "Hennessee's *primary* goal is to give an occupant what they desire so they will return the favor by engaging with it. The house enjoys having company and socializing. I'll use myself as an example.

"I said I wanted to find 'secrets in the walls'; it gave me a crawl space *and* a hidden passageway. I called it '*my* haunted house' before; it had *Paranormal Activity*–style temper tantrums in the hall. I challenged it to up the ante; it showed me specters. The house gave me what I asked for every single time. Without fail."

"Can we hear another example?" Maverick looked unconvinced, brow furrowed like the skeptic she needed him to be. "We've all noted that the house treats you differently. Those things made you happy, but what about everyone else?"

"How about Xander?" she offered. "First, I need to explain the function of a specter and how it communicates." She hit the next slide, which gave them a thorough overview. "Xander was very close to his deceased stepmom, Brightly. He's still actively grieving—he *wants* to see her again. He's always thinking of her. So, that's who Hennessee presents as. Specter-Brightly asks him when he's getting married and about his job. It's initiating conversation, which Xander freely engages with, reinforcing the house's belief that this is a desirable interaction.

"However, Hennessee doesn't recognize that this is also tremendously painful for Xander. It's as if he's being haunted with no understanding as to why. He feels sorrow, but the house doesn't recognize that emotion. It knows something is wrong, just not what exactly."

"Okay, wait." Maverick held up a hand. "If the house talks through the specter, why can't it explain its motivations on its own? Clear the air for him."

"It has been—or at least trying to."

When Hennessee House spoke, it wasn't cruelly mocking them. It was being *literal*.

"*are you not happy*" Am I giving you what you wanted?

"*will you stay—will you run*" Was this right? Did I mess up again?

"*give me what I want*" Talk to me, please. I'm lonely.

"*you will stay*" I know you won't leave me.

Lucky suspected Hennessee House's sentience was a fairly recent phenomenon that possibly started with Brightly. Because she never lived there full-time, the house had been alone more often than not with no one to teach it. It was still in the mimicking language stage, trying to learn how to express itself.

She continued, "Hennessee presenting as a loved one, deceased or alive, who looks and acts the part perfectly is devastating. Asking someone to stay forever is sinister icing on the uncanny cake. *Of course*, it makes everyone want to leave."

"Except you."

"I considered it," she reluctantly admitted with a sigh. "The first night I saw my specters, my strongest desire was to be able to share my family with you. Unfortunately, my family talks to me like I'm garbage so that's what the specters did. The house can only mimic memories. It doesn't understand that some of the ones it used were painful for me because I kept going. Every night I came back for more."

Neither Maverick nor Rebel had a response to that, other than staring as her words took root. That was the first time she'd openly talked about her family, barely saying anything at all, but it'd clearly been enough.

Rebel raised her hand. "What happens if you think of someone who made you happy and was nice to you instead?"

"That's most likely who I would see. Hennessee will make a specter of them."

"You should do that, then." An order, not a suggestion. Her little face looked so serious, Lucky had to stop herself from smiling.

"Don't worry. I plan to give it a try soon."

"You can think of me. My specter would be really, extra nice to you and if she's not, I'll beat her up."

Maverick scoffed, squeezing her into a side-hug. "You can't fight a house, honey," he said softly.

"Yes, I can! I will!"

"Okay, okay." He kissed the top of her head again, gently saying, "I'm sorry. I believe you."

"That's very sweet, thank you." Lucky did smile then, and had to stare at the back of her computer to get herself together before she started crying. Rebel, her tiny defender—she wasn't quite sure why that made her so emotional, but it did.

She quickly wiped under her eyes, cleared her throat, and moved on to the next slide. "The unknown phone calls. Sleeping there at night creates a connection between humans and the house. We know this. What I didn't know was how extensive it was. The longer you're there, the more intense it becomes, but it also doesn't stop when you leave. It has to fade over time. Until that happens, it can use the connection to make calls."

"How can a house make phone calls?" Rebel snorted with laughter. "That sounds like a joke on a popsicle stick."

"You're right—it does. In any case, Hennessee has seen our memories. It knows our phone numbers. There are phone lines in the house. It can make the call, but that's about it so far. It doesn't have vocal chords and I don't think it knows Morse code," she mused. Although, it did make clicking noises when she answered. Hmm. "My connection to Hennessee is abnormally strong. Yesterday it discovered I'd been hiding my true desire when I opened Rebel's present. I *think* it realized it didn't need to show me a specter because it had the means to potentially give me the real thing."

Maverick's solemn expression dipped into a frown before understanding set in. "So, the house called *me*?"

"It seems so. Do you have your phone?"

He checked his pockets. "I think it's in my room."

"I'll get it," Rebel volunteered and took off down the short hall. She came back suspiciously fast, as if she'd known exactly where it'd been. "No missed calls."

Lucky checked her phone and had three. "See? I'm not there. It doesn't have a reason to call you *unless* it's for me."

"*Jesus.*" Maverick rubbed his forehead. "I can see why you got drunk last night."

"Believe it or not, that came before." She laughed. "I didn't figure everything out until *you* told me you got those calls—my big light-bulb moment. It was the only thing that made sense. Why else would the house call you and not, let's say, Stephen? Everything fell into place when I started reconsidering everything I knew."

"Have you told Xander yet?"

Lucky shook her head. "I still need to do a final test and create a long-term solution to giving Hennessee what it wants."

"Which is?"

Lucky hit her last slide. "A permanent resident or permanent access. So, what do you think?"

"It was a good presentation. Nothing's confusing. Seems solid." Maverick bit his lip, hesitating. "Overall, though, I'm not sure yet. I need to think it over a little longer."

"Oh," Lucky said, surprised and decidedly not going to *push*. "Sure. Yeah. Of course."

"*I* think you're right about everything," Rebel said, quickly coming to stand by Lucky. "Do you want to see my room now?"

"I'd love to." Lucky grinned.

Rebel's redecorated room had pale pink walls and an early-sunset pink-and-blue ceiling. She gave Lucky a full tour of her bookcases, desk fully stocked with colorful pens and art journals, laptop covered in cartoon stickers, and her brand-new reading corner—an oversize armchair right next to her window, surrounded by her stuffed animal collection.

"You did such a good job," Lucky said. "Your room *feels* like you. That's pretty hard to pull off."

"My dad helped. He gave me the money for everything."

"Good job, Dad. Very nice."

"Thanks," he said dryly. Maverick was watching them from the doorway.

Rebel asked, "Are you sleeping over? Do you want to watch a movie? I usually read a book before bed but we're in the middle of one right now. You'll be too confused to follow along."

"Well, I've already broken the rules. I could stay a little longer."

They both turned their attention to Maverick for confirmation, who suddenly looked genuinely startled. "Oh Jesus, not *together*." He swiftly left the room, laughing. "I wasn't ready!"

Rebel chased after him. "What's so funny? Dad! Can Lucky stay or not?"

When she rejoined them back in the living room, Rebel was accepting the remote from her dad to pick a movie, settling on an epic high fantasy clocking in at over two hours. "This one is my *favorite*," she told Lucky, settling in next to her on the couch. "Have you seen it?"

"Not yet."

Maverick sat on Rebel's other side and draped a blanket over her. "She's gonna talk through the whole thing."

"It's not talking, it's *commentary*. I know *all* the behind-the-scenes stuff. It's *important*."

"It's fine." Lucky laughed. "I don't mind."

Rebel ended up falling asleep in under twenty minutes—out cold before the flashback sequence even ended. Maverick carefully picked her up, carrying her off to bed. Lucky met him in the hall as he was closing her bedroom door.

"We have a pretty strict bedtime schedule," he explained. "There isn't much that keeps her up."

"I should've called first," Lucky admitted. "After I put everything together, I think my brain stopped processing rational thought. All I could think was how much I wanted to see you. Sorry."

"How are you so beautiful?"

"That's—"

"Don't you dare."

Lucky pressed her lips together, fighting her smile.

"You're beautiful." He stepped forward, placing his hands on either side of her against the wall.

Her hands trembled as she placed them flat against his chest.

She hadn't been able to touch him in weeks. She'd been in his apartment for over an hour, silently timing how long she had to continue to wait. "If you were allowed, would you come see me?"

"During the day. *Am* I allowed yet?"

"Xander wouldn't give me a straight answer. What if I'm wrong about the house? What if I'm not done and I have to go back to square one? I'm tired of being alone," she confessed. "I miss you. I miss everyone."

"Your work is important to you. We understand."

"I liked it better when it was our work. When we were together, as a team."

Maverick nodded. "It's late. You should stay." He gently tugged her hips, pulling her toward him. They walked together to his bedroom farther down the hall.

37

Maverick closed his bedroom door and said, "We can't."

"I figured." Lucky nodded solemnly.

"I can't risk Rebel hearing us," he explained. "Even thinking about it stresses me out."

She grinned. "I understand, but for the record, I do know how to be discreet. I'm not loud."

He cocked an eyebrow and kissed the space in front of her ear, whispering, "If I have my way, you will be."

"Oh." Well. All right, then.

He chuckled as he kissed the corner of her mouth. She forced herself to hold still, waiting for him to ravish her properly, but he seemed intent on tormenting her instead. He kissed under her jaw and down her neck—hardly a poor replacement. She happily helped by tilting her head back for him. It'd taken her some time to realize it, but when she thought of romance, his were the kind of kisses she'd always imagined. His comforting touch lingered on her skin *and* in her mind. It was perfect where perfection wasn't supposed to exist. The most divine combination of physical intimacy and mental pleasure.

"I want to take a quick shower before bed," she said absently.

Maverick suddenly met her gaze, eyes alight. "We could do it in there? My shower isn't near her room, and if we put on music with the water running, it might . . . no?"

Lucky was shaking her head and frowning. "Shower sex might be okay, but maybe not the first time? I don't think I'd like that."

"Gotcha." He kissed her temple. "Would you be open to having company?"

"In the shower? Why?"

"You said all I had to do was ask." He took her hands and looked into her eyes. "I'm asking to join you. I want to take a shower with you."

"Oh. *Oh.* I've never done that before."

"Would you like to?"

"If you think *you'd* be okay just showering, I'd be fine with that. I mean, I'd be naked, so I completely understand if that's—"

"Let's go." In one fluid turn, he steered them both toward his bathroom.

She snort-giggled at his sudden eagerness. "Are you sure?"

"Positive. Let's go."

Maverick's sink and mirror were outside of the bathroom itself—Lucky waited there while he got the water started. Her travel toothbrush was still on the counter, next to his in the holder. Same for the toothpaste she liked and the rest of her toiletries. She didn't expect him to throw her stuff away or anything, but . . . maybe she did. Seeing them made her chest tighten. She shook out her hands and took a deep breath to steady herself. Little things like that always meant more to her than they probably should have.

She began pulling her braids up into a high bun. Her gaze lingered a second too long over a prescription bottle as he sidled up to her.

"I take them for anxiety," he said, kissing her shoulder.

Lucky suspected as much, but he never mentioned it before. "Have they been helpful?"

"I think so. It's easy to fall into the cycle of feeling like I'm doing great and then wondering, *Is it me or is it the pills?* Then I go off them and almost immediately it's like, *Oh no, it's the pills too*." He laughed. "I need to attack it from all angles. Exercise, staying busy, meditation, and medication. All of it, together, really makes a difference for me."

She watched him through the mirror, trying to gauge if he was okay talking about it, ultimately deciding to change the subject. "How are you so wonderful?" she asked. "You're wonderful."

He scoffed. "Sure. Come on."

"I'm serious," she said as they walked into the bathroom.

"Uh-huh."

"Accept my compliment," she demanded.

"Already done."

She narrowed her eyes at him before letting go and immediately noticed a distinct lack of steam. "It's not hot enough."

"I'm not interested in burning my skin off," he complained.

"You'll be fine," she promised, slightly adjusting the temperature. "You're taking a shower with me, which means we do it my way."

"What else does that include?" He laughed. "Because I was thinking I could undress you . . ."

Her stomach flipped and she stared at him wide-eyed. Being naked in front of Maverick didn't feel like a big deal. Him taking her clothes off, though? Big deal. Huge. Massive. In her mind, taking a shower together wasn't inherently sexual unless there was a choice to make it that way. Letting him undress her was definitely a *choice*.

"Or not," he amended softly, holding up his hands. "Can I ask for one thing?"

"Okay?"

"I'll wait in the bedroom. You go in first." He gently stroked down her arms. "Tell me when you're ready. Face front and don't turn around."

"Why?"

"Because that's what I'm asking for. You can trust me."

Lucky undressed quickly, neatly folding and setting everything on top of the hamper. In the shower, she concentrated on how soothing the hot water felt on her tense muscles and took a few moments to check in with herself. Old habits and fears died slow painful deaths. She wanted to do this. She wanted to be there. This wasn't too much. She felt comfortable saying otherwise.

"Ready!" She did as requested, not turning around when she heard him step in behind her.

"All good?"

"Yep."

"Tell me if it's not."

"I will," she said, smiling because she trusted him.

Maverick reached past her, wetting a washcloth. She gasped, surprised as he began washing her back. Using gentle circular motions, he skillfully moved across her shoulder blades and down the curve of her spine.

Lucky closed her eyes, allowing herself to relax and revel in the feeling of being cared for. No one had ever done this for her before. She never even would've thought to ask. It just didn't seem like something she'd be into. She'd been wrong—this felt indulgently marvelous. He placed one hand on her hip to keep her steady as he neared her lower back. His touch became firmer, movements more like a massage. Her happy sigh suspiciously resembled a moan.

"Still okay?" he whispered.

Hoping to make him laugh, she wiggled her ass right as he reached it and was rewarded with a low chuckle.

Unable to stop smiling, she asked, "Are you feeling shy?"

He snorted. "No."

"Embarrassed?"

"No."

"Then why can't I turn around?"

"Because you're not attracted to me."

She didn't mean to laugh but the disbelieving cackle had a mind of its own. "Oh, yes, I am. What are you talking about?"

"Not sexually."

She scoffed. "That one doesn't count."

"Why not?" The sincerity in his tone caught her off guard.

"Because it's not something I can change, Maverick. I'm attracted to you in all the ways that matter to me. Would you like me to list them? Because I absolutely *will*." She turned around before he could stop her. "Stop being so—oh, *wow*." Not wanting to be rude, she forced herself to look him in the eye, cheeks burning like hellfire. "That is definitely not little. Yeah."

"This is so strange." He laughed and then clarified, "Not bad. Just different than what I'm used to. You're very . . . calm right now."

Personally, she would've gone with *startled*, but a win was a win. She noticed he was also keeping his eyes on hers. "So are you."

"Yep." He nodded and they burst out laughing. "But really, looking at me—you're not turned on? At all?"

Instead of answering, she asked, "Would it be too much if I touched you? Above the waist?" He consented and she grabbed the second washcloth he'd brought.

She began washing his chest with the same mindfulness he'd shown her. Slow, methodical circles. Gentle kneading in tense areas. All while trying to keep a ridiculously pleased grin off her face.

"Seeing you naked isn't going to magically change me. Although"—she paused to look him up and down—"your body? One hundred out of ten. Beautiful. You have no idea how giddy I feel looking at you. I'm attracted to your body because it's your body. Try thinking about it like that without the qualifiers. I like *all* of you. Every single part, inside and out."

He casually placed his hands on her hips, and without missing a beat, she began washing his arms, from his shapely shoulders down to his wrists. She glanced at him while continuing the purposeful rhythm she'd created. He was watching her closely, a pensive look on his face.

"What are you thinking about?" she asked.

"Trying to wrap my head around everything. You enjoy sex, right? Not just liking it or thinking it's fine. You enjoy it?" His voice sounded strained—hoarse and concerned. "Because if you don't, please tell me."

"I can, yes." She wanted to be honest, and tried not to sound negative, but the truth was far more nuanced than that.

"I think I might've read too many accounts of people confessing that they only had sex because their partner needed it. They didn't even like it. I don't want that for you or for us."

"I see," she said. "Stripped down to basic parts, I like the way it feels. But I don't think I'd ever ask you to have sex with me, if that's what you're getting at."

"No, that's not what I mean."

"Switch places with me," she said, moving around him. "You in front." She added more bodywash and started on his back. He truly was a sight to behold. And touch. "Please continue."

"Basic parts. Okay," he echoed, thoughtfully. "For me, your enjoyment isn't optional. I want you to . . . uh, have a good time. I need to feel it. That."

She kissed his neck. "Say it however you normally would."

"Uh, no, I *really* don't think I should do that. We're not there yet." He turned his head to look at her, laughing nervously. "I'm very . . . exacting. I don't want to have any doubts. So, let's say, I tell you to look at me. In that moment, I want to see how hard it is for you to do what I ask. But once you do, I'm going to"—he stopped himself again—"*reward* your efforts. And then I'm going to ask again."

"Ah." Lucky began focusing on the shower wall in front of them. He was being cautious again, testing the waters, and she knew he'd barely skimmed the surface.

While slightly unexpected, she wasn't too shaken. She wrapped her arms around his waist and pressed her body firmly against his. "I think I understand what you mean. Would it always be like that? Because I enjoy . . . gentle." It took a moment for her to work up enough nerve to look him in the eye, but she did it. "Slow and steady wins the sensual race kind of vibe with kissing. Would that be okay too?"

"*Yes.*" He answered so enthusiastically it instantly put a smile on her face. "Now we're getting somewhere. What else do you like?"

"That's the only thing that's stood out so far," she said. "I only really know what I don't like."

"That's okay. We'll work on that," he said, holding her arms in place like a promise.

"You want to help me?"

He gave her an incredulous look. "I will do *whatever* you want."

"Even roleplaying? I think you might've been right."

Roleplaying seemed fun because they'd both be in on the joke. They'd be playing characters *together*. And when it was over, they'd go back to being perfectly happy as themselves.

"Especially that."

"Even—"

"What. Ever. You. Want. I do not care. I will do it." He laughed. "I highly doubt *anything* you genuinely want to do will shock me."

She narrowed her eyes to mess with him. "I'll see about that."

EARLY THE NEXT morning, Lucky woke up naturally on her own. No alarm. No phone call. Nothing tugging at her mind. She sighed into a stretch, happily rolling over inside of Maverick's embrace. He was still sleeping, serene and peaceful, breathing deep and even. She delicately brushed her thumb across the line of his bottom lip and smiled at his sleepy groan. She could get used to waking up next to him every day. But she had a job to finish first.

Lucky wanted to return before Hennessee woke up looking for her. She was almost finished getting ready when she heard Maverick shift in bed. "I can feel you brooding. I'm not supposed to be here, remember?"

"So, you were gonna sneak out?" he asked, tone more sonorous than she'd ever heard.

She grinned, glancing at him. "Maybe."

"You should stay."

"As tempting as that is, you know I can't."

Maverick grumbled in protest as he got out of bed. He kissed her cheek on his way to the bathroom. While she waited for him, she checked her phone to count the missed calls and filled out her spreadsheet.

He put on a shirt before sitting next to her on the bed. "Last night, you said you have an 'abnormally strong connection' with the house. What did that mean?"

"I've been there consistently, longer than anyone has in years." She explained the depth of the connection with examples to give him a better idea of her progress. "I also have a memory palace full of first impressions. It gets to meet new people as often as it likes and learn more about us. I suspect that's part of why it treats me differently."

"And you're just . . . fine with that? Not worried at all?"

She regarded him for a moment, trying to figure out where he was going. "You seem to think I should be?"

"I stand by what I said last night: your presentation was very good. Extremely thorough." He paused, gaze dropping to his lap. "The questions that I have are about you."

Lucky sat up straighter, rolling her shoulders back and giving him her full attention. She didn't have much time left but could spare a few minutes to reassure him.

"I don't understand how you're fine with the house constantly being in your head," he continued. "What makes it any different than a ghost?"

"Oh, well for one, Hennessee is far more powerful. It destroyed the ghost. It's not in my memory palace anymore."

Maverick's eyes widened—and Lucky knew she'd said the wrong thing. "Did you ask it to do that?"

"Not exactly, no," she admitted. "We have an agreement now. It hasn't done anything like that since."

"Lucky. I think you need to leave that house for your own good." He held her hands in between his and pressed them to his mouth. "I think you might be possessed."

38

Lucky laughed so hard she doubled over, gasping for breath. "Oh my god, Maverick, stop! I am *not* possessed."

Maverick's expression clearly disagreed. "I think the house might be influencing you, making you feel sorry for it. Making you think you're in control when you're not."

"I am not possessed. I have *always* been like this," she said, laughter dying down.

He stared at her, unconvinced. "That's exactly what a possessed person would say."

"All Hennessee wants is to not be alone anymore. Highly relatable if you ask me." She shook her head. "If I were possessed, do you really think the house would've let me leave last night to come see you? It spent the whole night calling me."

"It might. Maybe it plans to use you to lure more people in and this was a test run. The calls are a diversion so people like me won't get suspicious," he said. "It hijacked your body and made you walk barefoot into the orchard. Who's to say it can't do more? Who's to say it already hasn't? You're there, alone, day and night."

Lucky could not for the life of her tell if he was being serious. He was joking—he had to be. "Stop being ridiculous." She smooshed his cheeks. "Look into my eyes and listen to my words. I am not possessed."

"Because it's sunrise. House can't hold you right now," he said.

Her hands fell into her lap. "Do I really seem that different to you? Did I last night?"

"No," he admitted. "If specters are supposed to be near-perfect copies, do you think it would be able to trick me?"

"Specters don't exist outside of the house," she said carefully.

"But if it used your body, do you think it would be able to trick me?" he asked.

Lucky refused to answer that. "I'm not possessed. I'm in full control during my experiments."

"I believe you." But he sighed as he said it. "I just think you could stand to be a lot safer than you're being."

"I *am* being safe." She stood up and so did he.

"I don't think you are," he said calmly. "You can't even be objective. You refuse to even entertain the idea that there could be something wrong with that house. Maybe it isn't some big misunderstanding. *Maybe* it just likes watching people suffer."

"Well, I don't believe that." She raised her chin in defiance. "Any other questions? I need to go soon."

"No," he said, looking away. "That's it."

Maverick walked with her to the parking lot, neither of them speaking. She threw her bag in the back seat and was holding the driver's-side door open when she turned to say goodbye—and read what he wanted to say in his eyes before he said it.

"Lucky, wait. Maybe you should take a day off. Get some distance and go back in with a clear head. Xander will understand."

One last plea to see reason. Lucky wanted to smile but couldn't bring herself to fake one. "I don't need to do that," she said. "I'm hoping tonight can be my final experiment."

He looked taken aback, surprised even. "Are you—are you honestly planning to give that house *permanent* access to you?"

She scoffed. "It's just an option. I never said that's what I'm doing."

"Then what are you doing?"

"Being myself," she said honestly. "This is who I am. These are the kinds of risks I take and that you signed up to deal with. I'm going back to Hennessee House to finish what I started. I'm sorry you don't like it."

She wasn't surprised when Maverick had nothing to say to that.

Lucky knew from the beginning their personalities were like oil and water. This moment became inevitable from the second she agreed to be his, but she never would've guessed that it'd go down like this.

To be fair, were his concerns *really* that far-fetched?

Possession wasn't impossible. Improbable, but not outside the realm of possibility. He didn't know Hennessee the way she did. She condensed weeks of research into a twenty-minute presentation and *asked* him to be her skeptic. Not to mention she *told* him her worst fear was being possessed. Of course, he was going to check.

That wasn't what was upsetting her. All she'd ever wanted was to be believed.

He believed the supernatural was real, but he didn't believe in *her*.

She wasn't a "useless" twelve-year-old "psychic" anymore. She'd grown up, forging her own path one uncharted step at a time. But those devastating memories remained, lingering in the way that scars did, and those scars were half as old as she was. So, why did they still hurt like fresh wounds? How did they split open so easily because of a simple conversation that made perfect sense?

Lust wasn't the only thing capable of playing people for fools, apparently.

"I've put one hundred and ten percent of myself into investigating Hennessee House," she said. "I sacrificed everything to get here. This opportunity is supposed to be the start of my life's work." Tears rudely sprang out of her eyes, making her jaw ache and voice tremble. *Shit.* She managed to continue anyway. "I broke the rules because I missed you. I came here because I wanted to share the most important thing I have in *my* life with you. Gonna be honest, really wasn't expecting you to kind of diminish everything I've done by implying I don't know what I'm doing. That I'm just some possessed puppet who doesn't know any better."

Lucky waited for Maverick to say something, anything, and he didn't. She watched in real time as words left him and he retreated into himself, overwhelmed and needing time.

"Call me later, okay?" She kissed his cheek before hopping in the car. "If you want."

LUCKY WANTED TO bring everything full circle. She waited patiently as the sun began to set, standing with her back pressed against Hennessee House's front door. Ending where she began.

This time, however, Gengar supervised her from the staircase next to the camera she set up. A much welcome addition.

Despite wishing she had a team with her, she was ready. At sunset she'd hit the ground running on pure instinct. Tonight would make or break her stay in Hennessee House.

"Hello, Lucky."

"Hello, Hennessee House. I've been thinking a lot about you lately."

Specter-Maverick wore her favorite blue sweater and glasses. "Why am I not surprised?"

Lucky had to turn away to clear her head. Too late to change her mind now. She should've picked Xander for her specter—honestly, what was she thinking? Once again, she'd done this to herself by spending the day indulging in her thoughts about the real Maverick. Was he okay? She said what she needed to say, but did it upset him? Would he call tonight?

He needed time. She'd be fine waiting, just as she promised, because she trusted him to be honest and always come to her when he was ready.

"Can we talk? Please? I don't want to make you glitch if I don't have to." She kept her gaze fixed on his shoes.

"Yes."

She had her questions memorized and wanted to start off swinging for the fences. "Out of all the caretakers, why did you treat me differently?"

"You're a know-it-all."

She couldn't call it—could be the specter or the house. "So, it was my ability?"

"Your presence brings me much contentment."

She quickly glanced up—its face was blank, expressionless—
and regretted it. She didn't like seeing Maverick like that. At all.
It felt wrong, like something crawling under her skin. "That's
quite the sentence."

"This form is better. I remember it."

"Interesting."

Lucky was positive the house remembered Brightly too, but
Specter-Brightly didn't speak with that level of precision. Xander
didn't mention it saying anything out of character either. It was
possible the "it" Hennessee referred to was the connection, and
not the person. Did having a connection alter the specter's capa-
bilities? Maybe it relied on Lucky to generate it and used its own
connection to strengthen it.

"You are eager to understand," Specter-Maverick said. "Amusing."

"Are you laughing at me because I'm wrong?"

"I am embracing you because you care."

"Who made you?" Lucky nervously shuffled her feet. "You
never answer when I ask."

"I exist here. I am home."

"Does that mean you don't know?"

"I know what it is to wait. I want more."

"More what?" She tried to keep her frustration in check. This
was the best conversation they'd had so far. She had to be patient
with it. "I can't read you so you're gonna have to help me out here."

"*Could* you give me a home in your palace?"

"I could try. You're not human. It might not work," she said.
"You'll also have to let our connection go first. Are you willing to
do that?"

The first two times she overloaded were accidents and her

ability barely prevailed. She might be strong enough to stand against Hennessee House, but that didn't mean an abnormal reading wouldn't damage her in the process. She was alone. She needed to be safe.

Maverick would've been proud.

Meanwhile, Specter-Maverick considered her request for quite some time before saying, "Yes. I will give you my eyes."

Lucky very nearly recoiled—again with the sinister vibes. At this point, Hennessee had to be doing that shit on purpose. Years of isolation must've warped any and all chances of it having a normal sense of humor. She performed a quick self-check—all systems go—and then braced herself to perform an impossible reading.

"I will let go." Specter-Maverick held out its hand. "You must follow."

"All right. I'm trusting you, Hennessee. Don't hurt me." She took its hand—it was smooth, soft to the touch, and as cool as peppermint—and expected to walk to some hidden corner deep within the house where it hid the thing it considered to be its eyes.

Instead, she took its hand and saw *everything*.

Hennessee House read like a . . . television? A giant flat-screen mounted onto a wall covered in Hennessee's floral wallpaper. The white static on the screen clicked through the speakers and was the only light in the otherwise pitch-black room.

Lucky gasped, fully enthralled by the concept coming through. "*Whoa*."

Because the house didn't *have* eyes. It didn't have a core for her to read. But it knew how her ability worked and created an alternative that allowed her to see.

Each channel allowed her to watch a different chosen memory.

Owner after owner moving in and moving on. Being empty for long stretches of time—a *For Sale* sign staked in the overgrown front yard. Neglect and decay and a loneliness so profound it made an old house realize it existed. Learning how to open the doors and windows. Experimenting with electricity and wires. Moving the curtains to entertain itself when neighbors walked by. The Hennessee family on a house tour—*Brightly*. Endless, painful renovations. Brightly alone, knitting in the parlor room late at night, seemingly talking to herself until the lights flickered in response. Language and numbers and concepts. Observing Xander and Brightly in the orchard and assigning them a word, *family*. Discovering that disabling the cameras meant more people would visit. Extra dust and dirt made people stay longer. Unruly bushes and too much fruit made people stay longer. Gengar, as a kitten, curled up in a corner on the porch.

Silence, so much silence, when connections cut out.

Lucky sighed with her entire body, slouching against the door as she let go of Specter-Maverick's hand. Finally, she got it right. Companionship had always been Hennessee's goal.

And if it hadn't been for Maverick, she never would've figured that out.

Maverick caring enough to call her every night led to her asking him to help with her experiment.

Maverick falling asleep gave Hennessee the boost it needed to create the perfect specter to help her understand. Lucky's desire for him directly led to her success. She laughed to herself, heart feeling fuller than it ever had. He'd changed her life, and what a life it was becoming.

Hennessee's true voice resonated inside Lucky's head. *"you see me."*

"I do. You are both fascinating and deeply unimaginative," Lucky teased out loud. "A TV? Really? You didn't have anything more creative to use?"

"*you will stay.*"

Letting go of their connection so she could safely perform the reading had been a tremendous act of trust. All those severed connections were the only things that haunted Hennessee House.

"Well, Xander did say my residence here could last for as long as I needed. Do you have more secrets to discover? I've obviously figured out the why but not the how you're able to do what you can. We'll have to convince him to let us continue." She wanted to give as thorough an answer as possible without upsetting the house. It had serious abandonment issues—she didn't want to add to them. "I'm not leaving like tomorrow, but I will leave someday. And I won't be able to come back. I need you to accept that."

"*i accept—you are family—family visits.*"

Lucky instantly thought of Reggie. "Yeah. Sometimes."

"*i will sleep.*"

"What? Why? What's wrong?"

But Specter-Maverick disappeared.

Lucky pushed off the door, spinning in a pointless circle. "Hennessee? Where did you go?"

The doorbell rang. She hesitated for a split second before answering it.

Maverick Phillips was standing on Hennessee's front porch.

"Hi." Lucky had been humbled enough to admit that not only was she flustered, but she was thrilled to be so. Even now, seeing Maverick still did that to her. "What are you doing here?"

A black duffel bag hung from his shoulder, and he wore *the* blue sweater. Her brain momentarily *glitched*, thinking that

Hennessee was trying to trick her. She might have truly believed it and despaired, if she hadn't also spotted Maverick's car in the driveway.

"I wanted to—I was *hoping* to spend some time together. Right now. If you'll have me. May I come in?"

"No, you can't."

"Right, uh, I know Xander doesn't want me here." He quickly cleared his throat. "But you came to my place and—"

"Xander? I said no because you're too close. Hennessee's reach spans the entire property. From the sidewalk to the back of the orchard. You shouldn't be here. It'll know— *Oh*."

Oh.

This was why the house suddenly said it was going to sleep! Hennessee was giving Maverick, who refused to be inside at night, space to be comfortable. Lucky stepped onto the porch, closing the door behind her. *Thank you*, she thought, hoping that Hennessee could hear her.

The porch light flickered beside them.

"That's actually *why* I'm here. I want you to show me the progress you've made with the house," Maverick said. "And I'm also going to beg for forgiveness." He dropped to his knees to prove it. "I am so sorry. I've never been so sorry in my entire life."

"Oh my god, *stand up*," she said, laughing as he held her hips looking up at her. "I forgive you, please get up before you give the neighbors the wrong idea."

"I didn't mean to diminish your work, but I did and I'm sorry," he said. "You were right about everything. You said 'your caution will be your undoing' and it almost was."

"Okay, you know what?" She grabbed his hands to give herself room to kneel in front of him. "I need you to stop. My heart cannot take it. I will pass away, perish, cease to exist if you keep groveling like this."

"You're so strong, all the time," he continued. "It's too easy to forget how fragile you are."

"I'm not fragile. What are you talking about?" Lucky laughed, but he didn't.

"Because you patched yourself up, but the cracks are still there," he explained. "You still have to live with them. I still need to be careful. I can't talk to you like that without being clear what I'm doing. I shouldn't have assumed that you knew what I *wasn't* saying.

"I've interviewed dozens of self-proclaimed psychics, mediums, empaths, and not a single one even comes close to touching you. You're *good* at this. You're as brilliant as you are compassionate, and extraordinarily talented. I've told you how truly remarkable you are. I always have, since the very beginning, and I always will."

Lucky felt like she couldn't breathe. She balled her hands into fists, pressing her nails into her palms. "You're so important to me," she began, voice breaking. "The thought of my feelings for you being used to hurt me scared me so badly I figured out how to hide them. I held on to seeing my brother every night. I held on to my misery because I thought it gave me more control.

"If I hadn't met you, I don't know if I ever would've figured this out. I would've been spinning in haunted-house circles forever because I had no one. The house wouldn't have been able to create a specter for me."

"I think you're giving me too much credit." His short, skeptical laugh made her smile. He really had no idea how important he was.

"You are who I desire most. If you had somehow been my specter too early, I can't say with one hundred percent certainty that I would've made good choices." She shook her head. "Wanting to keep you to myself, hiding you from Hennessee House, was the decision that ultimately put me on the path to discovering the right answer."

Because Maverick had taken the time to get to know Lucky in a way no one ever had before. His connection with Hennessee gave the house access to everything he thought and felt about her. That combined with Lucky's desire for Maverick, and having a working knowledge of her ability allowed the house to create a perfect specter. It inherently understood them both because of their connection and learned a new skill. Together, they gave the house clarity.

"I was your specter?" He sounded alarmed. "It made you see me?"

"I know that might be hard to hear, but yes. Hennessee needed both of us. It's okay if you're not interested in what I do. I'd like you to be, but I know this isn't for everyone. As long as I *feel* like you're supporting me, I'll be fine."

"I don't think that's enough. Not for me. I need to show you. That's why I'm here." His hint of a smile was tinged with regret. "When I tell you *everybody* yelled at me? Rebel heard almost everything. She said, and I quote, 'I am very disappointed in you, Daddy! I'm staying at Riley's!' She hasn't called me that in years."

Lucky giggled. "Oh, Rebel."

"Georgia too. After Rebel called her to tell on me, I thought she was going to drag me here herself to apologize for pushing back too hard." He laughed softly. "I don't know what I was thinking. What happened at Penny Place got in my head."

"What do you mean?" She held his beautiful face in her hands.

"You didn't feel it like I did. That entity followed you," he said. "You attracted it like a magnet. You were talking and I could feel it pouring into me, judging the shit out of me. It didn't believe in us—it believed in you, and you wanted me, so it let me go. I wasn't worthy of you. And then I went and proved it."

"You didn't prove anything. That's not how the legend works. It's all or nothing. You can't twist the rules however you want," she reminded him. "Can we stand up now, please? My knees are killing me."

"Mine too," he admitted.

After they stood up, she kissed both of his cheeks, and then nodded to the door. "Are you sure you want to do this? You don't have to."

"I'm sure. If this is where you're standing, then so am I."

On its own, Hennessee House's front door swung open, inviting them in.

Epilogue

Early the next morning while Maverick was still asleep, Lucky snuck downstairs to call Xander.

She explained everything as thoroughly as she could and ended up pacing from the parlor room wall to the sitting room wall and back again while waiting for him to remember how to speak. Every so often she checked her phone screen to ensure he hadn't hung up. Six minutes so far.

Lucky yawned, throwing her head back and stretching her face muscles. "Are you going to say something? Anything?"

"You mean to tell me, that all I had to do was *think of someone else?*" Xander asked.

"Anything else, really, but preferably a person." She shrugged. "It became a haunted house for me, but I suspect that was an exception, not a rule."

"I cannot believe we were all so completely off base," he said. "It speaks volumes that we immediately assumed the worst. In hindsight, in what world would having a few final moments with a guinea pig be considered a torment?"

"It was the same with Eunice. The house didn't do anything except try to calm her with her favorite scent until she decided to leave. It knew she wasn't going to stay the moment she walked in."

However, Hennessee most definitely found scaring people amusing because it liked exaggerated emotional responses. There was a fine line between annoying and spooky—the house won either way.

Xander asked, "Were you able to discover what happened with Brian?"

Lucky sucked in a breath. "Turns out Hennessee was not a fan. Didn't like him at all. It was genuinely and aggressively trying to evict him. I couldn't read any of the people I saw in the house's memories, so unfortunately, I don't know why. But I highly recommend *never* getting on the house's bad side."

Xander made a noncommittal noise. "What of the names on the wall?"

"Easy," she said, still pacing for no particular reason. "By engaging with its chosen memory, it felt comfortable engaging with ours."

"Chosen memory?"

"Hennessee has very fond memories of a certain small, pale, and dark-haired boy giving it a *tattoo* once upon a time. It didn't use that word but that was the impression I got," she said. "It wanted to relive the moment you wrote your name. It was only fair that it then allowed us to experience some of our memories too."

"And it believed it was using our memories to make us happy. A peace offering that would hopefully lead to companionship."

Xander laughed, airy and brief. "Ah, Lucky Hart, you are a wonder."

"Stop flattering me like that. It's gross," she joked.

"Have you decided what's next for you now that *The Caretaker* is technically wrapped?"

"I have immediate plans to collect all the beautiful money you owe me," she said. "I was also hoping to stay with Hennessee for a little bit longer. It feels wrong to up and leave it right now." The house had already reestablished their connection. She fully expected to feel that familiar tug in a few hours.

"I unfortunately agree. It may take some time to find a permanent live-in caretaker. I appreciate your willingness to continue."

"With pay." She cleared her throat. "Willingness to continue *with pay*."

Xander was silent for longer than she liked. "Of course."

She punched the air. "You also wouldn't happen to have any leads on wealthy acquaintances in need of someone with my particular skill set?"

"An associate of mine may have something in the works you'd be interested in," he said. "But I'd rather hear what you would like to do."

Upstairs, Maverick rounded the corner and began descending the steps. She grinned at the sight of him, topless in plaid pajama bottoms that matched the shirt she wore. His second night inside Hennessee House had been nearly sleepless again, but easier overall.

The house didn't *actually* go to sleep. It had just said that as shorthand, so she spent some time coaching Maverick on how to choose his specter just in case Hennessee wanted to talk to him.

She also gave him some tips based on her own experiences—he wouldn't like seeing Rebel and he probably shouldn't think about Lucky either because she was already there. But as the hours passed, it became apparent the house would keep its word and let them be. So, they shifted their focus solely to each other.

Without breaking his stride, Maverick gestured for her to follow and continued toward the kitchen.

Lucky nodded. "Keep investigating," she admitted to Xander. "But with a team I can mentor. Maybe try getting into contact with young ESPers who are having a hard time like I did. Having someone to look up to would've been life-changing for me."

"That's ambitious."

"Yeah. I mean, it's not like I can establish a summer camp for gifted youngsters." She laughed. "It's just something I've been thinking about lately. I have to go. Maverick is up now. So."

"Up where?"

"Oh, did I not mention that? Maverick spent the night—okay, talk to you later, bye!"

Lucky sprinted to the kitchen, sliding the last few feet on the hardwood floor thanks to her socks. "Good morning." She stepped into his space, sliding her arms around his lower back and lifting her head to kiss him. Dizzy and breathless from happiness, she knew she was down bad and wouldn't have it any other way.

He whispered, "Are you hungry?" against her lips and kissed her again.

She hadn't been to the grocery store in a while. The refrigerator was crying out for help, and the pantry was a picked-over wasteland. "I think I have some eggs left."

He snorted. "I can work with that."

"So can I," she said to defend herself. "I've been learning how to cook. One new recipe every day."

"Is that so?"

She nodded. "I'll even cook this morning to prove it."

Lucky kept an eye on Maverick as she made eggs Benedict, noting the lingering tension in his posture, the tightness around his eyes, and how much he worried at his palms. He insisted he was fine but nervous, convinced Hennessee was waiting for the perfect moment—for him to drop his guard—to launch the perfect jump scare.

But he trusted her more and would stay until noon. They had plans to pick Rebel up and take her out for the day. After plating their breakfast and feeding a yowling Gengar, they sat at the kitchen table together.

"I'm impressed." He chuckled. "I thought recipe meant like . . . avocado toast."

"I have a recipe for that now too. Well?" she asked expectantly after his first bite.

"It's good. Really good." He smiled. "I have some news. I didn't get to tell you last night that they released the shooting schedule for the next season of *BARD*. It's going to be the final one."

"Did you?"

"I did. I'm retiring from hosting and transitioning to the new production unit as lead writer. Guess who's our producer?"

She gasped. "Not Georgia?"

"The one and only. *Shortcake* came together beautifully. She got a promotion."

"She didn't tell me that," she said with a slight pout.

"I don't think she's told anyone. She's happy about it, but a little overwhelmed too. It's a lot of responsibility. She'll be fine."

Lucky made a mental note to text Georgia later to check in. "When do I get to see the finished episodes? I can't wait."

"It's officially set to go live two weeks before *The Caretaker* and that depends on when you wrap up here. But I'm thinking about hosting a private premiere for family and Rebel's friends before it goes live. Make it extra special for her."

"Any ideas for potential venues?"

"My apartment."

"What if you held it here? Having a party would make Hennessee's entire year."

"I'd have to think about that." He began pushing the food around on his plate. "Rebel would love it, but my family might not come. They wouldn't understand. It would just freak them out."

"Ah, got it." She gently nudged his foot under the table and rubbed along his calf, nervous and needing to touch him. "Does the rest of your family know I have ESP yet?" Odds were good they did by now. Rebel or Silvia might've told them, and they already changed their minds about her and—

"You're not a house, Lucky. You're a person. They'll deal." Maverick stared at her, quietly contemplative. "Does your family really talk to you like you're garbage?"

"Yeah. I mean, they did. I don't talk to most of them anymore." She sucked in a shaky breath and cleared her throat. "I don't bother with my extended family at all. With my mom, it's complicated but it's also not. I decided I needed to let go and she let me. She didn't fight for me. I realized I didn't want her to. I'd like to talk to my brother, but I don't think that feeling is mutual. I sent him an email the other day."

His expression brightened. "Did he reply?"

"Yeah." Xander had convinced her to send it after Specter-Brightly disappeared and they'd gone back to drinking. Reggie responded within an hour.

"What did he say?"

"I don't know. I haven't read it."

"Lucky—"

"I know! I know! I just . . . I'm worried." She whined, unable to help it. "What if it says *Fuck off and never contact me again* and I shatter into a million pieces?"

Maverick's eyes flashed, his entire body tensing. She'd never seen him look like that before—fearsome with barely concealed anger. "It better not," he rumbled. The implied threat was sure and steady as stone.

Lucky giggled, completely surprised by the sudden appearance of Maverick's protective side. He wasn't a fighter by nature. She had never even heard him raise his voice before. He thought and overthought until he was ready to talk things out, but he'd fight for Rebel and for her without hesitation. She got up and walked around to his side of the table. He opened his arms and she sat on his lap, holding him tightly and pressing their cheeks together.

"You should read it," he murmured, relaxing against her. "What happened to almost fearless?"

Love honestly *ruined* that. It was easy to be almost fearless when she had nothing to lose but herself. Now the things that scared her made her feel alive in a way few things ever had.

"Do you want to read it together?" he asked.

"Okay."

Lucky pulled out her phone, opening her email.

"Reggie," Maverick read. "So many *R* names in our lives."

"I know, right?" She laughed even as her hands shook.

"Whatever it says, you still have me," Maverick promised. "I'm not going anywhere unless you tell me to."

Lucky kissed his temple, strengthened by his familiar scent and being in his arms. "You better get comfortable then."

Reggie had only written three sentences:

Call me. It's been too long. I miss you, Lucky Bug.

Acknowledgments

I started writing the first seeds of this story while recovering from surgery. The entirety of this book, every word on every page, is dedicated to Dr. Nakamaru. You believed me when I said I was so miserable and in so much pain I was ready to give up. Thank you for saving my life and giving me a second chance.

This book is also dedicated to my ace comrades, to my passionate believers in magic and the supernatural, and to all my alt-Black babes who have only ever wanted to be themselves. Your families might not understand you, but I do.

As manuscripts do, this one has changed so much from first draft to final book and there many people to thank for helping me getting it there: Carrie Pestritto, my agent; Kristine Swartz, my editor; and the entire production team at Berkley.

Mom, thank you for dropping everything to take care of me post-surgery. Twice.

Anna, Sandy, Shani, Jenn, and Sarah, thank you for being my friends.

SHINee, my loves, thank you for the *Atlantis* album, a no-skip masterpiece.

And Bebe, my cat, thank you for being a hunter.

Keep reading for a preview of

THE ROMANTIC AGENDA

a contemporary romance
from Claire Kann

THURSDAY

Dreams are such strange things to have and to hold.

They can be as big as wanting to be the next Naomi Campbell—the bougie-on-a-budget version. As outrageous as hoping to find true love in a seven-billion-person haystack. Or even as innocuous as hitting that fabled Inbox Zero before the end of the workday.

Forty-seven emails to go.

Joy doesn't know what happened. One second, she was wasting on-the-clock time by searching for and deleting junk email, and the next, she'd become intensely obsessed with seeing the number in the red notification bubble drop lower and lower and lower . . .

Her intercom beeps, breaking her concentration. "Joy?"

"This is, and you're bothering me," she answers playfully, holding the phone between her ear and shoulder to keep her hands free. Forty-three emails now.

"It's Meg. Do you think you could come to my office for a second?" Her voice sounds too high and strained.

Joy frowns, but says, "Be right there."

Down the hall and five seconds away, Megan sits at her desk, face crumpled in despair as she stares at a pile of papers. Her office is a mirror image of Joy's—from the slate gray pair of chairs for guests to the corny-as-hell inspirational wall art. Most employees at Red Warren added personal touches to make the space theirs. Megan brought in her adorable cross-stitch creations, displaying them everywhere.

Hanging on to the doorjamb, Joy says, "You rang, my dear?"

"I did." She looks up—her hazel eyes dominate her light brown face, with her patchy freckles coming in a close second. As if she isn't already cute enough, loose brunette curls cascade over her shoulders like a Rapunzel-in-training. "Is that a new outfit?"

Joy twirls into the room, ending in a pose. "New-ish." She'd bought the chic olive green pantsuit—flared high-waisted slacks and sleek blazer, both tailored to perfection, and paired with a tasteful plaid crop top—a few months ago, but this is the first time she's wearing it to work.

"Special occasion?"

As far as Joy is concerned, fashion is life, but Megan clocked the situation correctly. Her hopes are sky-high for something about to go down, most likely in the next hour. It's why she abruptly decided to devote her immediate future to securing Inbox Zero.

Approximately sometime around two hours, thirty-seven minutes, and twenty-four seconds ago, her focus had shattered from anticipation after her boss, Malcolm, sent a short email.

He asked if she had plans for the holiday on Monday.

He hinted about clearing everything from her calendar for Friday *and* the following Tuesday.

He needed to talk to her about something important.

"Hopefully?" Joy answers. It's a miracle her heart hadn't spontaneously combusted after she finished reading the email because her brain moved at the speed of light, jumping to the only possible conclusion: her time has finally come.

A reluctant laugh bursts through Megan's stress. "Well, I'm rooting for you, whatever it is. Come look at this, please." She's holding a signed contract with some questionable language around distribution and follows it up with pictures of the product itself: a line of craft beers with an explicit NSFW label.

"Huh." Joy's eyebrows are nearly at her hairline. The image is so realistic, she can't tell if the model's 3D or not. If she's real, despite her excellent, perky posture, she most certainly has back problems from having boobs that big and a waist that small. How she managed to hold a perfect spread-eagle side split would have been a small miracle on set.

The image slides straight past comical, bypassing artistic expression, and ends up a little too close to exploitation. Red Warren Nightclubs pushes the envelope here and there, but this kind of advertisement isn't in line with the brand.

"You approved this?" Joy asks.

"*No.*" All the color drains from Megan's horrified face. "I was there because I was filling in for Johnny. Remember when he got sick and was out for two weeks?"

"I do."

"I remember the product they showed us. I can literally see it in my head and it's *definitely* not this."

Joy nods, keeping her cool. "I've always wondered if people are born with a photographic memory or if they have to develop it."

"It's eidetic memory, not photo— *Oh, Joy*, oh no."

Joy grins, chuckling at her brilliant pun. She isn't above doing that. Everyone teases her for laughing at her own jokes, but it isn't her fault they don't appreciate her humor.

The most important thing is to calm Megan down. This mistake isn't the end of the world. Or her job. Situations like this happen all the time on the back end because Malcolm prefers working with a smaller team he knows he can trust. When one of them is out, they band together and fill in the blank even when they're not exactly sure what they're doing.

Red Warren nightclubs have a somewhat infamous reputation in the local industry for being *the* places to be and work. They meet every code and regulation, have enough staff, supervisors, and managers, and pay them well enough to avoid burnout. Everyone who works for them is the best of the best: dancers, DJs, bartenders, and security.

Red Warren the office, however, runs with a skeleton crew in a modern office building. Megan handles all things human resources, Allie watches their money like a hawk in accounting, Nikkiee networks like a cult leader in talent and communications, and Johnny uses his keen senses in development and acquisitions. Joy fills the role of manager to an unholy amalgamation of office, operations, and finance, and at times, doubles as an executive assistant. And Malcolm is the CEO—the dreamer, the face, and the heart of the company.

Megan says, "Johnny was reviewing everything and spotted the discrepancy."

"That must have gone well."

"He was so mad, oh my god. I thought steam was going to start whistling out of his ears."

Joy laughs, and Megan continues, "But it's not just me, though. Malcolm missed it too. He was *there*. He *reviewed* the contract before I signed off on it." Her gaze is practically a laser beam of sincerity aimed right at Joy. "It seemed like he'd been doing better lately."

Malcolm hasn't really been the same since Caroline (the Cruel) called off their wedding a year ago. A Virgo through and through, Malcolm lives and dies by planning and micromanaging every detail he can get his hands on. He likes order and precision, needs structure and control.

Joy had seen Malcolm heartbroken before—he played fast and loose with his heart on a regular basis. He's in love with love, always searching for The One, but that breakup broke him. Completely and utterly. Afterward, he missed important meetings, left work early on the days he even bothered to show up at all, overlooked major and minor details that caused everyone headaches later. Mistakes like this contract were a dime a dozen. Red Warren survived by staying in red alert mode.

But in the past couple of months, glimpses of the *real* Malcolm began to break through. His focus and dedication to Red Warren returned. Missteps became less frequent, nearly disappearing. He seemed better, lighter, and happier for some reason.

Joy fidgets at her side. "He's okay. He, um, I think he might be a little distracted right now."

Everyone knew Malcolm and Joy had originally met in college. A classic story of boy sees girl first, girl meets boy but then has an immediate revelation about her sexuality and completely ignores boy for two weeks before randomly popping back up into his life. They've been best friends, for better and for worse, in sickness but mostly in health, ever since. And she's deeply in love with him.

But no one at Red Warren needs to know a single shred of truth about her feelings for Malcolm. None. Nada. Over her dead and cold body. Hers is the kind of workplace secret you take to the unemployment line after promising to keep in touch even though you know that won't happen. Because you've had and left enough jobs to know better than to make false promises.

"I had a feeling." Megan nods. "Do you know what's up?"

"I don't," Joy lies. There are perks to moonlighting as an executive assistant. All signs point to Malcolm planning something big for the weekend. "Anyway"—she gestures to the contract—"this is fine. Everything is fine. Even if I have to go old school, pay them a *visit*, and remind them who they're dealing with. I'll take care of it."

"Knock, knock." Malcolm stands grinning in the doorway. Tall, dark, and ever handsome—in the literal sense. None of that thinly veiled colorist propaganda. Rich brown skin, black curly hair cut short, and deep chocolate eyes.

Joy unconsciously gives him a bright smile in return, just like she always does because she can't help it. Her brain recognizes him and there's an instant hit of dopamine to all the receptors that make her happiest.

He asks, "Joy, can I borrow you for a second?"

"Wow, I am *popular* this afternoon," Joy jokes to quiet her sudden nerves before looking at Megan. "Consider it handled, okay?"

Back down the hall in her office, Joy sits at her desk. Unlike Megan, she hasn't bothered with personal touches, preferring to keep her office sparse and clean. The cool grays and bursts of navy blue have a soothing effect on her. Something she relies on when she's forced to hop on one too many phone calls and her daily avalanche of emails start pissing her off.

All six feet and two inches of Malcolm collapse into the chair in front of her desk with a *thud*. The chair and his temperamental knees are probably swearing at him in a pitch only dogs can hear. "What are you doing this weekend?"

In case she was wrong about Malcolm's intentions, Joy had made a backup plan to visit her sister, a quick ninety-minute flight away. "My usual. A little of this, a little of that."

"No, you're not."

"I'm not?"

Malcolm's grin escalates to *devastating*. A true weapon of mass destruction, it has an impact radius of twenty paces and a ninety-seven-percent fatality rate. He's always wielded that perfect face of his like a formerly shy and gangly boy who just discovered the right side of puberty: completely earnest and unaware of how handsome he is.

Even after all this time, it still shocks Joy how much he can affect her. A quiet thrill ripples through her bloodstream, making her heart flutter. *It's happening, it's happening, it's happening.*

Two weeks ago, Malcolm scheduled himself out of the office on Friday *and* the Tuesday after the holiday—the exact same days he asked her to clear on her schedule today. After that, Joy spotted several browser tabs open on his laptop with telltale keywords such as "hot-air balloon" and "vineyard," and catering packages from her favorite restaurant. And most damning of all, Joy always helps him with his plans—business and personal. This time, he hasn't even mentioned a single thing about it to her.

Malcolm "King of Grand Romantic Gestures" Evans is about to make a comeback. And Joy has a sneaking suspicion it might *finally* be for her.

"Nope." He shakes his head. "Because you're going on a trip with me."

"Again?" Joy snort-laughs, playfully rolling her eyes. "Where are we going this time?"

Ever since Caroline-ageddon, Malcolm's been traveling non-stop, Joy being his companion of choice. They've driven to the Grand Canyon, watched the northern lights in Iceland, flown to remote beaches on private islands with sunsets to die for, visited museums and art shows, and attended fancy parties in skyscrapers that have no earthly business being so tall. A perpetual homebody, globetrotting has never been a dream of Joy's. But hey, if it's on someone else's wealthy dime with someone she loves, who is she to say no?

Besides, every time Malcolm asked, she was mostly shocked that he even wanted to spend time with her at all. Because according to Caroline, the main reason why she left him was . . . Joy.

"I know you figured out that I've been planning something. I can barely hide anything from you." Malcolm leans forward, locking her in his sights. No other human on the planet can make her feel like she's the center of their universe. No one has ever made Joy feel the way Malcolm does. "But I'm keeping everything close to my chest this time. I don't want anything to go wrong."

Joy frowns. "What do you mean?"

"I have this plan."

"A plan?"

"Yeah." He clears his throat. "I met someone. Summer."

A record scratch screeches in Joy's ears. "Summer?"

"We're friends. We've been hanging out for a couple of months now."

Everything suddenly feels blurry and detached, like she's watching a reflection of the moment instead of living in it. "Months?" When? How? She literally saw his calendar every day, they spent an ungodly amount of time together after work, and when they weren't together, they texted constantly. How in the hell did he squeeze a Summer into his life without her knowing?

"Two, to be exact." He laughs again. "I think there might be something there. I've been wanting to ask her out, and I'm positive she's into me, but it feels different this time."

"Different?"

"I don't want to just come out and ask. That's boring. I want to make her feel special, you know? So I thought: What if I planned a trip specifically for her? We'd do everything that she loves, a whole weekend in her honor, and then at the end, I'll stage a moment when it's just the two of us and I'll ask her."

This is how Malcolm, a hopeless romantic and serial monogamist, dates—he doesn't.

All his ex-partners came from their friend group. It always starts casual, hanging out and getting to know them, no pressure or pretense. Malcolm gets his patented "feeling," and one sincere heart-to-heart later they go straight from friends to being in a relationship. It's like a light switch flipping, friends to lovers so fast there should probably be a scientific formula to measure it.

Joy would know. She's witnessed the shift enough times. What's that saying? Always the bridesmaid, never the bride? That's her. By his side for ten years and he's never once made that record-breaking shift with her. After the past year, after every-thing they've been through, she really thought—

"Joy? Are you listening to me?"

"Of course I'm not." She frowns for a second before forcing herself to smile to keep him from reading her face, which he's an expert at. He's figured out how to guess her moods with ease, so she's learned how to trick him.

"Anyway, so Fox is coming too."

Joy discreetly reaches for the stress ball on her desk and holds it in her lap. Aiming for disinterested, she asks, "And who the hell is Fox?"

"I just told you. Were you really not listening?"

"I *said* I wasn't."

"I assumed that was a joke."

"You know what they say when you assume," she says. "You make an ass out of you, Malcolm Evans."

"Joy."

"*What?*" Joy snickers, giving the stress ball a mighty squeeze. Dad joke humor would get her through this hellacious situation one way or another. "Sorry. Please continue. You have the full remainder of my divided attention."

Malcolm levels a glare at her that doesn't last, softening in seconds. "When I invited Summer, I told her she could bring someone too because I thought she'd pick Fiona or anyone else besides Fox Yes-That's-My-Real-Name Monahan. But appar-ently it's his birthday." He rolls his eyes.

Not just Summer—there's also a Fox and a Fiona and an any-one else. It's like he suddenly has an entire second life he didn't tell her about. Why would he do that? She tries to not feel hurt. It's not like he isn't allowed to have friends, or he must introduce her to every person he meets. But it's just . . . that he usually does. He always has.

"And I take it you don't like this Fox person?"

"Let's just say we don't see eye to eye."

Joy stares at him. "What did you do?

"Nothing." He's lying. Malcolm's tell is always looking quickly to the left and then making direct eye contact. "But that's not the most important part. Summer wants to meet you. She asked me to ask you to come along."

Joy presses her lips together so her jaw doesn't fall open and slam into her keyboard. Her mouth barely moves as she asks, "You told her about me?"

He nods. "Of course. She can't wait to meet you."

"So. You're not inviting me? Summer is?" She unclenches her left hand and transfers the stress ball to her right, immediately putting it back into a death grip.

"No, no, it's not like that. Of course I want you there."

Joy's heart drops as she watches Malcolm look to the left and to her again. He continues, "It's just . . . I don't know if you'd have a good time. That's all. But. If you do come, I was hoping you could do me a favor? Fox is . . . a lot. Maybe you could keep him company."

"Oh, I've always wanted to try being an escort." She hates how breathless, almost winded from shock, she sounds. "Will I be getting paid?"

"Joy, that's not funny."

"What? I think I'd be good at it. I happen to be an excellent companion."

"I'm aware." And there it is—the smile that never fails to light up her whole world. Even when she's been plunged into suffocating darkness, he's there to lift her back up with hardly any effort. "I'd like to spend as much time with Summer as possible, but I know her. She's going to spend all her time making sure Fox doesn't feel like a third wheel because she knows we don't really get along."

"And if I'm there, it'll be four-wheel drive."

Malcolm gives her a rare laugh. Puns and wordplay aren't exactly his favorite thing about her. "We could just sort of naturally pair up for some of the activities I have planned."

"Natural. Organic. Not at all from concentrate or staged."

"Joy."

"What?"

"Will you please come and spend time with Fox?"

Malcolm waits for her to say something. She doesn't. Her voice feels shaky, so it'll probably sound worse. How could she have been so wrong about everything? The secret trip isn't for her, he isn't planning to ask her to be with him, because there's a Summer, and he wants to pawn Joy off on a Fox.

This is hell. Hell truly is other people.

Joy trains her gaze on the ceiling, exhaling into a horrible-sounding sigh. She closes her eyes and focuses on her breathing before turning back to him. He looks concerned but patient. "Why haven't you told me about Summer before now?"

"I don't know." Malcolm shrugs like it's nothing. "We met on this forum called Jilted Hearts. It's full of people with failed engagement stories. She planned a local meetup for a bunch of us, but we were the only two who showed up."

Malcolm doesn't even glance at Joy while he tells the rest of his story. His eyes are unfocused and lost in a memory. She takes in his wistful, effortless smile. His relaxed posture. The awestruck cadence of his words as he talks about Summer and the past two months he's spent getting to know her.

Joy has never heard him talk about *her* like that. Never seen him go soft when people ask how they met, how they managed to stay friends for so long. Joy always faithfully by his side because that's *her* spot, pathetically hoping that someday he'll see she's *right there*.

And then, it's like Malcolm suddenly remembers she *is* there, locking her in his sights again. "I just wanted to find someone to talk to who would understand what I've been through, and there she was. I'm convinced we could be more. I think that's why I've been waiting for the perfect moment to introduce you. This weekend is it."